BLOCK BY BLOCK

A Rome London Novel

XANN-SHAPELLA SMITH

Amazon KDP

This book is a work of fiction. Any reference to historical events, real people, or real places are used fictitiously. Other names, characters, places, and events are products of the author's imagination, and any resemblance to actual events or places or persons, living or dead, is entirely coincidental.

Copyright © 2017 by Xann-shapella Smith

All rights reserved. No part of this book may be reproduced in any form or by any electronic or mechanical means, including information storage and retrieval systems, without written permission from the author, except for the use of brief quotations in a book review.

Cover design by Doug & Sherry Walker and Xann.

ISBN:
978-0-692-89986-1

Acknowledgments

Sherry and her love of story. Ever grateful, my friend.
Tel and her 'mad' formatting skills, etc.
Michelle for being my Kiwi voice of wisdom.
Saafe' for the Austin kickoff and so much more.
Mom and Dad for passing on the creative genes.

Prologue

When your name is Rome London, there's only one career that seems fitting: that of a travel writer. And travel she does...

Current assignment: Port Arthur, Tasmania, Australia.

Logistics/Itinerary: NYC to LAX, economy, 5 hours. Read book on British convicts sent to Australian Colony. LAX to Sydney, Australia, business class upgrade, 14 hours. Sleep, sleep and more sleep. Customs. Sydney to Melbourne, economy, 1 hour. Brush teeth and try to fix hair. Arrive in Melbourne, borrow friend's second car, catch ferry across the Bass Strait to Tasmania.

Dock in Devonport, drive an estimated three hundred and thirty-three kilometers, taking approximately three hours and forty-two minutes (on the wrong side of the road and the wrong side of the car). Arrive in Hobart, check into hotel, sleep. Wake up, drive to Port Arthur, 1.5 hours. Research and write article on Port Arthur, one of the largest and longest running convict settlements in Australia's history.

Remember to breathe!

As Rome stared out the window of the Boeing 777, she fantasized of endless summersaults in the clouds, but quickly dismissed the whimsical thoughts as her attention turned to the crowd-pleasing announcement being broadcast throughout the aircraft. "The flight attendants will be making one last pass through the cabin to collect any remaining garbage."

One might think a travel writer to be footloose and fancy free, a bohemian by nature, but the opposite couldn't be more true of Rome. Logistics, itinerary, deadlines and the ticking of the clock are what motivate her, not only in her profession, but in her personal life as well. Somewhere deep inside, however, a familiar question continues to beg an answer. What would it feel like to be completely unrestrained? A fanciful thought to ponder when one is belted into a seat which can also be used as a floatation device.

Rome has spent the majority of her adult life writing for the magazine, *Trekking the Globe*, a career that has allowed her to walk the same paths that the feet of many have trod for thousands of years. It's not only through the annals of history and the recitations of tour guides that Rome has learned of otherwise forgotten lives. She also hears them, literally. Not through a psychic or Ouija board or any other type of mystical method, but through the dead's own voices. She's tried to reason it out, to explain it scientifically, physiologically and even existentially, but there's no rational explanation. She merely inherited a gift.

It's only been the last few years that Rome's begun to take her gift seriously. Maybe it's her age. Maybe it's her mood. Or maybe it's the point we all come to in life when our huge stack of questions outweighs that precious but tiny pile of answers we hold so dear to our hearts. That moment of epiphany where things happening on the inside become more fascinating than the events going on around us. Where the meaning of life suddenly becomes more important than the promotion at work, the nicer car, the bigger house or the pictures we post on social media.

Or maybe this time... it's as simple as a persistent voice, impossible to ignore.

So back to logistics and the real reason Rome chose to cover Port Arthur as opposed to other convict sites in Australia: the Isle of the Dead. A small island located just off shore and home to over one thousand graves, mostly prisoners.

This tiny island at the bottom of the world has been calling to her from thousands of miles away and she can only imagine the whisperings awaiting her down under.

Chapter One

The double doors swung open as a parade of khaki-clothed, Australian guides rushed from the room and scattered in every direction. The morning meeting had gone longer than usual, putting everyone behind schedule. Focused on their assignments, they scampered about preparing to meet a new onslaught of anxious tourists.

The last one to leave the room was Beverly Hucker, a forty-five-year-old, amazon of a blonde bombshell, who has spent most of her adult life guiding tourists through the ruins of Port Arthur. A fixture that's as much a part of the tourist site as the history she shares with the visitors. She loves her job and on any given day it shows. But this is no ordinary day. Today is the arrival of Rome London and everything has to be just right. "What are you still doing here, Jen?" asked Bev impatiently as she approached a female guide filling her water bottle at the drinking fountain.

"By failing to prepare, you're preparing to fail," proudly responded the young guide as she continued to fill her bottle, not realizing the urgency of the moment. "That's what you always say."

"I also say... If you don't meet Ms. London as soon as the gates open, you'll be cleaning toilets for a month!"

Sensing the seriousness of her supervisor's tone, the clueless guide grabbed her half-filled water bottle and ran for the door.

Bev continued into her office, stopping abruptly as she passed her window. Taking a few steps back, she looked out across the grounds and noticed a woman walking up the hill overlooking the prison site. Grabbing her binoculars, she quickly returned to the window and focused in on the female guest. Recognizing the presence of her favorite travel writer, she lowered her binoculars. "Toilets it is." The ringing of her phone pulled Bev's focus away from the window and back to administrative matters. She'd been waiting for a call from maintenance and knew it had to take precedence. With any luck, she could resolve the problem before Jen made it back with her American V.I.P.

REACHING the top of the hill, Rome lowered her bag to the ground and breathed in the ocean air. Taking a moment to give Port Arthur a quick 360, she pulled her thick, dark brown, shoulder-length hair back into a low pony tail and secured it with the band from her wrist. She left it loose to dry while she drove from her hotel in Hobart down the Tasman Peninsula to Port Arthur. Blow dryers require too much time, as does make-up. Fortunately, her dark brows, long black lashes and olive skin provide a natural beauty, saving her the time it takes to put on a face each morning. Nights are a different story. And as for style, she feels as comfortable in her casual v-neck t-shirt and knee-length shorts as she does in the designer labeled clothing hanging in her New York City closet.

Measuring up at a fit five-foot-five, Rome appears to be average in every way. A fact that works in her favor when she needs to blend into a crowd. Her relative obscurity allows her to capture the vibe and atmosphere of the guests within her tour group without tipping them off to her true identity. Simply put: she's more interested in authenticity than sycophants who tell her what they think she wants to hear.

After a quick survey of the once-thriving prison site, she sat down on the grassy hilltop, crossed her legs at the ankles and quietly stared at the ruins below. For a good travel writer, this moment is key. This is the moment where a tourist site either speaks to her or lies in silence. That crucial point in her visit where she waits to see if the location has a voice. That brief interval of time when all of her senses unite in a melody that sings to her soul.

And there it was. Port Arthur's eerie beauty began to wash over her. She wondered if it was the ocean breeze blowing through her mind or a choir of unfettered voices calling from beyond the grave. Whatever it was, Port Arthur had a unique voice and she wanted to find out what it had to say. Little did she know her wish would be granted immediately.

"Take a walk with me," a male voice whispered in her ear.

A cold chill trickled down Rome's spine and out of habit she reached back and grabbed the base of her neck. It was a practice she developed as a teenager to protect herself from what she couldn't see approaching from behind.

"Take a walk with me," he whispered again.

Twice was enough to get Rome off the ground and at full attention. As she looked around she saw exactly who she expected to see: no one. This wasn't Rome's first experience listening to a disembodied spirit, but that didn't make it any easier.

"Follow me," coaxed the voice again from farther down the hill, causing Rome to move in his direction.

"Where are we going?"

"To the water's edge," enticed the voice as he led her to the shores of Mason Cove.

As she walked toward the water, her fear of the unknown began to penetrate deep into her chest cavity causing the beats of her heart to pick up in speed. She wanted nothing more than to turn and run in the opposite direction as she had done most of her life. But there are no answers to be found in running.

"The Isle of the Dead awaits your arrival," whispered the spirit.

"That is why I came."

"I know."

"You're the one who called me here, the voice in my dreams."

"Yes."

Reaching the beach, Rome looked toward the island. It was beautiful, yet dreadful at the same time. She could only imagine what staring at the Isle of the Dead, day after day, meant to the convicts who once occupied Port Arthur.

"What do you see?" asked the spirit, standing directly behind her.

Rome breathed deeply, then quietly exhaled in an attempt to slow the pounding within her chest, but it didn't seem to help. "An island," she replied, uncertain of his motives.

"Look deeper."

Rome stared at the island intently, but continued to see only trees and a shoreline. "I'm not sure what you want."

"Look closer. You've got to want to see beyond the physical," encouraged the voice.

Rome closed her eyes for a moment to calm her racing heart. It took a few minutes, but eventually the labored breathing disappeared. With new eyes, she narrowed her focus. Slowly, she felt herself shift to a different level of awareness. Rome was entering new territory and wasn't sure how much farther she should go, but the spirit's voice urged her on. "That's right, Rome, search for it. Seek it. The ability is within you." All at once, she saw men begin to appear on the shoreline of the island. Ten, twenty, fifty, a hundred, soon she lost count. The spirits of the dead filled the island and lined the dock. Rome gasped as she stepped back in amazement, feeling the weight of their collective stare. The loose sand beneath her feet made it difficult to find solid footing as she worked to gain control.

"What do they want?" whispered Rome in quiet desperation, but there was no reply. The spirit was gone. He had left her to face the hoards of ghosts on her own. Although there was plenty of water between her and the island, a wave of fear overwhelmed her. Her instincts told her to run, but she couldn't move. The beach beneath her felt like quicksand, holding her captive before the hundreds of men staring her down from across the water. She had become the prisoner and there was nothing she could do.

Suddenly, the spirits let out a giant yell. The level of their unified cry was so strong that a pressure wave of audible sound launched toward Rome, parting the water as it traveled. The sound was deafening to Rome's ears and she quickly covered them with her hands. Again, her instincts screamed, "run," but she was incapable of moving. There was no escaping the ripple effect coming straight for her. It hit her like a speeding truck and threw her backwards onto the ground.

Conscious, but disoriented, Rome laid still as she tried to regain some focus. The loud yell of the spirits was instantly replaced with the sound of hundreds of birds squawking and flying erratically through the air. Rome watched in astonishment, realizing she wasn't the only one who had experienced the phenomena. After a few minutes, she found the strength to sit up on her elbows. She looked toward the island and was relieved to see nothing but trees and shoreline. Rome had never experienced anything like this and was more than 10,000 miles away from the paranormal expert with all the answers: her mother.

"G'day, I'm Jen. Welcome to Port Arthur."

Rome's attention quickly turned to the out-of-breath guide blocking her view. "You are the travel writer from America, right?"

"I'm sorry, what?" replied Rome, still a bit punchy.

"Are you all right?"

"I'm fine."

"Are you sure, cause it kind of looks like you've seen a ghost."

"Excuse me?"

"Are you sure you're okay?"

"It's just jet lag."

"I hear drinking water can help," said the guide as she held out her water bottle, while making loud smacking sounds with the chewing of her gum.

"Thank you, but I'm fine."

"I apologize for not meeting you at the gate."

"Not a problem."

"So you're not upset?"

"Of course not."

"Would you mind mentioning that to my supervisor when you see her? It might save me a toilet or two."

"I could do that," replied Rome, totally confused by her request.

"I'll take you to see her whenever you're ready. Sooner would be better than later, but it's totally up to you. I can wait if you need to rest a little longer."

Rome slowly crawled to her feet then slipped her bag and camera straps over her shoulders. "Lead the way, Jen."

Turning toward the visitors' center, the guide began to recite her prepared information. "All two day passes come with a forty-minute, guided walking tour. We also have an after hour Ghost Tour, lit only by lanterns. That ticket will need to be purchased separately." Facts and information poured out of her bubble-gum-chewing mouth as though the words were chained together, unbreakable by even a breath.

"Can you hit pause for a minute?" asked Rome as she limped alongside.

"Am I going too fast? I can go slower."

"No! The quicker the better. Like removing a bandaid."

"Okay," replied Jen in confusion.

"Beverly Hucker is still scheduled to be my guide. Is that correct?"

"Yes. She's the best guide here. She should be... she's been doing it for-ev-er. I'm not saying she's old or anything. I mean she's way older than I am, but that doesn't mean she's old, old. She's just really... experienced. Like you."

"Experience is exactly what I need."

"Then you two should get along great," responded Jen as she continued toward the visitors' center, leaving Rome shaking her head in disbelief.

A great guide is a necessity for Rome. Jen was not that. She had killer memorization skills but lacked everything else. A guide worth following is passionate, sharing everything a writer needs to know and more. It's usually somewhere lost in 'the more' where things get really interesting. Over the years, Rome's had the good fortune of working with some amazing guides, and because of her firm belief in leaving people better off than when she finds them, she's built up quite a network of 'informants.'

Feeling a need to do some guiding of her own, Rome decided to share a bit of wisdom. "Someday you'll reach the age of 'experience' and you'll realize that being in your late thirties isn't as awful as it seems at your age."

"If you say so," responded Jen as she blew a bubble then continued toward her destination. Rome continued to follow as she listened to the loquacious guide share more memorized information about toilet facilities, ATM's, foreign exchange and traveler's checks, proper smoking areas, lockers for a small hire fee, and of course food, drink and the proper disposal of rubbish. With the entrance to the visitor center growing near, Rome felt her feet picking up speed, causing the young guide's pace to increase as well. The end of her time as a captive audience was in sight and she wanted nothing more than to cross the finish line.

As they entered the office, Bev sat at her desk fielding a phone call she had no desire to continue. "Well, mate, if you keep complaining about it, I'll come down there and show you how much better I can do your job. I expect to see results within the hour." Hanging up the phone, Bev turned to her new guest and expressed her thoughts in one word. "Men!"

Smiling, Rome validated her view. "It's truly amazing that the world survived so long with them in charge."

"I knew I'd like you, Ms. London. I had a good feeling about you from the conversation we had a few weeks ago."

"Please, call me Rome and I share in that good feeling."

"Beverly Hucker, but you can call me Bev."

"Nice to finally meet you, Bev. So where shall we begin?"

"I was thinking about hitting one of the morning tours of the Isle of the Dead."

"No!" responded Rome defiantly, surprising Bev with her boldness. "I mean, not yet. I'd like to leave that tour till last. It would also help if we could make our visit to the island a private tour."

"We can do that. So why don't we start with the buildings that are currently not being toured? Then we can spend this arvo..."

"This arvo?"

"Aussie for afternoon... on a stroll through the Government Gardens. Following an evening meal, we'll join in on one of the Ghost Tours. And that's just today's itinerary."

"Sounds wonderful. Lead the way."

Bev stood up and put on an authentic leather, outback-style hat then handed her a cheaper, touristy version of the same thing.

"You'll need some shade."

Without question, Rome placed it on her head and quickly followed Bev out of the office, her short legs moving twice as fast to keep up. A feat not easily maintained given the lengthy stride of Bev's long legs.

The day went as her guide had described. Rome jotted down a bit of this and that, took a picture here and there as they made their way through several buildings, including the civil officers' cottages and the commandant's house.

Taking a break, they grabbed a couple of salad rolls and drinks and headed toward a quiet spot in the gardens. While Bev's attention was focused on returning an urgent text message to maintenance, Rome watched curiously as a newspaper floated out of the garbage can, across the yard and landed on a bench. The same bench they were walking toward. No voice accompanied the movement of the paper, but Rome guessed it was the same spirit she had encountered that morning. The same spirit she'd like to slap upside the head for abandoning her at the shore.

Looking up, Bev grumbled as she spotted the newspaper and assumed it was left behind by a careless tourist. "There's a bin not three meters away, yet still they leave their rubbish lying about. A good-sized breeze off the ocean and these pages become airborne litter."

Before Bev could grab it from the bench, Rome caught a glimpse of the picture and headline plastered across the front page.

"May I see that for a moment?"

"Help yourself."

As they sat down, Bev handed Rome the paper, piquing her

curiosity as she read the headline out loud. "Castle Jones Taking Shape. What's this all about?"

"Some billionaire decided to transport a castle from its original home in England all the way down here to Tassie, block by bloody block."

"What kind of person buys a castle in England and has it shipped to the bottom of the world?"

"Someone with more money than sense," replied Bev sarcastically as she took another look. "From the picture, the outside finally looks finished."

"What about the inside?"

"I doubt anyone will ever see the inside of that fortress. I hear the man who bought it is a recluse at heart. A loner worth billions of dollars."

"And he plans to live in the castle?"

"What better way to lock yourself away from the world, than in a fortress made of three meter thick walls and an iron gate?"

"Three meters? That's nearly ten feet."

"I don't actually know how thick the walls are, but I do know castles in general are designed to keep people out."

"Why would someone with that kind of money want to lock themselves away from the world?"

"Sergio Arturo would have you believe it's a sign of instability."

"Who's Sergio Arturo?"

Bev opened the paper to Arturo's column on page four.

"*Arturo: Off-the-Wall*. He's a syndicated columnist who covers celebrity gossip and bizarre occurrences throughout Australia and New Zealand. I love reading his stuff. Most people do. It's everyone's favorite topic of conversation on Monday morning. He lives in Sydney, but our local paper carries his column."

"I'm always skeptical of these so-called reporters. I've seen my fair share of lies and false statements spun to sound like the truth too many times."

"Then we'll just have to knock on the door of Castle Jones and find out the truth for ourselves. But we better be careful."

"Why?"

"We may get tossed into the moat."

"There's a moat?"

"Not yet, but I wouldn't put it past him. My cousin's husband was working on the plumbing team for a while before he got fired for having no idea what he was doing. I think he tried to steal something as well."

"Sounds like a winner."

"Before he got fired, my cousin's husband discovered that the owner of the castle also purchased most of the original paintings and antiques. It's all in some secure storage area waiting to be placed throughout the castle."

"That does seem a bit obsessed," said Rome, growing more intrigued with each new fact.

"According to Arturo, the owner spent most of his adult life in the shadow of his father, and when his father died, he withdrew from everything except the family business. Then his obsession with the castle began and no one understands what that's all about."

"What's his name?"

"Jones is the last name."

"As in Castle Jones?"

"Correct. Let's have a look."

Bev took the paper back from Rome and quickly scanned the article. "Here it is… Marshall Heath Jones Jr. From what I've heard, he goes by Heath. Marshall Jones Sr. was his father, an enormously successful shipping tycoon and philanthropist, as well as the handsome face of his company. I met him once. He was hosting a charity gala that took place down here at Port Arthur. He told me I looked like a woman who knew what she wanted. He was right about that. I would have taken him in a heart beat, right then and there—age difference and all. You should have seen the way he filled out that tuxedo."

"So meanwhile, back at the castle."

"Sorry. I got a little distracted. After Marshall died, his son Heath stepped into the role of CEO, but that's about the only footsteps he's filled. He sold his dad's estate up in Sydney and moved back down here to Tasmania to the house he lived in while his mother was still alive. Now he commutes between here and Sydney on his private jet."

Rome took the paper back and began studying the photo intently. Noticing her great interest in the picture sparked an idea that even Bev didn't see coming. "Would you like to see it?" enquired the adventurous guide.

"I would love to."

"The day after tomorrow is Sunday. What do you say we swing by for a look?"

"That's a great idea. And who knows... maybe Mr. Jones will be home," she said with mischievous delight.

"Or better yet, maybe he's not and I can work my 'feminine wiles' on the builders and get us our own private tour of the place."

"Even better," agreed Rome.

"Did I mention the castle's haunted?"

"No, you did not," replied Rome with a better understanding as to why the spirit wanted her to find the newspaper.

"That's the rumor anyway. My cousin's moron-of-a-husband claims the same thing."

"Maybe your cousin's husband should consider a career in private investigation, rather than plumbing."

"Don't even get me started."

"So what makes people think it's haunted?" enquired Rome.

"The butler can't keep any of the newly-hired staff on for more than a few days because of the ghostly antics."

"Really?"

"But enough about the castle. You're here to learn about Port Arthur and I happen to have all the answers."

"I do have a question."

"Ask away."

"It's a rather serious one."

"I can handle it."

"It requires a great deal of expertise."

"Bring it on."

"How does one... 'work their feminine wiles?'"

"Eat your sandwich!"

"No, I'm serious. Do your 'feminine wiles' include the use of those crazy long legs?"

"God didn't give 'em to me for nothing."

Rome started to laugh as she made a failed attempt to take a bite of her sandwich. Unable to contain herself, Bev burst into laughter as well, slugging Rome in the upper arm as they both enjoyed a good-sized dose of nature's best medicine.

"I knew I'd like you, London."

"Right back at you, Hucker."

"Most travel writers don't have your sense of humor."

"You can thank my dad for that, as well as endless rounds of comebacks and one-liners. Humor was his way of escaping the rigidity of military life."

"Sounds like a fun way to grow up."

"Boxing and making each other laugh were our favorite father-daughter activities.

"You must have had one patient mother," commented Bev as the ringing of her phone stole her attention.

Bev pulled the work phone from her belt clip, signaling to Rome that she'd be right back. As Bev walked away from the bench, Rome's attention turned back to the picture and article on Castle Jones. Obviously, the spirit wanted her to see it and that left her wondering if there was a link between the Isle of the Dead and the castle. If so, she could only hope that it wouldn't be as frightening as her morning encounter.

Chapter Two

Sunday finally arrived, and as Bev pulled up to Rome's hotel, she saw her waiting near the entrance. Rome opened the passenger side door and hopped in the car. "Thanks for driving today. I didn't expect the water pump to go out on my friend's car on the way back from Port Arthur yesterday."

"When will it be fixed?"

"They had to order the part. Hopefully they have it fixed by Tuesday so I can catch the ferry back to Melbourne. I gave them your number as a back up in case they can't get a hold of me."

"I'll make sure they don't jack up the price," vowed Bev as she entered the highway and drove out of town, eventually taking an exit onto a quiet winding road. As she drove along, Bev continued to do what she does best: share information. Stories and facts were flying at Rome faster than she could type, but Rome wouldn't have had it any other way. She loved to find out as much detail as she could about the places she visited.

Eventually, her fingers slowed as thoughts of Castle Jones and the familiar question that kept playing over and over in her mind took precedence. "What kind of man buys a castle in England and has it shipped to the bottom of the world?"

Rome had come across some eccentric characters in her travels, but Heath Jones may top them all. Switching from coach to business class on her recent flight to Australia was as impulsive as she'd ever been. Yet at the same time, Rome was intrigued by the audaciousness of such an enormous undertaking. There was an unrestrained freedom to Mr. Jones' decision that Rome found intriguing and even coveted.

Suddenly, without taking a break between topics, Bev spotted the castle. "There she is. Castle Jones in all her British glory."

Rome had visited hundreds of castles during her career. She once spent an entire year writing nothing but articles about castles. But the intrigue surrounding this one was more about the 'why' rather than the structure itself.

"It looks like any other castle, so what makes it so special?" asked Rome.

"Other than the fact that it may be the world's biggest souvenir?" sarcastically replied Bev.

"Good point."

Bev noticed the large iron-barred gate stretched across the private drive leading to the castle, so she pulled off to the side of the road and parked the car. "That gate's definitely designed to keep people out."

"Looks that way."

"My cousin's imbecile-of-a-husband said that once you get past the gate, the security is pretty much obsolete."

"You mean the winner who got fired for stealing, while pretending to be a plumber?"

"Spot on."

"Sounds like he was casing the place?"

"I wouldn't put it past him. You can pick your friends, but you can't pick your in-laws."

"I think I'll snap a few shots," said Rome as she pulled out her camera and reached for the door handle.

Bev and Rome left the car, crossed the road and walked up the driveway. They reached the large gate and stood in awe of the striking edifice standing in the distance. It looked to be two stories tall and had all the makings of an authentic castle: rugged gray blocks of stone, turrets with pointed roof tops and walls topped with battlements. Rome half expected the drive to be cobblestone rather than paved. A flag pole stood on the impressive tower with an Australian and Tasmanian flag patriotically flapping in the breeze.

"This is no home. It's a fortress," said Rome in amazement.

"I wonder if it's as cold on the inside as it appears to be on the outside."

"That would probably depend on the personality of the owner," responded Rome as she positioned her camera between the bars and took a few shots.

"From what I've read about him in Arturo's columns, the inside's probably dark and dreary."

"He can write what he wants, but what this guy's done is pretty remarkable."

"Seeing it in person, I have to agree. Mr. Jones just saved me a trip to England."

The more Rome studied the castle, the more familiar it felt. "I can't shake the feeling that I've seen this castle somewhere before."

"With all your travels you probably have."

Unexpectedly, a large delivery truck approached from the inside, causing the gate to open. As it passed by, Bev took Rome by the arm and walked through the open gate like she owned the place.

"What are you doing?"

"Being your guide."

"I'm not sure about this," fretted Rome as Bev continued undaunted toward the castle.

"At this point, the only way out is in," responded Bev as the gate closed behind them and locked.

Arm in arm, they continued the long walk through landscapers, construction workers, stone cutters and roofers, all slowing their work to take a look. Bev enjoyed the attention and began to flirt back, but Rome remained focused on the familiarity of the castle. Suddenly, a memory brought them both to a complete stop. "I have been to this castle before! My friend and I got lost one day in the English countryside and ran into it by accident. All that was left were the inside and outside walls. The roof had caved in and filled up much of the center with rubble. There were trees and bushes growing up through the debris, making it a part of the forest that surrounded it. Even then it felt haunted."

"Does that make this a coincidence or fate?"

"Coincidence. I don't believe in fate," replied Rome.

"Well, lucky for you, I do."

More determined than ever, Bev zeroed in on her target and continued her march toward the castle. As they grew closer, Rome secretly wondered to herself if the ghosts currently haunting the castle were the same ones she briefly experienced in England. Of course, she didn't bother to mention that she'd heard voices in the ruins of this very castle back in the UK or that she'd experienced a feeling that the family who once lived there suffered a great tragedy.

As they approached the castle, they stopped to take in the large wooden, arch-shaped door, held together by a series of bolts and ornate, iron straps. It was a door designed to keep people out and neither Rome nor Bev had packed along their battering rams. Gaining access was also complicated by the labyrinth of scaffolding that stretched across the wall above the impermeable door. Laborers stood on separate levels scrubbing moss from the rocks, using brushes, steel wool and several large buckets of water.

"When we get in... play it stealth," advised Bev.

"Don't you mean 'if' we get in?"

"We've made it this far, so why not go all the way?"

"I'm having second thoughts, Bev."

"We can't stop now."

"But we're trespassing."

"So we either get arrested or escorted back to the gate."

"I thought bad things come in threes?"

"The place is haunted," implied Bev.

"Are you going to knock?"

"I'm only the guide."

"Then we should definitely leave. I'm sure one of these nice gentlemen would be kind enough to open the gate for us," she said, still thinking about her experience with the ghosts on the Isle of the Dead.

"You want to leave after making it all this way?"

"Then you knock. You're Australian."

"We all speak the same language, Rome."

"You're better at this kind of thing."

"This kind of thing?"

"I'm not adventurous like you."

"Maybe not, but you're an American and that accent might be the key to getting us in the door."

"Fine! Take my camera just in case something interesting happens."

"Or that third bad thing," Bev mumbled under her breath as she held the camera in position while Rome walked beneath the scaffolding, took hold of the large door knocker and struck the base three times.

"Speaking of threes," joked Rome, trying to ease her nervousness.

"And you think you're not adventurous, London."

Their laughter ended abruptly as the large door slowly opened. Mr. Sheldon Burns, a distinguished British butler in his late forties, stepped into the light wearing a dress shirt, tie, vest and perfectly creased slacks. "May I help you?"

"My name is Rome London and I'm currently…"

"Whatever you're selling, we're not interested. Good day," declared Mr. Burns as he shut the door in Rome's face.

"That was rude," exclaimed Bev.

"In a proper sort of way," joked Rome.

"Knock again. He should at least hear you out. That's just common courtesy."

"There's no way we're getting through that door, Bev."

"What will it hurt?"

"Only our pride," responded Rome as she took hold of the door knocker and slammed it three times as hard as she could, hoping the noise echoed throughout the castle.

The door opened more robustly this time and the look on the

butler's face showed no intention of being courteous. "You will leave the grounds immediately or I will have you forcibly removed," warned Mr. Burns.

Just as he moved to close the door, one of the buckets from above tipped over, sending gallons of dirty, mud-filled water down through the scaffolding, drenching Rome from head to toe.

Click went the camera.

The laborers immediately responded with confusion as to how the bucket tipped over by itself, while Mr. Burns jumped back in shock.

"Good heavens, Miss! Are you all right?"

"She's just been drenched in liquid sludge. Of course she's not all right!" retorted Bev taking advantage of the situation by pushing Rome through the open door and into the castle. "Can we get a towel or is that too much to ask?"

Corralling them in the entrance way, Mr. Burns quickly called for one of the maids as he watched the filthy water and chunks of mud and moss drip off his unexpected house guest and onto the brand new tile. "Miss Lemmons, come at once!"

Miss Lemmons, a young, perky gal, dressed in a proper maid uniform and just happy to have a job, rushed to the top of the stairs located across the great hall, followed by two other maids of the same age. Out of view from the entrance way, Miss Lemmons' voice echoed through the empty castle as she responded to her employer's request. "Yes, Mr. Burns."

"Bring a towel. Quickly!"

"But they haven't been unpacked."

"Locate the boxes and get me several towels immediately, Miss Lemmons!"

"Right away, sir."

Miss Lemmons and the other maids quickly ran from the top of the stairs as Mr. Burns contained the fallout within the entrance way. He had no reason to trust the two strangers, so restricting their access seemed the logical course of action. Especially with all the ghost speculation running amuck. As far as he knew, the two women could be spies working for Sergio Arturo, a risk he was not willing to take. Confident he had the situation under control, he was content to wait for the maid's return. Unfortunately for Mr. Burns, Beverly Hucker was not content. "Are you just going to let her stand here like a drowned rat or should I dial Triple Zero and wait for the ambulance to arrive?"

Locked in a stare-down, Mr. Burns realized he may have met his match as he took a moment to weigh the consequences of her ultimatum. It didn't take him long to reach the conclusion that allowing them minimal access would make less of an impact than a hoard of emergency responders converging on the castle. So with a roll of his eyes and a guttural groan, the butler relinquished his stance. "You may enter, but only until the towels arrive."

"Ta," responded Bev as she flashed a victorious smile, while escorting Rome passed the butler.

Bev and Rome couldn't believe their eyes as they walked out from beneath the ceiling of the entranceway and into the open, two-story grand hall. The filtered light created a bright, museum-esque look to the enormous space. Quite a contrast to the rugged, dark blocks of stone on the outside.

They squeezed each other's arms in disbelief as their heads rotated from left to right, astonished by the grandiose beauty of the massive room. White marble tiles with natural gray veining covered the entire floor, giving it a regal and polished look. The two distant parallel sides of the grand hall were separated by rows of large mahogany pillars connected to a series of individual archways at the top. There was no furniture in the hall or the two connecting sitting areas except a few antique wooden chairs and a couch covered in plastic near the wall.

Next, their attention was captured by the centerpiece of the room, a stunningly enormous staircase. The steps were covered with the same tile and lined by a dark mahogany banister, which connected to the railing that ran along the second floor balcony. A balcony that was perfectly suited to a scene out of Romeo and Juliet or any other Shakespeare play.

Holding fast to each other, both Rome and Bev privately imagined themselves standing on the balcony in a formal gown, perfectly accessorized, as the man of their dreams waited at the bottom. Of course, neither of them would ever admit to such a fantasy, but their collective sigh was evidence to their thoughts and witnessed by a very impatient butler.

The balcony was only a warm-up as their heads bent back, allowing their eyes to fixate on the circular, frosted-glass dome above them. A gasp escaped both their mouths as they studied the detail and size of the overhead window. The pattern in the massive skylight was exquisite and had the appearance of vines and leaves extending in all directions. Keeping her eyes fixed on the ceiling, Bev leaned sideways and whispered in Rome's ear, "Now this is worth getting a bucket of sludge dumped on your head."

"What bucket of sludge?" replied Rome as she stood in awe of the creme de la creme of skylights.

Lowering their heads, they took one last look around before collecting themselves and returning to reality.

The hall was abuzz with activity as electricians on lifts continued to install lighting fixtures and carpenters worked to finish up the crown molding. Maids and laborers crisscrossed the floor carrying boxes, cleaning supplies and buckets, racing the clock to ready the castle.

"Can you at least make her comfortable while we wait?" Bev insisted.

"You may be seated. For the moment."

Just as Rome made an attempt to sit on one of the antique chairs, Mr. Burns intercepted her and gently moved her across the floor to the plastic-covered couch.

Click went the camera again.

Frustrated, Mr. Burns returned to Bev, leaving Rome alone on the couch. Or at least he thought she was alone. "This is private property, not a tourist site. Pictures are not allowed!"

"You should want people to see this place. It doesn't look haunted at all."

"Please tell me you two are not reporters."

"We just dropped by for a look."

"The last thing Mr. Jones needs is more bad press."

"In all honesty, she does work for a magazine."

"So you are reporters?"

"Beverly Hucker's the name. I'm a guide down at Port Arthur and this hot mess is Rome London, a travel writer on assignment from America."

Bev and Mr. Burns' attention immediately turned to Rome, who appeared to be in her own little world, moving side to side and forward as though reacting to someone or something. Mr. Burns made the first assumption as he watched with curiosity. "Perhaps she has water in her ear."

"Or maybe she's been possessed by your ghosts," responded Bev facetiously.

"Don't be ridiculous!"

"Or worse yet," Bev whispered to Mr. Burns, "whatever chemicals they're using to remove the moss have soaked into her brain."

"That's ludicrous!"

"Is it?"

Suddenly, Rome realized she was being watched. Nonchalantly, she stopped reacting to the ghostly conversations taking place around her and sat still as though she were waiting outside the principal's office.

"Enough distractions. Are you reporters or not?"

"She's a travel writer. A famous one at that."

"So much for being stealth," chimed in Rome.

Bev and Mr. Burns turned to see Rome picking large pieces of moss from her hair and dropping them to the floor as she leafed through several framed paintings stacked against the wall.

Horrified at the sight of the moss covered tiles, Mr. Burns walked toward a large construction garbage can, picked it up and placed it next to the couch. "You're in a castle, madame, not a barn." Shaking his head, he turned and walked back toward the foot of the stairs. "Miss Lemmons! We haven't all afternoon!"

Rome returned to the plastic-covered couch and started to shiver from her cold clothes as Mr. Burns approached. "If your intent is to write an article on Forest Gate, you'll need to seek permission through the proper channels."

"Forest Gate? I thought this was Castle Jones?" replied Rome curiously.

"Castle Jones is a term coined by the press, more specifically that obnoxious columnist, Sergio Arturo."

"*Arturo: Off-the-Wall.* I love that column," responded Bev.

"Of course you do," said Mr. Burns sarcastically.

"A-choo!" sneezed Rome loudly as her teeth began to chatter.

"Are you just going to let her sit there, wearing those soaking wet clothes until she catches her death?" enquired Bev with ulterior motives.

"Of course not. I'll have your car brought to the castle immediately."

"Why not let her take a quick shower?"

In protest, Mr. Burns moved back across the room to contest with Bev and remove the antique vase that had found its way into her hands. "Don't be absurd! She can't take a shower here."

"I have a change of clothes in the boot of my car that I keep on hand for emergencies. I'll go get my vehicle while Rome jumps in the shower and we'll be out of your hair before you know it."

"We don't have a shower."

"Who doesn't have a shower?"

"We made the mistake of hiring a plumbing company who employed a thief masquerading as a plumber."

"Don't look at me. The marriage wasn't my idea."

"Excuse me?"

"Sorry. Auto pilot."

"Needless to say, we're behind schedule. The only bath in the entire castle that has more than a working sink is the master bedroom, and I cannot allow her to take a bath in Mr. Jones' private chambers."

"The only way you're going to get rid of us, without any 'bad press,' is to be a gentleman and allow this lady to clean up before we leave."

Mr. Burns analyzed the situation as he checked the time on his pocket watch, then finally gave in with a dramatic exhale of disdain. "Fifteen minutes. No longer."

"Now that's chivalry, Mr. Burns, and I have to say it's kind of sexy," responded Bev.

"Have you no boundaries, Ms. Hucker?"

"I'm Australian."

"Clearly," sneered the British butler in a patronizing tone.

Bev winked at Rome and gave her the 'A-okay' sign behind his back as Mr. Burns walked toward the couch. "Shall I assume you can find your way to the car, while I show Ms. London to the bath?"

"I'll need the code to get through the gate."

"George!" yelled the butler.

Mr. Burns helped Rome off the couch and the three of them waited for George, while listening to the chatter of Rome's teeth echo throughout the grand hall.

Suddenly, George burst into the room wearing an over-sized suit beneath a dirty apron and rubber gloves. Carrying a bucket full of rags and cleaners, he approached Mr. Burns with a youthful enthusiasm. "Yes, Mr. Burns."

"I see you've resorted to hiring teenagers?" noted Bev, mocking Mr. Burns recent difficulties with keeping his staff employed.

"I'm older than I look, ma'am," said George as he leaned toward Bev, "and I'm actually the gardener."

"Escort this woman to her car and privately use the code to open the gate," ordered his boss.

"Got it, Mr. Burns," responded George happily. "Allow me to get the door."

"Such a gentleman," complimented Bev as they walked across the floor.

"I have no idea what I'm doing, so I've been secretly studying Mr. Burns," whispered George in return.

"I wouldn't study him too closely."

"You're not getting paid to chitchat," said the butler in frustration.

"Sorry, sir."

"And leave the bucket."

"Yes, sir," replied George as he placed the bucket inside the door and left the castle with Bev.

Shaking his head in disapproval, Mr. Burns turned his attention back to Rome and helped her climb the stairs. "Due to staffing issues, George, the caretaker for the grounds, is playing butler. It's so hard to acquire good help these days."

"Especially with all the spirits making such a racket around here."

"You've heard about that have you?"

"Heard about it?"

"The ridiculous stories about the castle being haunted."

"Oh, you're referring to the newspaper."

"Weren't you?"

"How much farther to the bathroom?" responded Rome, trying to change the subject.

Suddenly, Miss Lemmons appeared at the top of the stairs with her uniform disheveled and completely out of breath. "I found them!" Before Mr. Burns could get a word out, Miss Lemmons quickly descended the stairs and met them halfway. "I'm so glad you're staying. You're our first real guest."

"She is not staying, nor is she our guest. We're simply rectifying an unfortunate accident. Now take the towels to the master suite and draw a bath. Ms. London will be cleaning up before she leaves."

"Right away," she said smiling at Rome, then disappeared into the second floor as Mr. Burns continued to help Rome up the stairs.

Suddenly, a loud noise came from the direction of the kitchen, sounding like a tray of plates and glasses hitting the floor. Mr. Burns stopped for a moment, shook his head, then continued to climb the stairs.

"Like I was saying... It's difficult to find good help."

"How long has she been working for you?"

"She started yesterday morning."

"And George as well?"

"George is a good gardener, but his domestic skills are non-existent."

"I think their enthusiasm is adorable."

"But their skills are deplorable."

"How many staff members have you gone through?"

"More than I care to recall."

Mr. Burns and Rome cleared the stairs, crossed the long balcony and entered a dark hallway. Daylight poured into the hall through a few open doors, providing enough light to find their way. "As you can see, the wall sconce lighting has yet to be installed."

"Lighting would be helpful."

"Especially at night."

As they entered the master suite, Rome stopped just inside the doorway and instantly fell in love with the picturesque beauty of the room.

"This and the library are the only finished rooms. Excuse me while I check on the bath and Miss Lemmons. I'm certain another training opportunity awaits."

Mr. Burns walked to the bath as Rome continued to take in the beauty of the space. She walked toward the open window and noticed the light fabric of the curtains blowing in with the breeze. She did not expect that from a rumored recluse or to find those type of curtains in a castle. Tapestry and heavy fabric seemed to be more the norm.

As she began her own private tour around the enormous room, she found herself wanting to touch every dark wood surface of each piece of furniture and open every drawer. She walked toward the wide vanity located beneath a large antique mirror with a masculine design. Rome looked closely at the design on the wooden border and ran her fingers across the polished top of the vanity, then touched the intricate lion head imprint on the drawer knobs.

She continued past the other furniture, taking in the detail of each one until she came to the wardrobe armoire. She found herself compelled to open all four doors concealing an organized closet half full of dress shirts, suits, ties and shoes. Before she shut the last door, she caught her reflection in the full length mirror. She couldn't help but wonder what it would be like to live in such extraordinary surroundings as she stood looking at the disaster she'd become.

Then her eye caught the focal point of the entire room, reflected in the mirror behind her. She turned to see a beautiful, four post bed that completely mesmerized her with its antique beauty. She walked toward it and slowly ran her hand down one of the dark wood posts and across the foot board. It too shared a very masculine design, but its beauty was undeniable. It was obvious that the owner had impeccable taste, as well as a boatload of money.

"This must have cost a fortune," she thought to herself as she walked up the side of the bed to examine the detailed workmanship on the headboard. Rome continued in fantasy mode as she dreamed of what it would be like to fall asleep and wake up in such a beautiful bed and gorgeous setting. And why not? It was a castle, after all: the type of structure built for military purposes that predated the Palladian classic architecture of the Jane Austen novels Rome grew up reading. All Rome wanted to do was leap onto the bed, sink into the luxurious duvet and pretend she was a character in one of the books she loved so much.

Mr. Burns must have read her thoughts as he left the bath. "Don't even think about, Ms. London."

"But it's so tempting."

"The bath is drawn and waiting. Thank goodness for the speed of modern-day water pressure."

Miss Lemmons walked out of the bath behind Mr. Burns, smiling and waving at Rome as she left the room. Mr. Burns walked toward the door, but stopped just short of closing it, reminding Rome of the terms. "Fifteen minutes, Ms. London, no longer. I'll have Miss Lemmons bring your clothes up as soon as Ms. Hucker returns." With that said, Mr. Burns shut the door and left Rome standing alone in the silence of the room.

"Fifteen minutes will never be enough, but it will have to do," uttered Rome as she unbuttoned her shirt, entered the bathroom and shut the door behind her.

Once inside, she nearly melted from the sight of the master bath. "You've got to be kidding me!" she marveled as her thoughts of the bedroom were quickly replaced by the grandeur of the antique-inspired, modern, claw-foot bathtub setting before her. "Even if it's only fifteen minutes, I'll take it," continued Rome as she quickly removed her clothes, eagerly stepped over the high wall of the tub and fully immersed herself in the warm water. Disappearing beneath the surface, Rome felt as though she'd died and gone to heaven.

JUST AS MR. BURNS and Miss Lemmons reached the bottom of the stairs, George entered the grand hall, carrying Bev's bag. His eyes lit up at the sight of Miss Lemmons and she responded with a flirtatious smile and a wink. The moment quickly ended with the abrupt request of Mr. Burns. "Where is Ms. Hucker? Please tell me you did not leave her unattended."

"She was right behind me."

"Very well. Give Miss Lemmons the bag and get back to your duties."

"Right away, sir."

As George handed the bag to Miss Lemmons, their hands purposely touched and George whispered in her ear. "Are we still on for tonight?"

"The south side of the castle at ten," responded Miss Lemmons with great anticipation.

With a spring in their step and a smile on their faces, they quickly separated and went in different directions. Miss Lemmons watched George disappear below as she slowly walked up the stairs. Once she lost sight of him she hurried up the rest of the way.

Bev entered the door and closed it behind her. Secluded in the entranceway, she adjusted her clothing and combed her fingers through her blonde hair. Wanting to make the most of her visit to Castle Jones, or Forest Gate as it were, she set her sights on the man with a key to everything, the butler. Entering the grand hall, she nearly collided with Mr. Burns, who was on a direct path to find her. "So, Mr. Burns, what's a girl got to do to get a tour of the castle? We do have fifteen minutes to kill."

"Thirteen minutes and counting."

"Which will feel like an eternity if we just stand here staring at each other. Tick tock."

"One room, but no pictures."

Mr. Burns held out his hand and she handed him Rome's camera. "Follow me and do not deviate."

Bev slowly pulled out her cell phone, silenced it and started snapping shots behind Mr. Burns's back as they left the grand hall. Walking down a long hallway, she wondered what was behind each of the doors they passed. "Obviously, Mr. Burns does not possess the guide skills of a seasoned professional," Bev thought to herself as she followed him without deviating from the course.

As they entered the library, which doubled as the owner's private study and office, Mr. Burns stopped in his tracks. His temperature began to rise as he saw boxes of books covering the floor yet to be placed on the empty shelves. Mr. Burns walked back to the open door and yelled at the top of his lungs, "George!"

"You may want to consider an intercom system," said Bev as she gently rubbed her ears.

Mr. Burns rolled his eyes at her ridiculous suggestion and walked toward the large wooden desk covered with boxes. No sooner had he reached his destination, but George rushed into the room. "Yes, Mr. Burns."

"Look at this desk. It's a disaster! And why haven't the boxes been unpacked?" demanded the butler.

"I was working on it when you called me away to help the kitchen staff."

"That was three hours ago! You were only supposed to help them pack boxes in from the truck, then you were to return to your previous duties."

"I thought I was supposed to help them unpack the boxes as well."

"The kitchen's appearance is irrelevant. The two rooms that must be completed by the time Mr. Jones returns this evening are the library and the master suite."

"I'll get it done, Mr. Burns," vowed George as he rushed to the boxes covering the floor, opened the lid to one and began pulling out stacks of books.

Highly irritated, Mr. Burns turned his attention to the boxes on the desk and began unloading the contents as he shared his frustrations. "Between the constant rehiring and endless training I've had to do these past few weeks, I simply haven't been able to get it all done."

Bev, seeing an opportunity to extend their stay, made an offer she knew he couldn't refuse. "Then you're in luck. I happen to be very good at organization, not to mention, my alphabetizing skills are unparalleled. Where would you like me to start?"

"Why would you want to help?" suspiciously asked the butler.

"Consider it the price of admission."

Surprised by her willingness to assist, Mr. Burns swallowed his pride and accepted her offer. "You're welcome to help George, while I continue with the desk."

"Happy to help."

"It pains me to admit, Ms. Hucker, but those are the most wonderful words I've heard all day."

Reinvigorated by Bev's offer, Mr. Burns quickly began unloading the desk accessories from the boxes as Bev walked toward George who was kneeling on the floor near the wall of bookshelves.

"How are you at alphabetizing, George?"

"I can recite it."

"You do the bending and lifting and I'll do the organizing. Deal?"

"You got it, Ms. Hucker. And with your height, we probably won't need to find a ladder."

"That should speed things up as well."

Smiling a victorious grin, Bev surveyed the room as George handed her his first grouping of books. As they began to work, the silence was more than Bev could endure so she decided to test the waters by dropping a few random facts about the convict history of Tasmania. Neither George nor Mr. Burns complained, so she continued to educate them on her country's history. Beverly Hucker was born to be a guide, no matter what her surroundings or size of audience.

Chapter Three

As his private jet touched down at the Hobart International Airport, Heath Jones was eager to see the progress made on the castle in his absence. His business trip took a week longer than expected, but some things are necessary when you command a shipping and ship building empire. Once the jet taxied to a stop, Heath exited the plane and paused at the top of the stairs to locate his car and driver. Still dressed to make an impression on the international business community, he reached up, loosened his tie, unbuttoned the collar of his shirt and removed his suit jacket.

Noticing the approaching car, he began to walk down the ramp, never more grateful to be heading home. Before he reached the ground, the wind picked up, playing games with the locks of his sandy blonde hair and revealing a touch of gray. A daily reminder that he was nearing forty and there was no turning back. As he reached the ground, he wearily walked across the tarmac, his six-foot-three, athletic build drooping from fatigue.

Heath's pace slowed to a crawl as his phone began to ring. He looked at the screen and quickly dropped his head forward. His Uncle Roger, the COO of Jones Shipping and Ship Manufacturing,

Inc., was calling again. "Hello, Roger," he said with a thick Australian accent.

Annoyed at the phone call, Heath rubbed his forehead as he put his briefcase down and listened to his uncle's litany of concerns. It took everything he had not to disconnect the call and pretend the service had failed, but Roger was family and deserved his respect. As Heath listened to Roger's endless list of tasks to be done, he watched the steward roll his luggage toward the car. The chauffeur opened the trunk and helped him load the bags as they exchanged their usual pleasantries. Eager to get home, Heath finally took control of the conversation. "I left the contracts on my desk and my secretary will get them to legal in the morning."

Again he listened before responding. "We can discuss it further next week." Then he listened some more before sharing his thoughts for the last time. "I'm not going to make an important decision like that over the phone, Roger. I'm only here for a couple of days." No longer tolerant, Heath ended the call and walked toward the door, patiently being held open by his chauffeur.

"Welcome back, Mr. Jones!"

"Thank you for meeting me earlier than expected."

"Happy to get the call, sir."

Heath handed the chauffeur his briefcase then crawled through the open door and into the back seat of his luxury car. "Take me home, Max."

"To the family home or the castle?"

"The castle is my home now."

"Very well, sir."

Maximillian Snavely, a personable young man of Aboriginal-Australian descent, loved being a chauffeur and took his job very seriously. He loved to navigate the roads and highways of Tasmania, especially the Hobart area where he grew up. Not only was he a confident driver, but he was also quite the ladies man and dressed himself according to the latest business style of the day. He enjoyed the perks of being employed by one of the richest men in the world, but more importantly, he loved working for Heath and the relationship they had developed over the past three years. Crawling in behind the wheel, Mr. Snavely began with the same question he used each time his boss returned home. "Did you have a good trip, sir?"

"I accomplished what needed to be done," Heath responded as usual, "now I'm anxious to get home and take a long hot bath in my brand new tub."

"Should I call ahead and have Mr. Burns turn on the water?"

"Sheldon has no idea I arrived early. He'll figure it out soon enough. I just want to get home."

"A man's home is his castle," responded Mr. Snavely, adjusting the rear view mirror to see his employer's reaction.

"How long have you been waiting to use that line, Mr. Snavely?"

"At least a fortnight, sir."

"Well, I hope it was as satisfying as you thought it would be."

"The delivery and timing felt pretty good."

"Did I mention how eager I am to get home?"

"On our way, sir."

Continuing to feel the fatigue of travel, Heath laid his head back, stared out the window and watched the sun set, smiling at Max's attempt at humor. "It was a pretty good line, Max. And you're right... the timing was excellent, as always."

Pleased as punch, Mr. Snavely smiled to himself as he drove off the runway and onto the main road leaving the airport.

As Heath watched the silhouetted scenery roll by, the ongoing list of ends to tie up continued to traipse through his mind. A love of business had never been Heath's thing, but after an Oxford education and twenty-plus years of working by his father's side, he had become extremely good at it, whether he wanted to or not.

Heath's father, Marshall Heath Jones Sr., was a brilliant shipping tycoon and philanthropist. He ran the business like a well-oiled machine and Heath reaped the benefits of his genius. Not only did they have a great working relationship, but their father/son bond was just as solid. They worked together, they sailed together, they watched rugby together and almost every meal they ate at his father's home or on his sailboat was centered around the barbecue. When his dad passed away, a hole was left inside of Heath that nothing since has been able to fill.

Their close relationship began to form after his mother passed away on his tenth birthday. Up until then he only saw his father on the weekends. Business always came first in their family until the loss of his mother changed his dad's priorities. Rather than leaving Heath with a nanny while he travelled for business, Marshall made the decision to have his son accompany him wherever he went. He hired the best tutors to educate Heath while he attended meetings and business lunches, then hired a young British butler with an old name to see to their personal needs.

Heath even had his own study space at Jones Shipping. He was probably the only child in the world to have a private office—name plate on the door and all. In between the meetings and his own workload, Marshall spent as much time possible with his son.

When Heath turned fourteen, his father felt it was important to enroll him in a private school so he could benefit from sports and other social activities suited to boys his age. Marshall worked more from home during those years, splitting his time between business and his son's needs. Once Heath graduated and began attending Oxford University in England, Marshall threw all of his passion back into his business, growing his company to one of the largest international shipping entities in the world.

Marshall Heath Jones Sr. will always be remembered for his business prowess and charitable work, but if there were awards given for father of the year, he would have been a worthy recipient.

As the car slowed down and began to turn, Heath sat up with new life and stared through the windshield. He watched as the gate opened and revealed Forest Gate in the distance. A sight he hoped would never get old.

"Mr. Burns is going to be surprised at your earlier than expected arrival."

"And we both know how much Sheldon hates surprises, so this should be entertaining."

Mr. Snavely pulled up alongside the door, popped the trunk, grabbed his employer's briefcase and got out of the car. Before he could reach the passenger door, Heath opened it himself, took the briefcase from his chauffeur's hand and hurried toward the house. "Have a good night, Max."

"To you, as well, Mr. Jones. Enjoy the bath," responded Mr. Snavely, his words falling on deaf ears as his employer vanished from sight.

Entering the grand hall, Heath paused for a moment as he placed his briefcase on the floor and looked around. He couldn't help but be impressed with the progress made on the interior of the castle. "She's finally coming together." Heath seemed to find new energy as he bounced up the stairs, turned at the top and quickly disappeared.

Mr. Snavely entered the castle expecting to find his employer still in the grand hall, but all he found was his briefcase. "That must be some amazing tub," he said as he put the bags down in the middle of the floor just as Mr. Burns walked into the room.

Surprised to see him, the butler looked at the chauffeur, then at the bags, then back at Max as the realization hit. "Please don't tell me he's back early."

"Surprise! You just missed him. He's probably already in the tub."

"No!"

Suddenly, a lengthy, blood-curdling duet of screams echoed through the castle and reverberated down the stairs. Mr. Snavely and Mr. Burns looked at each other as Bev and George ran into the room from one direction and Miss Lemmons and several maids quickly entered from the opposite way.

"That can't be good," remarked Mr. Snavely.

"Oh, it's not," replied Mr. Burns, dreading what would come next.

Bev, feeling somewhat responsible for the situation, approached Mr. Burns with every intention of repairing the damage. "This is our fault. I'll take care of it."

Mr. Burns grabbed her arm and stopped her from going any

further. "As head of the household, the responsibility falls to me." Mr. Burns let go of Bev's arm and headed toward the stairs just as Heath appeared at the top. A deep silence filled the room as everyone waited for him to speak. But nothing came. He just stood there, staring down at them, trying to piece together the events of the last thirty-seconds. Finally, Mr. Burns broke the silence. "Sir, if I may..."

"Why is there a woman taking a bath in my brand new tub?" demanded Heath.

Before his butler could respond, Rome joined Heath at the top of the stairs, wearing his robe and attempting to dry her wet, messy hair with his towel. "There was an accident and Mr. Burns was kind enough to allow me to clean up in your bathtub."

"You're an American."

"Rome London."

"But you sound American."

"I am."

"So you're an American who lives abroad?" asked Heath frustrated by the conversation.

"Rome London is my name. I thought you might recognize it."

"Should I?"

"Only if you like to travel or read about it."

"I only travel for business."

"I could say the same."

"You're wearing my robe."

"It beat the idea of running out here naked."

Unable to control himself, George smirked out loud but quickly regained composure after receiving an icy glare of inappropriateness from Mr. Burns.

"Do you have clothing or do we need to provide that as well?" enquired Heath with an air of contempt.

"I do. I'll just head back to the bedroom and get dressed."

"That's probably the best idea you've had all day."

Unsettled, but remaining composed, Heath turned from Rome and descended the stairs. He was not used to chaos within the walls of his own home. Escaping the situation was the only way to avoid furthering the circus act that he and Ms. London had become to the audience at the bottom of the stairs. As he reached the floor he walked through the staff and continued across the great hall. "Mr. Burns, please accompany me to the library."

"Of course, sir."

As Rome and Bev made eye contact the guilt of the butler being taken to task was written all over their faces. Rome raised her shoulders, shook her head and walked back toward the bedroom. Bev paused for a moment then turned to the others who appeared unsure of what to do next. She reverted to the number one 'guide rule' used to handle awkward moments: remedy the situation with humor. "Nothing like making a great first impression," remarked Bev, trying to lighten the mood.

No one laughed. They were still in shell shock and awaiting orders from Mr. Burns, hoping they still had jobs.

"If anyone needs me I'll be in the car."

With the lonely sound of her shoes striking against the marble tile, Bev walked across the floor of the grand hall and came to a stop near the entrance way. Glancing back for what she thought would be the last time, she saw the uncertain look on the staff's faces as they slowly waved goodbye without uttering a word. She had crossed a line and she knew it. Bev came to Castle Jones out of curiosity, but her departure was filled with a sense of culpability. "So much for being stealth," she said to herself as she left the house, gently closing the door behind her.

HEATH ENTERED the library and walked to his desk as Mr. Burns silently followed. He sat in his chair and began rearranging the items on the top of the desk in an attempt to remain calm while gathering his thoughts. "You know how important my privacy is to me, Sheldon, especially with all the bad press I've been receiving."

"Yes, I do."

"Then why allow complete strangers into my home?"

"There is an explanation, but that's not the point. I should have exercised better judgment and never allowed them through the door. This is my fault and I take complete responsibility."

"Why is Ms. London here in the first place?"

"From what I can gather... curiosity about the castle, like everyone else. It all happened so fast. One minute I was answering the door, the next, she was being drenched from above with filthy water."

"I have less problems running a billion-dollar company than I do my own home anymore!" Highly irritated, Heath stood up and crossed the room to the window. Parting the curtains, he looked through the thick-walled window pane to see Bev staring at the engine of her car, surrounded by construction workers and laborers. He watched curiously as she flirted with the men while they did their best to assist. Her relaxed behavior in dealing with car trouble humbled Heath enough to realize he could have handled the previous situation with better form.

"I'm sorry, Sheldon."

"You have nothing to apologize for, Heath."

"I created the monster and now we both must live with it."

"Monster?"

"This castle."

Heath watched curiously as Bev tried to start the car again but was unsuccessful. Soon she left the men and walked back toward the house.

"What's your impression of them?" asked Heath.

"They seem harmless enough."

"It appears the tall one may have car trouble."

"I'll handle it," assured Mr. Burns as he walked toward the door.

"Do whatever it takes, Sheldon. I want my privacy back."

Mr. Burns promptly removed himself from the library leaving Heath disappointed that his return home had turned into such a fiasco. In an attempt to clear his mind, he pulled the cell phone from his pocket and began checking his emails.

BEV ENTERED the castle and walked into the center of the grand hall, finding George, Mr. Snavely, Miss Lemmons and the other maids still standing in the same place. "My car won't start and it's brand new. Nothing like adding insult to injury."

Bev looked up to see Rome quickly moving down the stairs toward her. Her pants, on loan from Bev, rolled up to compensate for their differences in height. Without stopping, she grabbed Bev by the arm and hurried them both toward the door. "Let's go before we cause any more problems."

"We can't go," said Bev as she stopped Rome from pulling her any further.

"What do you mean we can't go?"

"Remember how bad things come in threes?"

"Oh, we're long past three."

"The car won't start."

"Why?"

"I'm a guide, not a mechanic."

"First my car and now yours."

"Coincidence or fate?" said Bev jokingly.

"Or a poltergeist," responded George without thinking. "Did I just say that out loud?"

"That would explain the bucket tipping over and covering you with gunk," surmised Bev. "The worker claims it just tipped over on its own."

Silence filled the hall as they each considered the possibility of paranormal activity. Rome, knowing it was a probability, attempted to refocus the group on the problem at hand. All she wanted was to put distance between her and the owner of Castle Jones.

"Does that mean we're stuck here?" asked Rome.

"Not if we want to choose any one of the ten offers I just got from the guys in the construction crew."

"I think I've had enough impromptu fun for today."

"I'll call a taxi and have a tow truck pick up my car tomorrow."

Mr. Burns entered the room just in time to hear the conversation. "In order to expedite your departure, might I recommend the use of Mr. Snavely's services."

"And what exactly are 'Mr. Snavely's services?'" enquired Bev with a level of skepticism attached.

"Mr. Jones's driver will take you home tonight and I will deal with your car tomorrow."

"Why would you do that?"

"The why doesn't matter. Mr. Snavely will show you to the car."

Impressed by Mr. Burns's generous offer, Bev kept her eye on him as the chauffeur crossed the floor toward them. Reaching the entranceway he opened the door and waited for them to exit the castle with him.

"Thank you, Mr. Burns. That's very kind of you," acknowledged Bev.

"The kindness belongs to Mr. Jones."

"Difficult to believe, but I'll take your word for it."

With that said, Bev walked toward the door and left the castle. Mr. Snavely followed her out, leaving the door open for Rome.

Satisfied that the situation was contained, Mr. Burns walked toward the staff, prepared to resume his schedule as though the arrival of Ms. Hucker and Ms. London had never happened. "Did it slip your minds that you're all still on the clock?"

"No, sir," responded the staff in unison, as they scattered in different directions, followed by Mr. Burns, leaving Rome standing alone in the grand hall.

As she turned to leave, a silver pitcher holding a bouquet of flowers slid from the center of a small end table near the plastic covered couch and fell to the ground. She looked around the room suspiciously then walked toward the vase.

Unbeknownst to Rome, Heath arrived at the end of the hallway, still focused on his phone. Realizing he was not alone, he hid himself in the shadows and curiously watched.

Rome bent down, picked up the vase and placed it back on the end table, arranging the flowers as best she could. "If you're trying to get my attention, you have it," said Rome to the suspected ghost. In response, she heard the same male Australian voice whisper into her ear.

"Help them."

"Help who?" asked Rome out loud.

"He needs your help."

"Who needs my help?"

"You're the only one who can."

"A name would be helpful," enquired Rome, wanting more details.

With his curiosity turned to suspicion, Heath perked up causing him to accidentally drop his phone. Rome's attention quickly turned from the ghost to the sound heard from across the room. She watched as Heath picked up his phone and walked into the light of the grand hall.

"I was just leaving," said Rome as she crossed the floor.

"Who were you talking to?"

Rome stopped in her tracks, realizing Heath had heard one side of her brief conversation with the spirit. Her only option was to think fast. "I was admiring your vase."

"Do you often talk to inanimate objects?"

"No, but I have been known to talk to myself about them."

"Since when do vases have names? You said, 'A name would be helpful.'"

"Brand name," answered Rome cleverly.

"It's a hand forged antique from the early 1800s."

"It's beautiful."

"Yes, it is."

Heath could tell she was hiding something and doing her best to evade his question. He'd seen the technique used in business countless times and had employed it himself when it served his purpose. "So you expect me to believe you were talking to yourself?" asked Heath in an accusatory tone.

"Do you see anyone else in the room?"

"No, do you?"

"I shouldn't keep your driver waiting."

"He gets paid whether he waits or drives," replied Heath, exercising his authority.

"Before I leave I want to apologize for causing so much trouble.

That was not our intent," responded Rome in an attempt to change the subject.

"What was your intent, Ms. London?"

"Honestly, I wanted an answer to my question."

"What question is that?"

"It's no longer important."

"Humor me."

"Maybe another time."

"I highly doubt there will be one."

"All right. What kind of man buys a castle in England and has it shipped block by block to the bottom of the world?" asked Rome confidently and with a touch of sass.

Heath paused for a moment, surprised by the audacity of her question and the tone of her voice. "Did you get your answer?"

"I'm beginning to."

Ending the conversation in control, Rome departed the castle leaving the door open. Heath walked to the doorway and watched curiously as Rome took one last look at him then got into the car. Heath shut the door and leaned up against it, thinking about Rome's short conversation with what he believed to be a ghost. Intrigued by the prospect, he walked toward the center of the grand hall and looked around the room. "Hello. Is anyone there?"

Receiving no answer, Heath continued to walk toward the stairs. Unexpectedly, the same vase of flowers slid to the edge of the end table and fell off again. Heath stopped and slowly looked in the direction of the vase, finding it lying on the floor. His heart skipped a beat or two as he took a moment to inspect the room. "Sheldon? Sheldon."

Sensing he was being watched, the speed of his steps increased as he made his way to the top of the stairs. When he reached the balcony, he looked both ways, then again called for his butler as he disappeared down one of the dark hallways. "Sheldon!"

Mr. Burns entered the grand hall and saw the flowers lying on the floor. "Not again." He walked toward the bouquet and accidentally stepped in the puddle of water causing him to slip, but not fall. He picked up the vase of flowers and walked out of the room, muttering to himself as he went, "This castle is going to be the death of me. Miss Lemmons!" Clearing his throat, he felt the toll of all the yelling on his esophagus and for a moment he actually considered Ms. Hucker's recommendation for an intercom. But only for a moment. "Miss Lemmons!"

Chapter Four

*D*ay Five on Rome's assignment to Tasmania found her practically comatose in the center of her hotel bed. She'd stayed up too late the night before watching Bev drown her sorrows. At least she thought she was only watching. Buried beneath a pile of bedding, Rome's sleep was suddenly disturbed by a knock on the door that Rome had no intention of answering. "Go away!"

Unwilling to give up, the unknown visitor knocked again. This time a bit louder.

"What?" yelled Rome from beneath the covers.

"Ms. London. It's Heath Jones."

"Heath Jones?" Rome muttered to herself as she poked her head out of the covers.

Realizing who was knocking on her door, she sat up and tried to reach a coherent state. Raising her sleep mask to the top of her head, she was instantly blinded by the light coming in from the window. Covering her eyes, she crawled out of bed, stepped on one of her heels and fell to the floor, groaning in pain.

"Is everything all right in there?" asked Heath out of curiosity more than concern.

"I'm fine!"

Rome pulled the bedspread off the bed and wrapped it around her as she stumbled across the floor. Opening the door, she was blinded by the bright sunlight, causing her to further shield her eyes with her hands.

Shocked by her wild hair, partially contained by the sleep mask and her use of a bedspread for a robe, Heath spoke before he thought. "I think 'fine' might have been an overstatement."

"I went with Bev to a pub last night."

"Never go drinking with an Australian: we'll drink you under the table every time."

"I stopped drinking years ago, so I'm not sure what happened last night."

"Chalk it up to a cultural experience."

"What are you doing here?" asked Rome, already annoyed by his pompous presence.

"I came by to take you to an early lunch."

"Don't even mention food."

"Sorry."

"If it's close to lunchtime, I'm running late," said Rome as she began to close the door.

"Late for what?" enquired Heath as he put out his hand and stopped the door from being shut.

"This is my last full day in Australia, or at least what's left of it, and I need to see a few more sights out at Port Arthur."

"How are you getting there?"

"Taxi, I suppose."

"I could take you."

"What?"

"Do you want to go like that or did you want to... you know... maybe comb your hair?"

"Why would you want to take me all the way out there?"

"It's a nice day for a drive."

Rome took a minute to think about his offer, but due to the cloudiness of her head she wasn't terribly successful. "Okay. I'll meet you in the lobby in a few minutes."

"Is that a realistic time frame?"

Rome ignored what she considered to be a smart aleck response to her appearance and closed the door. Walking toward the bathroom she caught a glimpse of herself in the mirror and realized he was being honest rather than smug. "Oh! You answered the door like that? Have you no shame?" Realizing she needed more help than she thought, Rome entered the bathroom, turned on the shower and stepped into the center of the spray. She wanted nothing more than to stand in the hot water and allow the pulsing massage to beat down on her back for as long as she could. Unfortunately, time was of the essence and she was already way off schedule. As she poured on the shampoo and began washing her ratted hair, she couldn't help but question how she let her trip to Tasmania get so out of control. This was not like her. She was organized. She was disciplined. She was a six hour a night sleeper, no more. Rome lived and died by her itinerary and stuck to her plans like glue—part and parcel to being raised by an officer in the Navy and a mother who made the systematic structure of military life look like child's play. "What's done is done," she thought to herself, knowing that soon she'd finish up the last of her sightseeing research and be back on track. This may be one of those times where Rome had to pull it off at the last minute.

"Pull it off"... three words Rome detested for obvious reasons. She expected a high standard from her work and the idea of throwing something together at the last minute was amateur at best. However, Rome had never missed her editor's preprint deadline and she wasn't about to start now.

HEATH WALKED into the hotel lobby and approached the main desk. He pulled out his wallet and tossed some money onto the counter. "Can I get a newspaper?"

"Of course, sir."

The attendant handed him a copy of the Mercury's Sunday edition, then picked up the money and turned toward the cash register. "Keep the change," said Heath as he glanced at the front page of the newspaper on his way to the lounge area. The headline read: A Man and His Haunted Castle, byline, Arturo: Off the Wall. He cast the paper aside, muttering his feelings about the columnist as he found a suitable place to sit. Heath's attention quickly turned to a commercial on the television, advertising an evening entertainment news show boasting of several upcoming interviews with former employees of Castle Jones. Employees who quit their jobs due to an unsuitable work environment involving ghosts. Unable to take the bombardment of sensationalism, Heath stood up and left the lobby.

Outside he found a bench across the drive from the entrance and made himself comfortable in the shade. The sights and sounds of nature were a nice distraction for Heath as he waited for Rome. Unfortunately, his solace was quickly interrupted with the ringing of his phone. "This is Heath."

It was his secretary, Jane, calling to remind him of his upcoming appointments. Jane had been with Heath for most of his business career, and because of their close working relationship, she knew him as well as anyone could. Lately, she had grown more and more concerned with Heath's well-being, especially since he made what Jane and anyone else who knew Heath considered to be an irrational decision to purchase the castle.

"You'll need to reschedule," responded Heath. "Something came up and I won't be able to take that conference call this afternoon. Also, I left a couple of contracts on my desk that need to be sent to legal. Make sure that happens today so my uncle doesn't blow a gasket. Thank you, Jane."

Heath ended the call. Placing his phone in the inside pocket of his suit jacket, he noticed a scarlet robin building a nest in the fork of a tree branch. He watched as she floated from the tree to the ground, gathered a beak full of dried grass and twigs, then flew back to the nest construction site. He couldn't take his eyes off of the bird as she repeated the process over and over again. The robin knew exactly how she wanted her nest to look and was making it happen on her own terms. Soon she'd have a home built where she and her mate could raise a family. And the best thing of all... there are no other birds setting on the limbs, spying on her, taking pictures, writing articles and calling her eccentric for building her nest how and where she wanted it built.

Realizing he was getting a bit carried away, Heath quickly stood up to clear his head. "Let it go, Heath. Just let it go," he said to himself out loud as a form of relaxation therapy, then he turned around just in time to see Rome exit the lobby. His thoughts quickly changed direction when for the first time he saw Rome dressed in her own clothes, with her wet hair contained. Unable to take his eyes off of her, he stood speechless, watching her sundress and scarf blow in the breeze.

Carrying a large tote with her souvenir hat sticking out the top, a bottle of water and a light sweater over her arm, Rome looked around for Heath through a pair of dark sunglasses. She finally located him standing near the bench and crossed the drive toward him. She set her bag down and put on her sweater.

"That was a quick transformation."

"And you thought I couldn't do it."

"A mistake I will not repeat."

"The wonders of a shower and the brilliance of a hair clip."

"You look... very suitable."

"Wow, suitable. That's not a description you hear every day. Thank you, I think."

"Should we go?"

"The sooner the better," encouraged Rome.

Awkwardly, they both reached for Rome's large bag, nearly colliding with each other. Rome straightened up, allowing Heath to be the gentleman. She smiled to herself as she watched him pick up her bag, not expecting it to be as heavy as it looked.

"This is quite a bag you've packed for one afternoon."

"I like to be prepared."

"For everything it would seem."

"I'm not a fan of surprises."

"As proven by yesterday."

"Let's forget that ever happened."

"Would you like to stop for lunch on the way?"

"I think I'll just hydrate for now. I'm in a bit of a hurry. But if you're hungry, feel free to stop."

"I think I saw a cherry ripe between the seats."

Having run out of conversation, Heath turned and walked toward his vehicle. On his way he pulled out his remote key and started the Land Rover.

"No Mr. Snavely today?"

"I do own a government-issued driver's license and every now and then I like to dust it off."

"How average of you."

No response from Heath as he opened the passenger-side door and helped Rome step onto the running board and slide into the seat. "Buckle up."

"Oh, I plan to, especially with a novice at the wheel."

Rome again waited for a smile or even a laugh from Heath, but without comment he shut her door. She sat quietly as he opened the rear door and placed her tote in the back seat. "This one's a charmer," Rome commented to herself after hearing the back door shut. Her opinion quickly changed as she watched him walk around the front of the vehicle. All of a sudden, she found herself becoming intrigued by his smooth, confident stride and handsome demeanor. She tried to stop staring, but her eyes would not obey. She continued to watch in slow motion as he ran his fingers through his ample hair while waiting for a passing car. Soon, Rome found herself wishing that his personality equalled what she saw on the outside.

Embarrassed by the thought, she tried to shake it off, but it was no use. As he turned and walked to drivers' side door, Rome's eyes continued to follow behind the privacy of her shades. Never before had Rome been more thankful for a pair of dark sunglasses.

The door opened and Heath crawled into the driver's seat, buckled himself in and started the engine. "Safety first," he said as though he were a driving instructor.

Still intrigued by the one-man-show she just observed through the windshield, Rome responded the only way she could.

"Uh-huh."

"Are you all right, Ms. London?"

Realizing the gravity of his simple question, Rome quickly refocused herself on the conversation at hand. "Yeah, I'm good."

"I don't think we were properly introduced last night. Marshall Heath Jones. Call me Heath."

Unexpectedly, he extended his hand. Rome took hold of it and they slowly shook. "Rome London."

"An American with two international cities for a name."

"My country did begin as a melting pot," said Rome, making another attempt at humor. Or at least she thought so. Still no laughter. Not even a smile.

"So you were named after your country's roots?"

"Nothing that deep. My father's last name is London and my mother is from Italy. They met while he was stationed there in the Navy."

"So it's not your pseudonym?"

"No. It's the real deal. My great-great-grandmother was named Rome as well."

"It certainly is unusual."

"You'll get used to it. Everyone does."

"I'm sure I will," said Heath, finding himself not wanting to let go of her hand.

"I realize you don't drive a lot, but I'm pretty sure two hands are better than one. Safety first," said Rome, taking another stab at getting a laugh. But no laughter was heard, other than her own, halfhearted giggle.

In response, Heath snapped back to reality and let go of her hand. He turned his attention to the rear view mirror and adjusted it properly, then he gripped the steering wheel, put it in gear and pulled out onto the road.

Rome reached around to the back seat and pulled her laptop out of her bag. "I still need to look into some of the accommodations available near Port Arthur as well. I opted to stay in Hobart to get the feel of what the city has to offer, but I should inform my readers of some other options. You know, the small and quaint type. Bev has been great in providing plenty of information, but I'd like to physically see a few of her recommendations and I definitely need to take some more photos."

"Bev would be the woman who was with you at the castle?"

"Yes. She's been my personal tour guide at Port Arthur."

"So what haven't you seen down there?"

"The main thing is the Isle of the Dead. I saved it till last. Bev's taking me on a private tour this afternoon."

"You should be able to see it from shore."

"But I can't write about it unless I tour it."

"And there's no other reason?"

"I will admit that it's one of the main reasons I chose to highlight Port Arthur for next month's article."

"Why is that?"

"Now you're getting into trade secrets."

"I'm just curious."

"More incentive to purchase next month's issue of *Trekking the Globe*."

Even as she worked to deviate Heath from the truth, Rome felt the strangest thing happening. For the first time in her life she felt compelled to tell another person about her gift. She knew the risk of people finding out her secret and had kept it hidden her entire life, even from her closest friends and associates. Yet here she was, constrained to tell a perfect stranger about her ability to listen to the dead. Fortunately, Heath took the topic in a slightly different direction. "My great-great-great-great-Grandfather Jones was a prisoner at Port Arthur."

"Have you toured the site?" enquired Rome.

"I've been to Port Arthur, but not the Isle of the Dead. When I was a kid, my parents and I used to sail around the peninsula. One time we cruised into the cove and had a look at the island from the boat."

"Add it to your bucket list."

"Speaking of lists, what else do you need to see?"

"Some more sites on the Tasman Peninsula, but I'm not sure if I'll have time to see them in person. I may just have to write about them from the information Bev has given me.

"It would be a shame for you to miss them."

"Unfortunately, I'm on a schedule."

"You're on vacation."

"No, I'm on the job," said Rome emphatically.

"A job without appointments or meetings."

"Schedules are just as important in my line of work as they are in yours."

"I'm sorry if I insinuated differently," apologized Heath.

"I suppose it's an easy conclusion to draw."

Relieved that the change of topic ended Heath's curiosity about her visit to the Isle of the Dead, Rome laid her head back to get some rest. Heath's implication about her career allowed a familiar question to creep back into her thoughts as though it were being whispered in her ear. What must it feel like to be completely unrestrained?

As they drove passed the beautiful forests of eucalyptus trees, she knew that if she wasn't careful she could answer that question by getting lost in the unique beauty of this land. Or maybe the real threat was sitting in the seat next to her. The idea of relinquishing control and losing herself to anything or anyone scared Rome more than she was willing to admit.

Abruptly leaning forward, Rome shook off the invading thoughts as she removed the lid from her water bottle and took a drink. Within the hour she would part ways with her new acquaintance, Heath Jones, severing the unsolicited connection she was beginning to feel toward him, and by tomorrow she would say goodbye to this captivating land. Soon all would be as it should in Rome's world, that was until Heath decided to throw a monkey wrench into her plans. "Would you mind if I crashed your private tour of the Isle of the Dead this afternoon?"

"Do you have that kind of time, running a large business and all?"

"I'm the President and CEO. I can make the time."

"The tour may take a while."

"I can fit it in."

"What about your schedule?"

"Schedules are designed to be changed."

On that point, Rome definitely disagreed. But the larger problem at hand was that she was quickly running out of reasons for him NOT to accompany her on the tour. "My guide's not planning on a third person. That could complicate things."

"Complicated like... finding you in my bathtub last night?"

"Touché," responded Rome, realizing she just lost the argument. "I suppose we do owe you one after 'storming' your castle yesterday."

Again, no laughter other than her own.

Thankfully for Rome, Heath's phone began to ring allowing her the breathing space she needed.

"Hello, Jane."

As Heath conducted business over the phone, Rome found herself more confused than ever as she wondered why a billionaire would want to spend his valuable time on the Isle of the Dead. At this point there was little she could do about it, so she sat back and stared out the window. Her only remaining hope was with Bev and some kind of a guide policy that would limit the number of people on a private tour. A thought Rome quickly dismissed due to its own ridiculousness.

HEATH PULLED into the parking lot at Port Arthur and stopped the vehicle. He got out and walked around to the passenger side of the car as Rome pulled the hair clip from her hair and swapped it for the hat in her tote. Then she pulled out a tube of sunscreen and the visitor pass Bev gave her and put it around her neck. Turning back, she was surprised to see Heath opening her door and extending his hand. Rome took his hand and he gently helped her out of the car. Once outside, she put on her hat and began rubbing some sunscreen on her arms and chest.

"An official visitors pass," remarked Heath acting impressed.

"You are in the presence of a V.I.P."

Heath reached into the back seat and pulled out Rome's bag,

then escorted her to the Visitor's Centre. Rome felt a familiar welcoming from her surroundings and was glad to be back as she strolled across the grounds. In the distance, they saw Bev running toward them, waving enthusiastically.

"She's quite the presence, your friend."

"That she is," Rome said as she smiled with pride. "That she is."

A sound from Heath's phone alerted him to a text message and he began to respond instantly as Bev approached. Slightly out of breath, she wrapped her arm around Rome's shoulder and gave her a big friendly squeeze, dwarfing her in size. "I've had lookouts taking turns waiting for you. I was getting worried."

"I've had better mornings. You look no worse for the wear."

"I'm Australian."

"So that's the secret," said Rome jokingly.

"I see you brought someone with you."

"Actually, he brought me."

Unexpectedly, she turned to Heath, took him in her arms and gave him a quick hug. Continuing to interrupt his messaging, she followed it up with a robust pat on the back.

"Didn't think I'd see you again," joked Bev.

"Nor I you," responded Heath in a more serious tone as he continued to text.

"Thanks for taking care of my girl."

"I wouldn't go that far," mentioned Rome.

Turning back to her friend, Bev reached into her pocket, pulled out a set of keys and waved them in the air. "Ready to go? We're borrowing the maintenance boat."

"It's now or never," said Rome nervously, knowing what might be waiting.

"Would you mind if I tagged along?" asked Heath as he continued to respond to incoming text messages.

"As long as your mobile gets turned off."

"No problem," he responded as he continued to text.

"Now."

Heath realized that Bev meant business, so he stopped typing and lowered his phone.

"Did you turn it off?"

"Is that really necessary?"

"Only if you want to join us on the island."

Heath realized he was in a no-win situation, so he powered down his phone and tucked it securely in his pocket.

"What do you say we stop by the cafe on our way to the harbor and pick up something for afternoon tea? Have you eaten?" asked Bev.

Heath quickly answered the question before Rome could comment. "No! We haven't."

"Sounds like somebody's hungry. Come on."

The three of them continued across the grounds as Bev jumped back into the role she knew best—that of guide. Pulling out a notebook and jotting down notes here and there, Rome took in the endless flow of information about the Isle of the Dead.

Soon, they reached the cafe and Bev led them through the restaurant and into the kitchen. She picked up a basket and handed it to Heath, as she began filling it with assorted pre-prepared lunch items. She placed several bottles of water in a plastic bag and turned to the person running the kitchen to settle the bill. "What do I owe you for this 'V.I.P.' lunch?"

"Leave a fifty at the counter."

"A fifty? What about the employee discount?"

"That includes the employee discount."

Heath pulled out his wallet and laid a generous sum of money on the table next to Bev and the kitchen worker.

"Put that back in your wallet," objected Bev. "I'm not done negotiating here."

Heath placed his hand gently around Bev's shoulder and did one of the things he does best: problem solve. "Maybe you two can continue this debate at a later date."

"Oh, I'm just getting started."

"I sense that. However, time is of the essence."

Bev quickly recognized that Heath had a point and responded accordingly. "Don't be thinking this is over." Then she gave him the evil-eye and walked out of the kitchen.

Heath picked up the basket and whispered to Rome as he passed her by. "If she ever gets tired of being a guide, I could use someone like that at corporate." Rome smiled as she envisioned Beverly Hucker thrown into a mix of white-collar desk jockeys. "Now that would be worth seeing," she thought to herself.

Walking around the harbor, they finally reached the dock. Heath stopped next to the maintenance boat and placed Rome's tote and the food basket inside the vessel, then offered his hand to help a surprised Bev onto the boat. She approvingly took his hand and stepped over the side, carrying her sack of water bottles. Next he helped Rome onto the boat, making sure she steadied herself before he let go. "I'll get her untied," said Heath as he unwrapped the rope from the mooring cleat, tossed it back into the boat and stepped over the side just as Bev started the engine and propelled the boat away from the dock. The thrust of the take-off was so unexpected, it threw Heath and Rome into the padded seat at the rear. Bev glanced back at them and smiled a cheeky grin. "Time is of the essence," she yelled, then laughed out loud as she steered the boat toward the Isle of the Dead. As far as Bev was concerned, she was simply facilitating a private tour of the island, but for Rome and Heath it was much more than that.

They each had their own hidden agenda for visiting the island. Rome came for answers as to why the spirit's whispers had called her to Tasmania. Heath, on the other hand, was banking on a theory, a theory born from what he witnessed the night before at the castle. He too was seeking answers, not in the form of tales or old headstones, but from Rome herself.

Scared to move, Rome and Heath remained seated for the short trip as the cool breeze balanced out the warmth of the sun. The accelerated ride came to a halt as Bev pulled the boat up next to the dock. Heath grabbed the rope and jumped onto the dock then tied it off. Turning back, he accepted the food basket and tote that Rome had in her hands and put them down. He then extended his hand to Rome and helped her out as Bev waited patiently. Normally, she would have hopped over the side and had the boat tied off without a bit of help, but today she figured she'd play it like a lady. When with Rome, after all.

And there it was, the chivalrous extension of Heath's hand. Bev took hold and stepped over the boat, then began her spiel as she led them down the dock toward the island. Facts rolled off her tongue as she shared the history of the Isle of the Dead including stories about some of the over one thousand people buried there. Rome knew from her research that some historians believed the number of dead to be closer to sixteen hundred. But that was secondary to why she was really there.

Rome handed her camera to Heath to play photo journalist as she took notes. The majority of the head stones on the island were located on the high northern end. Of course, these belonged to the military and free men who ran the prison. The low southern end of the island was full of mostly unmarked graves belonging to the convicts who died while incarcerated at Port Arthur between 1833 and 1877.

While Heath and Bev continued down the trail ahead of her, Rome felt a presence begin to surround her. It was thick and heavy, making it difficult to walk. Forced to slowly come to a stop, she closed her eyes and began to listen. Soon the sound of the waves crashing against the shore was replaced by sonance from a choir of mismatched voices. Hundreds of words and portions of sentences were coming at her from all directions, making it impossible to understand.

Next, the physical force accompanying the voices began to spin around her, trapping her inside a whirlwind and pulling her upward. She tried to scream but was unable to speak. "Stop! Let go of me! Get away!" she yelled in her mind, but nothing seemed to have any effect on the power in control. Eventually, she became trapped in what felt like a full-body straight jacket, unable to move her arms or legs. Panic and fear began to set in as she felt her feet leave the ground. She tried to call out for help, but even her jaw was immovable. The chaotic and frightening voices grew louder and louder until everything came to an abrupt stop.

Rome dropped from the air and hit the ground with great force, propelling her forward. To control the impulse to scream, she dug her fingers deep into the earth until her grip was full of dirt. The pressure of pushing into the soil provided an outlet for the tension cresting inside, desperate for escape. Finally able to catch her breath, she remained on her hands and knees until the shaking stopped and she felt secure enough to release the dirt from her clenched fingers.

Sitting back on her heels, Rome opened her eyes to see a man staring at her from a safe distance, just to the left of the trail. He was dressed in the Australian convict uniform of the mid-eighteen hundreds commonly referred to as the 'Magpie.' She rubbed her eyes to make sure he wasn't a figment of her imagination, but there was no mistaking the fact that he was real. His heavy wool trousers were half black and half yellow and had buttons that ran down the outside of each leg which made it easy to remove while wearing leg irons. His trousers matched the color scheme of his yellow coat and woolen cap. Beneath his open coat he wore a shirt and a vest, dingy and worn from use.

Surprisingly calm, Rome crawled to her feet and faced down the man who continued to stare back at her. This was the first time she had come face to face with a spirit and wasn't sure what to do. Spirits had spoken to her over the years, but never had she experienced physical contact. The gift of listening to the dead had been passed down through her mother's side of the family for generations, but the only person who ever saw them in spirit form was her great-great-grandmother and namesake. Still unsure of what to do she continued to stare at the man waiting for him to say something, anything, but he never spoke.

Rome screamed out loud as Heath took her by the arm from behind. "Did I frighten you?"

She quickly looked back to the spot where she had seen the convict's spirit, but he was no longer there. Bending over and resting her hands on her knees, Rome breathed in the good air and let out the bad as she tried to collect herself. She'd worked hard to keep her ability a secret and despite her previous temptation to do so, she wasn't about to divulge it now. The last thing she wanted was to be labeled a freak or diagnosed as mentally unstable.

Hearing the scream, Bev quickly ran toward them, arriving just as Rome straightened up and brushed the messy hair from her face.

"Are you all right?" asked Bev.

"I'm fine."

"This island can be an intense experience. We can leave anytime you need to," said Bev, concerned for Rome's well-being.

"My imagination just got carried away for a moment."

"That's all it was?" asked Heath suspiciously.

"Like Bev said, this island can be an intense experience."

"For some more than others," implied Heath as he picked up Rome's hat, dusted off the sand and placed it on her head, tightening the small chord that hung beneath her chin. "That should help to keep it on." Then he gently patted the top of her hat.

Loosening the cord, Rome halfheartedly thanked him then turned toward Bev and rolled her eyes. A clear sign of the irritation she felt from being treated like a child.

Confused by the tension building between Heath and Rome, Bev decided to play referee and call a time out. "This may be a good time for afternoon tea. There's a beautiful spot down by the water where we can eat. Come on."

As she followed Bev down the trail, Rome felt a strong temptation to look back toward the spot where she saw the spirit. Trying to be nonchalant, she turned her head to the side, unsure of what to expect. Surprised to see the spirit standing in the same spot, Rome inadvertently allowed a small gasp to escape her mouth. She watched him for a bit longer then turned her head forward and continued down the trail, unaware that Heath was watching.

Heath surveyed the opening, searching for what captivated Rome's attention but saw nothing. Click went the camera as Heath took a picture in the direction Rome was staring. With his curiosity in overdrive, he was now more determined than ever to find out the truth about Rome. He truly believed that she was the answer to his castle's ghost problem and all he needed was enough evidence to prove his theory correct. Something had happened back there and Heath wanted to know more.

As they walked onto the beach, there couldn't have been a more picturesque location to dine. The two large, naturally-placed pieces of driftwood made the perfect seating arrangement as they sat down and took a break from touring. Bev placed the basket next to her and began handing out sandwiches and other assorted lunch items, until she realized what she forgot. "I left the water bottles back in the boat."

Rome jumped up from the driftwood in the hopes of finding more time to spend with the unknown spirit that had appeared to her. "I'll get them."

Unwilling to let her out of his sight, Heath quickly stood up alongside of Rome. "I'll go with you."

"It's one small bag. I doubt it requires the both of you to carry."

"Then I'll get it," volunteered Heath as he turned and ran back up the trail.

"And the day just keeps getting more and more interesting," Bev pointed out, hoping to start a conversation.

"Agreed. The tour of this island has certainly proved to be that."

"I'm not referring to the sightseeing. That man's on this island for more than a tour."

"That's what concerns me."

"You got a billionaire who lives in a castle interested in you and that's what's causing you concern?"

"What are you talking about?"

"I'm talking about the same thing you're talking about."

"Oh! You think, I think, he's interested in me romantically and that's why I'm concerned," said Rome, a bit floored by her observation.

"What else?"

"No. You're right. I'm totally thinking what you're thinking," Rome responded, hoping to distract Bev from what she was really thinking, that Heath suspected something about her ability and wanted proof. "Would you mind helping me off with my sweater?"

"So?" enquired Bev, pulling Rome's sleeves over her dirty hands.

"So... what?"

"Do you feel the same way?"

Rome pulled several paper napkins from the food basket, walked to the water's edge and squatted down. Lowering her hands into the water, she began to vigorously scrub the dirt from her palms and fingers. "I'm here on assignment, Bev. By tomorrow I'll be gone. Not to mention the fact that I'm seeing someone back in the states."

"How serious is it?"

"Are we really going to have this conversation?"

"We're stuck on an island full of dead people. I doubt any of them are interested in conversation."

She would like to have enlightened her new friend, but she knew the potential danger in opening up that can of worms, so she decided to play along. "Jamie and I have been seeing each other for about two years now."

"Two years is quite a while."

"It's not that long."

"How did you and this Jamie meet?"

"He works for the State Department as a DS agent..."

"A what?"

"Diplomatic Security agent. They ensure the safety and security of everyone involved in US foreign policy."

"How did he get that job?"

"He was a Navy SEAL."

"With a job like that he probably travels as much as you do. No wonder two years doesn't seem that long. You barely see each other."

"Actually, our lives fit really well together."

"Where did you meet?"

"In South Africa. I was there writing an article and he was running a security detail for some State Department official. I'd just returned from a hike of the Amphitheater in the Drakensberg Mountain Range and we literally ran into each other in the lobby of the hotel."

"How romantic."

"It would have been if I weren't covered in dirt and sweat. I figured if a guy were going to ask me out for a late supper looking and smelling like that, he was worth saying, 'yes' to."

"Does he live in New York City as well?"

"He lives in D.C., but he keeps a home in New York. He inherited the house he grew up in when his folks passed away and now he uses it as a weekender. It's a short commute from D.C. to the city."

"So how often do you guys see each other?"

"A couple times a month, but it's usually for a few days at a time. It also helps that all of his favorite sports teams reside in New York. Our dating schedule tends to revolve around the Rangers, the Knicks, the Yankees and the Jets' games."

"So you're both sports fans?"

"I'm fine with it as long as he lets me drag him to whatever I want to do."

"Are you in love with him?"

"And there it is, the most loaded question in the world."

"If it's that complicated, my guess is you're probably not."

Rome dried the water from her clean hands, then dipped the napkins into the ocean and began to scrub the dirt from her knees. Although she lacked the answer Bev was searching for, her silence was equally informative to both of them. Standing up, she brushed the remaining dirt from her sundress and made her way back to the driftwood, "I love Jamie for many reasons and we have a great time when we're together."

"But?"

"There is no but. Like I said, our lives fit really well together."

"Call me crazy, but I'm pretty sure that being in love is more than just two lives fitting well together."

"It seems to work for us."

The sound of Heath's feet running down the trail ended their conversation as he burst onto the beach, water bottles in hand and out of breath.

"I've been spending too much time in an office chair."

"You didn't need to sprint both ways," remarked Bev as she took a bottle of water from Heath's extended hand.

"I didn't want to miss out on the conversation," Heath joked as he handed Rome a water bottle and sat down on the driftwood next to her.

"Nothing but girl talk," Rome assured Heath as she turned her head and winked at Bev.

"I'm starved, so let's dig in."

Bev passed out the lunch items and they began eating while enjoying the beauty of their surroundings. She continued to share stories and information about the history of the island, but in the forefront of Rome's mind played the image of the spirit she had encountered. She just couldn't shake it. The sadness of his eyes. The fatigue of his posture. The look of torture on his face. "How could I have seen a spirit?" she asked herself as she sat next to Heath, pretending to be interested in the conversation. Why here of all places? Why now?

"It's getting late, we should probably get back," announced Bev as they wrapped up their picnic and prepared to end the tour of the island.

Feeling trepidation about the walk back, Rome needed to prepare herself for what may lie ahead. As she stood up and reached for her tote, she found that Heath had already claimed it. "Thank you," she said, accompanied by a smile. "After you." Rome was hoping he'd take her up on her offer to follow Bev and allow her to bring up the rear, but his response ended that possibility. "After you. I insist."

Heath wanted the best vantage point as they made their way back across the island, so Rome knew she had to find another way to spend time with her ghost. "I think I have a pebble in my shoe," she said, diverting Heath's attention.

Rome sat back down on the driftwood and started to remove her brightly-colored, canvas sneaker, but Heath beat her to it. He gently removed her shoe and tipped it upside down, while Rome secretly slipped her notebook behind the driftwood.

"I didn't see anything fall out," Heath said as he proceeded to slip the shoe back on her foot and tie it up in a bow.

"Thank you. That feels much better."

Rome stood up and headed for the trail, leaving the notebook hidden from sight. Thinking he had the upper hand, Heath followed her up the path.

As they approached the spot where Rome had seen the spirit, she discreetly moved her eyes toward the opening without turning her head. Just as expected, the same ghost stood in the same place, wearing the same clothes with the same look on his face. Much to Heath's disappointment, Rome continued down the trail as though nothing had happened.

When they reached the dock Rome used her best acting skills to make her announcement. "Huh! I left my notebook behind." In unison, both Heath and Bev offered to walk back after it, but Rome insisted she be the one to go. "I know just where I left it. I'll be back in a minute." Then she turned and ran back up the trail.

Bev, unaware of what was really going on, continued down the dock to the boat. Heath, on the other hand, suspiciously watched Rome disappear into the trees. She had outsmarted him, leaving him disappointed, yet somewhat impressed.

"Come along, Sir Heath," Bev called from the end of the dock, "This island's too small for her to get lost and all the criminals are dead."

Heath, realizing he had no more cards to play, turned back toward the dock and followed Bev to the boat.

ROME QUICKLY MADE her way back down the trail, finally reaching the opening and finding the spirit standing in the same place. "I'll be right back. Don't move!" As quickly as possible, she continued down the trail, ran onto the beach and grabbed her notebook.

When she returned to the opening, Rome began searching desperately with her eyes, but this time the spirit was nowhere in sight. Out of desperation, she decided to break the rules and leave the trail. As she walked toward the spot where he once stood, she stopped and made a slow 360 degree turn. Without warning, they met face to face as she came to the end of her rotation, causing Rome to lose her footing.

"How can you see me?" asked the spirit.

"Gift or curse... call it what you want," responded Rome.

"Somehow I feel a connection."

"With me?"

"Possibly?" replied the spirit.

Feeling a bit more comfortable with the situation, Rome got off the ground and dusted off the back of her dress. "Not a good day to wear white," she thought to herself. Looking up, she held her position as the spirit walked toward her. Rome waited for him to continue the conversation, but nothing came, then he turned his attention to the Port Arthur convict site across the bay.

"Who are you? enquired Rome.

Unexpectedly, he turned back to Rome and blurted out the answer as though his name were being called by a prison guard. "Jones, William! Jones, William!" yelled the spirit.

Shocked at first by the tone and volume of the spirit's voice, Rome gained control as he softly spoke his name a third time.

"Jones, William."

"I've come a long way to see you, Mr. Jones. What can I do for you?"

"Nothing."

"You must want something. Why else would your friend have called me here?"

"I have no friends."

"But you must want something from me."

"No one can give me what I want."

"At least let me try."

The spirit turned his attention back to Port Arthur and again stood in silence.

"Let me help you," said Rome in desperation.

"No one can help me." Without warning the spirit disappeared from Rome's sight.

"Wait, Mr. Jones! We're not finished!"

"Finished with what?"

Responding to the unexpected sound of Heath's voice, Rome turned around to see him watching her from the trail. She could only imagine what was going through his mind: either she's crazy or talks to the dead. At that point, Rome wasn't sure which would be worse.

"Finished with what?" asked Heath a second time.

"With the tour. It's unfortunate that we don't have more time." With that said, she bent down, picked up her notebook and brushed the sand from the pages. "I found it," proclaimed Rome, attempting once again to throw Heath off the trail.

"And in such a bizarre place."

"Go figure."

"Who were you talking to?" asked Heath.

"No one."

"Then why did you call my name?"

"What?"

"I heard you say 'Mr. Jones.'"

Rome paused as she connected the dots between Heath and her ghost. He had mentioned that one of his ancestors was imprisoned at Port Arthur and she may have just met him.

"Rome?"

"I'm sorry, what?"

"You said my name like you were talking to me."

"I was talking to myself. I do that sometimes."

"Like last night at the castle?"

"It helps me to formulate."

"Formulate?"

"Part of the writing process. But enough about that. Bev's probably eager to get back," said Rome as she attempted to walk past Heath.

Taking hold of her arm, Heath stopped her from going any further. "Why not finish your conversation? I'll wait."

"I can have a conversation with myself anywhere. That's the beauty of talking to yourself," said Rome as she pulled her arm away from Heath's grip and started back down the trail.

The return walk to the boat seemed to be the longest yet. Rome could feel Heath's eyes watching every step she took. The feeling was so intense that if Heath had Superman's powers the stare from his eyes would probably had already pierced a hole through her skull.

Reaching the dock, Rome and Heath made their way to the boat, but this time there was no outstretched hand to help her aboard. He simply walked to the rope and began untying it from the mooring cleat. Fortunately, Bev came to the rescue once again. "All aboard, people. We need to get the boat back while I still have a job."

Rome stepped over the side, followed by Heath. As Bev started the engine, Rome found her way to the seat in the back and waited for Heath to join her, but he stepped to the front, staring forward as Bev steered the boat away from the dock.

For the first time since she had arrived in Tasmania, Rome wanted nothing more than to return home. Her trip to the Isle of the Dead had become a confusing disappointment. All the way back to Port Arthur she thought about the spirit, but with Heath's suspicions, she knew she couldn't risk pursuing another encounter. She had to accept that it was over. William Jones believed that no one could help him and Rome's only option at that point was to accept his opinion—at least that's what she told herself. In the end, she'd tried her best and that's all anyone could ask.

The boat ride came to an end as Bev gently parked near the dock. Just as before, Heath jumped out and tied her off then offered his hand to Bev as she stepped from the boat, carrying her basket. "I appreciate your help today, Heath. If you ever feel like a change of pace, feel free to apply," remarked Bev, half-jokingly.

"Right back at you. You're very good at your job, Beverly."

"Few people get to make a living doing what they love. I'm one of the fortunate ones."

Heath extended his hand to Rome as he continued his conversation with Bev. "Thanks again for allowing me to come along for the ride. My fourth great-grandfather was a prisoner here. Unfortunately, he never made it out."

Rome stepped onto the dock and turned to Heath for more clarification. "So he did die at Port Arthur?"

"I told you he was a prisoner here on the way down."

"I just assumed he was released after he served his time."

"No, he passed away before his sentence expired. William Jones is buried somewhere on that island," said Heath. "Mr. Jones."

Although Rome had released her grip on Heath's hand, he continued to hang on, staring into her eyes, waiting for her to respond, hoping she'd share in his moment of discovery. But the moment passed without a word of admittance from Rome.

"Fortunately, most prisoners survived and were able to start new lives here in Australia," Bev interjected, inadvertently giving Rome some much needed breathing space. Rome caught up with Bev and walked alongside her toward the end of the dock, leaving Heath behind to formulate his next move. She could feel her heart pounding inside her chest as she replayed the events of the last twenty-four hours. How could she have been so careless, both on the island and at his castle the night before? How could she let it go this far? This time the evidence may be too overwhelming to simply dismiss, so she did the only thing she could: find a way to distance herself from Heath. "Could I get a ride back to the hotel with you?" Rome asked Bev quietly.

"My car's still in the shop. I caught a ride with a co-worker this morning. Is something wrong?"

"No, I just thought we could check out a couple more places on the peninsula."

"I'm sure Heath would be happy to make a few stops on your way back," suggested Bev, loud enough to bring Heath into the conversation. Rome breathed in a quick shot of oxygen and held her breath.

"I'd be happy to help with that."

"Problem solved," responded Bev with a twinkle in her eye.

Feeling a sudden chill, Rome pulled the sweater from her tote with her free hand and awkwardly tried to put it on while keeping up with Bev's pace. Without warning, she felt Heath slip the sweater gently onto her shoulders, then reach down and take the tote from her hand. "We better get a move on. We've got a lot of ground to cover," he whispered with newfound enthusiasm, allowing the side of his face to brush past hers.

Bev couldn't help but recognize that the temperature between Heath and Rome had grown colder as the outing progressed. Unsatisfied with how the day was ending, she decided to take a last stab at fixing things once they reached the parking lot. "I need a word with Rome. Do you mind, Heath?"

"Not at all. I'll get the car."

"It was lovely to see you again," Bev hollered as Heath walked away, then she quickly turned her attention to Rome. "All right, what happened out there?"

"Nothing!"

"This is Beverly Hucker you're talking to. Not some amateur. Now spill."

"I think I upset him."

"How?"

"He wants something from me."

"We know that."

"Something I can't give."

"Right now or with time?"

"It's more complicated than you realize, Bev."

"Is it fixable? 'Cause it better be fixable. I saw the way he looked at you. He's hooked, Rome."

Their conversation ended with the approach of the Land Rover. For the first time since they met, Heath's timing could not have been better. Bev wrapped her arms around her new friend and whispered one final piece of advice in Rome's ear. "Use the drive back to fix what needs to be fixed. Regret will make the flight back to the States even longer."

Bev let go of Rome as Heath rounded the back of the vehicle and opened the passenger door. She stepped into the car and Heath shut the door. Before Heath could get very far, he felt Bev's arm wrap around his, escorting him around the back of the vehicle. "Not that it's any of my business, Heath, but I hope you realize that there's more to you and Rome's story than this."

Bev opened the door as Heath took a moment to ponder what she said. He took one last look at Bev, smiled in agreement, got into the car and started the engine.

"Where to?" asked Heath as though nothing had happened.

"My hotel. I think we should call it a day."

"What about the other places you wanted to visit?"

"I have enough information."

Heath did as she requested and drove down the road, knowing that even if he confronted her he'd never get a straight answer. Time was his enemy and without it, he'd never be able to confirm his suspicions or get the help he needed. He needed a new plan or at least a revision to his old one.

Dusk began to settle in as Heath reached the turn-on point for the highway. Unexpectedly, he pulled to the side of the road and made an offer he hoped she could not refuse. "I have a friend who has a beach house sitting empty up in Nubeena. It's a short drive from here. Just across the peninsula."

"And?"

"We could stop and pick up some groceries on the way and anything else we might need. Not that you don't already have everything in that bag of yours."

"Are you suggesting we spend the night there?"

Heath paused for a moment then continued his take-over strategy. "Obviously, you're not finished yet."

"What?" asked Rome, thinking he was referring to the last words she spoke to the spirit on the island.

"The list of things you wanted to accomplish. For your article."

"Oh, that."

Heath and Rome sat in silence for a moment as Rome pondered Bev's final advice, then chose to ignore it. "Just take me back to the hotel. I have more work to do on my article and I still need to pack for the ferry tomorrow evening."

Defeated, Heath slowly turned back toward the steering wheel and thought for a moment. Knowing he had only one more shot at the 'win' he pulled out his last bargaining chip: his friend's sailboat. "Would you stay on the peninsula if I threw in a small sailboat?"

"You're giving me a sailboat?"

"A tour aboard a sailboat."

"That's very generous, but I really do need to get back to my hotel."

"So you're telling me that a world-renowned travel writer, like yourself, would give up the opportunity to take a private cruise around the Tasman Peninsula?"

"It's not part of my itinerary."

"Just think of all the photos you could take for your article, for your readers. Unique photos that aren't normally seen."

"Do I need to call a car service?" asked Rome, determined to end the conversation.

"So the famous Rome London would walk away from an opportunity to see all the sights on her list, just to go back to her hotel so she can spend the majority of tomorrow writing and packing? Are you really so committed to your itinerary that you'd pass up an opportunity like this?"

"Yes, I am."

Stunned by Rome's direct answer, Heath sat back in his seat, knowing he had nothing left to offer. Short of kidnapping, he'd used every strategy available and had come up empty-handed. He'd run out of bargaining chips and was about to give up, when something unexpected happened: Rome revived Heath's topic of discussion. "Do you really have access to a sailboat?"

"My friend keeps his boat docked in the marina just down the road from his beach house."

"And you know how to sail this sailboat?"

"We sailed it down from Sydney together."

"And your friend wouldn't mind?"

"We use each other's stuff all the time. I use his beach house and he uses mine."

"Of course, you would have a beach house as well as a friend who owns a beach house," said Rome sarcastically.

"The beach house was my dad's. I inherited it."

Rome sat for a moment, seriously pondering the consequences and possibilities of the choice she was about to make. Officially, she'd come to Tasmania to write a top-notch travel article and somehow let her ability to listen to spirits take precedence over her assignment. Rome knew she'd be a fool to turn down his proposition, but she also knew the reason behind the offer. Whether Heath learned the truth or not was completely within her control and no one had more self-control than Rome. Ultimately, she had the upper hand and wanted to make sure Heath knew it. "If I say yes, there can be no talk of what I said at the castle last night or about what happened on the island today," demanded Rome.

Heath thought for a moment then responded the only way he could to finalize the negotiations. "Deal."

"We have to get back in time to pick up my friend's car from the mechanic and catch the ferry."

"We'll get an early start," responded Heath happily as he turned onto the highway and drove toward Nubeena.

Feeling cautiously optimistic and grateful for more time with Rome, Heath began to plan. So far his skills and persistence had paid off, but he was still determined to get the truth from Rome. This was business, plain and simple, and no one was better at business than Heath. He was used to closing the deal and getting what he wanted, so why should this time be any different?

Chapter Five

Sydney, Australia.

Roger Ash entered his office at Jones Shipping and Ship Manufacturing, Inc., just as he did every morning. A cup of black coffee in one hand, his briefcase in the other and a newspaper tucked under his arm. Unbuttoning the suit jacket to one of his many pinstriped, three-piece suits, he sat down at his desk, allowing his protruding gut to expand as far as his vest would allow. Before he could get settled, his secretary, Olivia, stormed through the door. "There's a man waiting to see you. He's been here for over an hour, a very excruciating hour. He has no appointment, yet refuses to leave. Would you like me to call security and have him removed from the building?"

Roger made her wait as he woke up his computer and began checking the emails that came in overnight. Without making eye contact, he responded to Olivia in a very impersonal way. "Send him in."

"Excuse me, Mr. Ash?"

"Send him in!"

"Right away."

Before Olivia could clear the doorway, Sergio Arturo, the egocentric, self-imposed celebrity writer of the weekly column, *Arturo: Off-the-wall*, stepped into the doorway and pointed at Roger with a cheesy grin saying, "I'll have what he's having."

Invading the secretary's personal space with his ultra-skinny body, he eyeballed Olivia from head to toe, then back up again before placing his order. "And make mine a double."

"Of course," she responded, wishing she had a can of disinfectant spray. Olivia left the office having no intention of bringing anything back.

Arturo remained in the doorway, sliding his thumb and forefinger down the two skinny sides of the pencil mustache lining his upper lip, a perfect pairing to the soul patch located just beneath his lower lip and his slicked-back, thinning, strawberry-blonde hair. Watching her walk away, he couldn't help but call out one last order. "And bring a couple pastries as well, sweetie." Still watching her from behind, he took one more opportunity to vocally prove his ladies man status to Roger and anyone else within the range of his voice. "You get to work with that every day? I guess it pays to be rich."

Sergio Arturo was not the type of person anyone with an ounce of self-respect would ever choose to spend time with or even admit to knowing. He was vulgar, boorish and crass: the type of person that made others want to take a shower after being in the same room. Unfortunately, he had a huge readership who loved the sensationalism of his weekly column and that added fuel to the fire that powered his vanity.

For Roger, Arturo was nothing more than a means to an end, a way to get what he had wanted for the better part of his business career: control of Jones Shipping and Ship Manufacturing. Roger had struck a deal with the devil of yellow journalism and now he was stuck with him. Wanting to get this impromptu meeting over as quickly as possible, Roger demanded his attention. "This is a business, not a pub. Sit down, Arturo."

Acting like he owned the place, Arturo crossed the room and

planted himself in one of the large chairs across the desk from Roger.

Staring at his computer screen, Roger refused to give Arturo his full attention, sending the unspoken message that he had better things to do with his time. While simultaneously responding to a long list of emails, Roger got right down to business, the business of a corporate coupd'etat. "What's so important that you couldn't just tell me over the phone, like usual?"

"What? No small talk, Ash?"

"I run a billion dollar business. I don't have time for small talk. You've got five minutes."

"I'm the one doing you the favor."

"We're both benefitting from this unholy union and you know it! Now why are you here?"

Arturo reached into the large pocket on his safari-style bush jacket and pulled out a five by seven envelope containing photographs. He tossed it onto the desk in front of Roger, drawing his attention away from the computer screen. Roger opened the envelope and pulled out three photos. He immediately recognized that they were pictures of his nephew's castle at night.

"Who took these?"

"I used some of your slush fund to..."

"That 'slush fund' isn't a free-for-all."

"I know that."

"At the rate you're burning through it, I question whether you do."

"That slush fund is the only thing keeping the ex-staff from sharing details of the ghosts with everyone and their dogs. Does the word 'exclusive' mean anything to you? That's my end of the deal, remember?"

"Fine. But I expect a detailed expense report when this is all over."

"You business types are all the same."

"Just get on with it, Arturo."

"Fine. I got one of the electricians to take some photos the other night. He'd been working late all week, so it worked out perfectly."

"What's that glowing in the windows?" Roger asked as he analyzed the first picture closely.

"Apparitions," Arturo replied with a sly grin on his face.

"You're never going to get your readers to believe they're ghosts. I'm staring right at the photo and they don't look like ghosts."

"That was my first attempt."

"Attempt at what?"

"Look at the next two."

Roger put down the first photo and picked up one of the last two. Instantly, he saw the silhouette of a person, contained within the bright light of one of the windows.

"Is that what I think it is?"

"A ghost. At least that's what my readers will believe. Pretty good, huh?"

Unresponsive, Roger picked up the last photo and immediately noticed not one, but two ghostly silhouettes.

"So this is the question: Is one ghost enough or does it look better with two? I can add as many as I want," bragged Arturo.

"You doctored the photos?"

"We're living in a visual world. Photos sell the news. Words are only a backup these days."

"We're not going to manufacture evidence when there's already enough first-hand reports out there to prove the castle is haunted."

"I'm simply enhancing the story through visual stimulation."

"It's impossible to take a picture of a ghost. Your readers are never going to believe this," argued Roger.

"My readers want to believe it, and because they want to believe it, I can get them to believe anything I want. I'm that good!"

"And this is the world of news?"

"If you want your nephew to appear too unstable to run the company, we've got to go big. That is still what you want, right?"

Roger stood up and walked toward the window of the high-rise building overlooking the harbor. He took a moment to collect his thoughts before replying to Arturo's question. "I just need the board to see Heath as compromised and no longer able to make good decisions. At that point, they'll be forced to make me President and

CEO, which they should have done after my brother-in-law's death. I can finally take the company in the direction I want it to go."

"From what I hear, Heath's pretty brilliant at business himself. A chip off the old block."

He's young and idealistic. His latest idea is to venture into deep sea submarine building and increase the commercial ship building here at home. I want it all shut down and the manufacturing moved to China. Can you imagine the money we'll save?"

"Money that will most likely be lining your pockets?"

"Stick with journalism and leave the world of business to me, Arturo."

"Fine. Two ghosts or one?"

"If one is good, two must be better. Especially with your gullible readers."

"Go big or go home. Words I live by."

Arturo reached over the desk and placed the photos in the envelope and put them back into his pocket. "I'm running a teaser in the Thursday edition of the papers that carry my weekly column. That should bring plenty of interest and cause enough chatter to sell quite a few newspapers come Sunday. Every large paper in Australia will be running my column on the front page of their Sunday edition."

"Onto phase three of our plan," Roger said as though the destruction of Heath's career was nothing more than a hostile takeover.

"Phase three is advancing nicely on my end. I'm heading down to Tasmania tomorrow morning to work out some details and gather more intel."

"I may be headed there as well if I can't get Heath to return my calls," responded Roger. "I also have a board meeting this afternoon, where I plan to advance my cause. In order to keep myself from being implicated, the board must reach the decision to replace Heath on their own."

"We both have our work cut out for us," said Arturo as he stood up and walked toward the door. Halfway there, he couldn't resist leaving the room without a final display of his manliness. "Looks like I'm going to have to track that little kitten of yours down to get my coffee and pastries... and anything else I can get my hands on. Me-ow," panted Arturo, shutting the door behind him.

Roger walked back to his desk, picked up the phone and dialed the building security. "This is Roger Ash. A man in a khaki jacket just left my office. Make sure he leaves the building immediately." He hung up his office phone, pulled out his cell and dialed Heath's number. Waiting for Heath to answer, he leaned back and combed his fingers through the loose, salt-and-pepper waves of his thick hair. Per usual, the phone went straight to voicemail, forcing Roger to leave a message. "Heath, this is your uncle, again. You still haven't told me what day you're planning on being back at work. I have some important meetings to set up, so I need to know as soon as possible. Give me a call or have your secretary contact mine with the details."

Roger tossed his phone onto the desk as he returned to his emails, feeling confident that he'd only have to put up with his nephew for a short time longer. He cared for his nephew, but his jealousy had buried those feelings deep inside. In order to justify undermining Heath, he fooled himself into thinking his nephew would be better suited to a life of philanthropy. But that was not his to decide.

Unfortunately, Roger saw himself as more than an equal to his late brother-in-law, Marshall Jones. He'd waited for years to prove his case on a global level, but if truth be told, Roger Ash would be nowhere in life without Marshall and his own sweet sister. It was his sister who talked her husband, Marshall, into giving Roger a job at Jones Shipping. Previous to that, he had made a series of bad business decisions that led to the downfall of the company he inherited from their father. Of course, Roger never saw it that way. It was everyone else's fault. He refused to accept that his failures were the consequences of his own decisions.

Built from the ground up, his father's business was a small but successful company until Roger took the reigns and ran it into the ground. When Marshall brought him aboard he started him out in a position where he could do no harm to his company. Over the years, he allowed him to slowly rise through the ranks but always kept a tight rein on his decision-making power.

Now, in some twisted reality, Roger felt that his time had arrived. He truly believed that it was his duty to fill Marshall's shoes as CEO of their multi-billion dollar company and in some bizarre way as a father figure to Heath. And why wouldn't he think that?

With the exception of a few distant cousins on his mother's side of the family, Roger was his nephew's only surviving relative. Having never been married or had children of his own it only seemed right that the guidance and direction of Heath's well-being would fall to him.

His nephew, however, would disagree completely. Heath was closer to his long-time butler, Sheldon Burns, than he'd ever been to Roger. Mr. Burns was only twenty when he was hired by his father after the death of his mother, so he seemed more like an older brother. What he lacked in experience he made up for in kindness. It was Sheldon who helped raise him and who was there to pick up the pieces after his dad's unexpected death. Roger was too busy pitching a fit after finding out he would not be Marshall's successor, but all that was about to change.

Chapter Six

Opening her eyes, Rome woke to the sound of waves crashing against the shore. She thought of the night before and how much she enjoyed relaxing on the porch, listening to the waves and eating some pretty tasty bachelor food cooked on the barbecue by Heath. Morning had arrived as it always does and Rome knew she had to watch the clock in order to make it to the ferry on time. She reached for her cell phone, only to find her battery dead. "Great. The one thing I didn't bring is my phone charger." She tossed the phone back on the night stand and stretched her arms toward the ceiling, making the decision to pull herself out of bed.

With the exception of the sounds of nature, the house was quiet as she moved from room to room. Opening the outside door she found Heath sitting on the porch, staring out toward the ocean. At the risk of interrupting his alone time, Rome enquired, "Did you sleep out here last night?"

"I'm an early riser. How did you sleep?"

"Like a baby."

"Good."

"I can't seem to find any clocks in the house and it appears my cell phone battery died."

"We're doing good for time. I've already packed some food and water so we're ready to go whenever you are."

"I'll grab a quick shower."

Rome turned to walk back into the house but stopped to ask on more question. "Why are there no clocks in the house?"

"Everyone should have a place to go where time stops."

"That's a nice theory, but not realistic when you're on a schedule."

"What's the point in having a house on the beach or a cabin in the mountains or a tent in the woods if you can't leave your schedule behind, even for just a little while?"

"Why don't I believe that?" replied Rome.

"Are only travel writers entitled to enlightenment?"

"I'm going to grab that shower now."

"And I'll get the food."

Rome entered the house followed by Heath. As he walked through the living room he saw a small, decorative clock setting on the end table. He picked it up, carried it into the pantry and placed it inside a drawer with all the other clocks he removed before Rome entered the house last night. He needed the day to go his way and since he was used to being in control, hiding the clocks came naturally.

CARRYING a couple of large tote bags, Heath led the way as he and Rome walked down one of the docks in the marina. Coming to the slip where his friend's boat was docked, Rome's jaw dropped as she saw the size of the vessel.

"You said it was small."

"This is small."

"Maybe in your world," quipped Rome.

"She's a forty-two foot keelboat. I had them fuel her up this morning, so we're set to go," said Heath as he placed the tote bags in the boat then took Rome's bag and put it inside as well. He helped her over the side and she walked to the front of the sailboat while watching him untie the ropes holding the boat in place. Rome turned her face to the blue sky above allowing the warm sun to shine down on her skin. "It looks like the weather is going to cooperate," happily remarked Rome.

Heath stepped from the dock to the boat and agreed with her assessment of the weather. "Mother Nature is definitely smiling on us today." Taking a minute to check everything out, he started the engine and backed the sailboat out of the slip. "Get ready to see some of the most beautiful scenery in the world."

It didn't take long for Rome to fall in love with the gorgeous view of the coastline and the relaxing feel of the sailboat. The scenery was as breathtaking as Heath had described, but the bigger story for Rome was the continuing change in Heath. It was as though the sailboat and Heath were one, working in unison, turning here and sailing there. In the short time since they met, she'd never seen him more comfortable and relaxed than in this setting. In Rome's mind she could not have imagined a more perfect outing.

She was also impressed with how invested he was in making sure she got the most from her tour. Heath pointed out the different sea cliffs and other sights along their journey while Rome snapped photos and recorded information on her laptop. Trivia continued to flow off his tongue, not only about the geography of the coastline, but of pirate tales from Tasmania's past and sailing stories from his own childhood. They also shared tidbits about each other and discussed things they had in common. Surprisingly, they shared more interests and pursuits than Rome thought possible.

Not only was their outing affecting Rome's view of Heath, but he was growing more fascinated with her by the minute. Admittedly, he hadn't made the best first impression or second for that matter, so he wasn't sure what to expect when they set sail. However, things were changing, evolving. Not only in their relationship, but inside Heath as well. He could feel his heart softening. The same heart that had grown hard over the past several years while dealing with the loss of his father and the pressures of business.

Maybe it was his love for sailing or the splendor of the beautiful scenery that allowed Heath to lower the wall he had built. Or most likely it was the introduction of Rome into his life. Whatever the case, he was beginning to feel a deep connection with her that was beyond his own explanation. He couldn't remember a time when he enjoyed being with a woman as much as he enjoyed being with her. She was easy to talk with, inquisitive, knowledgable and funny—in her own way. Not to mention her unpolished beauty that captured Heath's attention the minute he found her in his tub.

Still, Rome had a secret that he needed to uncover, a key to fixing a problem he had no idea how to solve. She was hiding something and it was up to him to either gain her confidence or expose the mystery she kept hidden. He just never planned to fall victim to his own strategy.

On their return trip, Heath lowered the sail as they approached his previously-planned destination. The boat slowed to a crawl and began to rock gently with the waves as he lowered the anchor. "Maingon Bay looks like a good place for afternoon tea. We're not far from the marina, so it shouldn't take us much longer to get back."

Heath pulled out random containers of leftovers from the previous night's barbecue and some items he picked up during his morning stroll to the marina. He began setting the table as Rome made one last installment in her notes then slid her computer to the side. She smiled to herself as she watched Heath fill the table with a unique assortment of food.

"As you can see, we have quite a few options to choose from in today's buffet," announced Heath, mimicking a server at a restaurant.

"A girl could get used to these bachelor buffets. Where to begin?"

"I'm going for that leftover snag from last night. There's only one left, so you're going to have to fight me for it."

"You take the sausage and the sausage roll if you like. I'm more interested in this amazing assortment of fruit you have here. And what are these?"

"Pasties. They had a couple left in the warmer at the shop last night. If I remember right this one is meat and that one is veggie."

Rome picked up the veggie pastie and took a bite.

"That's good."

"I forgot the most important ingredient," said Heath as he reached into the bag, pulled out a bottle of tomato sauce and squeezed a blob onto her paper plate. "Here. Dip it in the tomato sauce."

"You mean ketchup?"

"Not in this part of the world."

He squeezed a bunch onto his bun then paused for a moment. "It's hard to eat a snagger smothered in tomato sauce without thinking of my dad. He was the king of the barbecue."

"How long has he been gone?"

"Three years in January," said Heath right before he took a huge bite.

"You miss him a lot, don't you?"

Heath responded by shaking his head up and down, signaling to Rome that his mouth was too full to reply.

"So why the castle?" asked Rome curiously.

Heath finished chewing his bite and followed it up with a swig of ginger beer. "Several months after Dad died I was trying to find a document at his home office in Sydney. In my search, I found several files labeled 'Jones Family Genealogy.' I took them with me and spent the next several weeks going through the files. Dad never told me that he hired a professional genealogist to research our family tree. The dates indicated it was during my years at Oxford."

"Finding those files must have been quite a surprise."

"It was."

"Why didn't he show them to you?"

"I'm not sure. Maybe he forgot about them."

"Did you find anything interesting in your family tree?"

"There's so much information. Some of it dates back to Twelfth Century England. The files contain church records, legal documents, birth certificates, death certificates, burial sites and headstone information. It appears the Jones family were well-respected members of the upper class."

"So you come from a long line of successful people. Must be genetic."

"Or luck."

Rome smiled as she watched Heath stick several slices of kiwi fruit into his mouth then begin to peel and quarter a Granny Smith apple. She couldn't believe the transformation from the Heath she met at the castle to the one sitting across from her. She found herself hoping that this was the real Heath as he continued to share his family history.

"The thing I found most interesting was a diary kept by Lady Jones, wife of Lord Hubert Jones. They were married in the early eighteen hundreds and lived until the summer of 1840."

"Did they live at Castle Jones?" enquired Rome.

"Forest Gate was the name of the castle and estate originally owned by the Jones Family. It had been passed down through generations, long before Lord Hubert was born. Unfortunately, they were the last of the Jones family to live there. Apple?"

Heath offered Rome a slice on the blade of his knife, which she happily accepted.

"What happened to their children?"

"They had one son... William Jones."

They both paused at the mention of his ancestor's name until Rome moved the conversation forward with a lighthearted response. "He must have been the apple of their eye."

"William grew up knowing who he was supposed to marry from the time they were kids. Her name was Meredith Hampton, the daughter of an upper middle class magistrate. The arrangement had been made by their parents, who had been friends for years."

"A prearranged marriage would never have worked for me. There would have been blood in the streets."

"Somehow I believe that," gibed Heath.

"You were saying?"

"According to Lady Jones's diary, each summer they would send

William up north for a month to stay at the country estate of a close friend of the family. What they didn't know..."

"Let me guess. The friend of the family had a gorgeous daughter and they fell madly in love," interjected Rome, finding a clean place on the table to rest her elbows.

"Close."

"I knew it!"

"William did fall in love, but with the cousin of a clock maker, who owned a little shop in the small town nearby."

"Second guess: they met while William was out riding his horse through the countryside. Am I right?"

"Jane Austin fan?" asked Heath with a tone of sympathy in his voice.

"What woman isn't?"

"True."

"So how did they meet?"

"There's no mention in Lady Jones's diary of how they met or anything to do with Helen's past other than the fact that she belonged to a different class, the lower middle class."

"I've seen enough English movies and watched enough BBC to know what that means."

Heath stood up, tossed his peelings into the water and leaned his back against the railing.

"Long story short: William and Helen got married without either of their families knowing."

"I bet that didn't go over well with the folks."

"That was the least of their problems. After their wedding Helen was arrested in London for stealing a brooch and sentenced to serve seven years as a female convict in the Australian colony of New South Wales."

"I did not see that twist coming!"

"It gets worse. William tried to stop them from taking her aboard the convict ship and in doing so he attacked a policeman. Next thing you know he was sentenced for assault, loaded onto a ship and sent to Port Arthur as a convict himself."

"Are you kidding me?"

"It's true," Heath assured Rome.

"So William was your fourth great-grandfather who's buried on the Isle of the Dead."

"Yes. Both he and his wife Helen ended up in Australia, but in two different places. They never saw each other again. I doubt William ever knew that his wife gave birth to a son eight and a half months later."

"That's the saddest ending to a love story I've ever heard."

"It gets worse."

"How is that even possible?" asked Rome in amazement.

"William's parents, Lord Hubert and Lady Jones, died on the very day William was loaded onto the convict ship and sent to Australia. I doubt William even knew his parents were dead before the ship sailed."

"Are you sure Nicholas Sparks didn't do your genealogy?"

"Who?"

"Never mind."

"After I discovered the family files I went on a business trip to England. While I was there I took some personal time and tracked down Forest Gate or 'the Devil's Castle' as the locals referred to it."

"So it has a third name. Where did that one come from?"

"The castle switched hands many times through the years, but each new owner was frightened away by the ghosts. Soon rumors began to spread that Forest Gate was inhabited by evil spirits.

"You didn't take that into account before you bought it?"

"The place was abandoned and practically in ruins. There wasn't that much left to haunt. The last owner sold all the furniture and belongings to a private collector and just let the place go. Fortunately, the walls were still intact and we were able to remove entire sections by binding them together, but most of the castle arrived here block by block. It's now three years later and Forest Gate has been rebuilt on a different continent," said Heath proudly.

"Why do it? Why go to all that expense? You could have just built your own castle from scratch."

"I was grieving the loss of my dad and trying to deal with the mixed emotions that came with it. I knew I had to channel them into something and the family business wasn't enough. Making the decision to take back what originally belonged to our family felt right. It felt good. I thought by bringing the castle to Australia, to William and Helen, I could somehow make it right. Wow! Saying that out loud makes me realize how absolutely bonkers that sounds. No wonder the press are having a field day with me and my castle."

Rome stood up and joined Heath next to the railing.

"I think it's a sweet gesture. A little over the top. Maybe a lot over the top, but very thoughtful."

"You're probably the only one who sees it that way."

"You've answered the question I had when I came to the castle Sunday night."

"What kind of man buys a castle in England and has it shipped block by block to the bottom of the world?"

"You remember that?"

"I do. So what's the answer?"

"The type of man I would like to know more about."

Unexpectedly, Heath took Rome into his arms and kissed her. Although she was surprised by Heath's bold move, she abandoned her defenses and gave in to the moment as the sun began to set.

"What time is it?"

"I think you're going to miss the ferry."

"I think I am too."

The two of them continued to kiss, silhouetted in each other's arms as the sun slowly disappeared over the horizon. Eventually, however, logic and logistics took control and Rome pulled herself away from Heath.

"What are we doing?"

"What's wrong?"

"This. This is wrong."

"How is this wrong?" asked Heath confused by her reaction.

"I got caught up in the moment."

"So did I, but what's wrong with that?"

"What isn't wrong with that?" responded Rome.

"Is that rhetorical?"

"We live half a world apart on two different continents, not to mention hemispheres."

"You're a travel writer."

"Yes, but I always return home. No strings attached."

"There's a first for everything."

"I'm not going to start something that I can't finish."

Rome walked toward the table and began putting the food back into the bag, but Heath wasn't going to let her off that easily. He was a problem solver. A negotiator. A business man who never left a meeting without some kind of resolution on the table. "And by 'finish' you mean...?"

"Commitment. A relationship."

"And those are bad things?" asked Heath, now seriously confused.

"I live in the States. You live in Australia. My job is there. Your business is here. A relationship with those kinds of circumstances and that much distance would never work."

"I think we're getting a little ahead of ourselves, Rome," responded Heath, trying to calm the situation so they could have a rational discussion. Unfortunately, his good intentions backfired when Rome experienced an epiphany.

"You're right. It was just a kiss. I'm getting carried away over nothing."

"I wouldn't go that far," responded Heath, disappointed by her casual dismissal of what they shared.

"No, you're right. I took a simple kiss and practically turned it into a marriage proposal."

"I'd say it was more than a simple kiss."

"Now who's getting ahead of themselves?"

Heath leaned down and kissed her again.

Rome felt her inhibitions lowering as the items in her hands dropped to the floor. She knew in her heart that this was more than just a simple kiss and that Heath was more than a temptation to resist. The flood of emotions accompanying the moment was proof positive. Frightened by that realization, she once again pulled away from Heath.

"It was just a kiss. Let's leave it at that," said Rome as she walked away from Heath.

"I think this is worth discussing."

"There's nothing to discuss. This would never work."

"Your parents were from two different countries and they made it work."

"They were young and just starting out."

"A starting point is a starting point. Age and circumstances are just details."

"Are you even listening to yourself?" Rome asked in frustration.

"Yes, I am," countered Heath boldly.

"You can't honestly believe it's as simple as just picking a 'starting point.'"

"I start new deals all the time."

"This isn't business!"

"No, it's an argument."

"A discussion!"

"An irrational discussion."

"A fervent discussion," Rome clarified.

"And where is this 'fervent' discussion leading us?"

"When did we become an 'us?'"

Heath paused for a moment as he felt the sting of Rome's last comment. Realizing he was on the losing end of the argument, he decided to engage one last tactic. "So today means nothing to you?"

"Of course it means something to me. It's been a wonderful day, but to think we could have some kind of future together is completely unrealistic when framed by the circumstances of our lives."

"What's wrong with discussing the possibilities?"

"Possibilities are for dreamers."

"Don't you dream, Rome?"

"No! I have a life plan. I think it's time we head back."

Beaten and disappointed, Heath turned and walked back to the boat's control center. As he stood next to the wheel he realized the gravity of what he had done. He allowed himself to fall for Rome which would now compromise his original intent. He had to clear his head. More importantly, he had to clear Rome from his head. A relationship was not in the plans when he showed up at her hotel room yesterday morning. He was there to satisfy his curiosity and solve a problem.

Her strange behavior was the reason he convinced her to come on a sightseeing tour of the Tasman Peninsula in the first place. It had nothing to do with her article like he pretended. He simply wanted a confirmation to his suspicions and the only way to do that was to get her back to the Isle of the Dead and let her finish what she started.

How did he get so off track? He wanted to blame the beautiful scenery or the warmth of the ocean breeze or the sunset showing up at just the right time, but he knew they weren't the cause. Heath had let down his guard and he had no one to blame but himself.

Now he stood at the crossroads, trying to decide if he should stick with his original plan or return to the beach house with the slim hope of furthering a relationship with Rome. It wasn't long before necessity and rational thought overpowered what he was feeling with his heart. Once his head took control, his inner dialogue convinced him to stick to his original plan. "We have one more stop to make," announced Heath, much to Rome's surprise.

"It's practically dark. We won't be able to see anything."

"You've already seen this place."

Rome walked toward Heath as he started the engine and steered the sailboat deeper into the inlet.

"Where are you taking us?"

"You have unfinished business on the Isle of the Dead," asserted Heath emphatically.

"Are you crazy? That's trespassing."

Undaunted by the risk of breaking the law, Heath continued toward the island. "We'll anchor the boat behind the peninsula and take the dinghy ashore. No one will even know we were there."

"Turn the boat around, Heath. I'm not doing this."

"I heard you say you weren't finished on the island yesterday."

"I told you I was talking to myself."

"You were talking, but not to yourself."

"What about our deal? You promised me we wouldn't discuss what happened there yesterday," argued Rome.

"I'm not discussing it. I'm simply giving you a chance to finish what you started. I'll stay on the beach with the dinghy."

"I already missed the ferry. I'll just come down in the morning and catch one of the tours out to the island," lied Rome in a desperate attempt to mislead Heath and avoid returning to the island.

"What you need to do can't be done in a crowd of people!"

Suddenly, everything stopped.

Rome's arms, once folded against her chest in defiance slowly fell apart as she turned and lowered herself to the railing, gripping it tightly with both hands. The rhythm of the waves slapping the side of the boat created a calming effect as she stared into the dark water below. For the first time in her life, someone had discovered her secret and she needed a moment to consider her path forward. Unfortunately, hindsight refused to let that happen as Rome began to retrace the day's events. Realizing she'd been played, she released her grip on the railing, then turned to confront Heath. "Returning to the island was your plan all along. This whole 'sightseeing' idea was just a rouse, a way to make me miss my ferry. You pretended to care, you romanced me, just to keep me out here until it got dark enough to sneak onto the Isle of the Dead."

"What happened between us was not part of the plan."

"Of course it was! You've been using me from the minute you knocked on my hotel door. I can't believe I fell for this. No one knows how to avoid getting suckered when traveling better than I do. I've written articles on it for crying out loud!" yelled Rome angrily.

"I'm just giving you a chance to wrap up what you started on the island yesterday. Don't tell me that someone who talks to the dead is scared of cemeteries at night?"

"Right now, it's not the DEAD who are scaring me!"

"Then there shouldn't be a problem," responded Heath as he throttled up the engine and proceeded deeper into the bay.

Rome turned from Heath and wrapped her arm around the

mast. In an attempt to calm herself, she pursed her lips together, slowed her breathing and began to think in terms of pros and cons. Rome knew she had the skills to put up a fight, but Heath was a good foot taller and in decent shape. She could dump him over the side but didn't know enough about sailing to make it back to Nubeena. She could swim to shore, but that would mean a long walk back to the highway in the dark. After exhausting all of her options, she knew there was no other alternative to Heath's plan.

Unexpectedly, Rome was struck with an epiphany: Why not return to the island? For the first time ever she had seen a spirit. Not only that, but she actually had a two-way conversation with him. This was new territory and, yes, it made Rome a bit nervous, but her fear of this new development was secondary to the betrayal she felt from Heath. How could he have lied to her like this? How could she have been foolish enough to believe him?

As the boat moved closer to the peninsula, Rome found herself shivering. She walked past Heath with not so much as a glance in his direction and pulled a sweatshirt out of her bag. She put it on hoping it was the cool night air that was causing her to shake and not the thought of what may be waiting for her on the island. Feeling a need to be even more prepared, she changed her sandals out for socks and the pair of sneakers she'd packed in her tote.

Heath slowly steered the boat toward the tip of the small peninsula located near the Isle of the Dead. There he anchored it far enough up the coast from Point Puer and the golf course that it wouldn't be seen. He unhooked the dinghy and dropped it on top of the water, then turned back to Rome and extended his hand with a promise. "I won't let anything harm you."

"Any more than you already have?" countered Rome. Ignoring his offer to help, she crawled over the side and lowered herself into the small craft, leaving Heath wounded from her accusation. Next, he lowered himself into the dinghy, started the quiet engine and steered her around the tip of the peninsula toward the Isle of the Dead. As the island grew closer, Rome could feel her heart speeding up in anticipation of furthering her conversation with William, despite her feelings of betrayal from Heath. There was a reason

William had appeared to her and she was determined to find out what it was, whether he wanted her help or not.

Reaching the beach, Heath jumped out and pulled the dinghy ashore. Rome climbed out on her own as Heath tied the dinghy to a large piece of driftwood.

"I'd offer you a torch, or a flashlight as you would call it, but I think it's better to use the light of the full moon."

"You being the expert and all," responded Rome with one more stab as she left Heath behind and walked toward the trees. She'd been hesitant to come to the island, but now that she was back, Rome was determined to finish the conversation she started yesterday.

"I could come with you!"

"I need twenty minutes alone. You come looking for me any sooner and I'll be taking that dinghy back to the sailboat by myself. And don't think for a moment that I'm not capable of that."

Taken aback by the seriousness of Rome's tone, Heath knew she meant business and pushing the envelope would not be a wise move, so he asked one more question, "And when the twenty minutes are up?"

"Come and find me... or what's left of me," responded Rome beneath her breath as she walked away.

Heath looked at his phone and noted the time as he watched Rome disappear into the darkness of the trees. Sitting down on a piece of driftwood, he began to wonder if he made the right decision in bringing her back to the island, especially in the middle of the night. "Stop second guessing," he told himself, but then he remembered something his father taught him when he was younger.

He had wanted to play mini rugby on a city team as a nine-year-old-boy, but his father felt he should wait until he was a little older and his bones had reached the proper stage of growth to handle the impact. He'd played tag rugby and really enjoyed it, so he continued to beg until his Dad said yes. In his third game he broke a bone, which came close to damaging a growth plate. If he had waited a year or two, he may not have had the added complications of surgery. He remembered his father sitting him down and telling him that playing rugby was a good decision but would have been a better decision if he had waited a couple years. In the meantime, he could have practiced his running and passing skills.

As he waited on the beach, he continued to hear his father's words play in his memory. "People seem to think second guessing a decision is a sign of weakness or failure, a lack of commitment or faith. But if that second guess leads you to learn something about yourself in regard to the choice you made and why you made it, then there's no harm in taking that journey. No man is perfect and no choice is always the right one to make, no matter how good it seems at the time. The same choice may be better when made at a different time or under different circumstances. Most people think it's the choices we make that define who we are, but a person interested in truly knowing themselves understands that it's the 'why' behind the choices that tell us who we really are. Especially if we are wise enough to be truthful about why we made the choice in the first place."

With his Dad's words ringing in his ears, there he sat second guessing his decision to send Rome into a cemetery in the middle of the night by herself.

Although his motivation stemmed from a desire to find out if Rome could talk with the dead, his decision was a selfish one and this was not his finest hour, proving that his dad's advice on second guessing was accurate. Although he couldn't change the decision he made, he had learned a valuable lesson.

As he continued to monitor the time, the clock on his phone became the proverbial watched pot that would never boil. The passing of time slowed to a crawl as each second ticked by more slowly than the previous one. At this rate, the twenty-minute mark seemed like an eternity away. Heath knew the reason for his impatience was two-fold: one, he wanted to quench his obsession for the truth; and two, his worry and concern for Rome's safety were intensifying. No longer able to sit still, Heath began to pace the beach. He was committed to the twenty minutes, but not just because of Rome's impressive threat. Heath knew he was way out of his league and the best he could hope for was a positive ending to the situation and Rome's safe return.

EVERY SOUND WAS HEIGHTENED and every shape drew Rome's attention as she walked through the shadows created by the moonlight. Soon she reached the spot where she had seen the spirit the day before. She left the trail and walked into the opening. At this point, the idea of not seeing the spirit was beginning to sound like the best conclusion of all. Instantly the spirit's silhouette appeared only a few feet from her. As he stepped forward, the moonlight captured his face, displaying the same misery that was present the day before.

"Why have you returned?" asked the spirit.

"Because a controlling, egotist thinks we have some unfinished business—and so do I."

"Many have come and gone over the years, but no one has ever been able to see us. Why now?"

"I'm not sure, but I'd like to find out. My name is Rome London."

"What type of name is that, pray tell?"

"For the sake of time, let's save that explanation for another day."

"Very well."

"You mentioned before that you felt a connection. What kind of connection?" asked Rome, probing for more details.

"Your guess is as good as mine."

"I see from your uniform that you were a convict at Port Arthur."

"I arrived in 1840 and was incarcerated until my death in 1852."

"Twelve years is a long time."

"Longer than twelve years should ever feel."

"May I ask what you were imprisoned for?"

"I stabbed a man."

"Murder is a serious crime."

"I was convicted for assault, not murder."

"Why did you stab a man, William?" enquired Rome, happy that his story coincided with the one Heath told aboard the boat.

"In an attempt to save the woman I love."

"Your wife, Helen?"

Astonished, the spirit stepped back from Rome. "Is it by magic that you're able to do what you do?"

"No, but it does have to do with the connection you're feeling."

"I'm listening."

"The man I was with earlier today, his last name is Jones. Heath Jones."

"Many people share common surnames."

"Helen gave birth to a son not long after reaching Australia."

"A son?"

"Heath is a direct descendent of your son."

"My son," responded William, shocked by the news. "Helen and I had a child?"

"Yes."

The revelation of a son had an immediate impact on William. His tortured countenance began to fade, revealing a transformation from despair to optimism. The darkness in his eyes glimmered with signs of hope. His mind raced with curiosities to be resolved and Rome was his only source. "What did he become, my son? What did he do with the life given him?"

"I don't know, but there are other spirits who do, including your son," replied Rome.

"Are you confined to this island, William?"

William stared into the shadows, unresponsive to Rome's question. The sadness on his face slowly returned as feelings of anger began to grow in his heart.

"William?"

"There are places where spirits gather. Some in families. Some with friends," responded William, his tone bitter and cold.

"Why don't you gather with your family?"

"I prefer the solitude of this island, not that I'm by myself."

Rome looked around wondering how many spirits were watching. "Are there others here now?"

"They're allowing us our privacy."

"Have you been able to locate Helen or the rest of your family?" enquired Rome, wanting to find out as much as she could before Heath came looking for her.

"Billions of people have died. That's a great deal of spirits."

"But that's not why," argued Rome, rejecting William's logical reasoning.

"Do you fancy yourself a mind reader as well, Miss London?" taunted William, becoming irritated by her invasive questions.

"I've had my fair share of one-sided conversations with the dead. Regrets seem to come up often."

"They hold a certain power," William scoffed, his tone of voice reflecting the wrath growing inside him.

"Only if we let them. We are not our regrets."

"Words easily spoken."

"I'm only trying to help," Rome shot back.

"I don't need your help or anyone else's!"

"So that's why you've isolated yourself?"

"How can I face her? How can I face any of them?" roared William.

Rome felt the force of William's rage blow toward her, but she held her ground. She was instantly reminded of her first day at Port Arthur and her experience with the collective residents of the Isle of the Dead. Hesitant to make things worse, Rome took a moment to think about her response. She'd pushed William too far and the only way to move forward was to clear the air. "I'm sorry, William. I have no right to open old wounds."

"They've never closed," replied William in a way that nearly broke Rome's heart.

Unable to speak, Rome defied the ticking clock and stood in silence. She'd come to this country, to this island, thinking she was the answer to someone's problem. Through sheer ignorance, however, Rome had dismissed the tragedy of William's life and over a century and a half of regret. As the tears welled in her eyes she gave into the power of humility and her gift of a listening ear. Standing in the moonlight on an island at the bottom of the globe, Rome made an epic decision: to operate according to someone else's schedule. She would wait on him.

After a few minutes of silence William turned back toward Port Arthur. "Locked away, I longed for correspondence from home, but nothing came. The shame of my crime must have been too much for my parents to bare. Society would have seen to that. I chose selfishly and it caused the people I loved great pain."

Rome longed to tell William the truth of his parents' deaths, but without knowing the circumstances surrounding their demise she worried it could make matters worse. Her best option was to steer William in a more positive direction. "You loved Helen."

"And I still love her with all my heart, but it would have been better for her if we'd never met."

As Rome listened to William, she sensed the heavy load of guilt he'd been carrying for over a century and a half. Instinctively, she found herself moving closer. In an effort to console him she reached out and took hold of his hand. What a strange feeling, she thought to herself. There was substance, but not like flesh and bone. It was like nothing she'd experienced before.

Beyond that was the image she saw when she took hold of his hand. She saw a young woman standing in a small church dressed in a simple white gown and holding a bouquet of wild flowers. Her dark hair was contained by a beautiful wreath of flowers and greenery that gracefully surrounded her head. Her smile reflected her hope for a future together with the man she loved.

"She's beautiful."

"Who do you speak of?"

"The woman in your memories."

"You truly are a mind reader."

"For the moment it would seem so," said Rome, just as astonished.

"They took everything from me but my memories."

"Why stay on this island of death, staring across the harbor at where you spent the worst years of your life?"

"My bones are here and a spirit maintains a strong connection to their bones. I'm standing over mine right now."

"You're buried right there?"

"Beneath my feet. There's a couple more bodies below me, but I don't see those spirits come around very often."

"Below you?"

"Why dig three holes when one would suffice?"

Before she could respond, Rome heard the snap of a twig from behind. Turning back toward the trail she saw a figure moving toward her.

"It's been twenty minutes. I'm just following your instructions," Heath said as he emerged from the shadows, not knowing what to expect.

"I need more time. Go back to the beach."

"Is everything all right?"

"I'm fine, but you need to leave now."

"I'm not leaving without you."

With that said, Heath walked toward Rome and took hold of her arm. Instantly, he saw William's spirit standing in front of him. Reacting in fear he let go of Rome's arm and stumbled backwards, falling into the bushes on the other side of the trail. Unsure of what just happened, Rome ran toward him and tried to help him up, but Heath wouldn't let her touch him. "Stay away from me! Don't touch me!" Heath got to his feet, yet refused to leave the safety of the bushes. He stared sheepishly past Rome, using her and the bushes as a barrier between him and what he thought he saw.

"What are you doing?" asked Rome impatiently.

"Someone else is here! I saw him! He was right there. He just disappeared."

"What?"

"It was a ghost! He was standing right in front of you wearing one of those old prisoner uniforms!"

Heath continued to take cover from the apparition, but Rome was too preoccupied to help him. She was still trying to wrap her head around her own self being able to see William, let alone Heath being able to as well. "How is this possible?" she muttered to herself as she turned from Heath in an attempt to process. "How is any of this possible?" Desperate for an answer, she ran down the possibilities. "Maybe it's the full moon or the island itself that's causing this anomaly. Could it be Heath? Or possibly William?" She continued to grasp at straws until she was interrupted by a calm voice of experience.

"You'll go mad searching for an answer where there's none to be found. It took me years to learn that."

Rome nodded at William in confirmation then turned her attention back to Heath. He now had proof positive of her gift, a fact she was not happy about but needed to accept. Based on earlier events she doubted she could rely on him to keep her secret, but at this point, she had no other option. Rome was forced to make the one decision she did not want to make: trust the man who recently betrayed her. "Heath, I need you to calm down and listen to me."

"I'm calm!" responded Heath, clearly not as calm as he thought.

"You were right. There was unfinished business here, but it's not mine."

"What are you talking about?"

Rome walked back toward William, stood by his side, then turned around to face Heath. "Guess whose grave I'm standing over?" Before Heath could answer, she turned her head to William with an apologetic look on her face and said, "I hope you don't mind me standing on your grave."

"You wouldn't be the first."

"You're talking to him, aren't you?" whispered Heath from the bushes.

"Yes, I am. Now come over here," responded Rome, as she took a moment to enjoy watching Heath in distress.

"I don't think he's going to listen to you. I know I wouldn't," said William.

"He's going to have to listen to me. Stay here."

"I have nowhere else to be."

As Rome walked toward Heath he backed up until he slammed into the trunk of a tree. Rome stepped toward him and grabbed the front of his sweatshirt, making sure he stayed put while she delivered an ultimatum. "You either come with me or I'm taking the dinghy and leaving you on this island by yourself! Well, not entirely by yourself."

"I can't."

"We're just taking a few steps in that direction," said Rome, thinking that it might be proximity to the grave that caused Heath to be able to see William.

"What's going to happen?"

"That's what we're going to find out."

Heath stepped out of the bushes and cautiously followed her, sweeping the area with his eyes as he walked. Every sight and sound drew his attention as the anticipation continued to build. The snapping of twigs beneath his feet, leaves rustling in the breeze, shadows being cast by the moonlight, all seemed to bring the island to life. But still no sign of the ghost as he came to a stop next to Rome.

"Well?" enquired Rome.

"Well, what?"

"What do you see?"

"Nothing but you and a bunch of trees."

"That doesn't make sense."

"It's fine with me. Let's go!" As Heath grabbed Rome's hand to pull her in the opposite direction, he immediately saw William standing in front of him. "There he is!" declared Heath.

"You can see him?"

"He's standing right in front of us."

Rome, wanting to further test this new phenomenon, let go of Heath's hand. William's spirit disappeared from Heath's view. "Where did he go?"

Confirming her theory, Rome reached out and took hold of his hand again, causing William to instantly reappear to Heath.

"You're back."

"He never left. You can only see him when we're touching."

"How is this possible?"

"Your guess is as good as mine."

"Who is he?" whispered Heath.

"Heath Jones. Meet William Jones. Your great…"

"Great-great-great-grandfather," said Heath, finishing her sentence.

"Pleased to make your acquaintance," responded William as he extended his hand.

Heath cautiously lifted his hand and took hold of William's while continuing to hang onto Rome. Spellbound, he studied the spirit intently as they shook hands.

"I've seen you before. The painting."

"Painting?"

"There's a portrait of you."

"The painting commissioned by my mother on my eighteenth birthday."

"It took me a while to track down the family art pieces, but I finally did," said Heath proudly.

"Track them down? Are they no longer hanging at Forest Gate?"

"There have been a few changes since you left England."

"I'm sure the castle's been redecorated many times."

"Redecorated, refurbished, rebuilt," said Heath, adding one more description under his breath. "Relocated..."

"I've not found the courage to return home. The distance has grown too far."

"The distance may be shorter than you think."

Although William and Heath spoke the same language, Rome couldn't help but chuckle at how lost they were in translation. Here were two men discussing Forest Gate from two completely different perspectives. Eventually, the inevitable happened: a lull in conversation. Heath and William turned their attention to Rome for help, but Rome would have no part in it. "This is your family get-together. I'm just here to facilitate the connection."

Heath turned back to William and asked the first question that came to mind, "Where's Helen?"

"Helen?"

"Weren't you reunited after death?"

"The time has come for my departure," replied William soberly. Without hesitation, he disappeared from sight.

"Wait. Don't go! Did I say something wrong?"

"Unfortunately, that's about as far as I got. William is consumed with guilt and regret. He keeps himself isolated on this island as a form of personal punishment."

"Get him back here so we can straighten him out," demanded Heath impatiently.

"I don't control any of this. Spirits talk to me when they want to, not the other way around. There's nothing more we can do here."

"There's got to be something," said Heath as he lowered himself to a squat position and silently began picking twigs off of William's grave.

Rome bent her knees and joined Heath near the ground in an attempt to explain why. "I'd have to camp out and wait for William to show up again. I'm pretty sure the authorities from Port Arthur would frown on that. Let's go back to the boat and I'll tell you what I learned from my conversation with William."

"I can't leave him."

"He left us."

"We can't leave him on this island alone."

"We don't control where a spirit chooses to reside."

"Let's take him with us."

"You're not listening to me. You can't force a spirit to go where you want them to go. It just doesn't work that way."

"I'm not talking about his spirit. Let's take his body."

"There's no way I'm letting this little adventure of yours go from trespassing to grave robbing!"

"It's not robbing. I'm a family member who simply wants to exhume a loved one's remains and have them moved to a different location."

"Tomorrow you can fill out the proper paperwork and go through the right channels to make it happen."

"And how am I going to prove that I know where the body of William Jones is located? You heard Bev yesterday. There are thousands of bodies buried on this island. My paperwork would get tossed before it even gets considered."

"You have a point, but there's got to be a different way."

With new determination, Heath looked Rome straight in the eyes. "I need to tell you something, but I don't want you to freak out."

"Then don't tell me."

"I recently had Helen's remains exhumed and shipped to the castle."

"I told you not to tell me," said Rome as she stood up and walked away.

"I know it sounds crazy and maybe it was crazy, but I just felt like she needed to be here... closer to William. I was able to back door the whole thing from getting the paperwork okayed to having her body exhumed and shipped to Hobart. Money helped expedite the process, of course, but it was all done legally. I'm burying her remains tomorrow. The hole's being dug in the morning. If we dig up William's body tonight and take it back with us, we can bury them both in the same place. Side by side. Finally, reuniting them... or at least their remains."

"What if William doesn't want that?"

"Sometimes it takes someone else to show us what we really want."

"You actually believe that, don't you," responded Rome.

"I plan to build a memorial garden around the grave site. It's going to be beautiful."

"Heath, it's dark and I'm getting cold. Not to mention the fact that we don't have anything to dig with."

Heath removed his ripped, outer sweatshirt and held it out for Rome to put on as he constructed the next phase of his plan. "By the time we get back to the sailboat, get a shovel and return to the island, the moon should be right above us. We're just going to have to work with what we have."

Before Rome could disagree, Heath grabbed her hand and ran down the trail, pulling her behind.

"What will we put the body in to carry it back?" asked Rome, still trying to deter his plan.

"There's an extra set of sails on the boat. We can use part of that."

"And how are we going to cover our tracks?"

"Fortunately, his grave is located in a spot where not much grass is growing. We'll fill the hole back in and cover it with some dried leaves and twigs."

"The other two occupants will appreciate that."

Heath came to a sudden stop and turned back to Rome with a look of horror on his face. "Other two occupants?"

"At least they're below him."

This time Rome took off, leaving Heath to follow behind. Together they made their way down the trail and back to the beach. Heath pushed the dinghy from the shore into the water, then helped Rome step into the craft. He boarded the dinghy, started the motor and steered her back to the sailboat.

"So this is what if feels like to be a criminal," Rome thought to herself as the dinghy rounded the tip of the peninsula and headed back toward the sailboat. Aiding and abetting in a crime was not something she ever thought she would do, yet here she was doing it, hoping she wouldn't find herself on an Australian version of 'America's Most Wanted.'"

When they reached the sailboat, Heath had Rome stay in the dinghy and handed her the materials they would need. Using a knife, he cut off a portion of the extra sail and handed it over the side to Rome, then crawled down into the dinghy, started the engine and steered toward the Isle of the Dead.

Carrying their supplies they made their way back up the now familiar trail toward William's burial sight. Heath took his short-handled shovel and scraped off the top of the grave site. After moving the light-colored dirt and debris aside, he began to shovel.

"How do you know which direction to dig?" enquired Rome.

"I don't. I reckon I'll just keep going until I come to a bone or something. At that point we can figure out which direction the body is lying."

"Great!"

"If you don't think you can handle this you should probably wait down at the beach."

"I wasn't the one hiding in the bushes at the first sight of a ghost," replied Rome.

Offering no comment, a more humbled Heath returned to digging as Rome's attention split between watching him dig and glancing around for William to reappear.

After digging about three feet down, Heath pulled up a hand with his scoop. Startled, he fell back against the side of the hole, but quickly contained himself as Rome watched with amusement. He pulled the cell phone out of his back pocket, bent down into the hole and used the flashlight option to view the skeletal hand more closely. Rome quickly tossed the canvas sail over Heath and the entire hole to hide the light from view as he studied the remains. The hand was still in the proper position next to the two bones of his forearm and now Heath knew what direction to dig. He turned off his phone light and popped his head out of the canvas, startling Rome with his sudden appearance.

"Are you trying to give me a heart attack?"

"The living scares you, but not the dead?"

"In more ways than one."

Heath ignored her obvious implication and returned to excavating William's bones. "Thanks to the hand, I know which direction to dig."

"Good. The sooner we get off this island the better," responded Rome as she pulled the sail toward her and laid it flat.

"One thing's for sure... Exercise needs to be a bigger part of my life," admitted Heath.

Eventually, the entire skeleton was exposed and they carefully lifted the bones out of the hole and onto the piece of sail. Heath went back to shoveling as Rome wrapped the ends of the canvas around the remains, cut pieces of rope and secured it like a Christmas present. "Some gift this would be," Rome thought to herself as she continued to secure the rope. After finishing the body bag she dragged it onto the trail, located all the supplies and put them on the trail as well. No evidence of their crime could be left behind.

Daylight was encroaching which meant time was running out.

Fortunately, filling in the hole went much faster than removing the dirt. Heath paused every so often and walked over the loose dirt to pack it down and keep it from settling at a later date. He continued the process until he used every last bit of dirt and then some from beneath the bushes where no one would notice. After he packed the final layer, he scraped the lighter dirt over top of the dig site, then sprinkled some leaves, twigs and other natural debris over the disturbed ground.

Completely finished, Heath handed his shovel to Rome then found a broken-off tree branch and drug it about as he walked backwards toward the trail, ridding the ground of footprints. Once he reached the trail, he tossed the branch back into the bushes.

Without a pause, Heath and Rome picked up the tools and body bag and headed back to the beach where they loaded the dinghy and powered toward the sailboat.

Again, Rome felt the familiar night air blowing against her face. She couldn't help but wonder if they were doing the right thing. She knew William would find his bones in their new resting spot, a fact she'd neglected to share with Heath, but had no idea how he would react to being buried alongside Helen. Burying their remains together would definitely add a twist to this centuries-old love story and hopefully provide a happy ending. After all, what else could possibly go wrong? With that thought in mind, Rome reached out to the shovel and knocked on the wooden handle three times for luck.

Approaching the side of the sailboat, Rome was grateful they were in the home stretch. All they had to do was load everything back into the sailboat, head back to the marina, unload the evidence before daybreak and return to the beach house.

And that's exactly what they did.

Chapter Seven

Opening her eyes and stretching her hands to the ceiling, Rome once again woke to the sound of waves crashing against the shore. Only this time it was early afternoon. As Rome lay on her back staring at the ceiling, reflecting on the events of the night before, she found herself speculating if last night actually happened or if it was just a dream. "It really happened," concluded Rome, amazed she was saying the words out loud.

For better or for worse, her time on the island would be a night she would never forget. The rush of adrenaline she felt during their 'covert operation' was thrilling to say the least, but when she weighed the thrill against the consequence of getting caught, she knew it was reckless, and Rome London was not reckless.

She'd spent much of her adult life traveling the world, writing about adventure, but never truly understood the meaning until last night. Adventure requires a free spirit and the ability to switch gears at the drop of a hat, similar to Heath's decision to remove William's remains. Rome would never have made that choice nor even considered it. She was far too disciplined.

Crawling out of bed, she felt the effects of the physical exertion from their moonlit antics. She stretched her body as far as the pain would allow, then put on her robe. As she walked toward the door, she paused for a moment to prepare herself for what would come next. The last person in the world she wanted to see that morning was Heath, but there was no getting around it. His manipulation and betrayal had left her wounded and nursing a massive amount of mixed emotions brewing inside her. An eruption was eminent and Rome was no volcano. She was far too controlled.

Looking in the mirror, Rome knew from her reflection that not all the blame could be placed at Heath's feet. She was upset with her choice to get on the boat in the first place, but it went deeper than that. She was angry at herself for dropping her guard long enough to develop feelings for Heath. It was unprofessional and unbecoming a travel writer of her experience. Leaving the honesty of the mirror behind, she took a deep breath, opened the door and left the bedroom.

She walked through the quiet house, expecting Heath at every turn, but he was nowhere in sight. Without notice, he bounced through the front door carrying a box of pastries and some fruit juice. "I come bearing afternoon tea. No doubt you're as hungry as I am." Heath picked out a couple of pastries and a lemon square and loaded his plate then placed a couple of pastries and a fruit tart on Rome's plate. Rome remained silent as she watched him go about his routine as though nothing out of the ordinary had happened the night before.

"Still not talking to me?" said Heath nonchalantly as he sat down at the table and dove into his pastries, stuffing his mouth full of delight as he filled their glasses with juice. "I went down to the marina and finished securing the sailboat in its slip. She's all cleaned up and stored properly. We can stop by your hotel on the way home and grab a change of clothes so you can clean up at my place."

Unable to take it any longer, Rome ended his fantasy. "No! You can drop me by my hotel and drive away."

"Don't you want to be there for the burial?"

"I'm in Tasmania to write an article for my magazine, not play sidekick to a spoiled manchild with more money than brains." Trying to hold back the hot lava, Rome contained herself before any more hurtful words escaped her mouth. "I'll get dressed, so we can leave." Rome walked away but Heath wasn't about to let things end on that note. Standing up, he proposed another offer in an attempt to recapture her attention. "My internet connection dwarfs anything you'll find at the hotel."

"Why is that relevant?"

"Come back to the castle and use my office to finish up your assignment. You can upload your article and pictures without the frustration you'll have to deal with at the hotel. That should make your editor happy."

"Like that's possible at this point."

"If you need to be in the States to save your job, I'll fly you to Sydney first thing in the morning on my private jet. I'll buy you a first class ticket to the States as well. I'll even have Max take your friend's car on the ferry back to Melbourne. I owe you at least that much."

Unwilling to give Heath another chance, Rome put an end to what felt, yet again, like a business negotiation. "What I did last night I did for William, not you." Rome felt a crushing weight come to rest on her heart as she walked away. This was not like her, but the molten fluid rock was so close to the surface.

"I'm still grateful, Rome, and always will be."

Surprisingly, Heath's words of gratitude caused the volcano to cool just enough to allow the practical side of her mind to take control of her inner dialogue. She knew that his office was the best place to finish her article, as well as swim through an ocean of photos, and she was foolish not to accept his offer. Unable to erase the last few seconds of their conversation, she continued down the hallway.

"Rome, wait!"

There it was. The two words that would hopefully give Rome a chance to choose differently without having to swallow her pride. So she did wait, both of them waited. Frozen in place, neither opting to move. Finally, Heath broke the silence. "I can't change yesterday or last night, but what I can do is try to repair the damage and lessen the impact."

"A line right out of a Business 101 textbook," Rome thought to herself as she continued to listen, but then he got personal and Rome wasn't expecting personal.

"For the first time since my dad died, I feel like I'm engaged in life rather than just going through the motions. I woke up this morning looking forward to my day. I haven't done that in years and I have you to thank for it. I'm sorry for deceiving you, Rome. Tell me what to do to make up for it and I'll do it."

Heath's words dripped with sincerity, causing the lava within Rome to recede. The last thing she wanted was to open her heart to him again, but she began to feel something tug and then something pull as she humbly replied, "The use of your office would be a start."

"I'll call Sheldon and make sure you have access to whatever you need for however long you need it. You'll have the run of the castle."

"Every modern woman's dream," responded Rome jokingly.

The return of her sense of humor and the calming effect that it brought was a good sign. Rome walked to the table, picked up the fruit tart and began eating it as she walked down the hallway. With her emotions in check, her mind began to plan the rest of the day accordingly. She would finish up her article, get it to her editor and say goodbye to Heath for the last time, a plan she'd attempted twice in the past twenty-four hours.

Heath was also pleased with the outcome of the conversation but had a different goal in mind. Shoving the last bite of pastry into his mouth, he cleaned up after themselves and left the house. Progress had been made with Rome, but gaining her help with his ghost problem was still a concern. Not to mention the fact that last night's adventure had prompted within Heath an even deeper adoration for Rome.

Heath had put himself between a rock and a hard place. His only hope was to have enough time to reverse the damage he had caused and rebuild his relationship with Rome. "But where to start?" he thought to himself as he sat on the porch evaluating his performance over the past couple of days. Slowly, humility began to set in making Heath its pupil. Although unintentional, he had hurt Rome deeply, a fact that was painful to admit even to himself. He knew better, but more importantly, Rome deserved better. After further contemplation, the answer was clear. No more manipulation. No more deception. He would move forward with honesty in the hopes that Rome would forgive his trickery and see him through new eyes. He would never hurt Rome again.

THE CAR REMAINED quiet for the first half hour of the drive back from the beach house as Rome's thoughts debated how her mother would have handled the conversation with William. No matter where the Navy stationed them, the strings of her mother's heart seemed to have no end as they wrapped themselves around those in need. Rome considered her mom to be a saint and continued to hold out the hope that a morsel of her mother's compassion would someday rub off on her. But in order for that to happen, Rome would have to lessen the tight grip she held on the reins of her life as well as the strings of her own heart. A grip that allowed her to maintain the restraint she relied on to keep the itinerary of her life moving along as planned.

At the same time, Heath was building up courage to ask the question that had been swirling around his head since the first night they met in the castle. Finding the guts necessary, he posed the question. "How are you able to do what you do?"

Trust was still an issue, so Rome took a moment to weigh the consequences of allowing Heath deeper access to her long-kept secret. She recalled the inexplicable urge she felt to tell him about her ability on their drive down to Port Arthur. She'd never felt that before, especially with a stranger. She had yet to tell Jamie and they'd been dating for over two years.

"You don't have to answer, Rome," said Heath in an attempt to alleviate the pressure building with the silence.

"The cat is kind of out of the bag at this point," responded

Rome, "but before I can answer your question, I need you to promise to keep it a secret."

"It'll go with me to the grave."

"This is serious, Heath. Beyond myself and Mom and Dad, you're the only one who knows about my gift. I need you to protect our family secret. No one else can ever know."

"I owe you that and more," promised Heath sincerely.

Feeling satisfied that he wouldn't betray her, Rome attempted another first. "It's hereditary, through my mother's side of the family," responded Rome, knowing her decision to trust Heath didn't make sense on paper.

"How far back?"

"According to my mother, my great-grandmother, who was also named Rome, had the ability to communicate with the dead, as well as generations of women before her. My ancestors were gypsies who emigrated to Italy in the sixteenth century from northern Europe. When I think of my great-grandmother, I picture the classic gypsy fortune teller, sitting in front of a crystal ball, with a scarf wrapped around her head and big gold hoop earrings hanging from her ears."

"The classic grandma portrait," said Heath, in an attempt at humor.

"Was that a joke?"

"I'm sorry. I didn't mean to make fun of your family."

"I was referring to the fact that you may actually have a sense of humor."

"I tend to keep it on a short leash."

"Feel free to lengthen it."

"Noted. So back to this thing you do..."

"The ability to listen to the dead skipped my grandmother, who was grateful to not have to deal with what she considered to be a carnival act. Her feelings stemmed from the fact that my Great-Grandma Rome was quite well known for her gift in the village where she lived and that was an embarrassment to her daughter, my grandmother. As a teenager she ran away, leaving her family behind in the hopes of fitting in as a normal Italian. Her wish came true when she married an Italian man and began living a normal life.

When my mother was born and it became apparent at an early age that she could hear voices, my grandmother forbade her to speak of it. When Mom turned seventeen, she left home in search of her roots, eventually finding her Grandma Rome. She was able to spend the last six months of her grandmother's life getting to know her and the rest of her relatives. She also had the opportunity to learn about what her grandmother considered to be a gift, the ability to listen, and for some, talk with the dead. After her grandmother's death, Mom said goodbye to her newly discovered people and returned home. Once all her questions were answered, my mom and grandma's fragile relationship began to heal. Mom was able to accept the differences in how she and my grandma viewed the family gift."

"Those must have been some powerful answers," responded Heath.

"Sometimes answers don't always come in the form of words. Once Mom saw the unconditional love her Grandma Rome had for her daughter, a daughter ashamed of her own mother, she learned the true meaning of love. Rome taught her that true compassion allows people with differing opinions to have a conversation without passing judgment as to who's right or wrong. When Mom returned home, she saw her mother through new eyes. That, coupled with everything else she had learned, made a difference in their relationship. Eventually, Mom met my dad and they began a marvelous life together."

"Did you ever meet your mom's mother, your grandmother?"

"We visited Italy many times over the years until Grandma and Grandpa passed away, but the family gift was never discussed out of respect for Grandma. I loved them both very much, and in terms of how I view my ability, I probably have more in common with my grandma than I have with my own mother. I'm still hoping some of Mom's selflessness rubs off on me one day."

"Does your mother use her gift?" enquired Heath.

"All the time, no matter how much the inconvenience. Growing up, our family plans for the day were often diverted because a voice whispered in Mom's ear."

"What did your dad think of that?"

"He's learned to deal with it, but he's never been really comfortable following my mother into the great unknown. His life is one of order and discipline, while my mom is more of a free spirit, a gypsy by nature. Over the years, they've rubbed off on each other and learned to respect their differences, but they still have to work at it."

"You seem more like your dad."

"Definitely. Even though I have the same gift as Mom, I like to be focused and in control. Life is easier that way. It makes sense to me."

"I hope I'm not being too nosy, but I find this whole thing fascinating."

Rome assured Heath that his queries were not intrusive but did not share how strange it felt to freely answer. For the first time since she developed her gift, Rome felt liberated. She realized that this must have been what her mother experienced when she visited her family village and was able to discuss her gift openly with her grandma. Rome wondered if this could be a sampling of what it feels like to be unrestrained. More food for thought as her focus returned to Heath's next question.

"What was it like growing up with a mother like that?"

"After school I would accompany Mom on her 'special errands' as she called them.

She'd leave notes for people in regard to lost items such as keys, family records, contact information, precious heirlooms, safe deposit boxes, words of advice and the list goes on and on. It was just a normal part of our day, like doing laundry or cooking dinner. As the official lookout, I was always aware of the people around us. Mom had seen firsthand the price her Grandma Rome's family paid from the public knowledge of her gift. She didn't want that for us, so she found ways to use her ability that didn't come as a cost to our privacy or reputation."

"You must have some amazing stories to tell," said Heath, sincerely impressed.

"I do. Her favorite errands were when a spirit wanted a special memento, card or flowers delivered on a certain occasion. Mom would ring the doorbell then take my hand and we'd run and hide so we could watch the person's reaction. I saw every emotion possible, but they never matched the expression I'd see on my mother's face. As much as I hate to admit it... that was always the best part."

"When did you realize you had the same ability?" asked Heath.

"It came slowly at first and mostly while I was sleeping. As a kid, I remember waking up in the middle of the night wondering if it was a dream or the voice of a spirit. Once I started hearing the whispers, as my mom calls them, she began tutoring me just as her Grandma Rome taught her. She wanted me to fully understand the responsibility that came with the family gift, but I was a teenager and the last thing on my mind were the needs of others, especially dead people. Sometimes I'd tell Mom what I heard and she would take care of it for me."

"Sounds like a teenager. I remember those years," remarked Heath, finding common ground with Rome.

"It gets worse. In college, I became really good at shutting out the voices, thanks in part to the Walkman. When I started my career the last thing I had time for were 'special errands,' but that didn't mean the voices stopped."

"How do you feel about your gift now that you're older?"

"I'm more accepting of it. I wouldn't be in Tasmania right now, if I weren't. To be honest, my greatest fear is ending up like a circus act. I couldn't deal with the chaos. I could not live that way."

"At least you'd have your own tent... and lots of scarves."

"Another joke. You're on a roll."

"Sorry. I couldn't resist."

"I did open the door to that one."

"Are you going to tell your mom about your experience on the island?"

"My parent's anniversary is next month, so I'm headed down to Florida for that weekend. I have to share this in person. A phone call would never do the story justice."

"How do you feel about being named after your great-grandmother?"

"I consider it an honor, mostly because Mom cherished the months that she got to spend with her."

"After my experience last night with William, I feel the same way. I've never known any family on my dad's side, so that meant a lot to me. Thank you for that, Rome."

"Don't thank me. I came to Port Arthur because a relentless spirit continued to call me here."

"It couldn't have been William; he seemed as surprised as we were."

"Agreed."

"Then who was it?"

"I have no idea."

"Maybe someday you'll find out."

"Maybe," responded Rome as she turned her attention to the passing scenery and slowly closed her eyes.

Heath, on the other hand, was as alert as he'd ever been, reflecting on the magnitude of what he just learned. Astonished by her ability, Heath became even more intrigued with the woman resting in the seat next to him. Rome wasn't just growing on Heath—she was becoming his sole focus, his obsession, a thought that surprised him more than all the ghosts in his castle.

THEY REACHED the hotel and Rome felt like a new woman after taking a shower and putting on a clean change of clothes. Heath spent the entire time on his phone, putting out fires and taking care of business. They were back to the real world now which meant dealing with the matters at hand. Rome repacked her bags with what she thought she would need and off to the castle they drove.

Heath pulled up to the door and Rome was relieved to see the scaffolding gone. Mr. Burns met them out front and opened the car door as Rome gathered her bags and got out of the vehicle.

"Sheldon will help you get set up while I drive down to the shed and unload the cargo," instructed Heath before he drove away.

"Welcome back, Ms. London. Hopefully, this visit won't be as eventful as the last," said Mr. Burns as he opened the door, took Rome's bags and led her into the castle. "This way to the library."

Rome followed him down the hallway and entered the room. Impressed with all the books and the gorgeous furniture, she almost forgot why she was there in the first place.

"You should find everything you need here to finish your work," exclaimed Mr. Burns professionally as he placed her bags in the desk chair.

Rome walked to the large desk and slid her hand across the beautiful wood. Turning to her bags, she removed her laptop, placed it on the desk, then plugged it into a power source. Next, she unloaded her camera and connected it to her laptop, then she pulled out an external hard drive and plugged that into her computer as well. Anticipating countless missed calls from her editor, she hesitantly plugged in her charger and connected the phone.

Mr. Burns waited patiently for any request she might have as she pulled out her notebook, a pencil and a bottle of water and placed them perfectly on the desk. With her work space organized, she removed her bags and sat down in the wing-backed leather desk chair, then rolled herself forward.

"Is there anything else I can get for you, Ms. London?"

"I think I'm good, Mr. Burns."

"Then if that's all, I'll check in on you later."

"Thank you."

"My pleasure."

Mr. Burns turned and walked out the door, closing it behind him. Rome opened her notebook and turned to the proper page, pulled up her work-in-progress article and began to read. With her deadline approaching, Rome felt the urgency to get her article and photos submitted before the end of the day. She also knew that would soften the blow for when the time came to return an overdue phone call to her editor. Reading through her notes, Rome's fingers raced across the keyboard, doing what they were trained to do: entice her readers to dream. She knew the most adventurous part of her trip would never grace the pages of the magazine, but she would take the memories with her wherever she went.

Suddenly, she heard someone in the room with her. "Where are they? What have they done with them?" said the panicked voice. Rome's attention turned to the books sliding in and out as the voice continued to ask similar questions. "Where are they? Why can't I find them?"

As much as she wanted to help the spirit, Rome knew she had to remain focused. She'd never let her boss down before and she wasn't going to start now. Returning to her work, she chose to ignore the rambling voice and the movement of books as best she could.

Unfortunately, the voice wasn't Rome's only distraction. She couldn't help but let her thoughts wander to Heath and his preparations for the sunset burial. In his own way he was writing the final chapter in the love story that was William and Helen's, a modern-day ending that involved two strangers on a small island in the moonlight.

HEATH CAREFULLY OPENED the lid to the coffin and looked in on the remains of his fourth great-grandmother. As he stared respectfully at the corpse, he couldn't help but wonder if her spirit was nearby. Gently, he moved her remains to one side, picked up the canvas bag and laid it on the table next to the casket. Using a knife, he cut the ropes and laid the canvas material open, revealing William's bones in the light of day. Picking up a small whisk broom, he began to brush the dirt from remains. The last thing he wanted was to cover the beautiful satin lining with dirt.

Sliding the canvas close to the coffin, he gently picked up the bones and placed them next to Helen. Heath made sure the two of them were positioned properly by taking the time to arrange the limbs, then he shut the lid and locked it tight. After disposing of the used canvas and rope, he drove to the castle and entered his home, shocking Mr. Burns with his unkempt, dirty appearance. "No wonder you requested we draw you a bath."

"And how is that going, Sheldon?"

"Miss Lemmons is handling it as we speak."

"Then I'll see you when I'm more presentable."

With that said, Heath ran up the stairs before Mr. Burns could finish the conversation.

"Your clothes are laid out on your bed, just as you requested."

"Thank you, Sheldon!" responded Heath as he disappeared down the hallway.

Nearly colliding with each other, Heath entered his bedroom just as Miss Lemmons was leaving. "Excuse me, sir. I didn't see you."

"You must be Miss Lemmons."

"At your service, Mr. Jones."

"How's the bath looking?"

Miss Lemmons proudly held up her digital thermometer for Heath to recognize her diligent effort. "The temperature is just as you requested, sir."

Before Miss Lemmons could clear the doorway, Heath pulled his shirt out of his pants and began unbuttoning it. "Perfect," said Heath as he turned and walked toward the bathroom, removing his shirt on the way.

Smiling a school-girl smile, Miss Lemmons took one last peak at her employer's impressive physique before she shut the door behind her. Curious as to her own rising temperature, she stuck the thermometer in her mouth as she walked down the hall.

Inside the bathroom, Heath finished stripping off his dirty clothes and stepped into the bath, one foot then the other. "Just right," he said to himself as he lowered his body into the warm water. Laying his head against the back of the tub, Heath found himself at peace, not just from the past twenty-four hours, but from the past three years. Although he entered total relaxation mode, his thoughts wandered to Rome and the writing of her article. He smiled as he thought of their time together, then slowly submerged himself beneath the water.

FEELING BOTH RELAXED AND REJUVENATED, Heath left the bathroom and walked toward the bed expecting to find the gray metallic suit he had requested, but instead he found a sports jacket and a pair of jeans lying in its place. He walked to the armoire and opened the doors to find the suit he wanted still hanging in its usual place. "That's strange," Heath commented as he looked back at the clothes on the bed. "Sheldon must have had something different in mind."

Not wanting to take the time to change things around, Heath put on the more casual selection with the accompanying shirt and tie. Approving the outfit in the mirror, Heath shut the armoire door and left the room.

As he walked down the stairs, Mr. Burns met him at the bottom, examining Heath's unexpected attire. He leaned the broom he was carrying against the stair railing and commented on his casual outfit. "That's a different look for you."

"You're the one who picked it out."

"I laid out the metallic suit as you requested."

"This is what I found on the bed."

"Perhaps Miss Lemmons took some liberty."

"That's not what I pay her to do."

"The staff is young but trainable with time."

"Let's hope so."

"The strange occurrences that we've been experiencing have run off every seasoned professional I've hired."

"You take care of the training and leave the strange occurrences to me."

"I'll speak to Miss Lemmons."

"Very good. I'll be on the grounds if you need me."

Heath left the castle as Miss Lemmons entered the room, providing perfect timing for more training. "I didn't hire you to be a stylist, Miss Lemmons."

"Excuse me, Mr. Burns?"

"The changing of Mr. Jones' attire?"

"All I did was draw a bath. I didn't touch his clothes," responded Miss Lemmons, leaving Mr. Burns confused as he watched her walk up the stairs.

Turning to leave, he reached for his broom, but it unexpectedly dropped to the floor. When he reached down to pick it up, the broom eluded his hand and stood up by itself, alerting Mr. Burns to the presence of a ghost. "I am not amused." Following his comment, the broom moved from the railing to the butler's hand as though it had been placed there. "Thank you," he said, then decided to get something off his chest. "And while we're at it... it's my job to dress Mr. Jones, not yours." Pleased by the way he handled the situation, he swung his broom back and forth as he cheerfully exited the room.

ROME PUT the final touches on her article and photos, then pushed the send button. Feeling victorious, she stood up and stretched her arms to the ceiling, then looked at her mostly charged phone. Hesitantly, she picked it up and checked the international clock app to find out what time it was in the States. "Still early enough to call," admitted Rome disappointedly as she unplugged her phone and began scrolling through all the missed calls. "Don't know whose number that is... Looks like Bev left a message. I'll check that later... I'll get back to him tomorrow... Won't bother calling them back at all... Jamie called. Several times. That's strange. Why would Jamie be calling? I thought he was on a job in the South Pacific somewhere. All the rest are missed calls from my editor. That's a lot of missed calls." Rome took a deep breath and speed dialed Angelica Fontaine, one of the best editors in the magazine business. "Hi, Angelica. It's me," said Rome as she walked toward the window, moving her phone away from her ear as her editor grilled her as to why she didn't return her calls.

"I'm sorry. My phone died and I didn't have my charger. I was on a sailboat all day taking pictures of the coastline."

Again, Rome moved the phone away from her ear as her editor responded to Rome's excuses.

"The good news is, I just finished my article and it should be waiting in your inbox. Rome listened to the response which was much more subdued this time as her editor checked her email.

"I think you're going to love the photos. I'm very happy with how they turned out. You'll see I labeled the ones I thought would look best in the article and on the cover."

As her editor responded, Rome looked out the window and saw Heath talking to a group of laborers on the grounds. Losing interest in the call, Rome tried to wrap it up as quickly as possible. "So let me know what you think and if you want me to make any changes."

Before she could disconnect the call, her editor asked the most difficult question of all. "When will you be returning to the office?"

Rome thought for a moment as she watched Heath taking care of business on the lawn. "I have an event to attend this evening, so I'll give you a call tomorrow and update you on my itinerary."

Feeling satisfied with the answer, Angelica ended the conversation. Rome slowly lowered her phone and placed it in her pocket as she walked back to the desk, closed her laptop and left the room.

But Rome wasn't the only one watching Heath. Mr. Burns stared out the upstairs window of the master suite, observing Heath as he prepared his men for the sunset burial. The look on his face was that of concern. A look Sheldon never allowed to be seen outside the privacy of his own surroundings. His worry for Heath had continued to grow since the death of his employer, Marshall Jones. For the past three years, he had felt like a mother bird watching her young leap from the nest for the first time, not knowing if he would survive on his own or fall victim to the forces of nature.

He had become butler to the Jones family nearly thirty years ago, following the death of Marshall's wife. He was quite young but took the job very seriously. He loved serving both Marshall and his boy, Heath. They were good people to work for and he knew that was a rare thing to find in his industry.

Mr. Burns watched Heath grow from a boy into a man and

could not have been more proud if he were the boy's own father. He watched as Heath became exactly what his father wanted him to be, his protege' and apprentice. Neither of which was a bad thing, but he often wondered what Heath wanted or if he even knew what he wanted. With his father's untimely passing, Heath was forced to embark on a solo journey, an expedition without a map, guide or compass. An odyssey of sorts, into what Heath Jones truly wanted for himself and his life. Sheldon wanted Heath to dig deep and take an honest look without the titles of 'son,' 'CEO,' 'president' or 'sir' obstructing his view. He hoped that he would look beyond how circumstances and the positions he held defined him and find out what Heath Jones truly wanted from life.

So far, Heath had stuck to the world he knew best: the world of business. However, the personal path Heath had chosen to travel was a strange one and Mr. Burns did not know what to make of it or where it would lead. But that's the thing with this type of journey and why only the courageous attempt it without a safety net or parachute.

Mr. Burns's attention turned from Heath to Ms. London as she walked across the grounds toward Heath. It wasn't hard for Mr. Burns to see the connection between them, but he was curious as to why Heath had so quickly welcomed Rome into his life. That wasn't like him. Something had brought them together, but neither of them were willing to share the details and Mr. Burns wasn't used to being kept in the dark.

WALKING ACROSS THE BEAUTIFUL GROUNDS, Rome continued to make her way toward Heath. She approached him from behind and took a position by his side, staring into the deep hole in front of them.

"Does this mean another Rome London travel article is headed for the presses?" enquired Heath.

"That all depends on my editor."

"You don't have to be here."

"And miss the denouement to my first felony?"

"Only a writer would see it like that."

"So when will the burial of the evidence begin?"

"The men should be up with the coffin at any moment."

"It's a lovely evening for a funeral."

"I couldn't have timed it better. Look."

Both Heath and Rome took a moment to stare off into the beautiful sunset, reminding them of the afternoon they spent together on the sailboat. For Heath it was a fond memory, but for Rome it was unsettling.

"While we're waiting I could give you a feel for what the memorial gardens will look like," offered Heath.

"I'd love that."

He left Rome's side and began walking around the area pointing out the future locations of rose beds and flower gardens, fountains and reflecting pools, benches, two or three—an archway here, a gazebo there, and on and on. Fascinated, Rome watched Heath move about powered by his passion for the project. His presentation only added to her belief that Heath Jones was two people trapped in one body: the driven business man and the pensive, passionate adventurer.

Heath stopped what he was doing and hurried past Rome in order to guide the approaching truck to the grave site. They came to a stop and four men walked to the casket. They slid it off the back of the truck, placed it on the ground at the foot of the hole, then each man took a long rope and ran it through two of the handles on both sides of the coffin. Reaching down, they grabbed the handles and packed the casket over the hole. With the coffin in position, the four men took hold of their ropes and lowered it down, inch by inch, until it came to rest inside the plastic vault at the bottom. Letting go of one end of their ropes, they pulled the other end through the handle and out of the hole. Rolling up their ropes, the four men took their positions by the side of the grave, awaiting their boss's orders. Rome waited for Heath to say something, but no utterance came from his mouth. She waited a bit longer then finally whispered a suggestion.

"Are you going to say something?"

"I thought about it," replied Heath.

"And?"

Again, silence.

Rome realized someone needed to take control of the situation, so she turned to the men alongside the grave. "Would you gentlemen excuse us for a moment?"

The men nodded their heads and walked away from the grave, gathering together out of ear shot.

"I can leave as well if you'd like some privacy."

"No, stay! Please."

"All right."

Summoning his courage, Heath reached into his pocket, pulled out a piece of paper and held it tightly in his hand, uncertain as to whether or not he should open it. "I copied down what a priest would say. I personalized it. It's kind of sappy."

"I'd like to hear it."

He slowly unfolded it, and after taking a deep breath, began to read it out loud. "We therefore commit these bodies to the ground; in sure and certain hope of the resurrection to eternal life. For dust thou art and unto dust shalt thou return." He paused for a moment in an attempt to gain the courage he needed before he continued.

"Was that the sappy part?" asked Rome in uncertainty.

"No. That was the priest part."

"Go on then."

Heath took another deep breath, then committed himself to finishing his speech. "Ashes to ashes, dust to dust, here lie two lovers, beneath earth's crust. May their spirits unite, in peace and love, finding rest from their cares, high up above." Heath quickly folded up his paper and placed it back in his suit pocket, content that Helen and William's love story finally had a happy ending. Or at least he hoped so.

"That was lovely, Heath. Definitely sappy, but very sweet," commented Rome.

Heath smiled at Rome's review of his poem then continued to stand in silence until he dropped a bombshell on Rome. "You're the only woman I've ever met who really gets me. Would you consider staying for a while?"

Unsure of how to respond, it was Rome's turn to choose silence as they both stared at the same atmospheric phenomena that just twenty-four hours ago had them in each other's arms. Fortunately, rational thought entered the picture, replacing the effects of the mesmerizing display on the horizon and snapped her back to reality.

"What is it with Australian sunsets?" asked Rome in frustration, then she turned and walked back toward the castle, leaving Heath confused by her response.

Rome walked into the library and began placing her laptop and other items into her bag. In the process, she pulled out a copy of a recent issue of *"Trekking the Globe"* and dropped it on the desk as a memento of their time together.

Heath cautiously entered and stood in the doorway. Rome noticed him in her peripheral vision but continued undaunted.

"What will it take to get you to stay, Rome?"

"This may come as a shock to you, but some things you just can't negotiate."

Heath crossed the room and placed his hands on the opposite side of the desk, staring intently at Rome. "I disagree."

"We've known each other for seventy-two hours. That's three days. Have they been extraordinary days? Yes, when compared to my normal life. But three days is not long enough to warrant a request for me to stay. What did you expect me to say, Heath? What is it you want from me?"

"I don't know..."

"If you don't know, why ask me to stay?" replied Rome, cutting him off mid-sentence.

"You didn't let me finish."

"Okay, so finish."

"How can I finish when I don't know where to start?"

Frustrated, Heath straightened up while continuing to stare at her, then he removed his sports jacket and laid it over the back of the couch. Rome watched and waited as he loosened his tie and rolled up his sleeves. Again, he laid his hands on the desk and leaned forward in an attempt to explain. "I don't know how to say what I want to say." After a brief pause, his eyes lit up as he continued, "But I can show you." Without warning, he reached across the desk, grabbed onto Rome's hand and hurried toward the door, pulling Rome behind him.

"What are you doing?"

"Answering your question," responded Heath as he continued down the hallway and into the grand hall. As he began to climb the stairs, Rome yanked her hand away from his and demanded an answer. "I'm not going any further until you tell me where we're going."

"Aren't you the one who said answers don't always come in the form of words?" argued Heath as he reached out his hand for Rome to take hold. Again, the rush was on as they ran to the top of the stairs and across the balcony.

Heath pulled her down a long, dark hall, passing door after door until they reached the one facing them at the end of the hallway. By the look of the door, anyone would have thought it to be a closet, and for a brief second, Rome wondered if he was going to stuff her inside until she changed her mind. Not a pleasant thought!

Instead, Heath opened the door which led to a small room, just big enough to house a tall spiral staircase. Without a pause in his step, he began to climb the circular stairs with Rome in tow. Around and around they climbed until Rome's legs began to feel the burn. Reaching the top, Heath slid a large bolt lock to the right and opened the door. He walked through and helped Rome make it up the last couple of steps. Stepping through the doorway, it appeared she was standing on a patio of sorts.

"I had them construct this part of the castle first, so I could come up here and think," said Heath as he led Rome to the four-foot-high wall surrounding the area.

Bending over the wall, Rome realized she was in a tower overlooking the vast roof of the castle and the entire grounds. Although the sun had disappeared, she could still see for miles in every direction. The view was incredible and she found herself squeezing

Heath's hand in a different sort of way, this time not wanting to let go.

"This is why I want you to stay," he whispered into her ear, "Someday, I want to share this with someone. Someone like you."

"What?"

"I think I'm falling in love with you, Rome."

Taken aback by his unabashed honesty, Rome let go of Heath's hand in order to think. Finding the courage necessary, she returned to the conversation with new determination. "You're not falling in love with me. You're simply in a heightened emotional state due to the effects of the extraordinary circumstances we've shared over the last couple of days."

"I pour out my heart and that's your response?"

"I'm being pragmatic, Heath. I think our situation calls for some level-headedness."

"I'm the most level-headed person you'll ever meet."

"You bought a British castle and had it shipped to Australia."

"I'll give you that one, but as far as my feelings go, they're genuine and not the result of extraordinary circumstances. I'm falling in love with you, Rome, and that's the truth."

Rome reached out and wrapped her fingers over the outside of the thick wall. Gripping the block, she leaned backwards, breathing in the good air and letting out the bad as Heath continued to present his side of the argument. "I think if we walk away from this, we'll both regret it, and as educational as regrets can be, I'm not a big fan."

"No one is," replied Rome.

"Then why not start from here and see what happens?"

"A starting point is a starting point," said Rome as she stared into Heath's eyes, hoping to NOT see the sincerity she needed to see. Yet, there it was and now it was her turn to be honest with him. "I'm seeing someone back home, Heath. I have been for a couple of years now."

"And you're only telling me this now?"

"There hasn't been a reason till now."

"What happened on the sailboat wasn't a good enough reason?"

"It was a kiss. A long kiss but still just a kiss. I got caught up in the emotion of the moment, but you're right, I should have told you."

"Is it serious?"

"We're exclusive, if that's what you're asking."

"What does he do for a living?"

"Don't do this."

"Why not? He's the competition... Isn't he?"

"Actually, I think you're the competition."

"What does he do? Doctor, lawyer, accountant, mechanic."

"Jamie works for the U.S. State Department as a DS Agent."

"He's a secret agent?"

"Diplomatic Security Agent. He protects the people who travel the world on behalf of U.S. Foreign Policy."

"When do you and this 'Jamie' actually see each other?"

"We schedule time together."

"And you think I run my life like a business?"

"Call it what you want but it's worked for two years."

"And now?"

"I didn't expect this, Heath."

"Didn't expect what... to be falling in love with me?"

"To have feelings for you and that's all it is at this point."

"I'm not one to give up," countered Heath.

"You are formidable, but even Heath Jones can't buy true love."

"I don't want to buy it, I want to find it... with you," said Heath as he leaned down and gently kissed her lips.

As Rome kissed him back, she felt all of her inhibitions failing once he wrapped his arms securely around her. She was in trouble and falling deeper by the second. Rome knew that if she didn't leave the tower she might do something foolish that would lead to regret in the light of day. "I think it's time you take me back to the hotel," she said softly, walking away from Heath.

"So that's it?"

"For now."

"Spend the night with me, Rome."

"What?" she replied, surprised by his boldness.

"No! I meant it's getting late and I have a lot of spare rooms. We could have a nice dinner and I could show you around the place."

"Is this part of your original plan, your scheme to get me to fix your ghost problem?"

Heath burst into laughter, surprising Rome with his gusto and intensity, then he made an announcement she did not expect. "I say we ignore the ghosts."

"You can try, but I doubt they'll let you. They're here for a reason," warned Rome.

"Have you seen any since we've been back?"

"What happened with William was very unusual. I've never actually seen a spirit before my visit to the Isle of the Dead. It's usually a one-way conversation: they talk and I listen."

"With your ability, you could host your own reality show," joked Heath.

"On that note, I think it's time to leave," said Rome as she walked toward the door.

"Unless I keep you locked away in the castle."

"And the jokes keep on coming," she said, trying to open the door. "You were joking, right?"

"Of course."

"Then why won't the door open?"

Heath stepped in front of Rome and took hold of the door handle. He pressed his thumb on the latch and pulled several times, but it wouldn't budge. "It's locked from the inside."

"And you want to ignore your ghosts," remarked Rome, lightly mocking his earlier idea. "So what now?"

"I'll call for help over the side. Someone might hear me."

"Heath, wait."

"For what?"

"Shhhh," said Rome as she listened to an Australian voice speak into her ear.

"Don't give up on him. Don't give up on him. Don't give up on him."

Before Rome could respond, they heard the inside lock slide to the right and watched as the door opened in front of them.

"Let's go before they change their minds," suggested Heath.

Rome agreed and entered the door followed by Heath, who took one last curious look around then shut the door and bolted it tight. Re-entering the castle, they continued down the dark hallway toward the light in the distance. Once they reached the top of the stairs, Heath stopped, turned toward Rome and said, "What happened up there?"

"A spirit spoke to me."

"And?"

"He said, 'Don't give up on him.'"

"Give up on who?"

"I'm not sure, but he repeated it three times."

"Why are the ghosts here?"

"I think they're attached to the castle somehow."

"This is getting stranger by the minute."

"Especially since the voice I just heard was the same voice I heard at Port Arthur when I first arrived. It's an Australian accent, not British like the others."

"Great! Now the local ghosts are moving in!" responded Heath in frustration.

"I've been to this castle before, back in England. I stumbled upon it by accident and spent some time inside the walls. I distinctly remember the sound of a woman wailing and moaning. It felt like something tragic had happened there, and now after hearing your ancestor's history, it all makes sense."

"So what do we do about it?"

"The only thing we can do... wait for them to speak and try to help whoever it is that needs help."

Mr. Burns entered the grand hall and breathed a sigh of relief as he saw Rome and Heath atop the stairs. "There you are. I've been all over the castle and the grounds looking for you."

"Sorry, Sheldon. I was showing Ms. London the view from the tower."

"The one place I did not look. Very well. Dinner is ready to be served in the dining room."

"We'll be along in a minute."

"I'll be in the kitchen."

Mr. Burns left the grand hall as Heath turned his attention back to Rome. "So how do you feel about my invitation to spend the night?"

Rome paused for a moment to weigh the consequences of her decision. She wanted to help Heath but knew it would be easier to leave than deal with his feelings, let alone her own. At the same time, she could hear her mother's voice reminding her of the great responsibility that accompanied the family gift. "I did pack an extra change of clothes, in case there was another accident."

"Then you'll stay?"

"If I do, it can only be about the ghosts, Heath, nothing else."

"I don't know if I can make that deal, but I'll try."

"Try hard."

Heath offered his arm, but Rome decided to play it cool and politely refused his gallantry. Together they descended the stairs and made their way toward the dining room.

As they entered the large room, Rome was taken aback by the size of the beautiful wooden table and chair set that appeared to seat at least twenty comfortably. Heath guided her to a chair near the end of the table and pulled it out for her. She took her seat, ever so impressed with the place setting. There were more dishes, glasses and silverware than she knew what to do with. Rome couldn't help but contrast the meal she was about to eat with the one aboard the sailboat made up of leftovers and deli items. "When in Rome," she thought to herself as she placed the linen across her lap.

"I think I'll have the staff bring the whole meal out at once, instead of waiting on each course," said Heath as he left the dining room. Rome watched him leave then curiously picked up a plate to check out the name of the china pattern. Glancing up, she nearly jumped out of her chair at the sight of a female spirit sitting directly across the table from her. Catching the tossed plate as well as her breath, she smiled at the ghost dressed in regal Victorian clothing. "How long have you been sitting there?" sputtered Rome.

"Much longer than you've had the privilege," the spirit

answered with a tone of superiority. "I will admit, however, that it's nice to have the table and chairs back where they belong."

"This table was originally yours?"

"I commissioned a craftsmen to build it not long after Lord Hubert and I were married. Not to speak ill of the dead, but his mother's taste in furniture was atrocious."

"Ill of the dead? But aren't you... Never mind. How long has the table been missing?"

"A week, if not near two."

"Don't you mean a century if not near two?"

"Don't be daft," said the spirit condescendingly as she looked around the room. "Where is he? Late for supper again."

"And who might that be?"

"The master of the house. My husband, Lord Hubert."

"So that makes you Lady Jones?"

"How much more of this conversation must I endure on my own? My husband most likely remains in the library, engrossed in one of his volumes of law. Those books are taking preference over everything these days. Not to worry. It will all be worth it when Lord Hubert gets our son back home where he belongs."

"That would be William, correct?"

"Are you acquainted with my son? Is that what brings you to Forest Gate?"

"In a way."

"Another woman vying for William's attention?"

"No, no. Just a friend of the family," responded Rome as she paused for a moment before testing the waters further. "I heard he got married to a woman named Helen."

"Do not speak that thief's name in this house! I will not hear of it! Once Lord Hubert secures William's freedom, he will have the marriage annulled and William will marry Miss Meredith Hampton as planned and all will go back to normal."

"May I ask how this proposed marriage between William and Meredith came about?"

"Lord Hubert and Mr. Henry Hampton, Meredith's father, were both enrolled at Eton as boys. Henry was the son of a gentleman, but of not much means. His father owned a quaint home on a small piece of property and that was enough to retain his status as a gentleman. Henry and Lord Hubert became best of friends and both went on to gain a higher education at Oxford, still maintaining their friendship. Both William and Meredith were born the same year and it was decided that they would one day marry, uniting the house of Hampton with the house of Jones, an increase of great value to the Hamptons. Just one of the many examples of Lord Hubert's great generosity."

"This may seem like another 'daft' question, but..." Rome paused briefly, wanting to tread lightly in order to not upset Lady Jones. "What year do you think it is?"

"I think it is the very year that it is, 1840. You seem a bit touched. Do you need to lie down?"

Again, Rome paused as she considered the theory that Lady Jones was still living in the same year that William was sent to Port Arthur. "Might I ask another question?"

"I shall endure it."

"How long ago was William arrested?"

"It has been weeks since the horrible day."

"Is that all?"

Lady Jones paused for a moment as she considered Rome's question, appearing to be confused. "I will admit that sometimes it feels longer than that... much longer." She drifted off into thought, until she caught herself and returned to the conversation. "My husband assures me that William's sentence will be reversed once the court has heard him argue on our son's behalf. The only reason William has been afforded an appeal is due to my husband's position in parliament."

"Is Lord Hubert a lawyer?"

"He was schooled in law at Oxford as was his friend, Henry Hampton, but rather than serve as a barrister or solicitor, his title of Baron allows him to serve in the House of Lords, both in the judiciary and legislative arms. Henry went on to serve as a solicitor, eventually becoming a magistrate. A respectable title, but of not much financial gain."

Heath re-entered the dining room and took his seat at the end of the table next to Rome. "Did I miss anything?" he said jokingly as Lady Jones reacted to his arrival. "I can't seem to keep up with all the people coming and going these days, making themselves at home as though they own Forest Gate. And in such strange dress. Might I enquire as to who this gentleman is?"

Rome stared back and forth between the two of them, trying to decide the best route to take, then finally decided to answer Lady Jones first.

"Sir Heath."

"Very funny," responded Heath. "Keep it up and there will be no dessert for you, Ms. London."

Offended by Heath's response and his clear lack of manners and propriety, the lady of the house responded. "I will be the one to decide when dessert is to be served and to whom it will be served, Sir Heath."

"As it should be," replied Rome to Lady Jones.

"Are you suddenly on a diet?" said Heath, not realizing Lady Jones was present.

Rome, barely able to control the urge to burst out in laughter, continued to find enjoyment in the absurdity of the conversation.

"How dare he ask such an absurd question," said Lady Jones.

"Completely absurd," agreed Rome, adding to Heath's confusion.

"I wasn't implying that you need to be on a diet. Feel free to eat as much dessert as you want," said Heath in an attempt to make up for putting his foot in his mouth.

Rome couldn't help but giggle as she responded to his generosity. "Thank you."

"It appears the responsibility of locating my husband has fallen to me. Clearly, the servants have abandoned their posts," announced Lady Jones.

Just as she was about to disappear, Rome got a wonderfully wicked idea, which led her to reach out and grab Heath's hand.

Heath let out a yelp and fell backwards in his chair as the ghost of Lady Jones appeared next to him.

"Such lack of decorum!" exclaimed Lady Jones as she disappeared from the table.

Unable to control herself anymore, Rome burst out in laughter as Heath stood up and sat back in his chair. Rome slowly gained control as she watched Heath calmly lift his silverware and place the linen across his lap. "That was not funny."

"Oh, yes, it was."

Unexpectedly, Heath began to laugh, causing Rome to start up again.

Just then, Mr. Burns entered the dining room, followed by Miss Lemmons and George, carrying dinner on trays. "Shall we come back at a better time?" asked Mr. Burns.

"Your timing couldn't be better, Sheldon. Rome was just enjoying some pre-dinner entertainment."

"Very well, sir."

As the staff placed the trays on the table, Rome and Heath began filling their plates. "This looks amazing, Mr. Burns. I'm absolutely starving," mentioned Rome as she ogled each dish, sampling as she went.

"So it appears,' replied Mr. Burns as he watched in astonishment.

"I'll take some of that chicken, George."

"You got it, ma'am."

"And those potatoes look delicious, Miss Lemmons."

"They are. I sampled some before I brought them out," Miss Lemmons whispered in response.

Impatient with the staff's lack of decorum, Mr. Burns rolled his eyes and motioned for them to follow him out of the dining room. "If you need anything else, we'll be in the kitchen," said the butler as he left the dining room, followed by George and Miss Lemmons, while Rome continued to load her plate.

"Is there a problem?" asked Rome, noticing Heath was lagging behind.

"How is all this normal to you?"

"I've been eating solid foods for a while now."

"You know what I'm talking about."

"It's not, Heath. Sitting across the table from a ghost and having a conversation is all new to me," replied Rome as she put down her utensils. "The good news is that I'm beginning to piece some things together. Hopefully, I'll know more by morning. Right now, that's really all I can tell you." Rome picked up her utensils and returned to eating her dinner as Heath slowly started to fill his plate.

"By morning?"

"Hopefully. How did they get this chicken so moist? I think I've died and gone to heaven."

"Speaking of heaven, what do you think the odds are of getting a few of our guests to head in that direction?"

"It's entirely up to them."

"You are the expert."

"No. I'm just a listening ear. Now can you pass me the rolls? And is that real butter?"

As he passed the basket of rolls, Heath was amazed at how nonchalant Rome seemed about this whole ghost thing, not to mention how voraciously she was going after her plate of food. Feeling his own stomach growl, he realized all they had eaten that day was a couple of pastries at the beach house so he dove in with equal enthusiasm.

HEATH PACKED Rome's tote as he led her down a familiar hallway toward his master suite. He opened the door and they both entered the room. "You can sleep here tonight," said Heath as he put down her bag and walked toward his chest of drawers."

"Where are you sleeping?"

"Sheldon has a daybed in his room, so I'll spend the night on the pull out mattress."

"I have no problem sleeping on the couch in the library, Heath."

"You're my guest and I owe you a good night's sleep. I'll just grab a few things before I leave you to your privacy."

"I'm sorry to be pooping out this early. It's not even nine o'clock and I can barely keep my eyes open."

"We didn't get much sleep last night, if you recall?"

"I do recall," responded Rome as she sat down on the side of the bed watching Heath make his way from the chest of drawers to the bathroom, then back again, carrying some clothes and his toothbrush.

"The house isn't as far along as it should be thanks to some unexpected staffing issues."

"House?" said Rome with a snicker. "That's a bit of an understatement."

"It's got four walls and a roof like any other house."

"Don't forget the tower," joked Rome.

"What's a house without a deck?"

"Perspective, I suppose. Any ideas on decorating?"

"Most of the furniture is still in storage, but I plan to get to it this week," said Heath, sitting down next to her on the bed, hoping to extend his stay. "Feel free to use whatever you need."

"Did you get everything?"

"What I didn't get, Sheldon will have."

The two of them sat quietly for a moment until Heath leaned in and gently kissed Rome on the cheek, taking in the smell of her soft perfume. No longer able to take the temptation of his presence, Rome stood abruptly causing Heath to stand as well. "I really am tired."

"Say no more. I'll see you in the morning."

Disappointed, Heath crossed the room toward the door then paused for a moment to check one more thing with Rome. "Are you sure you'll be okay in here by yourself... you know, with all the strange things going on?"

"If I need help, I'll come find you."

"First room on the right in the east hallway."

"Good thing your 'house' only has two wings or I'd never find you."

"Good night, Rome."

Rome waited for Heath to leave, pulled a new toothbrush from her bag and removed the wrapping as she walked toward the bathroom. Opening the medicine cabinet, behind the beautiful mirrored front, she located his toothpaste, then shut the cabinet door. "Ah!" yelled Rome, surprised by the reflection of a male spirit in her mirror. Growing a bit more at ease with the comings and goings of the castle's ghostly visitor, Rome turned around and faced the apparition with confidence.

He appeared to be a snooty sort, dressed in Victorian era, gentleman's-style clothing, which consisted of a white shirt with a tie around its collar, layered beneath a silk vest and covered by a black dress coat that extended to his knees.

"And who might you be?" the spirit demanded.

"A guest of Lady Jones."

"And in their bed chambers?"

"I take it you're not Lord Hubert Jones."

"Are you daft, woman?"

"That's the second time tonight I've been asked that question."

"The others will hear of this impropriety," warned the ghost as he disappeared from the room.

Nonchalantly, Rome turned back to the sink and squeezed the toothpaste onto her brush.

"The others? I think that was a movie, a horror movie involving ghosts. Great!" Rome began brushing her teeth, checking the mirror from time to time to see if anyone was standing behind her. After wiping off her face, she leaned her hands on the sink and continued her conversation with the mirror. "If he isn't Hubert Jones, then who is he? Or who was he? And more importantly, how is he linked to Forest Gate?"

Turning off the lights, she left the bathroom ready for a normal night's sleep. Rome smiled as she looked at the bed lit by moonlight. Releasing her inner child, she ran toward it, stepped onto the trunk and leaped through the air. The landing was perfect, soft with a decent bounce. Twisting and turning, she wormed her way into the center of the large bed, finding comfort in the luxury of the silk sheets and pillowcases. As her head sank into the pillow, she closed her eyes and let out a sigh of relief. After a few seconds her eyes popped open and took one last look around the room. Then she pulled the covers up over her head and disappeared from sight.

Chapter Eight

Feeling pleasantly rested, Rome poked her arms out of the covers and pulled the duvet down to her chest as she slowly opened her eyes. Not expecting to see Lady Jones sleeping next to her, Rome reacted quietly to the situation. "Oh, this isn't right." Suddenly, the sound of snoring from the other side of the bed caused her to freeze in place. She slowly turned her head to see a male spirit sleeping on the other side of her. "This is definitely not right." Rome pulled herself out of the covers and carefully crawled toward the end of the bed and over the trunk. She walked to the bathroom and splashed cold water onto her face, letting herself drip into the sink as she pondered the moment. Grabbing a towel, she looked back through the door to see the ghosts still sleeping comfortably in her bed... or their bed. Rome wasn't sure of anything at this point. Without warning, Lady Jones sat up as though an alarm had sounded and shouted, "Mr. Jones. Hubert! We've overslept!" Wearing the same clothes as the night before, she ran toward the window as Lord Hubert sat up in bed. "The courts will be open soon and I'm the first one on the docket. I mustn't be late!" he yelled, putting his jacket and top hat on over the clothes he wore to bed.

Lady Jones parted the curtains and looked below. "I don't see the carriage! We left explicit instructions to have the carriage ready by daylight and it's far past daybreak."

"I'm sure it will be waiting by the time we reach the courtyard," Hubert assured his wife as he put on his boots.

"Please, do hurry. Today is the last chance to appeal the ruling and reverse William's sentence before he is loaded onto the ship at noon. The very hour is nigh at hand."

"Where are my law volumes?"

"By now I'm certain you have them memorized. We must leave at once. Make haste!"

Lord Hubert rushed through the door, followed by Lady Jones, disappearing into thin air. Curiously, Rome crossed the room and took hold of the doorknob, carefully opening the door.

"Surprise!" yelled Bev as she leaped into the open doorway, scaring Rome and sending her backwards into a wing back chair located nearby. Breathing heavily, she placed her hand over her heart. "Not a good morning for that, Bev!" As Rome pulled herself out of the chair, Bev began checking out the room. "I see the two of you took my advice," she said, gloating as she continued her own private tour. "So where is the 'master' of the house?"

"He slept on a spare bed in Mr. Burn's room."

"He's got a hot-looking American in his bedroom and he slept with the butler? Maybe I was wrong."

"Definitely wrong."

Mr. Burns hurried into the room, slightly out of breath from his search for Bev. "I do apologize, Ms. London. I told Ms. Hucker that you were still sleeping and she assured me that she would wait. The minute my back was turned, she disappeared from my sights."

"It's fine, Mr. Burns. I was up anyway," replied Rome.

"Very well. Might I ask what time you prefer breakfast this morning?"

"What time is Heath eating?"

"Mr. Jones has already eaten. He's an early riser. He had some errands to attend to in the city but should be back in an hour or so."

"How about ten minutes?"

"Delightful. Shall we set the table for one... or two?"

Rome looked to Bev for a response.

"I did tell my boss I'd be late."

"Breakfast for two, Mr. Burns."

"Very well. We'll expect you and your guest in the dining room shortly." Mr. Burns turned and left the room, shutting the door behind him and prompting Bev to share her thoughts. "I think Sheldon's warming up to me. I have a feeling we'll be best of friends one day."

"I wouldn't get my hopes up," replied Rome as she pulled a change of clothes from her bag and walked into the bathroom, leaving the door open so she could continue the conversation with Bev. "How did you know I'd be here?"

"The mechanic couldn't get ahold of you so he called me. I went by your hotel, and when you weren't there, I figured Heath probably brought you back to the castle and locked you away in the tower. Did you notice the castle has a tower?"

"Yes, I've been on it."

"Oh, have you. Start from the beginning. I want every detail."

"What about the mechanic?"

"The mechanic?"

"My friend's car?"

"It's parked out front. I picked it up this morning."

"I really appreciate it, Bev. I got busy researching and forgot all about it."

"Researching, huh?"

"It's true."

"If you say so."

"How much do I owe you for the car?"

"We can settle up after we leave."

"Leave?"

"I need a ride back to work."

Rome left the bathroom and walked toward her bag, continuing to make plans with Bev. "That will work perfectly. I need to head back to the hotel anyway."

"Just so you know, I did come prepared to free you from the tower," replied Bev in earnest.

"Would that make you my knight in shining armor?" asked Rome jokingly as she opened the door.

"More like your 'guide' in boring khaki."

"What were you planning to do, scale the wall?"

"Absolutely. I threw a rope and grappling hook in the car."

"I have a feeling Mr. Burns would have cut the rope before you made it to the top."

"I could take him."

"I think you could take anyone."

"Thank you. I do try to keep in shape," Bev said as they left the bedroom and entered the dark hallway.

"Watch your step."

"What are they trying to do, save on electricity?"

"Just walk toward the light."

"Heath should give that recommendation to the ghosts supposedly haunting his castle. How much farther to the dining room?"

"Not far, unless we get lost on the way."

Bev and Rome continued chatting as they made their way across the balcony, down the stairs and toward the dining room.

THE MORNING HAD TURNED to rain as they finished their breakfast and left the castle. Bev held her hand over her stomach as she approached the driver's side door. "I think I'm going to burst."

Carrying an umbrella, Rome placed her bags on the back seat, concurring with Bev's condition. "I'm beginning to wonder if I'll be able to get the seat belt around me on the flight home."

"Mind if I drive?" asked Bev as she crawled into the car and put on her seat belt.

"You are in the driver's seat."

"Sorry, habit."

Just as Rome was about to get into the car, she noticed a woman in the distance, wearing a white, high-waisted, long, flowing skirt and standing at the foot of William and Helen's grave site.

"What's she doing in the rain without an umbrella?"

"Who are you talking about?"

From Bev's response, Rome realized she was looking at a spirit. Not wanting to miss an opportunity to gather more information, Rome came up with the best excuse she could on short notice. "I need to get a couple more shots of the castle. I'll be right back."

"In the rain?"

"It adds to the mystique," replied Rome as she pulled her camera out of the bag and started off across the grounds toward the grave.

"Hurry! I can't take the whole day off."

Approaching the spirit, Rome pretended to be interested in taking pictures of the view while she tried to make conversation. "It certainly is a rainy day." Getting no response, Rome turned and faced the spirit, instantly recognizing her as Helen from the image she saw in William's memory. Unfortunately, her beautiful face showed signs of worry similar to William's visage. Rome continued to snap a few shots of the castle as she waited for her to speak.

"Why was I brought here?"

Relieved to hear her speak, Rome wasted no time in continuing the dialogue. "You're Helen, aren't you?"

"How do you know that?"

"I ran into someone recently who spoke highly of you."

"In this day and age?"

"So you're aware that it's not 1840?"

"That's one year I never want to relive."

"The year of your wedding."

"I was a foolish, common girl, who had no business falling in love with someone like William. If I had a morsel of common sense, I would have refused his invitation and sent him home to wed the woman he was expected to marry."

"But you fell in love with him."

"A broken heart would have been much easier to heal than a

heart grown cold from betrayal, a heart that would have withered and died if not for the love I felt for my son."

"Betrayal?"

"I thought William would come for me, but he never did. I wrote countless letters but received no response, even to news of the birth of his son. I was left to the conclusion that Lord Hubert had our marriage annulled and William married Miss Meredith Hampton as planned. My punishment must have been too much of an embarrassment for William and his family."

"I've spoken with William..."

"You have?" responded Helen, with longing in her eyes, "You have seen him?"

"Two nights ago."

Helen's sudden enthusiasm quickly disappeared as she lowered her head to the ground.

"I have searched for him in vain, if only to know the truth. Clearly, he does not wish to be found." Then she disappeared from sight.

Disappointed, Rome reacted by throwing her empty hand in the air and shouting to the rainy sky. "Can't anyone stick around long enough to have a complete conversation?"

Rome looked toward Bev, surprised to see her standing next to the car, staring back at her with a very confused look on her face. Defeated, Rome started back just as Mr. Snavely pulled up next to the castle. Rome watched from afar as Heath beat his chauffeur out of the car and found refuge beneath Bev's umbrella.

"Sir Heath. So nice of you to join us."

"Ms. Beverly Hucker. To what do we owe this surprise?"

"Just delivering Rome's car."

"Can you stay a while?"

"Actually, we've eaten breakfast and now we're on our way back."

"We?" responded Heath nervously as Rome approached.

"I'm taking Bev back to work, then I need to check in with my editor and take care of a few things at the hotel."

"You're planning to come back, aren't you?"

"Can I talk to you for a minute?" responded Rome as she winked at Bev, then took Heath's arm and led him away from the cars.

"Don't worry about us. We'll just be right here... waiting," called out Bev as Mr. Snavely approached carrying his umbrella.

Once Rome and Heath got far enough away, they stopped and huddled beneath her umbrella. "We should probably discuss where we go from last night."

"I've been pretty clear on that," responded Heath.

"I'm talking about your house guests. I've had some more conversations."

"As in the 'other-worldly type?'"

"I definitely have more pieces of the puzzle, but I'm not sure how they fit together."

"That's more than I had a few days ago."

"I'm curious about the role Meredith Hampton plays in all this."

"The woman William was supposed to marry?"

"Yes. Could you contact the genealogist your father hired and see if he can get any more information on her?"

"What are you thinking?" enquired Heath curiously as they turned to walk back to the car.

"I'm not sure," replied Rome. "I just have a feeling."

"I'll take care of it before the movers arrive. In the meantime, why don't you let Mr. Snavely drive you and Bev into town, so you can check out of the hotel?"

"Who said I was checking out?" asked Rome coyly, knowing full well that she planned to check out of the hotel.

"Why pay for a hotel when you can stay at a castle for free?"

"You make a good point. I'll consider it."

"Max can drop you off at your hotel, take Bev down to Port Arthur, then pick you up on the way back. That should give you plenty of time."

"Is this your way of ensuring my return to Forest Gate?"

"Whatever it takes," responded Heath, determined to have his way.

"I will say the idea of not having to drive back on the wrong side of the road..."

"You mean the right side?" corrected Heath.

"...as well as the 'other' side of the car is enticing."

"I'll take that as a 'yes.'"

As they approached the cars, Heath announced the change of plans. "Mr. Snavely will drive you both to your destinations. If that's all right with you, Bev?"

"I'll do it for the people of Tassie. One less American driver on the road."

Everyone laughed at Rome's expense while Mr. Snavely opened the back door for Bev, who whispered a secret message as she walked past the chauffeur. "Grab the bags, but leave the rope and grappling hook. It may come in handy later." Mr. Snavely looked at Bev in confusion as she smiled and winked at him, then crawled into the back seat.

On the other side of the car, Rome and Heath weren't quite ready to say goodbye as they waited for the chauffeur to return to the driver's seat. "What do you have planned for this morning?" enquired Rome.

"Sheldon and I will be directing the placement of furniture for the better part of the day."

"Decorating a castle sounds like a lot of work."

"I could use the distraction," responded Heath as he opened the door and leaned in to bid Bev farewell. "It was good to see you again, Beverly. Come anytime."

"You can count on it."

Heath turned his sights back to Rome as Mr. Snavely started the engine. "I'll see you when you get back."

Rome folded up her umbrella, got in the car and responded silently by pressing her hand to the window as Mr. Snavely drove down the driveway. Her attention turned to the rear window and the sight of Heath, drenched by the rain, watching the car drive away. Approaching the gate, Bev turned and stared at the castle as well. "It really is amazing. Too bad it's haunted."

"I wouldn't believe everything you hear."

"Obviously, you didn't see the morning paper."

Bev pulled a folded newspaper out of her bag and showed it to Rome, pointing to a picture of the castle at night and the caption accompanying it: *Ghostly Images from Castle Jones Captured on Camera.* Below the picture, it read: *See actual photo in Sunday's edition.*

"That's a total lie."

"You haven't even seen the picture."

"It has to be a fake."

"Fake or not, it's generating a lot of talk."

"Maybe people need to mind their own business."

"I see it's getting personal," replied Bev, wanting to know more details. "Speaking of personal... Where did we leave off at breakfast...? Oh, yeah. You spent the day sailing and were eating afternoon tea as the sun set on the horizon."

Rome pressed her finger to her lips and leaned forward. "Mr. Snavely, would you mind closing the privacy window?"

"Of course, Ms. London."

Watching the privacy divider move into position, separating the front of the car from the rear, Bev couldn't help but do what she does best, speak her mind. "A girl could get used to this."

"That's why it's important I keep focused."

"You're a pragmatist, Rome London."

"I don't think that's a bad thing."

"Only if it keeps you from your passion."

As the car pulled out of the gate and onto the road, Bev got back down to business, the business of details. "So, back to the sailboat and the sunset."

"A very complicated sunset," Rome said with a twinkle in her eye.

"How complicated?"

There was no way Rome was going to share the intimate details of her time with Heath, but she also knew Bev wouldn't give up easily. Fortunately, Rome was a writer, a storyteller to some extent, and that came in handy as she began to thrill Bev with a colorful, yet condensed version of their romantic interlude aboard the boat. At this point, however, Rome's mixed feelings for Heath took a back seat to her concerns about the rest of his family, namely William and Helen. She'd been drawn into their world and the deeper she traveled the more preoccupied she became with the journey. Rome had become the bridge between Helen and William, a bridge that would hopefully reconnect them as husband and wife. But a bridge is only helpful if people choose to use it.

Chapter Nine

Circling the airport one last time, Roger Jones watched through his first-class window as the plane landed on the wet runway of the Hobart International Airport. He planned his arrival to be unannounced, hoping to catch an unsuspecting Heath at the castle. As he got off the plane and made his way through the airport, Roger rehearsed the plan in his head. Officially, he had arrived on company business, but secretly he was there to commence the third phase of his take-over. He felt bolstered by the uneasiness he felt from the board members during their meeting earlier in the week and would rely on that, as well as the company's dropping stock prices, to accomplish what must be done. He had the ammunition he needed and the element of surprise. What could possibly go wrong?

Exiting the airport, he opened his umbrella and walked toward the taxi stand. Sergio Arturo, disguised in a trench coat and hat, merged into the crowd and followed him down the sidewalk. Approaching from behind and trying to keep the conversation covert, he whispered in Roger's ear. "There's been a complication."

Roger attempted to look around, but Arturo stopped him from

making facial contact. "Keep walking. There are too many security cameras."

Although he recognized Arturo's voice, he played along until he reached the taxi stand, then he stepped toward the rear, allowing others to go around him. Arturo moved next to him and there they stood, side by side, staring toward the road in silence. "It appears your nephew may be involved with someone," said Arturo, barely moving his mouth.

"What?"

Arturo made another attempt to speak covertly, resembling a ventriloquist missing his dummy. "Your nephew might be involved with a woman."

"Speak up, man," said Roger in a frustrated whisper.

"Your nephew's got the hots for someone!"

Out of curiosity, the people waiting in line slowly turned and looked as Roger quickly lowered his open umbrella toward the crowd, hiding he and Arturo's faces.

"Heath's seeing someone?" asked Roger in disbelief.

"Not only that, but they're shacking up together at the castle."

"Super model? Actress? Socialite?"

"Unfortunately, no. She's a writer. A popular one at that."

"A writer of what?"

"She writes for a travel magazine, has for years. She's in Tasmania doing a story on Port Arthur and somehow they met. The problem is... she's well respected."

"Oh, great!" responded Roger embittered by the news.

"My thoughts exactly. An actress or a socialite would have been much more scandalous."

"And worthy of coverage," agreed Roger. "Not to worry. Everyone's got a few skeletons in their closet, a few secrets to hide."

"You do claim to be an investigative reporter."

"Actually, I'm a columnist, but that's beside the point. It might be faster just to get rid of her."

Panicked, Roger grabbed his arm and pulled him backwards. "Are you crazy? It's one thing to doctor photos, but I will not have a murder on my hands."

"That's not what I meant. She's an American who needs to go home."

Roger perked up as an idea popped into his conniving mind. "Or at least away from Tasmania until the job is done."

"What are you thinking?"

"How do magazines stay in business?" asked Roger.

"Revenue from sales."

"And advertising. What if Jones' Shipping and Ship Manufacturing were to take out a surprisingly large ad in a certain travel magazine?"

"Ad for what?"

"A public awareness campaign for our 'eco-friendly' shipping practices. In return, I'll request that their travel writer cover more convict sites for next month's issue."

"Taking her away from Tasmania."

"And away from Heath. Fortunately, I share an interest with her magazine in regard to Australia's penal colony history and I'm aware of at least eleven other convict sites."

"That many stops throughout Australia should keep her busy."

"And away from Heath until the job is done. I'll sweeten the kitty by offering to pay for the travel expenses... anonymously, of course."

"Of course," replied Arturo smiling as he crossed the street and disappeared into the carpark. Feeling confident after their impromptu strategy meeting, Roger closed his umbrella, pushed through the crowd and rudely took the next cab.

AS THE CAB approached the gate at the castle, the cab driver rang the buzzer to gain access through the gate.

"Yes," responded a voice from the box.

"Roger Ash to see his nephew, Heath Jones."

"One moment."

The box remained silent as the cab driver and Roger stared at it with great intensity, but nothing came. All at once, the gate opened and the cabby drove through and up the drive. As they approached the castle, moving trucks full of furniture, art and decor crowded the parking space near the front of the building.

"Looks like this is as far as I go," said the cab driver.

"Fine." Annoyed by the inconvenience, Roger tossed some money over the seat and got out of the cab. Holding a briefcase in one hand and his umbrella in the other, he began making his way through the obstacle course of moving men, chastising them for not watching where they were going. Just as he reached the door, Heath departed the castle, dressed casually in jeans and a t-shirt. "Sheldon told me you were at the gate. What are you doing here?"

"If the nephew won't come to the uncle, then the uncle must go to the nephew. A simple return phone call could have saved me a trip."

"As you can see, I've been a bit busy."

"From what I hear, this isn't the only thing keeping you busy. A certain travel writer comes to mind."

"How do you know about her?"

"Relax. I didn't come all the way to Tasmania to discuss your personal life."

"So why did you come?"

"Someone has to run the company while you're playing 'Lord of the manor.'"

"I'm sorry, Roger. I should have gotten back to you. We can discuss the schedule in my office."

They waited for the doorway to clear of men and furniture, then Heath and Roger quickly moved through. Once they gained entrance to the castle, Roger stood in the middle of the grand hall staring about the room and up at the ceiling as movers packed furniture and decor all around him and up the stairs.

"It's this way, Roger."

"I still can't believe you brought a castle all the way from England and you're actually living in it." Roger followed Heath down the hallway, continuing to study the details along the way. Once inside the library, Heath closed the door, shutting out the noise of the movers. "Take a seat at my desk."

Roger walked to the desk and opened his briefcase, noticing the *Trekking the Globe* travel magazine that Rome had left behind. He read the title of the feature article: "A lovely Getaway for Hopeless Romantics," then looked at the author's name: Rome London.

Before Heath could reach the desk, he was distracted again by a loud knock. Opening the door, he found a mover in need of further instruction. "Sorry to interrupt, Mr. Jones, but we need to know which bedroom you want the oak vanity to go in and where you want it located once we get it there?"

"Upstairs, left hallway, last room on the right. Just put it in the room and I'll be up when I can," said Heath as he closed the door and walked back to the desk. "As you can see, I don't have a lot of time, so let's get to it."

"Actually, Heath, I need to make a few phone calls to check on some details. Why don't you go back to orchestrating the move and I'll find you when I'm ready."

"Sounds good."

Once Heath left the library, Roger picked up the magazine and began leafing through it. "I love this magazine. I read her articles every month," remarked Roger as he laid the magazine down and turned to his tablet. He began searching the internet for the magazine's contact information, happy in the thought that soon Rome and Heath would be separated long enough to carry out phase three of his plan. After that, they could live happily ever after and so would he.

ROME PACKED her bag with precision, making sure everything was in its proper place and folded just right. As usual, she was taking home more than she brought with her, so she laid her body across the bag, squishing it enough to work the zipper around the three sides of the suitcase. Just as she reached the end of the zipper, her cell phone rang. Noticing it was her editor, she pushed herself off the suitcase and back onto the bed, getting comfortable before she answered the phone. "Hello, Angelica." Much to Rome's delight, her editor proceeded to tell her how much she loved the article on Port Arthur and the unique angle she chose to take. She continued to praise her for the beautiful photographs and shared which ones she has chosen to use in the magazine. Rome smiled at the accolades coming from the other end of the conversation, a completely different tone than their discussion the previous afternoon. Then the topic of conversation took an unexpected turn.

Surprised, Rome sat up as her editor shared her new plan to have her cover several more convict sites in Australia before she returned home. "This seems out of the blue, Angelica," responded Rome as she continued to listen to her editor's new plan to dedicate more space to the topic of touring Australian penal colony sites. "Where did this idea come from?" asked Rome as she got off the bed and began pacing the floor, trying to understand her editor's decision. Rome had known and worked closely with Angelica for years and this wasn't like her at all. She was all about deadlines, quality of work and most importantly, sticking to the plan, a trait they both happily shared. Angelica never veered from the plan and this was definitely a swerve. Finally, with two little words, everything made sense: advertising revenue.

Rome learned that an Australian company was willing to pay for a big ad space if more of the edition was dedicated to its country's convict history. It all came down to money and Rome knew that money signed her paycheck and greased the wheels of any type of publication. Deflated, Rome ended the call, sat down next to her suitcase and stared out the window at the tops of the trees swaying in the breeze. The rain had stopped, but the winds had picked up, and not just outside. The winds of change had blown Rome's plans in a totally different direction. With the final deadline fast approaching, she would have to leave immediately. This was not good timing. All that morning she'd been secretly kicking around the idea of taking some long overdue vacation time and spending it in Tasmania. She wanted so much to bring Helen and William back together again. Unexpectedly, she found herself getting teary-eyed at the thought of leaving so abruptly. She'd grown more attached than she realized and had no idea how to break the news to Heath.

All of a sudden, the beeping of Rome's phone snapped her out of it and alerted her to the fact that she'd received an email. Knowing it was the travel itinerary her editor promised to forward, she chose to ignore it. Rome laid the phone on top of the suitcase and crawled onto the bed. Grabbing a pillow and hugging it closely to her body, she closed her eyes in an attempt to escape the inevitable, even for just a moment. She hated the idea of William and his family waiting even longer, but at that point she had no choice. There was no escaping her responsibility.

ROGER WALKED THROUGH THE CASTLE, taking in the architecture of this recently transported structure. As he wandered from room to room, he couldn't help but be impressed with what his nephew had accomplished. Of course, he would never admit to being impressed. That would ruin the plan and Roger was far too committed to flush everything down the drain with sentimentalism. Eventually, he entered the same room as Heath and it was back to business as usual. "I'm ready for you now, Heath."

Heath turned from the man hanging the portrait and walked toward Roger. "Good timing. The men are just about to break for lunch." Heath left the room, followed by Roger. As they approached the stairs, they met Sheldon at the top, who had no intention of hiding his disdain for Heath's uncle. "Mr. Ash."

"Mr. Burns," replied Roger with the same tone of disgust.

"A lunch of sandwiches and appropriate sides and drinks have been prepared for the movers as you requested. Where would you like it to be served?"

"Here in the grand hall should be fine. They can sit on the stairs and eat."

"Very well."

"Roger and I will take our lunch in the library. We'll have the same thing the movers are having."

"Very good, sir," Sheldon responded as he turned and walked back down the stairs.

"I can't believe you still keep that fool employed," remarked Roger, just loud enough for Sheldon to hear on his way down the stairs.

"That 'fool' as you call him is one of the wisest men I know. I'd be the fool if I let him go."

Mr. Burns smiled to himself after hearing Heath's response, knowing how angry Roger would be after being put in place, yet again, by his much younger nephew. Happily, the butler made his way through the castle, informing the movers that lunch would be served immediately in the grand hall. As he walked back toward the kitchen, he passed the door to the electrical room, noticing it was slightly ajar with an intermittent light coming from within. He walked to the door and opened it wide, finding one of the movers using his flashlight to study the breakers and electrical panel. "This room is off limits!"

Shocked by Mr. Burns's loud voice, the mover quickly turned toward him, shining the light in the butler's face.

"What are you doing in here?" demanded Mr. Burns.

"I was just... checking out the power supply, making sure all the lamps had enough power."

"The lamps?"

"And other things."

"This room is locked. How did you get in?"

"One of your staff must have left it unlocked."

"I'm the only one with a key. George!" yelled Mr. Burns.

George quickly approached. "Yes, sir."

"Show this man to the door and make sure he leaves the grounds immediately."

"But I don't have a ride."

"Do you have a mobile?"

"Yes."

"Then call a taxi... from the other side of the gate. Now get out!"

The man picked up his bag and departed the electrical room. George followed him down the hallway, making sure he didn't deviate from the course. Sheldon stepped inside the room and turned on the light. He thoroughly checked out the breaker box, the computer server and the castle's security system. Feeling secure that all was fine, he turned out the light and locked the door, muttering a familiar theme as he continued down the hall. "It's almost impossible to get good help these days!"

REACHING THE LIBRARY, Roger delivered the first blow as soon as the door closed behind him. "I didn't just fly all the way down here for scheduling purposes. The board is concerned about the direction you're headed."

"Based on what?"

Roger walked to the desk and pulled out his copy of the Thursday paper, pointing to the teaser ad and picture of Heath's castle. "Based on this and all the negative press you've been receiving since you started this whole castle obsession."

"It's not an obsession! You're making me sound crazy."

"Call it what you will, but the board meeting did not go well this week and I've been fielding phone calls all morning in regard to this ad for Sunday's paper."

"I'll straighten everything out at our next meeting."

"It's not just the board. Have you noticed the drop in our stock price?"

"We're talking a few cents and what does the drop in stock price have to do with this castle?"

"No one wants to own stock or let alone buy stock in a company whose president looks like he's lost his mind."

"That's the most ridiculous thing I've ever heard!"

"With so many CEOs under scrutiny these days, buying a castle and having it shipped across the planet puts you and our company in the cross hairs. Why do you think the press is having such a field day with you?"

"That's what I'd like to know and I plan to find out."

"The only thing we can do now is try to turn this around," said Roger, hoping Heath would bite.

"I can't pack the castle up and send it back, Roger, nor would I."

"Fortunately for you, the flight down here gave me some time to think about the situation. And the thought that came into my mind was this: what would Marshal have done?"

"Do not bring Dad into this!"

"Let me finish. Your dad was the face of this company for most of his life and he was very good at it. He never shied away and because of that, the press wasn't always after him."

"Get to the point, Roger."

"I say we host a party, here in the castle and invite all the 'who's-who' of Hobart: the mayor, the city council, top business leaders, movers and shakers in local society, and possibly a reporter to cover the event."

Roger pointed to the picture of the castle in the paper. "This Sergio Arturo might be a good one to invite."

"And you think I'm crazy?"

"Keep your friends close, but your enemies closer. Your dad knew the importance of that."

"Yes, Roger, he certainly did," responded Heath, implying a reference to Roger's employment at Jones Shipping. "How would hosting a party for the upper class of Hobart fix anything?"

"It would normalize you and the castle, especially if we make it a charity event. It's hard to find fault with a fundraiser for the needy. After that, you'll no longer be seen as the eccentric and crazy CEO who bought a haunted castle to live in as some kind of hermit."

"I prefer the term recluse, but that has nothing to do with why I bought the castle and shipped it to Tasmania."

"I believe you, Heath, but I'm your uncle. We need to get everyone else to buy into it and the best way to do that is to stop letting some reckless reporter control the narrative. We need to take back the power and that's something you're very good at."

"I suppose it's not the worst idea you've had," conceded Heath.

Much to Roger's chagrin, Sheldon entered the room, followed by George, carrying a large platter full of lunch items. "Lunch is served. Where would you like it, sir?" Heath was grateful for the interruption and the breathing room it allowed. "Just leave it on the desk. Thank you, Sheldon." George placed the platter on the side of the desk, then turned and left the room. "Will there be anything else?"

"That's all."

Sheldon turned to leave, but before he could reach the door, Heath changed his mind. "There is one thing, Sheldon."

Sheldon turned back, anticipating Heath's need for a particular condiment or seasoning. "And what might that be?"

"What do you think about hosting a party in the castle?"

"Party, sir?"

"As a way to connect with the people of Hobart. We could make it a charity event."

"If that is your wish, then the staff and I will begin preparing at once."

"You didn't tell me what you think."

"May I be so bold to ask where this idea came from?"

"Roger thought it would be a good way to squelch all the rumors and bad press we've been getting which now appears to be impacting the company."

Sheldon paused for a moment before answering as he considered the source. He'd known Roger for many years and considered him no more than a worm attempting to destroy a perfectly good apple from the inside out. He put no trust in the man and found it very difficult to believe that Roger Ash had Heath's best interests at heart. "I follow him to serve my turn upon him," Sheldon said in answer to Heath's question.

"What type of British mumbo jumbo is that?" responded Roger.

"Shakespeare. Will that be all, sir?"

"Yes, Sheldon."

Mr. Burns turned and walked toward the door as Roger started loading up his plate from the lunch platter. Heath watched the butler leave the room, contemplating what he meant. Sheldon had a great love for the works of Shakespeare and had impressed that love on Heath from an early age. He knew the words were familiar, but couldn't place them. As Heath moved to the bookshelves surrounding the room, Roger began shooting off his mouth, yet again. "I will say this. The Pome sure knows how to throw a lunch together."

As Roger continued to fill his plate, while shoving his mouth full of food, Heath located the shelf containing *The Complete Works of Shakespeare*. He placed it on the corner of the desk, picked up a plate and started to fill it himself as he tried to move the meeting along. "Let's look at the schedule while we're eating. I don't have much time and you probably need to get back to Sydney."

"So what have you decided about the party?" enquired Roger.

Before he could answer, the Shakespeare anthology slid off the desk and hit the floor, opening up to the play, *Othello* and the very scene containing the line of dialogue belonging to the character Iago and quoted by Sheldon. With a quick glance, Heath vaguely recalled the scene where Iago begins to plot revenge against Othello, the general he served. Heath took an empty envelope and used it as a bookmark, then put the book back on the desk. "I need time to think about it."

"Make it quick. The sooner we get out in front of this thing, the better. I'm booked on a flight leaving at 4:00 this afternoon." Roger sat down, placing his plate next to his tablet and leaving a trail of crumbs across the top of the antique desk. His anger at Sheldon boiled inside him. He had Heath just where he wanted him until the butler walked into the room and spoiled everything. "Let's start with Monday of next week," suggested Roger as he pulled up his day planner. The two men began the toilsome process of scheduling meeting after meeting as they ate their lunch.

A KNOCK on the door signaled to Rome that her ride had finally arrived. She crawled off the bed and walked to the door, opening it for Heath's chauffeur. "Mr. Snavely. Right on time as expected."

"I aim to please, Ms. London."

"Please, call me Rome."

"Maximillian, but everyone calls me Max."

"All right, Max. I'll just take one more look around to make sure I haven't forgotten anything."

"Sounds good."

Mr. Snavely waited patiently just outside the doorway as any professional chauffeur would. He loved his job and took it very seriously. This was easily seen by his professional look and the rules of conduct he maintained.

Rome returned from the bathroom and checked the closet and night stand one last time. "I think we're good, Max."

"Then I'll take your bags to the car."

"Just take the big one. I'll grab the carry on and my bag."

"I may appear small, but beneath this sharp-looking suit lies a pretty buff physique," Mr. Snavely said as he took hold of both handles and pulled the suitcases out of the room. Rome took one last look around, grabbed her bag and followed. All the way down to the car, Rome's mind kept replaying the conversation with her editor, hoping to come up with a solution before she reached the castle. "How am I going to break this news to Heath?" she thought to herself, wishing it came as easy to her as it did to her editor, but that was not the case.

ROGER WALKED through the open door of the castle, followed by Heath, quickly stepping out of the way of two moving men carrying a large mirror.

"What did you do, buy out an entire estate sale?"

"Something like that. A lot of it's from Dad's house up in Sydney as well."

"What about your parents' house next door? What are your plans for it?"

"It'll set quiet for now. I don't want to interrupt the memories. Sometimes it's nice to go back in time."

"Be careful of too much sentimentality. It makes a person soft," warned Roger as they watched the approaching taxi cab wind its way through the parked moving trucks. While they waited, Heath attempted to get an answer to a question that had been on his mind since their first conversation of the day. "How did you know about my relationship with a travel writer?"

"Word just traveled, so to speak," responded Roger, avoiding the truth.

The taxi finally stopped, getting as close to them as it possibly could. Heath and Roger walked toward the car as they continued their conversation. "Sorry I don't have time to run you to the airport."

"It would have been nice to bring the corporate jet down."

"You mean the jet Dad purchased for his own private use and allowed the company to use as well. The one he left to me in his will?" Heath didn't like to play the 'will card' but he also didn't like his uncle's attitude. If he wanted to travel on the jet to Tasmania and leave it parked until his return to Sydney, then that's exactly what he would do and he wanted to make sure his uncle knew that.

"You're right. I apologize for the overreach," replied Roger, trying to control the tone of jealousy in his voice. Roger hated to be corrected by his nephew and this time was no different. It simply added more fuel to the fire of his plan to unseat him as CEO, take control of the company and buy himself his own corporate jet. "I hope to hear soon about your decision to host a charity event at the castle. Everyone's worried about the upcoming article in the Sunday edition and how it will impact the company."

"I'll let you know," Heath said as he opened the back door of the cab for his uncle.

"I fear we only have a small window of time to turn this around before the damage becomes irreparable."

"I said I'll let you know."

Roger got into the back seat, feeling disappointed that he couldn't get Heath to commit to the party. With his plan hanging in the balance, he had no choice left than to up the stakes. Before the taxi pulled away, Roger rolled down the window and gave it one last attempt. "I didn't bring this up before, but a few of the board members are questioning whether or not you're still fit to fill the position of President and CEO. This is serious, Heath, I'd treat it that way." Then he rolled up his window and directed the cabby to drive away.

As Heath watched the cab make its way toward the gate, he began to worry about the consequences of his choices, especially if things were truly as serious as Roger made them out to be. He thought of his father and grandfather, who both stood at the helm of Jones Shipping and Ship Manufacturing during their lifetimes, and what they might think if he lost control of the company. He even thought of his great-great-grandfather who became the owner of a small shipping company when his partner died and went on to name it Jones' Shipping. Heath had generations of great men to live up to and failing to do so was not an option. It was sentimentality at its best.

Without warning, the head of the moving crew and Mr. Burns approached Heath from behind to give a report on their progress. "We've got everything out of the trucks and into the house. The men are working on putting the beds together, but we still have quite a few furniture items to place."

"Thanks for the update. I'll be inside in a minute."

The moving man walked away, leaving Sheldon and Heath alone in the drive.

"Sheldon."

"Yes, Heath?"

"What is the smallest number of staff members you would need to run this house for a while?"

"Don't tell me we've run out of funds," Sheldon said attempting a bit of humor.

"Somebody is leaking information. Personal information."

Knowing the critical nature of Heath's comment, Sheldon took the question much more seriously. "The cook and two others should be sufficient."

"Pick the three you trust the most, then give the others a paid holiday as severance."

"Consider it done, Heath."

Sheldon immediately turned and entered the house, knowing exactly who he would keep and who he would send packing.

Heath turned and entered the castle as well, but this time with more on his mind that just moving furniture.

MR. SNAVELY PULLED though the gate and up the drive toward the castle, looking forward to dinner after a long round trip. At this point, the moving trucks were all gone, allowing him to pull right up to the door. Rome opened her door and stepped out of the car, feeling something strange and unexpected as she looked around. Somehow, she no longer felt like a guest visiting. Instead, she felt like she had come home. Like she belonged at Forest Gate. "This can't be right," she thought to herself, growing nervous about what she was experiencing.

Mr. Snavely removed the bags from the trunk and rolled them toward the door. Rome hurried and opened the castle door for him, allowing him to enter without stopping. Walking into the entranceway, she felt that same familiar, comfortable feeling. It just felt like the right fit. As she entered the grand hall, she was delighted to see that the furniture was no longer covered in plastic and stacked against the walls. It was arranged beautifully throughout the two connecting sitting rooms. She also noticed that the stack of art pieces had been divided up and placed on the floor around the room, leaning up against the walls where they would soon hang. Something magical had happened while she was away that had transformed the castle and made it complete. She was awestruck at the beauty and majesty of the room.

Heath's voice from the second floor snapped her out of her trance and turned her attention toward him as she watched him descend the stairs.

"So? What do you think?"

"Color me impressed. This is amazing."

"Come on. I'll give you the tour," said Heath, extending his arm.

Rome wrapped her arm around his and they walked down the hallway together as Heath pointed out the origin and history of each furniture piece. Rome had been on hundreds of tours throughout her life and listened to many guides, but she could not remember enjoying one nearly as much. She felt Heath's passion for every detail and it didn't take long for his passion to become hers. His enthusiasm for what he had finally accomplished after three long years was contagious and she caught the bug. As they moved from room to room, she complimented everything he showed her and validated everything he said. Finally, the tour wound up back at the top of the staircase. "My uncle thinks it's a good idea to host an open house here at the castle as a charity fundraiser."

"And what do you think?"

"I think it's too risky with our ghostly visitors, unless you're able to convince them to go home soon."

"About that..."

Rome sat down on the top stair and patted the floor next to her with her hand. Heath sat down, laying his forearms across his knees and folding his hands together in front. Her tone sounded serious and he wasn't sure if he could take any more bad news that day. Rome sat in the same position, staring forward, searching for the words. Just as she began to speak, Sheldon walked out of one of the hallways, but quickly pulled back into the shadows to avoid ruining their moment together. He turned to go back down the hallway and find another way around but stopped when he heard her first sentence. "So my editor called this morning and surprised me by extending my assignment."

"How much longer are you able to stay?" said Heath in excitement.

"She's decided to expand the topic and dedicate the majority of the issue to Australian convict sites."

"I won't pretend to know how magazine publishing works, but that seems a bit last minute."

"It's extremely last minute and not Angelica's style at all. Somehow word got out that I was here covering the Port Arthur site and it attracted some big advertising campaign out of Australia. They're demanding more coverage before they'll commit."

"So where is she sending you?"

Rome pulled out her phone and accessed her email. "There are a few more sites in Tasmania she wants me to cover. The Cascade Female Factory, Brickendon and Woolmer's Estates, the Coal Mines Historic Site and the Darlington Probation Station on Maria Island, just off the coast."

"That's not so bad. I can get you to all those places."

"This is where it gets tricky. She also wants me to visit Cockatoo Island in the Sydney harbor, Hyde Park Barracks and the Great North Road Complex, also both in New South Wales. After that, she wants me to fly to Western Australia and tour the Fremantle Prison. And to top it all off, she wants me to visit the Kingston and Arthur's Vale Historic Area on Norfolk Island."

"That's in the middle of the ocean between here and New Zealand."

"Yes, it is."

Sheldon shook his head as he eavesdropped on their conversation, a practice he knew any self-respecting butler would never think to do, yet something was fishy about this whole thing and he didn't like the smell of it. Deciding he'd heard enough, he re-entered the hallway and continued his duties.

After an extended moment of silence, Heath took the high road and chose to support Rome over his own situation. "This is your career and that needs to come first. My ghosts will just have to wait."

"I don't think they can. I feel like we have a short window of time to help resolve this family's issues, your family's issues. The relocating of this castle not only brought it back to life but is somehow bringing this family back together as well. I expect William to show up at any time, whether he wants to or not."

"What makes you think that?"

"He told me that spirits always know where their bones are buried. They're drawn to them somehow."

"You waited till after we moved his bones to tell me that?"

"Like that would have stopped you."

"True. So we can probably expect a visit from Helen now that her bones are buried here as well."

"I had a conversation with her this morning."

"They really are coming together."

"If we don't take advantage of what's happening right now, we may never get the opportunity back, but with my new assignment it's just not possible."

"So what do you want to do?"

"I have no idea. Where's Beverly Hucker when you need a guide?" said Rome jokingly, hoping to lighten the mood.

"That's it!" said Heath with a booming voice that filled the great hall. "What if we ask Bev to travel to Western Australia, Sydney and Norfolk Island to cover the convict sites for you?"

"She's not a writer. She's a guide."

"Exactly. All these sites you just mentioned are in her wheelhouse. She'll have access to all the information you need. She can take notes and pictures of everything she hears and sees. All you have to do is sort through it all and write the articles."

"Allowing me to be in two places at once."

"No one will ever be the wiser."

"But will she do it?"

"I say we invite her to dinner and find out."

"It's getting late in the day. Should I have her bring an overnight bag?"

"We do have a few more beds to choose from now."

"A few?"

"Quite a few."

"I'll give her a call," said Rome as she stood up and walked down the stairs.

"And I'll make sure Mr. Snavely is standing by." Heath slapped his hands on his knees and stood up, ready to put their plan in motion. "Sheldon," Heath hollered, "I'm going to need another bed made up for tonight." Not getting a response, Heath walked down the stairs and across the floor in the direction of the kitchen, making a mental note to put the installation of an intercom system on his list of things to do. "Sheldon?"

As Rome watched him walk away she felt a deep stir within her chest. Heath was making inroads that she was no longer able to block. Breathing deeply, she stood up in an attempt to shake it off, but knew it would take more than physical exertion to reverse what was happening on the inside.

BEV ARRIVED at the castle and Rome surprised Heath by inviting Mr. Snavely to stay and eat dinner with them as well. Not only did she invite Max, but she invited Mr. Burns, Miss Lemmons, George and Gladys, the cook, to join them around the dining room table. They were the only members of the staff left, the few that Mr. Burns trusted enough to be in the house. The night was lovely. They talked and laughed and ate to their hearts' content.

Following dinner, the staff went about their duties and Rome, Heath and Bev made their way to one of the sitting rooms. "I can't get over what you've done to the place since yesterday," said Bev as she found a comfortable spot on the couch.

"All thanks to an army of movers."

"Well, I'm impressed."

"Thank you."

"So on the phone you mentioned needing a favor from me."

Rome sat down on the coffee table, looked directly at Bev, and began her sales pitch. "This is a pretty big favor, so I'll totally understand if you can't do it. You've already done so much for me."

"I've had more fun since you came to town than I've had in years. If it's more of the same, just name it."

"The magazine I work for unexpectedly extended my assignment, but Heath and I are in the middle of something kind of serious right now."

"Serious, huh?" teased Rome with great delight as she looked back and forth at the two of them.

"It's not what you're thinking."

"Oh, I'm sure it's not," Bev responded with a wink. "So how can I help?"

"This is kind of huge, so prepare yourself."

"You're killing me, London, just spit it out."

Block by Block

"I need you to tour several of the other convict sites throughout Australia as well as Norfolk Island for me. The problem is, I need it done by Wednesday at the very latest. That barely gives you six days." Rome waited for a response from Bev, but nothing came. So she continued. "You'll need to take notes and plenty of pictures, so I have a lot to work with." Again, Rome waited for a response, but still nothing. "Just email me your notes after you've toured a sight and I can get a head start on the articles." For a third time Rome paused, but still not a peep from Bev, who sat frozen on the couch in front of her. Rome looked to Heath for some help and he quickly moved to the couch to offer some incentive. "Of course, everything will be paid for, so there will be no out-of-pocket expense on your part."

Still silence on Bev's end.

At this point, Rome figured Bev was trying to find a way to say, "no" and couldn't find the words, but she continued with the pitch anyway. "The places you'll need to visit are Cockatoo Island, the Hyde Park Barracks and the Great North Road Complex, followed by the Fremantle Prison in Western Australia and the Kingston and Arthur's Vale Historic Area on Norfolk Island." Again, Heath jumped in, trying to sweeten the pot. "And we'd like to pay you to do it; that way you won't lose any money taking off work."

"So what do you say?" asked Rome with great trepidation.

Bev burst into tears, which quickly turned into uncontrollable sobbing. Rome jumped up and sat next to her on the couch, wrapping her arm around her shoulders.

Heath watched in shock, having no idea what to do, until Rome motioned with her head toward the water pitcher. He jumped up from the couch, hurried across the room and poured her a glass of water. Returning to the couch, he offered it to Bev, who was still sobbing loudly and muttering words that no one could understand. Eventually, Bev took the glass and drank it dry, which seemed to help her gain some control.

"I am so sorry, Bev. I didn't mean to upset you."

"I'm not upset. I'm ecstatic. This is me being ecstatic!"

Bev started to cry again, but this time a bit more controlled.

Rome noticed a box of tissues and motioned to Heath, who quickly crossed the room and retrieved them. Bev pulled several out of the box, wiped her eyes and blew her nose, while trying to share her thoughts. "This is like a dream come true! I've wanted to see those other sites for as long as I've been a guide. You guys are the best!"

"So you'll do it?" enquired Heath, still a little confused by her overreaction.

"You had me at the first sentence. I was just too shocked to respond."

Rome hugged Bev and she returned the affection in her usual bigger-than-life way. Rome gave Heath the 'A-okay' sign with her finger and thumb and he nodded his head in response, then pulled out a tissue and wiped the sweat from his forehead. Rome gently pulled away from Bev and looked her in the eye. "There's just one more detail, but it's an important one. We have to keep this a secret, just between the three of us. If word gets out I could lose my job."

"My lips are sealed. I'm just taking an overdue vacation. I'm going to call my boss right now." As Bev leaped off the couch and hurried toward the door, she continued to make plans. "You can tell me exactly what you want me to look for at each site. Having Beverly Hucker on the ground will be just as good as being there in person."

With the departure of Bev, the room suddenly went quiet as they stared at each other in astonishment. Finally, Rome broke the silence. "I think that went well."

"She did say, 'yes,' didn't she?"

"Yes," Rome replied, "She said 'yes.'"

"Then we can continue with our plans."

Heath crossed the room and poured two glasses of water, thinking out loud along the way. "This couldn't have worked out any better. We're killing two birds with one stone. The articles will get written and my ghost problem will be solved. I think we should start Bev in Western Australia at the Fremantle Prison site and work our way back east," suggested Heath as he handed Rome a glass of water and began pacing the floor near the couch. "The castle is yours for however long you need it, Rome."

"Thank you."

"Should I let the staff go for the next few days?"

"They're still working here, so that means they must be used to the ghosts by now. We'll just have to make sure they don't find out about my involvement."

"Do you think we could have this all wrapped up by Sunday afternoon?"

"This isn't something you can put to a timetable, Heath. The spirits choose to come to me, remember?"

"Sorry, I'm used to projections."

"Why Sunday?"

"I'm flying up to Sydney Sunday evening. I have a bunch of meetings scheduled for the first part of next week as well as several important conversations I don't want to have."

"Speaking of conversations, I believe I promised to share a few 'other-worldly' ones that I've had recently."

"That you did," said Heath excitedly as he sat down next to Rome.

"So this is what I've been able to piece together. Lady Jones and Lord Hubert seem to be caught in a time warp of sorts. I think they're continuing to relive the days surrounding William's arrest and sentencing."

"That's a lot of years to be reliving such a small amount of time."

"I don't think the time warp started until the castle began to be rebuilt. Somehow it triggered the event and now they're stuck reliving the same time over and over."

"So you've spoken to both Lady Jones and Lord Hubert?"

"I've only spoken with Lady Jones, but I've watched them interact together."

"You were spying on the ghosts? Isn't it usually the other way around?"

"I just happened to wake up first and get out of bed before they woke up and... got out of bed."

"They slept in the same bed as you? In the master suite? In my bed?"

"Well, it is their bed or bed frame and it is setting in what was once their room. I slept so soundly that I didn't know they were there until I woke up this morning."

"So they just crawled right into bed with you?"

"Have you seen the size of that bed? I doubt they knew I was even there, especially since the lights were off and I had the covers over my head. They were just lying there on the top of the covers, like two dead bodies."

"But I slept in that bed Sunday night," said Heath as he stared off into the distance.

"So anyway... while I was at the hotel this morning, I called Mom and asked her if she had ever experienced a spirit reliving the same moment in time over and over again and she has several times. She referred to it as being stuck in a 'vortex' caused by extreme circumstances. Getting caught in a vortex usually stems from a person dying during a horrific situation that's beyond their control. According to Mom, it's very important that they break free of the vortex by themselves through their own awakening. The good news is that each time a spirit engages a human, the closer they get to snapping out of it. Of course, I didn't tell her that I'm having full conversations with these spirits and in person. I'm still keeping that as my anniversary surprise. Are you following? Heath?"

"Huh?"

"Are you with me?"

"Uh-huh."

"Have you heard anything I said?"

"I'm listening."

"You're freaked out about the ghosts being in your bed, aren't you?"

"Why do ghosts have to sleep at all?"

"They don't, but sleeping was an integral part of why Lord Hubert didn't make it in time to save William from being shipped to Australia. They're going through the same motions hoping for a different result."

"So you're telling me that they'll be in my bed every night until this 'awakening' pops them out of their vortex?"

"Most likely. Moving on. I mentioned earlier that Helen came to visit her new resting place, remember?"

"Yes."

"She has no knowledge of what happened to William after she sailed away on the convict ship. She thinks he married Meredith Hampton and they lived happily ever after."

"Did you enlighten her?"

"Mom made it very clear that it's not my place to tell any spirit the truth. They need to find it on their own. I can only help them along the path."

"It's too bad we just can't get the whole family in the same room at the same time and let them hash it out."

"That's a great idea, but the questions is how?"

"I got nothing," replied Heath.

"I think the key is William. He's the magnet that will bring them all together."

"How? He's spent the last one hundred and sixty-plus years hiding from his family."

"Now that his bones are here, we should expect him to show up at any time."

"So we're just waiting for a ghost."

"Pretty much."

"I wonder what my father would think if he could see me now."

"I'll ask him if I see him," responded Rome jokingly, not thinking what the impact of that statement might have on Heath. His sudden silence was Rome's first clue that she may have put her foot in her mouth.

"I'm going to go check on Bev and make sure she didn't get lost," said Heath as he got up walked toward the door. "I'll also have Max prepare to take your friend's car back to Melbourne on the ferry tomorrow."

"That would be great," replied Rome as she watched Heath approach the door and exit the room. She lowered her head in disappointment, upset with herself for making such a tactless joke. No sooner had Heath left the room, but Bev entered, joyful after her conversation with her boss and excited to share the news. "We're set. I just took the next ten days off of work. Ten days. Can you believe it? I haven't taken a vacation in years. I realize it won't take me that long to cover all the sites, but I may linger in Sydney for a while when I'm done."

"And your boss was okay with it?"

"He wasn't happy about the last-minute timing, but we were able to work it out. I practically run the place and he knows it."

"That's wonderful! Thank you so much, Bev. I owe you big time for this one."

"It's me that owes you and Heath. This will be a trip of a lifetime and I can't wait."

"Let's call it even."

"With pleasure."

"Did you see Heath?"

"I passed him in the hallway. I gave him the thumbs up as I passed, but he looked pretty serious. Is everything all right?"

"He had to take care of something."

Bev pulled a notebook and pen out of her backpack and turned to Rome, ready and waiting to be taught. "Tell me everything you want me to cover and how you want me to cover it."

"Wow. Where to begin? Heath thinks it's best if you visit the Fremantle Prison first, so let's start there."

Just as Rome proceeded to share her secrets of what to look for when visiting a site and what type of notes to take, Mr. Burns entered the room to make an announcement. "Mr. Jones has resigned himself to the library for the rest of the evening in order to make the travel arrangements for Ms. Hucker. He asked me to show you to your room whenever you're ready."

"We have some more details to discuss, so what if we find you when we're finished?"

"Very well."

"Mr. Burns," Rome called out, "Now that the other rooms are furnished, where will I be staying tonight?"

"Mr. Jones made it very clear that he'd like you to continue your stay in the master suite."

Rome smiled to herself, secretly knowing why Heath wanted her to sleep in his room and not him. "Please tell Heath I'm honored that he would allow me to continue to sleep in his own bed," replied Rome with tongue in cheek.

"Of course, Ms. London."

Rome hoped that her reply to Heath would help offset her earlier comment. If not, she would find a way to fix it later. That's the risk you take with humor: not everyone finds it as funny as the person making the joke. But for now, it was back to business—the business of turning a guide into a travel writer.

Chapter Ten

The lights of Hobart shone in the distance as Heath stared at them from his castle tower. The night air continued to grow cooler, but Heath had prepared himself by wearing a light jacket. He had finished Bev's travel arrangements but was unable to sleep. As he looked at the dark grounds below, he wondered if William had come to visit his bones, then he found himself wondering how any of this was even possible. Less than a week ago, stories of ghosts were simply that, stories. Fictional tales of the dead told around campfires, in the movie theatre and now in the form of reality television. Ugh, reality television, a form of entertainment Heath did not understand, nor ever wanted to understand.

Unexpectedly, the door opened and Sheldon entered the tower. "I thought you might like a spot of tea, sir." Following Mr. Burns through the door was an out-of-breath George, carrying a tray loaded with a tea pot, two cups and saucers, cream and sugar, two spoons and a dish of cookies. Heath quickly met George halfway and helped him get the tray to the outside wall, where they put it down.

"I think I would have made it, sir, but I appreciate the help all the same," George said, trying to catch his breath.

"Go to bed, George. Call it a night."

"But who will retrieve the tray when you're finished?" replied Mr. Burns in earnest.

"That's what I have your for, Sheldon," insisted Heath in jest as they watched George leave the tower. "Not to worry, I'll be the one carrying the tray down the stairs."

"How very kind of you, Heath."

"I notice there are two cups instead of one. Were you planning on sharing a pot of tea with me before you retire for the evening?"

"I wasn't sure if Ms. London would be joining you."

"It's late. I'm sure she's fast asleep at this point and I'm even more sure that you already know that. Would you please join me for tea, Sheldon?"

"If you insist. But first..." Mr. Burns reached into his pocket and pulled out a set of keys. "I keep forgetting to give these to you. Tomorrow I can show you which door each key belongs to. Shall I pour?"

"By all means."

Heath put the keys in his pocket as Mr. Burns picked up the tea pot and filled the two cups.

"Two sugars," said Heath as he dropped two cubes in each cup and stirred them around. "And just a touch of cream to lessen the heat."

"It appears you learned some culture in all those years of training."

"You were a wonderful teacher, Sheldon. I'd make an excellent butler."

"No, you wouldn't, but never mind."

Mr. Burns rolled his eyes at Heath as they both picked up their cup and sipped from the top. Mr. Burns picked up the saucer of cookies and offered it to Heath, who took one in his hand and dipped it in his tea.

"Any self-respecting butler knows you don't dip your biscuit in your tea. I was never able to break you of that habit."

"And you never will," said Heath as he dipped again.

"Australians."

"We are an uncivilized lot. So what's on your mind, Sheldon?"

"Whatever do you mean?"

"It's long past your bedtime, yet you made that poor boy climb a spiral staircase to the top of the tower, carrying a loaded tray of tea. Something is on your mind."

"I suppose I do have a thought or two roaming about."

"Don't keep me in suspense."

"Ms. London seems good for you."

"Agreed."

"But she's an American."

"Yes, she is."

"An American with her own life."

"True."

"And you're an Australian."

"As you so often remind me."

"That's quite a distance."

"Yes, it is."

Taking a break to process, they sipped some more tea and took another bite of their cookies as they stood in silence, staring out at Hobart.

"Tread carefully, Heath. Your heart has only recently healed from the loss of your father. I'd hate to see it damaged again."

"Thank you for your concern, Sheldon."

Again, they sipped their tea. After a minute or two of silence, Mr. Burns placed his cup back on the tray. "One more thought before I turn in and leave you to the silence of the night sky."

"And what would that be?"

"Beware of your uncle. He may be family, but I do not believe he has your best interests at heart. He never has. Nor did he have your father's."

"The castle open house has you worried."

"Only because it's his idea. Your uncle is not to be trusted."

"Thanks, Sheldon. You know how much I value your input."

"And I, yours," kindly responded Mr. Burns. "If I'm no longer needed, the time has come for this 'old man' to retire to bed."

With a pat to Heath's shoulder, Mr. Burns turned back toward the door.

"I trust you'll get the tea tray back to the kitchen tonight."

"Yes, I will. Good night, Sheldon."

"There is a marvelous invention out there that you may consider for accessing the tower. I believe it's called an elevator," suggested Mr. Burns before he entered the stairwell. "Even a dumbwaiter would be an improvement."

"I'll take it under advisement," said Heath as he returned to the saucer of cookies.

"And don't eat too many bickies before you go to bed," echoed Mr. Burns's voice as he descended the spiral staircase.

Defying Mr. Burns' recommendation, Heath dipped another cookie into his tea and bit off the softened part. Allowing the cookie to melt in his mouth, he turned his attention back to the distant lights of Hobart and considered the advice of his trusted friend.

ROME peacefully lay asleep in the master suite, until the mystery spirit from the night before appeared in the room, demanding answers. "Why are you still here?" he shouted at the top of his voice, causing Rome to wake up in a panic.

"What are you trying to do, give me a heart attack?"

"I'll do worse than that, you tawdry harlot."

"Who do you think you are coming into my bedroom, accusing me of being a harlot? And P.S. Mr. Whoever: nobody uses that word anymore."

"And to think my daughter nearly married Hubert's son!"

Realizing who he was, Rome got out of bed, walked right up to the man and stared him straight in the eye. "If your daughter was anything like you, who I assume to be Henry Hampton, then William was better off dying in a prison in Australia than being stuck with her for the rest of his life."

Completely offended, the man stepped back in shock that a

woman would dare talk to him in such a way. "The others will hear about this and it's Justice Hampton to you."

"Well, it's Ms. London to you and next time bring 'the others' with you so I can introduce them to the twenty-first century as well!"

"You're the devil, woman!"

"Why don't you throw the word 'witch' in the mix too, then we'll have a really wicked combination."

"Sacrilege! What are you?" demanded Justice Hampton.

"I am a modern woman, who leases an apartment, has a job and votes in elections."

"Such insolence!"

"I may be insolent, but I still have a body, which means I will sleep in this bed anytime I want to sleep in this bed. So take that back to 'the others.'"

With that said the man disappeared, leaving her to contemplate their bizarre conversation. "How did women survive back then?" uttered Rome as she walked across the room, poured herself a glass of water and took a drink. As she put her glass down, she heard a rumbling from behind. Turning around, she saw an angry mob of at least twelve male spirits surrounding Justice Hampton, all dressed in gentlemen's-style clothing. "You have impugned my character, Witch, and that of my daughter. Allow me to introduce you to her cousins."

"Let me guess... the others?"

"The other members of the Hampton family."

"What? You couldn't find any witch hunters from the seventeenth century?" replied Rome sarcastically as she stared at the intimidating group of spirits in front of her.

"Arm yourselves, men!"

Following orders, the men began to grab whatever they could find: a lamp, hair brush, blow dryer, vase, pillow, comforter, chair, valet stand, a small mirror, a large book, etc.

"Oh, this isn't good," exclaimed Rome as she ran from the room screaming for help, followed by the mob of angry spirits. She quickly made her way to the top of the stairs just in time to see

Heath at the bottom carrying the tea tray toward the kitchen. "Run!"

Heath looked up to see items from his bedroom floating through the air along the balcony as Rome descended the stairs in her nightgown. He carefully, but quickly, put the tray down and grabbed her hand as she hurried by. With the touch of Rome's hand, Heath was instantly able to see the angry spirits and demanded to know more. "Who are they?"

"Men on a witch hunt!"

"Who's the witch?"

"Take a guess!"

Bev ran to the top of the stairs just in time to see all the objects floating down the stairs and across the grand hall. "I knew it! The castle really is haunted!"

Sheldon joined her at the top of the stairs, just as alarmed by the spectacle. "Good heavens!" shouted the butler.

"Should we run, Mr. Burns?" asked Bev as they watched the objects float erratically toward the door.

"Your room or mine?"

"Whatever's closest."

Mr. Burns grabbed her hand and they ran across the balcony and down the east hallway.

Heath reached the door and found it to be locked. He pulled out the keys Mr. Burns gave him and began trying each one in the lock as Rome watched the angry spirits grow closer and closer. Unable to find the right key, Heath placed Rome between him and the door to protect her from the angry mob.

Just as they were about to attack, a loud voice boomed from the top of the stairs. "How dare you enter my home uninvited and declare war on my guests!"

All the spirits, as well as Heath and Rome, returned to the grand hall to see Lord Hubert standing at the top of the stairs, staring down at them. "Are we gentlemen or barbarians?" demanded Lord Hubert.

"You have a witch in your midst, Hubert. She has professed it herself. I am a magistrate and you are a member of the House of Lords. It is our duty to prosecute!"

"Witch trials are no longer a practice of England and you know that, Henry."

"Not to mention the fact that she is our guest," Lady Jones added as she approached from behind. "And I don't recall inviting you or your family for a visit."

Without further argument, Henry Hampton and the others began to disappear, one by one, allowing the items to drop to the floor, some breaking on impact, others surviving the fall.

Rome and Heath walked toward the stairs as Lady Jones and Lord Hubert descended toward them. "Thank you," said Rome.

"I may not understand why you're here, but you're more welcome than that lot," responded Lady Jones.

"I would like to help you understand why I'm here. Can we talk?"

"Perhaps another day. Our son's sentencing is tomorrow and we must spend tonight preparing," remarked Lord Hubert.

"Wait!"

Rome's plea fell on deaf ears as Lord Hubert and Lady Jones disappeared from view.

"Why were all those ghosts after you in the first place?" asked Heath.

"Women's suffrage."

"Huh?"

"Never mind," replied Rome as she walked back to the mess and started picking the items off the floor.

"Who were those spirits?" asked Heath as he joined her in picking through the clutter.

"Meredith Hampton's father and her extended family."

"The woman William was supposed to marry?"

"Exactly."

"What are they doing here?"

"No one seems to stick around long enough to find out. But I will say this... For being best of friends, it didn't appear that Lady Jones and Lord Hubert were too happy to see Lord Hampton."

Heath picked up pieces from the broken mirror and stacked them in a pile as he thought about what could have happened if Lord Hubert and his wife had not appeared. "I never meant to put you in danger when I asked you to help me."

"This isn't your fault. I'm not used to having discussions with the spirits. I could have used a bit more diplomacy."

"Just when I think we're making progress, more ghosts show up. How are we ever going to fix this?"

"My mother said that her Grandma Rome only had one rule when communicating with the dead."

"What was that?"

"To help them find their own solutions and not to solve the problem for them."

"Wouldn't a little 'show and tell' make things go a lot faster?"

"If you only have one rule, there's probably a reason for it." On that note, Rome stood up holding the lamp, hair brush, blow dryer, vase, pillow and carrying the comforter draped around her shoulders. Heath finished piling the glass and picked up the remaining chair with one hand and the valet and book with his other.

"I think that's everything. I'll have the staff clean up the glass in the morning," said Heath as they walked toward the stairs and began to climb to the second floor. "I'll make up another bed for you in a different room."

"The master suite is ground zero for paranormal activity, so that's where I need to be," responded Rome as an idea popped into her head, causing her to stop and ask, "Do you have any way of knowing which bedroom was William's?"

"I got the entire layout of the castle from the description in Lady Jones's diary. She was mad about details. She even sketched some of the room designs. That's how I knew where to put the furniture in each room."

"Are you up for some light reading before you fall asleep?" asked Rome with a twinkle in her eye.

"With all the adrenaline pumping through my veins, I could use a good bedtime story."

Once they reached the bedroom, Rome lowered her items to the bed and began placing them one by one about the room. Heath put down the chair and valet, tossed the book on the bed and turned back toward the door. "I'll run down to the library and grab the diary." Heath left the room as Rome continued to put the stuff back in their original places, then she turned her attention to the bed. As she began to straighten one side of the covers, she noticed the blankets begin to pull on the other side. Looking up, she saw Lady Jones carefully aligning the sheets with the blankets. Rome continued to make the bed, watching Lady Jones and waiting for her to speak.

"I'm beginning to see things more clearly."

"What do you mean?" replied Rome.

Lady Jones finished her side of the bed and sat down on the edge, facing away from Rome. "For years my husband and I have watched strangers come and go at Forest Gate."

"Strangers?" Rome enquired with curiosity.

"We tried to interact with them but the more we tried the quicker they left."

Rome realized the awakening had began just like her mother told her it would. Encouraged by Lady Jones's stroll down memory lane, Rome walked around the bed and sat next to her.

"All we wanted was help, but no one would listen to our pleas."

"What kind of help?"

"Help for our son. When the last of the strangers left, they took everything with them. No one came to stay after that."

"Why did you stay?"

"My husband would not let go and I could not let go of him."

"Let go of what?"

"The sorrow he felt for failing to right a wrong."

"Whose wrong?"

"He's never spoken of what happened and I've learned not to ask." Lady Jones stood up from the bed and walked to the window. Staring out over the grounds she took a moment to think as she continued to piece the past together. "Eventually, vagabonds moved into Forest Gate and in their attempt to stay warm they started a fire that practically destroyed our home. Only the walls remained."

"Yet you stayed?"

"Time passed then people began taking the walls away."

"And you went with them?"

"My husband and I were sitting on the remaining stone blocks when they came for the last load. We had nothing left, so we never moved."

"Now Forest Gate has returned to its original splendor," remarked Rome, trying to keep Lady Jones on her current path.

"That's not all that returned."

Rome left the bed and walked toward Lady Jones. Standing behind her, Rome stared out the window as she whispered into her ear. "What else returned, Lady Jones?"

"Somehow the rebuilding of Forest Gate triggered my husband's obsession and our desire to..."

"Right a wrong?"

Lady Jones turned back to Rome just as the final moment of her awakening hit. A recognition of the truth was finally allowing her to escape the fantasy she had been reliving over the past three years. The look on her face was honest and sincere but not without sorrow and Rome's heart ached for the pain she was feeling.

"I remember now. We were never able to save William."

"I'm so sorry."

"If only we hadn't slept in that morning. My husband feels such a tremendous guilt for not being able to stand by our son's side in court and present on his behalf."

"So that's why William's sentence was not overturned?"

"Our deaths put an end to our son's hope."

"May I ask how you both died on the same day?"

"Due to our late departure from Forest Gate, Lord Hubert was racing our carriage toward London in an attempt to make it to the courts before the ship sailed at noon. I'd never seen him drive so swiftly. Soon, the carriage lost control causing it to flip over and be dragged down the road."

"That's terrible."

"Lord Hubert laid next to me in silence, both of us pinned beneath the carriage. I called his name over and over, but no response came. Eventually, life drained from my body as well. My last thought was of my son and how he would think that we'd abandoned him."

"It was an accident. William would understand that," said Rome in an attempt to console Lady Jones.

"Hubert hadn't slept for days, so I convinced him to close his eyes for a couple of hours the night before. As a result of not waking up on time, we failed to save our son."

"Your son still needs saving, but in a different way."

Lady Jones turned to Rome with signs of hope replacing the sadness and despair in her face. "And you can do this?"

"I want to help, but this is a matter that needs to be dealt with as a family."

"Lord Hubert is calling. Let us visit this topic further at a later day." Lady Jones instantly disappeared from sight just as Heath entered the door, holding the diary in his hand as though it were a trophy.

"Got it."

He hopped onto the bed, landing on his belly, and began to slowly turn the pages of the fragile journal. Rome, feeling more optimistic from her conversation with Lady Jones, crawled onto the bed and joined Heath in looking at the diary. "This is amazing, Heath. I can't believe it survived all these years."

"After I purchased the castle, I began searching for more of the Jones' family assets, which led me to a private collection that had been warehoused for years. Following the death of the collector, his heirs put it on the market and I was able to purchase the contents before being acquired by a museum. Most of the furniture and art work in this castle came from that collection, including this diary."

"Wow. That's impressive."

"I needed to throw myself into something after Dad's death and the business just wasn't enough."

As Heath slowly turned the pages, scanning each one for information, Rome found herself staring at him rather than the pages of the book. The more time she spent with him the more fascinated she became. She was glad that he talked her into staying. It gave her the time to get past the cold, self-gratifying, business-like exterior she had first witnessed and find so much more on the inside, a place few people got to see.

Slowly, she turned her attention back to the pages of the book as Heath pointed to the different entries. Rome no longer found herself wanting to solve the mystery out of an obligation to her gift but as a partner sharing in his quest. She was secretly enjoying their little adventure, and after her recent conversation with Lady Jones, felt more assured that they were making progress.

Chapter Eleven

Friday morning arrived, finding Rome and Heath asleep in the master suite, lying next to each other on the bed. They had closed their eyes unintentionally the night before and were now peacefully wasting away the morning hours.

"Ahem," interrupted Bev, clearing her throat in an effort to wake them from their slumber.

No response.

"Ahem!" came a more pronounced throat clearing, but this time by Mr. Burns.

Rome struggled to lift up her head and open her eyes, finally able to focus on Bev and Mr. Burns standing at the foot of their bed.

"As enjoyable as I think a morning cuddle is," noted Bev, "my bags are packed and I'm awaiting further instructions."

Mr. Burns reached down and picked a pillow off the floor and placed it on the foot of the bed as he followed up on Bev's inquiry. "The itinerary, sir."

Rome realized she was lying next to Heath with his arm wrapped around her waist.

Causing her to panic on the inside, she quickly crawled out of bed as Heath more slowly rolled out in the opposite direction. "What time is it, Sheldon?"

"Half past eight, sir."

"I'm pretty sure your plane departs around ten. I'll go print out the itinerary while Sheldon calls Max and has him bring the car around."

"Max is unavailable. He drove Ms. London's car up to Devonport this morning in order to load it onto the ferry."

"That's right," said Heath, still trying to wake from the first deep sleep he'd had in a long time.

Rome picked her shoes up from the floor and began putting them on as she added to the morning plans. "I'll get the Land Rover and Heath and I will drive you to the airport."

"Might I recommend an alternate plan?" asked Mr. Burns.

"And what would that be, Sheldon."

"I could drive Ms. Hucker to the airport," he responded, stunning both Heath and Rome. "That would allow the two of you to properly begin your day. That is if I'm not needed here."

Heath looked to a surprised Rome as he responded to Mr. Burns' suggestion. "I think that would be a great idea. I'll meet you outside with the itinerary," said Heath as he hurried toward the door and left the room. Following suit, Rome hurried around the back of the bed past Bev and Mr. Burns, adding to their preparation. "I left my camera in the library. You'll need that for the pictures. I'll meet you down there."

Rome left the room as well, leaving Mr. Burns and Bev still standing at the foot of the bed. Without moving, Bev shared her thoughts in regard to his plan. "That was a brilliant idea and a rather gallant move, Sheldon."

"It only seemed fitting, Beverly, since recently I too have developed an affinity for the morning cuddle."

Mr. Burns picked up Bev's hand and raised the back of it to his lips. He gently kissed her hand and lowered it back down, then took hold of the extended handle on her suitcase and pulled it toward the door.

"Falling for the butler. Who would have thought?" she said to herself happily, then followed him out of the room.

EVERYONE RUSHED out of the castle. Bev hugged Rome goodbye and got into the passenger side, while Heath fiddled with the seat adjustment on the driver's side, making sure Mr. Burns's seat was in the right position.

"Need I remind you, Heath, that I've been driving longer than you?"

"Not that much longer. Be safe, my friend." Heath stepped back from the car and they both watched as Mr. Burns drove down the long drive and pulled through the gate.

"I think they're actually starting to warm up to each other," observed Heath.

"Who knows. They may end up being friends after all," replied Rome.

"Let's not hold our breath."

The two of them shared a laugh together as Rome glanced across the grounds at the grave site. She saw Helen standing in the same place at nearly the same time as she was yesterday morning. She reached over and took hold of Heath's hand, stopping him from entering the castle. "Come on. I want you to meet someone."

Heath looked in the direction he was being pulled and saw a spirit standing at the foot of the grave. "Is that Helen?"

"Yes. Now remember, it's very important that she make her own discoveries about the family and William. I may have already shared too much information when I told William he had a son."

Heath tried to prepare himself mentally as they crossed the grounds approaching Helen from behind.

"Hello, Helen."

"You again."

"My name is Rome and this is my friend, Heath."

"Hello, Helen. It's a pleasure to meet you," said Heath with reverence and respect, amazed that he was speaking to his great-great-great-great-grandmother.

"What is this place you've brought me to?" enquired Helen.

"You're still in Australia, but I moved your remains from New South Wales down here to Tasmania."

"Tasmania?"

"In your day it was referred to as Van Diemen's Land."

"I know of Van Diemen's Land. That's where they sent a great deal of the prisoners."

"Yes," Heath replied, "And now it's named Tasmania."

"The prison on Van Diemen's Land was said to be a terrible one, designed for the roughest of convicts. Is it still in operation?"

"No. It was closed in the late nineteenth century."

"And what century is it now?"

"The twenty-first century."

"It appears many years have passed since my death."

Unsure of how to respond, Heath and Rome waited for Helen to make the next move in the conversation.

"And this castle. Somehow it looks familiar to me."

Heath looked to Rome for help, uncertain of how much information he should share. She quickly took over the conversation. "It was shipped here from England. Perhaps you passed it in your travels growing up there."

"Perhaps."

Helen paused, trying to remember as she looked at the castle in curiosity. Heath and Rome waited for her to make a connection on her own, not certain if she had ever seen the castle or not.

"Might I enquire as to why one would ship an English castle to Australia?"

"It had fallen into disrepair when I found it and I wanted to bring it back to life," replied Heath proudly.

"What must it be like to live in a time when you can actually ship a castle across the great ocean to another land? I would like to have known a time like that."

"I'd be happy to give you a tour of the castle."

"Although I find myself drawn to it, I must leave now."

"No. Don't go. I'm so enjoying our conversation," responded Heath with all the sincerity of his heart.

"I shall visit again, soon." And with that, Helen was gone, leaving Rome and Heath standing in the afterglow of yet another completely unbelievable moment.

"I think we actually made a friend," said Rome as she turned her attention to Heath. "And you were a big part of that."

"I was just trying not to scare her off."

"Clearly, she feels comfortable enough to come back. I imagine we'll see her tomorrow around the same time."

"Thank you for this, Rome."

"Don't thank me. Thank whatever triggered the evolution of my gift. In the meantime, shall we see what we can scrounge up for breakfast?" enquired Rome as she wrapped her arm around Heath's and began walking him across the grounds toward the castle.

"Why would we scrounge something up? I have a cook."

"Of course you do."

"You're being sarcastic."

"Not at all."

"And there it is again."

"Just part of my charm, I suppose," responded Rome with tongue in cheek.

"So charming."

"Now who's being sarcastic."

"When with Rome..."

"Like I haven't heard that one before."

"And here I thought I was being original."

"So what's on the agenda for today as we wait for more spirits to make an appearance?" asked Rome in an attempt to move beyond the silly state of their current conversation.

"I still have a bunch of artwork to put up throughout the house as well as curtains and blinds to hang."

"Sounds like fun."

"Good."

"Right after breakfast."

"You're the only woman I've ever spent time with who isn't afraid to eat more than a plate of lettuce in front of me."

"A by-product of dating super models."

"I don't date super models."

"Nice try. I did an internet search of you a few days ago and there's plenty of evidence to the contrary."

"You're referring to some old pictures my college buddies posted from my days at Oxford. I hate the internet."

"You can't hate the entire internet."

Heath reached for the door of the castle, swung it open and waited for Rome to enter as he responded to her claim. "Fine. I hate most of the internet."

"We live in the twenty-first century, Heath. You may want to develop a more tech-savvy attitude."

"Why? I have people for that."

"Of course you do."

Heath shook his head as he entered the castle, happy to know that he'd finally met someone with as much unabashed honesty as himself. He knew he was falling for her. Take that back. He'd already fallen for her, despite the fact that there would be no net at the bottom to catch him if she didn't come to the same conclusion. But there was nothing he could do about that, so why not eat breakfast and enjoy the day?

Chapter Twelve

Sydney, Australia

Sergio Arturo walked through the busy copy room of The Sydney Morning Herald on his way to the editor's office. Ignoring the few people who actually cared to greet him, he remained focused on his objective. He entered the editor's office without bothering to knock and took a seat across the desk from his boss.

"Have you forgotten how to knock, Arturo?" asked his editor.

"You asked to see me, so here I am."

"In all your glory," responded his editor sarcastically.

"I'm a busy man. Can we make this short?"

"You work for me, Arturo. I'll make it as short or as long as I want to make it."

The editor picked up the photo of the castle that Arturo had doctored and tossed it onto the desk in front of him.

"This is a newspaper, not a tabloid."

"And I write an opinion column, not the news."

"We're not in the business of lies and conjecture."

"When did opinions become facts?"

"This photo is doctored and you know it. I wouldn't be surprised if you did it yourself."

"Careful. That sounds an awful lot like conjecture."

"A word that best describes your weekly column," accused his editor.

"A column that has sold a lot of newspapers."

"That may be so, but this crosses the line. I won't run it and if this paper doesn't run it, no other paper will pick it up either."

"Maybe you should check with the man who actually owns the paper. Last we talked, which was on the golf course yesterday, he mentioned how excited he was to read my upcoming column and see the picture in Sunday's edition."

"He may own the paper, but he pays me to run it."

Arturo stood up and buttoned his safari jacket as he responded with a threat. "I'd expect a phone call from him within the hour about running that photo." Arturo looked at his watch then back to the editor. "Make that two hours. We'll want to get through our lunch meeting first."

Arturo smiled at the win then turned and walked out of the office, leaving the door wide open. Angry at Arturo's threat, the editor picked up a stress reducing device and hurled it across the room.

ROGER ASH WALKED down the hallway toward the boardroom, knowing exactly what he must do to convince the board to see things his way. He entered and found the board members chatting amongst themselves, waiting for the meeting to begin. "Thank you all for coming on such short notice and so late in the day. I apologize for calling this emergency meeting so soon after our last meeting, but I felt I should report back on my trip to Tasmania."

"Has Heath returned with you?" asked one of the board members.

"Unfortunately, he had more pressing matters to attend to," replied Roger.

"More pressing than his own business?" enquired another board member.

"From what I saw, the decorating of his castle has taken preference over Jones Shipping."

"I don't believe this. What has gotten into him?" exclaimed a third board member.

"His obsession with this castle seems to be his only priority. I tried to talk some sense into him while I was there, but at this point he may be too far gone to be saved."

"Marshall would be turning over in his grave if he could see what is happening with Heath," said the first board member.

"There is some good news. He did agree to return to work next week for a few days. My hope is that we can talk some sense into him before implementing more radical measures," responded Roger.

"In the meantime, is there anything we can we do about this?" asked the second board member as he tossed a copy of Thursday's newspaper onto the table, pointing at the teaser for Sunday's issue.

"Unfortunately not. I've been in contact with Arturo's editor and he's fully committed to running the picture and column on the front page."

"What's our next move?" asked the third board member.

"I came up with an idea while meeting with Heath and I think it may solve a lot of the problem."

"And what would that be, Roger?" asked the first board member.

"I recommended to Heath that he host a charity fundraiser at his castle and invite all the movers and shakers in the Hobart community."

"Isn't that a bit risky with all the ghost rumors currently circulating?" asked the second board member.

"I highly doubt there are any ghosts in Heath's castle. If there were, he probably would have mentioned it during our meeting."

"Lies created by this Arturo character. I've long suspected that he manufacturers the majority of the content in his column," said the third board member.

"Agreed. It's evident that he'll do anything to maintain his celebrity status," responded Roger.

"Hosting a fundraiser would help to normalize the situation and show a more philanthropic side to Heath," proposed a fourth board member.

"Which would make him appear more like his father. Everyone adored Marshall. You most of all, Roger," agreed the first board member.

"It's because of my great fondness for my brother-in-law as well as my nephew Heath, that I'm willing to do whatever it takes to fill the void that Marshall's death has left behind," Roger assured the board.

"We will encourage and support the charity fundraiser idea in our Monday meeting," responded the second board member.

"Agreed," acknowledged the board members.

"Thank you. I feel strongly that we're making the right choice for Jones Shipping as well as for Heath. Now if you'll excuse me, I have another meeting to attend. I've been doing double duty in Heath's absence."

"When it comes time to reward you with your annual bonus, we'll remember all the work you've done for the company and on behalf of Heath," responded the third board member.

"Being of service to my family and this company is a reward in itself," said Roger, feigning humility, then he smiled at the board and departed the room to a round of applause. Once in the hallway, Roger pulled out his cell phone and dialed as he walked toward the elevator. "The meeting is over. I'll meet you in ten minutes." Roger disconnected the call and was off to yet another clandestine meeting with Arturo.

THE SUN SHONE brightly that Friday afternoon as Arturo sat down on his favorite park bench, situated perfectly for feeding the swans. He opened his brown paper bag and began tossing bread crumbs into the pool of water. The swans soon migrated to his end of the pond and began competing for each chunk of bread that landed on the water.

Roger Ash approached the bench and sat down on the other end.

"Bread crumbs?" offered Arturo.

"I didn't come here to feed the birds."

"They're not just birds, Ash, they're swans."

"Were you able to convince your editor to run the picture?"

"Front page, exactly as planned. Were you able to get the board to back you on the castle fundraiser?"

"The board is on board, so to speak. At this point, it shouldn't take much to convince Heath. I've already retained the services of an event planning and catering service and the invitations were sent out four days ago. Things are moving ahead as planned."

"I've met with my guys as well. They've already performed their recon and are in the final stages of preparation."

"And you can trust them?"

"I've used their services many times, anonymously, of course," assured Arturo.

"None of this comes back to me, Arturo."

"I never leave a trail to follow."

"For your sake, I hope not," threatened Roger.

"And the travel writer?"

"According to her editor, Ms. London is en route to Western Australia to tour the Fremantle Prison."

"Then she's no longer a threat to the plan."

"It appears we've covered everything," said Roger confidently.

"The next time we meet will be in Tasmania, dressed in black tie."

"Just as planned."

Roger stood up from the bench and walked away as Arturo continued to feed bread crumbs to the swans.

Chapter Thirteen

Rome finished placing the curtains on the rod then moved them back and forth, evening out both sides. Before she left the window she parted the curtains and noticed the sun beginning to set. "Where did the day go?" she said out loud.

"I don't know, but we sure got a lot done. How does this look?"

She turned around and looked at the painting Heath had just hung on the wall. "A little higher on the left."

Heath attempted to adjust the painting but moved it in the wrong direction.

"Your other left."

Heath, not used to making mistakes or being corrected, now took it in stride as he adjusted the painting in the opposite direction.

"Perfect. That really is a good likeness of William."

"It seems fitting to hang it in what was once his bedroom."

"You mean his bed chambers," responded Rome, attempting a British accent.

Suddenly, the heavy wooden door swung shut and locked itself. Heath and Rome looked at the door then back to each other.

"Are we not alone?" whispered Heath.

"I'm not seeing anyone."

"That's because I'm behind you," whispered a voice in Rome's ear, sending chills down her back. Rome jump forward then turned and looked back, seeing William standing behind Heath. Rome watched as William slowly began to circle around Heath. "It was his idea to move my bones. Was it not?" asked William with anger in his voice.

"Rome?" enquired Heath curiously, reacting to her sudden move.

"Just stay where you are, Heath."

"Good advice, Miss London. He would be wise to take it. Now answer my request."

Rome watched William reach into the tool box and slowly pull out an eight penny nail about two and a half inches long, then turn back toward Heath. She continued to watch with great trepidation, trying to think of what to say to stop William from harming Heath.

"It's done. What does it matter?"

"Do you know what prison taught me?"

"No."

"How to survive. Not just the brutality of the punishment of prison life and the endless hours of slave labor, but often surviving meant stopping someone else from killing you. I never realized there were so many ways to end a person's life until my time at Port Arthur."

Heath nervously watched the nail float up from the toolbox toward his neck but continued to stand still, putting his trust in Rome.

Trying not to show it, Rome grew more alarmed as she watched William raise the nail to Heath's neck and point it toward his carotid artery.

"Do you know what spending twelve years in that hell hole did to me and others like me?"

"I can imagine."

"People say that, but they truly can't. It was beyond the limits of imagination. It hardened my heart and stole my soul. I became a lifeless shell moving through day after miserable day."

"That was a long time ago, William."

"You should have left me on that island. That's where someone like me belongs. Promise to return my remains or he will die."

"No!"

Shocked by her definitive reply, William responded by pressing the nail into Heath's skin as he watched her walk toward Heath.

"I will do it, Miss London."

"No, you won't, William. There's still goodness within you. I've seen it."

Rome reached Heath's side and took hold of his hand, allowing him to instantly see William, who was standing face to face with him, holding the nail next to his neck.

"Hello, William," said Heath nervously, uncertain of what else to say.

"It seems Miss London would rather watch you bleed to death than return my bones to the Isle of the Dead."

"Don't you want to know why we moved them?" enquired Heath courageously.

"I'm not sure the 'why' is important at this point," responded Rome, uncertain as to whether revealing more information would make matters worse.

"On the contrary. I'd like to know why my great-great-great-great-grandson moved my remains without my permission."

"Tread lightly, Heath," reminded Rome, hoping Heath wouldn't expose too much of the truth at once.

"Before I knew where you were buried on the Isle of the Dead, I already had the remains of your wife, Helen, exhumed and brought to Tasmania from her original burial site in New South Wales. I had plans to bury her on the estate, and after meeting you on the island, I decided you should be buried with her. There's a great view of the burial site from your window."

"So much for treading lightly," said Rome beneath her breath as they waited for William's reaction.

William continued to stare Heath in the eye as he processed the information, then he slowly lowered the nail, tossed it into the toolbox and walked toward the window.

"It was my decision to dig up your bones and bury you here.

Rome had no say in the matter. Do what you want to me, but please don't harm her."

Rome looked at Heath, proud of the man she stood beside, a man of integrity and strong character, someone she could love with all her heart, if only their circumstances weren't so problematic. Each day she could feel him chipping away at her resistance, but Rome had worked too hard to allow herself to be vulnerable. Just some thoughts rolling around her head as she continued to stand next to Heath, holding his hand and waiting to see if William was going to kill them both. Finally, William spoke, relieving the growing tension in the air. "I only see the earth disrupted over the size of one grave site."

Hesitantly, Heath offered an explanation as Rome gripped his hand tightly to show support. "That's because I placed both of your skeletons in the same coffin, side by side. I wanted you to be together in death, since you couldn't be together in life."

"What a ridiculous notion," replied William.

"Excuse me for sounding rude, William, but I'm not buying this tough guy routine for one minute," responded Rome.

William turned from the window and began walking toward her, so she quickly decided to finish what she had to say. "You're not mean and hateful. You're racked with guilt for sure, but only because of the sorrow you feel for what happened to the ones you loved so long ago. The spirit I met on that island was tender and fragile and the last thing he wanted to do was to hurt anyone. That's who you really are, not the person you're pretending to be now."

"How dare you take the liberty of lecturing me on what type of person I am. You have no idea who I am!"

"I'm certainly not discounting the effects of what you went through during your time at Port Arthur, but aren't you tired of reliving it? Do you really want to carry this with you through eternity?"

"This is my eternity!"

Before Rome could respond with more of the same, Heath touched her arm, signaling that he would like to try. "I don't know exactly what your life before imprisonment was like, but after meeting Helen this morning, I think it had to be pretty good."

"I don't want to think about that!"

"You need to think about it. Tell us how it began, William," encouraged Heath, hoping he would bite.

"I can't."

"Show us how it began," said Rome as she took William's left hand in her right and Heath's right hand in her left, the three of them forming a circle.

"What are we doing, Rome?" asked Heath in confusion.

"Hopefully, you'll see. Literally," responded Rome, then she turned her attention back to William. "Start from the beginning."

"I don't know that I can speak of it after all these years."

"Of course you can. You're safe here with us," Rome assured him.

William took a deep breath, closed his eyes and began to speak. "I was to be wed to Meredith Hampton, the summer of my twenty-first birthday. It had been the arrangement since we were children, but I knew in my heart that I could not marry her, for I had fallen in love with Helen over the course of the many summers I had spent in the North as a youth. I tried in vain to get my father to end my predetermined betrothment to Meredith, but it was no use. As the day of nuptials approached, I resolved that I could not spend the rest of my life with a woman I did not love. So I contacted two of my best schoolmates, who lived north of London, and we hatched a plan. They were to make all the necessary arrangements at a familiar church within walking distance from Helen's home. I was to travel up from the South and meet them at the chapel."

Once again, Rome was able to see the memories playing out in William's mind, only this time they weren't just images.

"How is this possible? It's like watching a movie of the past," whispered Heath as he stood with his eyes closed, viewing William's memories as well.

Rome responded with a quiet, "Shhh," in order to not distract William, but he was too deep in memory to be stopped, and Heath and Rome were along for the ride.

Chapter Fourteen

England, 1840.

A small country church set quietly on a hill in Victorian England. The plains that surrounded it were alive with the beauty of green grass and wildflowers, waiting patiently for the next traveler to make their way through the countryside. The sound of horses striking the road with their hooves broke the silence as a small, single, horse-drawn carriage quickly approached the church.

William Jones, as a young twenty-one-year-old English gentleman, quickly hopped out of the carriage and tied his horse's reigns to the post near the church. Dressed in his best suit and finest hat, he appeared ready to attend a formal occasion.

Charles Mott and John Hughes, also English gentlemen in their early twenties and dressed in their finest, exited the church, happy to see the groom and their good friend, William, had safely arrived. They quickly greeted each other with handshakes, smiles and pats on the back. "Finally! We were about to form a search party and release the dogs," said Charles, having fun at his friend's expense.

"Apologies, my dear friends. It proved more difficult to get away than I had anticipated."

"Not to worry. The arrangements have been made and the priest is ready to begin," John assured William.

"Is Helen here? Did she make it all right?"

"More than all right. Wait till you see her," tempted Charles, gripping William's shoulder. "She truly is a beauty to behold."

"You are fortunate to marry for love, William," added John, "I do envy you that."

"But not the wrath to be unleashed by your father when he discovers what you have done," warned Charles.

"I refuse to let that ruin the happiest day of my life."

"As well you should, my friend. Now, shall we get to it?"

"At once. But first, thank you for coming, both of you. It means a great deal to have you stand with me."

The three men climbed the stairs to the door and entered the building. Once inside, William stopped in his tracks, surprised by the transformation that had occurred within the walls of the small country church he and Helen had visited so often. The floor of the aisle leading to the front was covered in flower petals, while overhead, garlands made of flowers and ribbon ran in all directions. Everywhere William looked he saw more flowers, ribbons and candles filling every nook and cranny.

"When I asked you both to make the arrangements, I had no idea you would go to such great lengths," said William as he continued to take in the appearance of the room.

"That's the beauty of it... we didn't do anything but make contact with the priest," responded Charles.

"The chapel was decorated earlier for a wedding which will be taking place in," John checked his pocket watch, "less than one hour. We're just giving it a practice run."

"We'd better get to it," responded William.

John nodded to the priest, who signaled to Helen, waiting behind a dividing wall next to the priest. Time seemed to stop for William as she entered the room, wearing a simple white dress, white boots and holding a bouquet of wild flowers. Her long, dark hair was crowned with a beautiful wreath of flowers and greenery, with a white scarf cascading down her back. Once she reached the side of the priest, she turned and faced the aisle, then with a smile, she stretched out her glove-covered hand, signaling for him to approach.

Without taking his eyes off of her, William began his walk down the aisle, followed by his two best men. Reaching the front, William took hold of Helen's hand and gently pulled her near to him.

"It's just as I always dreamed it would be, William. Don't you think it's beautiful?" she enquired of her fiancé.

"All the beauty in the world pales in comparison to the woman I see before me."

"Ahem," John cleared his throat, garnering their attention, "Time is of the essence." Helen and William both turned and faced the priest, who immediately began reciting the words that would unite them in marriage.

The ceremony ended beautifully as William took Helen into his arms and they kissed for the first time as husband and wife, then William walked her back down the aisle. John and Charles shook the priest's hand, thanking him for squeezing them in at the last minute and performing the ceremony. Once outside, William helped Helen into the carriage then walked back to speak to John and Charles, who were coming down the stairs.

"I cannot thank you enough, my friends."

"It is I who should be thanking you. I've not had this much intrigue in quite some time," remarked Charles.

"Nothing like a clandestine wedding to get the blood pumping, even the royal blood that runs through my veins," agreed John.

"When will you see your father?" asked Charles hesitantly.

"I've arranged to spend tonight at an inn just outside of London. Tomorrow morning I plan to meet my father in the city before he heads into parliament. I feel it would be best to break the news to him without Helen being present."

"Agreed. God speed, my friend," said Charles as he extended his arm.

"And to you both," William responded, shaking both of their hands, then walked toward his new bride.

William crawled into the carriage, kissed Helen and snapped the reigns, alerting the horse to begin the journey south. As the carriage continued down the road, Helen wrapped her arm around William's and laid her head on his shoulder. The future they had dreamed of for years had just begun and they could not have been happier.

THE NEXT MORNING, William rose early, got dressed and left the inn, but not before he kissed his new bride on the cheek, careful not to wake her. He made his way to the stable and paid the liveryman to ready his horse and carriage, then headed toward the streets of London. William knew his father had a penchant for kidney pie and stopped at the bakery near the parliament building each morning to indulge his fancy. So outside the bakery William waited.

Just as expected, William's father, Lord Hubert, arrived and ordered his morning pie, times two. He was feeling the need for solace and comfort after weeks of dealing with William's opposition to his upcoming union to Meredith Hampton, as well as his son's recent disappearance. With pies in hand, Lord Hubert turned back toward the door, spying William through the glass window. Quickly, he pushed his way through the morning crowd and left the bakery, looking in both directions for his son.

The waving of a hand caught his attention and he moved down the busy street, eventually ending up in an alleyway. There William stood, silently staring back at his father, unsure of how to break the news to him. He loved his father and didn't want to upset him, but his many attempts to break off the predetermined engagement to Meredith Hampton had fallen on deaf ears. William felt he had no other choice.

"William! Thank goodness you're all right. You've had your mother worried to death and so close to your wedding date."

"That's what I need to discuss with you, Father."

"Enough! You're a grown man, William, and it's time you take on the responsibilities of adulthood. You've been educated in both knowledge and culture and the time has come for you to take your place in society. This union between you and Miss Hampton will also mean the union of our two properties one day. She being the only child of her parents stands to inherit what small amount they possess, but according to the law she cannot inherit without a husband."

"Marriage should not be about obtaining more wealth and property. I am fond of Meredith and have been since we were children, but I am not in love with her."

"That will come in time."

"No, Father, it won't."

"Of course it will. That's how it works. That's what is expected."

"I see marriage differently than what society expects. Why get married in the hope that love will come, when the opposite brings a certainty of love?"

"Fanciful ideas placed in your mind through the examination of too many fictional works of literature."

"You're the one who had me educated, Father, and by its very nature, education brings advancement in thought and practice."

"Advancement is marrying within the proper class and station. Any fool can fall in love!"

"Then I count myself amongst the fools of this world, for I have fallen in love with Helen, Father."

"So you have told us over and over again, but none of that matters. For your own future and the sake of your family's name, you cannot marry a woman from a class so far beneath your own."

"It's too late, Father."

"What have you done, William?"

"Helen and I were wed yesterday in a small church, north of London, near her home. It was witnessed and I have the certification within my possession."

The two kidney pies immediately fell victim to the ground as Lord Hubert raised his hands to his head. Painfully, William watched as his father reacted to the news. The disappointment on his father's face was more difficult to watch than William had anticipated.

"I wanted so much for you and mother to be there, but…"

"Stop! You have said enough. Who else knows of this union?"

"The priest who married us and my two friends, Charles Mott and John Hughes. They have been sworn to secrecy until after we inform the Hamptons."

"You will speak of this to no one. You must allow me the time necessary to do what needs to be done."

"I had hoped to bring Helen home this evening to meet you and mother."

"Do as I say, William. You've already caused enough trouble. Where are you staying?"

"At an inn off the highway, just north of town."

"Go there and wait. I will send correspondence with a servant when it's safe for you to return home."

"I do not understand why this is necessary, Father."

"Just do as I tell you and wait for my word."

With that said, Lord Hubert turned abruptly and withdrew from the alleyway, leaving William standing alone with the weight of the situation resting heavily upon his shoulders. With his head down and his hands in his pockets, William made his way out of the alley and back onto the crowded streets of London. He knew Helen would wonder why they couldn't go to Forest Gate as he had promised.

She was so looking forward to meeting her new family and truly believed that everything would work out once they were wed. Helen was also very excited to see William's beautiful home. He had sketched her a drawing of Forest Gate Castle and she kept it tucked away inside the knitted drawstring bag which hung from her wrist. Although she knew the wedding was performed in secret, Helen had little idea of what was really going on behind the scenes. He had told her of his family's prearranged plans to marry Meredith Hampton, but not of how opposed his parents were to him marrying Helen. William wanted to spare her the difficult details, so he kept the majority of the truth hidden away inside himself. All at once, he remembered that Helen had mentioned wanting to give a gift to her new mother-in-law, in the hopes of a good first impression.

"That's it," he thought to himself.

William realized he could buy himself some more time if he took her shopping that afternoon and used the outing as an excuse to delay their arrival at Forest Gate. With his head no longer drooping with discouragement, he found a new spring in his step as he continued through the crowd. Things were back on track and he truly believed it wouldn't be long until he received word from his father to bring his new bride home.

Arriving back at the inn, he found Helen dressed and ready for travel. William told her of his plans to spend time in the shops of London before heading home, and although she shared her concerns with her husband, she agreed to his plan. After all, this was her husband's world and she was merely a visitor to the way the people of his station spend their days.

Not only had she left her cousin's small home and village, but she had left a life of working in the same type of shops that she would now be touring on the arm of her husband. However strange it may seem at first, Helen knew she would adjust and learn to fill the role and responsibilities she had accepted by marrying William.

After eating a lovely mid-morning brunch in the dining room, they embarked on their carriage ride into London. William enjoyed playing tour guide as he pointed out the different landmarks, sites and buildings to Helen as they traveled to the West End, where they would find the fashionable shops of the day. Helen had never seen anything so magnificent in size and commotion. She remained in awe of the large buildings, crowds of people and the traffic of horse-drawn carriages. In all her youth, she never dreamed she would see such a sight as London.

Finally reaching their destination, William parked the carriage and left the horse in the charge of a man paid to care for him. As they strolled down the streets together, William watched Helen's innocent enthusiasm as each new window display brought a new curiosity. To William, who had visited the West End shopping district more times than he cared to remember, it was a treat to see it through new eyes. As they approached a jewelers shop, Helen turned to enter in the hopes she would find a beautiful trinket for her mother-in-law at an affordable price. Looking across the street, William noticed a tobacco shop and thought of his father.

"Why don't you have a look around while I survey the tobacco shop for my father?"

Helen agreed and entered the shop as William crossed the street. Time passed and William finally found and purchased the perfect tobacco for his father. As he was exiting the store, he couldn't help but see the commotion being generated near the jeweler's shop. As he started to cross the street, he was nearly run down by the fast approach of a horse-drawn jail wagon which stopped in front of the jeweler's shop. As he rounded the front of the horses, he saw two policemen haul Helen by the arms toward the jail wagon.

"Stop! Where are you taking my wife?"

"William!" Helen cried out, as she tried in vain to release herself and run to her husband's safe arms.

"What do you think you're doing? Take your hands off of her at once!"

Two policeman grabbed William to restrain him as the other two loaded Helen into the back of the wagon and locked the iron-barred door.

"Unhand me! My father is a Baron who rules in the House of Lords. He will hear of this!"

The policemen released William and he immediately grabbed onto the bars of the jail wagon. As she wrapped her hands around her husband's, he could see the fear in her eyes yet was helpless to save her.

"I don't understand what's happening," desperately enquired William.

"They found a brooch in my purse, William."

"Yah!" With the yell of the policeman, the horses began to quickly pull away as William ran behind, unwilling to let go.

"Help me, William. Don't let them take me!"

"I will come for you, Helen!" With that said, the speed of the carriage no longer made it possible for William to hang on to the bars. Falling away, he dropped to his knees, watching Helen stretch her arm toward him as the wagon disappeared around the corner. William quickly got off the ground and began running toward Scotland Yard.

Once he reached the jailing facility, he found the huge crowd of people waiting to see their loved ones to be overwhelming. William had never experienced this side of London and was shocked that the policemen in charge would not let him see his wife.

Realizing he could do nothing more, he made his way to parliament, arriving just in time to meet his father exiting the building. Shocked by the news, Lord Hubert immediately summoned his carriage and together he and his son traveled to Scotland Yard. Lord Hubert's appearance made a difference in the tone of the policeman in charge, but they were still not allowed into the jail due to the great overcrowding.

They were informed that she would be brought in front of a magistrate in the morning and they would be able to see her then. Unsatisfied with the conclusion, William continued with his plea but to no end. His father pulled him from the jail and discreetly forced him out of the building.

"Listen to me, William. Things work a certain way and we must respect the process!"

"That's my wife in there, Father!"

"We'll find out more in the morning and I'll do whatever I can to help," Lord Hubert assured him, "now come home tonight and get some rest."

"How can I rest, knowing the circumstances and the danger that Helen faces?"

"Is your plan to sleep on the street tonight?"

"I have no plan," responded William in frustration as he turned and stepped away from his father.

"How can one day bring the greatest of joy, then be followed by such tragedy?"

"I must ask, William... Is she innocent?"

"Of course she is! How can you ask such a thing?"

"Did she tell you of her innocence?"

"There wasn't time before they hauled her away like a common criminal."

"Let's return to the jeweler's shop and enquire as to what happened."

"Yes, Father. That's a brilliant idea," William said excitedly as he hurried toward the carriage.

Not nearly as hopeful, Lord Hubert crawled into the carriage and instructed the driver to take them back to the scene of the crime.

THEY REACHED the shop just as the jeweler locked the door and turned his sign to the 'closed' position. Lord Hubert stopped William's abrupt exit with his arm and got out before him, approaching the jeweler with an air of authority. "I am Lord Hubert Jones of the House of Lords and I've come to elicit the facts of the alleged theft which occurred earlier. What have you to say?"

William watched from the carriage as his father did what he does best, deal with the law.

"Lord Hubert, sir, I don't know all the facts, but I will give you an account as I know it. I was helping a customer with a purchase when a man came near and privately told me that he had seen the woman in question place a brooch in her purse. I immediately approached the woman and asked to see the contents of her purse."

"Did she open her purse to you?"

"Yes, and with no argument," replied the jeweler.

"She did not contest your petition in any way?"

"Not all, sir. She was perfectly amiable to my request."

"Go on then."

"She removed the purse from her arm and opened the drawstrings. We laid it on the counter and removed the items, one by one."

"And the brooch in question?"

"It was there, sir, for all present to see. Just as the man had said."

"That's a lie! There was no reason for Helen to steal that brooch when we have more than enough to pay."

Lord Hubert quickly held up his hand, silencing his son until he could finish the questioning of the shop owner.

"And was it at this point you alerted the police?"

"It was not I who alerted the bobbies. The man, who claimed to have seen her place the brooch in her purse, ran from the shop as soon as the item in question was revealed. The policemen must have been nearby, for their arrival was very quick indeed."

Unable to remain in the carriage for a moment longer, William leaped to the ground and approached his father from behind. "Father, tell me you don't believe this man."

Lord Hubert turned to William in order to silence him as well as reassure his son. "I have no reason not to believe him, but the circumstances do seem curious."

"Is that all, sir? It's been a long day and I do hate to be late for supper," asked the shop owner.

"That will be all. If I have more questions, I know where to find you."

"That you do, sir."

The jeweler began to walk down the street but stopped and turned back to Lord Hubert and William. "In my business I've encountered many thieves and desperate people willing to do desperate things, but this woman was not like them. I wish the end result had been different."

"With any luck, the magistrate will uncover the truth."

"Then I bid you a good day, sir."

William and his father watched the jeweler walk away as they pondered their next move. Lord Hubert crawled back into the carriage and expected the same of William, but William remained on the street.

"There is no more to be done today. Get in the carriage, William."

"My carriage is parked just down the way. I will pick it up, then go collect our belongings from the inn."

"Will your mother and I see you at Forest Gate tonight?"

"The thought of leaving Helen by herself in London does not set well with me."

"If we don't see you at home tonight, I shall see you at court in the morning, bright and early. Drive on!"

William watched his father's carriage pull back into the street and disappear around the corner. He turned and walked down the now much emptier sidewalk until he reached the location of his carriage. He paid the man then crawled into the carriage, took the reins and headed out of town.

Chapter Fifteen

William let go of their hands, walked back toward the window and looked out at the ground below. Heath and Rome opened their eyes and stared speechless at each other, trying to adjust to the present. "That was intense," Heath whispered to Rome.

"To say the least," Rome concurred, then turned her attention to William. "Are you all right?"

"The rest is too painful," said William. Without warning he disappeared from the room.

Heath, still holding onto Rome's hand, sat down on the bed, encouraging her to join him. "I need to know more, Rome."

"I feel the same way, but there's nothing we can do but wait until he's ready."

"You could ask me."

Startled, both Heath and Rome jumped from the bed as Helen appeared a few feet in front of them. "I hope you'll forgive me, but I heard William's voice from the hallway and I couldn't pull myself away. I apologize for eavesdropping."

"No, please, make yourself comfortable... if spirits even do that," said Heath nervously.

"After our last conversation, I remembered where I'd seen this castle before. William had sketched a picture of it one summer. I kept it with me all the time. He was a wonderful artist, but few people knew that. No one knew William like I did and he would say the same of me."

"You said that we could ask you," Rome enquired, "do you remember what happened next?"

"I'll never forget it. The wagon arrived at the jail before I even had time to fully comprehend what was happening. They unloaded me into an over-crowded cell of women, many of whom had been there for days and others for weeks. Hundreds of women filled the cells lining the two walls. Most were just as scared as I was, while others seemed resigned to the situation, almost as though it were expected. The cell I was put in was so full that you didn't dare seek rest on the floor for fear of being trampled."

"What a terrible thing to have gone through," Rome said sympathetically.

"Growing up in the country, it was like nothing I had ever seen, but then hope came in the form of an announcement. A man walked through the door and climbed a set of stairs so all could see and hear him. He told us that the magistrates had decided to hold an impromptu court session that evening, due to the overcrowding of the jail. Some cheered and some wept.

Still in shock, I didn't know how to react, but I was certain my husband would be there and he would explain everything to the judge. In my naivety, I truly believed I would once again be spending the night in William's arms.

They began calling out the names of the women who had been incarcerated the longest. I found it strange that once they left, they never returned. I waited patiently, hour after hour, for my name to be called. Finally, when I was the only one left in the cell, the jail keeper entered and called my name. I was led out of the building and across the courtyard. As I entered the room, I looked around but saw no visitors, not even my William. I began to grow nervous as I was brought to stand before the bench, wondering why my husband was not present and who would argue my innocence.

My name and the description of my alleged crime, as well as the testimony of the man who accused me, were read for the court to hear and record. The three magistrates sitting on the bench gathered their heads together and discussed my verdict. Before I could speak for myself, the magistrate chairman's gavel struck the wood beneath it and I was pronounced guilty. The sentencing immediately followed: seven years to be served in the Australian Colony of New South Wales. I had no idea where that was or what those words even meant. Dazed and confused, I couldn't find the strength to fight back or even argue for myself as my hands were immediately placed in chains.

I only had one question going through my mind as they escorted me out the back door and loaded me into the crowded jail wagon: why hadn't my husband come to my aid?

As the wagon traveled through the dark streets of London, I wondered how long the wagon ride would be till we reached this New South Wales. You can only imagine my shock when we arrived at the harbor. Dawn was beginning to break and I heard a man yell to another that the ship was due to set sail within a few hours' time. The women from our wagon were lined up, waiting for the men who were taking supplies aboard the ship to clear the gangplank.

Several of the women tried to escape, but they didn't make it far and were severely beaten as punishment. Once the gangplank was empty, they marched us up the ramp toward the ship. Looking up, I saw a woman leap over the side of the ship's railing and into the dark water below. I never heard if they found her.

Once aboard we were chained to the railing in order to keep us out of the way of the sailors who were continuing to load the ship with supplies. It wasn't long until the shock disappeared, and the reality of my situation opened the flood gates to my emotions. The tears poured uncontrollably as I stared at the docks below, hoping against hope that William would still come to my rescue.

At daybreak, the dock below began to fill with family members who had received word of the trial and sentencing. Some were angry and fought with the policemen, while others proclaimed their love and their plans to join them in the new colony. Still, there was no sign of my William.

Soon, the gangplank was removed and the large ropes holding the ship to the dock were untied. Next came the sound of the first mate's voice, alerting everyone that the ship was ready to set sail for the Australian Colony.

Just as the men began pushing the ship away from the dock, I saw what I had almost given up hope in seeing: my husband, fighting his way through the crowd. I remember screaming his name at the top of my lungs as he ran toward the end of the dock, calling my name. My heart was pumping so strongly that I thought at any moment it would leap from my chest. William had come for me. He had come to my rescue!"

Helen began yelling William's name as though she was reliving it, shocking Rome and Heath who were waiting in suspense to find out what happened next. Tears streamed down Rome's cheeks as she observed the agony on Helen's face and heard the pain in her voice. After a brief pause, Helen collected herself and continued with the story.

"At that moment, I truly believed William had every intent of jumping into the harbor, swimming toward the ship and joining me aboard. But before he could reach the dock's edge, several policemen stopped him in his tracks.

As the ship pushed away and the distance between us grew, I watched as he fought with the policemen. A riot ensued and I saw William take hold of a knife left lying on a crate nearby and use it to strike one of the policemen. Enraged by the attack, several other policemen violently subdued William to the ground. That was the last I ever saw of my husband. I sent letters but never received a response."

Rome sat quietly, pondering Helen and William's tragic story, while Heath insisted on keeping the story going before Helen disappeared.

"How long did it take the ship to travel to Australia?"

"Eight months."

"That must have been miserable."

"It was even worse when I realized my seasickness was actually due to pregnancy."

Instinctively, Rome stood up, let go of Heath's hand and walked toward Helen. Although Rome had never been married or pregnant, she knew how to be a friend and was undaunted in her response to Helen's heartbreak.

No longer able to see or listen to Helen's part of the conversation, Heath was satisfied to let them share in the more personal part of the story. Proudly, he watched Rome show great compassion toward Helen, proving she was more like her mother than she thought.

As Rome approached Helen, she took hold of her hands and consoled her as best she could. "I can't imagine going through what you had been through, only to find out that you were pregnant."

Helen smiled at Rome, thanking her for her kindness, then continued with the story. "Needless to say, the motion of a ship at sea was not conducive to the sickness that accompanied my pregnancy. For the first four months, I spent more time leaning over the side of the ship than anywhere else. Fortunately, there was a midwife traveling with the crew and she took me under her wing. She was a free woman paid to travel to the Australian Colony to deliver babies in the female prison factories."

"Why would they need a midwife in the female prisons?" asked Rome out of curiosity.

"Because of the overcrowding, many of the female convicts who worked in the factories had to..."

Helen paused as she realized she was speaking in the third person instead of the first. "I'm speaking as though I weren't one of them, but I was."

"Go on, Helen," encouraged Rome, "show me why."

"Due to the overcrowding, many of us had to find our own accommodations. With no money to pay for their housing, many women were forced to engage in prostitution in order to afford their rent. Thanks to the midwife from the ship, I had the rare good fortune of finding refuge in the laundry room of a boarding house. The midwife was a tenant there and used her connections to get my son and I the room. I earned our rent by washing and hanging the boarders' bedding, clothing and towels. I spent the rest of the day in the prison workhouse. For seven years, that was my routine, until my sentence expired and I was made free of the factory."

Opening her eyes, Rome realized that Heath was missing out on the story. She let go of Helen's hands, walked to the bed and again took hold of Heath's.

"Did you ever remarry, Helen?" asked Rome.

"The governing body favored marriage between the male and female convicts and even encouraged it. Marriage produced families, which was a good way to further populate the Australian Colony. I was approached many times by men who wished to take me as their wife, but I only had enough room left in my broken heart for my son and the memories of William. I continued with my job at the boarding house until my death in 1860."

"You died so young," replied Rome as she quickly added the years in her mind.

"I was thirty-eight, but the years and the heartbreak had taken their toll. A cold set in one winter and I had not the strength to recover. It progressed into pneumonia, which quickly led to my death. My son had secured employment with a small shipping company and was away at sea when I passed away. We never got to say goodbye. Throughout his lifetime, however, I had the opportunity to peek in on him. He became a partner in a small shipping company and eventually went on to be the sole owner after the death of his partner. He met a wonderful Australian girl and together they had a beautiful family. As a mother, I could not have been more proud or more pleased. I only wished my husband could have seen what I saw."

"William certainly has a lot of catching up to do and hopefully we can help him with that," said Rome, in an attempt to cheer up Helen.

Rome had allowed herself to be drawn into their story as well as their lives beyond the grave. Heath had started something big, but Rome was the only one who could finish it. Now that she knew the story behind their tragic love affair, she truly believed that closure was possible—that was until she heard Helen's final words. "I've given up hope of ever seeing or being with William again. He has made his choice and we must both live with that forever."

Again, without warning, Helen quickly disappeared before Rome had a chance to respond to her statement.

"And I thought human relationships were complicated," Heath observed.

"I'm not giving up on those two," replied Rome as she let go of Heath's hand and began pacing the floor. "Clearly, they're soulmates."

"Clearly?" Heath responded, intrigued by Rome's observation.

"Can't you see it? It probably started long before they ever met."

"How is that possible?"

"As spirits before they were even born."

"You believe life doesn't just begin at birth?"

"Our physical lives do, but we lived as spirits for eons before that."

"And what makes you think that?"

"I learned it several years ago from a monk, or I should say, the spirit of a monk, while I was in Bhutan writing a feature article on dzongs."

"What?"

"Dzongs. Religious fortresses that were built centuries ago in Tibet and Bhutan. They were built on cliffs and hilltops and also used for military purposes."

"I know what a dzong is; I'm more interested in what the monk's spirit told you."

"I was hiking up a steep mountain with a monk as my guide..."

"Real monk or spirit monk?"

"Real monk."

"Just trying to keep up."

"We were on our way to a dzong called Paro Taktsang, otherwise known as the Tiger's Nest. The hike up was challenging yet beautiful and my guide taught me a great deal as we climbed. We reached the dzong outside of visitor hours, but because of my guide's connections, I was allowed a tour of the monastery, as well as the opportunity to spend some time in meditation. It was during my meditation that I listened to the spirit of a monk who nearly two centuries earlier had spent his life in service at the Tiger's Nest. He spoke briefly of how quickly the memories of his life prior to being born came rushing back to him after death. That information expanded my view and gave me new insight into my own mortal life."

"So let me get this straight. You think Helen and William had a connection before they were born?" asked Heath inquisitively.

"It's just a theory."

"Did this spirit teach you about soulmates as well?"

"No. That's my observation based on my own personal definition of what a soulmate is."

"And that would be?"

"You know. Someone you feel like you've known forever. A person who understands you and that you understand right back."

"I don't believe everyone has a soulmate. The idea that there is only one person on earth that's meant for you seems pretty limited," Heath argued. "I think most people are just looking for a companionship that works," said Heath.

"Two lives that fit well together," responded Rome.

"Like you and your secret agent boyfriend."

"Why did I ever tell you about him?"

"Is he your soulmate?"

"Not according to my own definition, but that's really none of your business."

"But it does give me hope, if I actually believed in soulmates, that is."

"May I ask you a personal question?"

"Depends on how personal."

"Why didn't your father ever remarry after your mother passed away?"

Feeling uncomfortable, Heath got up and walked toward the window before responding. "He was a busy man."

"No doubt. He had a son to raise and a billion-dollar company to run, but that's not the real answer, is it?"

Heath waited for a moment, trying to find the courage he needed to open himself up to Rome, then turned back to answer the question. "Not long after I returned from college, I started seeing a woman. After about six months she began talking marriage, but I kept dragging my feet."

"Why?"

"That's what I couldn't figure out. She was beautiful, well educated and we shared a lot of the same interests. I enjoyed spending time with her, but I didn't feel the same way about her that she did for me. I couldn't figure out why."

"So?"

"My dad and I were out sailing and I asked him for some advice."

"And?"

"He told me why he never remarried after my mom died. I mean, it's not like he didn't have plenty of opportunities. He was one of the world's most sought-after bachelors. He told me that he could never imagine being able to love someone as powerfully as he loved my mother and that someday I would understand what that type of love felt like."

"So what happened with the woman you were dating?"

"We ended it the next weekend. I've never come that close to a serious relationship since."

"No time to meet anyone?"

"I may have used work as an excuse a time or two."

"A time or two? It's been a few years since you returned from Oxford."

A knock on the door brought their conversation to an end. Rome opened the door and Mr. Burns enquired after them. "When would you like dinner to be served?"

"I don't know about Heath, but I could eat anytime."

"No surprise there," said Heath jokingly, passing by Rome on his way to the door. Rome playfully slugged him in the upper arm as she responded to his cheeky comment. "That's what happens when you put me to work all day."

"Like that makes a difference," said Heath, rubbing the top of his arm.

"You're just jealous because I have an exceptionally high metabolism," Rome rebutted as she followed Heath out of the room.

Mr. Burns rolled his eyes as he closed the door, muttering to himself. "Just get on with it, you two."

Chapter Sixteen

The next morning Rome woke early, feeling completely rested after a relaxing bath that prepared her for a long night's sleep. She quickly got dressed, brushed her teeth and proceeded to put her hair up in a clip, but stopped. Looking in the mirror, she made the bold decision to leave it down, unrestrained. There was a bounce in her step as she left the bedroom and walked down the hallway toward William's old room. Getting no response to her quiet knocking, she cracked open the door and looked inside. Lying in bed, with an open book containing the works of Shakespeare next to him, Heath appeared to still be asleep. Rome mischievously tiptoed across the dark room to the window near the bed and quickly threw open the curtains, allowing the rising sun to shine directly on Heath's face.

"Ah! Close the curtains, Sheldon."

"So much for being an early riser. It's Saturday and I have big plans for us today. Let's go! Rise and shine! Get the move on! Up and at 'em!"

Unexpectedly, Heath reached over, grabbed her around the waist, flipped her over top of him and landed her on the other side of the bed.

Completely shocked by Heath's move, Rome lay speechless as Heath stared down at her. "What plans could be so important to wake me at 6:00 on a Saturday morning?"

"Plans?" muttered Rome, forgetting why she even came into the room.

"That was the word you used."

"That's right. I had a plan."

"Had?"

Heath moved his head toward Rome, causing her to think he was about to kiss her, but at the last moment, he moved to the side of her head and lowered his face down to her shoulder, taking in the smell of her neck.

"What is that?"

"What is what?"

"That smell."

Rome turned her face toward her shoulder and took a whiff.

"Moonlight Lavender and Chamomile."

"Perfume?"

"Aromatherapy."

"Lotion?"

"Essential oils."

"Essential for what?"

"For the bath, I guess. It's supposed to relax you."

"Did it work?"

"It did last night."

"I haven't smelled that on you before."

"Someone left it by the tub yesterday."

"Sheldon."

"For a butler, he does have good taste."

"May I say that you smell amazing."

"Thank you."

"I'm sorry. I interrupted you."

"You did?"

"You were going to tell me your plans."

"My plans?"

"For today."

"Oh, those plans."

"Have they changed?"

"Why would they change?"

"Plans can change."

"Can they?"

"You're the planner. You tell me."

Rome knew he was talking about more than just changing her plans for the day, but she couldn't form the words to disagree. She wanted to argue her point, but lying in the warmth of his embrace, she found herself too impaired to move, let alone think straight. Suddenly, her cell phone began to ring. "Saved by the bell," she thought. That was until Heath decided to reach around her waist, pull her phone out of her back pocket and read the name 'Jamie' on the screen. "Your secret agent is calling. Shall I answer?"

Rome grabbed the phone from Heath, letting it go to voicemail then pushed him aside. She sat up on the other side of the bed and took a few seconds to breathe in the good air and let out the bad. Once calm, he stood up and attempted to start over as though nothing had happened. "So back to the plan. I thought we could get an early start on visiting the remaining convict sites here in Tasmania. You up for it?"

Heath stared at her in disbelief, then rolled to the opposite side of the bed and sat up with his back to Rome. "Wouldn't miss it."

"I'll see if Gladys can throw some leftovers in a basket and we can eat along the way."

"Whatever you want."

"I'll see you downstairs."

Rome walked back to the door but couldn't help noticing Heath's defeated posture. "I think it will do us good to get out of the castle."

"Whatever you think, Rome."

Rome turned and walked out, shutting the door behind her. She'd never felt what she was feeling for Heath and it scared her. Getting lost in him and his world was not an option. She had a life she loved awaiting her at home and returning to that life was her number one objective. All she had to do was reunite William and

Helen, as well as research a couple more convict sites, and her work in Tasmania would be complete. Feeling resolute, she continued to plan as she walked down the hallway.

Heath, on the other hand, stood up and stared out the window at the new day. In many ways he dreaded it. In other ways he longed for it. Spending time with Rome was everything he wanted, but her rejection of him was beginning to take a toll. Sunday afternoon was fast approaching and there was a real possibility that once he flew to Sydney, he would never see her again. He either had to close the deal or let it die. As businesslike as that sounded, it was the reality of the situation and Heath knew it.

The day went just as Rome had planned. She was a pro at logistics, which caused the events to play out flawlessly. They began by heading into the city, and after a quick stop at a pastry shop, they hit the road north for the approximate two-hour drive to the Brickendon and Woolmers Estates. They arrived just as they opened and were able to take the first tour of the day. It was enjoyable to visit the estates and learn of the history of how the convicts were used as farm labor on these two beautiful farms. From what Rome had seen and heard, places like these would have been far superior to a prison like Port Arthur.

Upon returning to Hobart, they drove to the Cascade Female Factory Historic Site in South Hobart. There they learned the history of a prison where thousands of women, along with their children, were taken in order to be reformed. The stories were heart wrenching as many died working within the walls of the prison, never to know freedom again.

With time quickly ticking away, they ate their picnic lunch as they drove down the Tasman Peninsula to Triabunna, then caught the ferry out to Maria Island and toured what was left of the Darlington Probation Center. Rome was surprised to see so many of the buildings still intact. She had sent her camera with Bev, so the pictures she was taking with her phone would have to suffice.

Arriving back on the Tasman Peninsula, they had only one more stop to make: The Coal Mines Historic Site. The sun was setting just as they arrived, so Rome only had a short window of time to snap some decent photos. Using the flashlight option on their cell phones, they took an evening tour of the unmanned facility. Heath's phone ran out of battery life before they completed the tour and Rome was down to a very small percentage. Once finished, they walked to the end of the grounds overlooking the ocean and collapsed on the grass as the darkness of night replaced the day. Staring up at the stars, there was no other place Heath would rather have been than lying beside Rome at the end of a pretty remarkable day. "You truly are a force to be reckoned with," he said out of pure admiration. "No one else could have accomplished what we did today."

"I wasn't a hundred percent sure we could do it, but thanks to you and your highly impressive driving skills, we made it."

"After about fifty different traffic violations."

"Sometimes extreme circumstances call for extreme measures."

"I doubt any policeman would agree that a magazine deadline is an extreme circumstance."

"They've never met my editor, Angelica Fontaine. Thank you, Heath. Today was definitely above and beyond the call of duty."

"Just another example of how good of a team we make," responded Heath after rolling onto his side to face Rome.

"To that point, I cannot disagree."

"But that's not enough, is it? You're not going to give, are you, Rome?"

"We've had an amazing time together, but that's all it is, a window in time that will eventually close when we both go back to our normal lives."

"Most windows are not designed to remain closed," countered Heath.

"It's only been six days, Heath. Six days. I've been dating the same guy for two years. That should tell you something."

"It speaks volumes. You demand honesty from me, yet you refuse to be honest with yourself." With that said, he got up and walked back to the Land Rover, leaving Rome to ponder what his words.

Block by Block

HEATH TOOK his time driving back up the Peninsula toward Hobart and eventually to Forest Gate. He had spent the entire day driving like a mad man to get Rome to each of her destinations, so the slower pace was a relief.

Believing there was nothing left to say, Rome closed her eyes and pretended to rest as Heath chauffeured her back to the castle. After only a few short days, Rome had begun to feel as though Forest Gate were her home.

How could she feel just as at home in an enormous castle as she did in her own Upper West Side apartment back home? She didn't feel this comfortable in her boyfriend's weekender house back in New York and they'd been dating for two years. More thoughts and feelings for Rome to contend with as they traveled down a quiet Tasmanian highway in the middle of the night.

It was late when Heath pulled into his driveway, finding the gate already open.

"That's strange," said Heath as he drove through the open gate and made his way up to the front door of the castle. Rome sat up in curiosity after hearing Heath's observation.

"Is everything all right?"

"Sheldon probably anticipated my arrival and left the gate open," responded Heath as he stopped the vehicle and parked it for the night.

"Thanks again for today. I could not have done it without you," said Rome in all sincerity.

"I'm glad it worked out."

Heath got out of the vehicle and walked around to Rome's side to open her door. Uncertain of what time it was, Rome checked her phone but found the battery to be dead. Too much GPS and flashlight use. As she got out of the car and walked toward the entrance, she couldn't help but remark as to how hungry she felt. "I'm hoping there are some leftovers in the kitchen, because I'm starved."

"Count me in. I could use a late night snack."

Heath opened the back door, pulled out the picnic basket and followed her into the house. Once inside the grand hall, they noticed something was wrong. All of the artwork from the walls and the decor was missing. Heath quietly put down the basket and whispered to Rome. "Go back to the car, drive to the street and call the police with your mobile."

"My phone's dead."

"And I'm pretty sure we don't have a land line installed yet, which means we have no access to a phone. I need to find Sheldon. Take the car down to the street anyway, so you'll be safe."

"I'm not leaving you here by yourself."

"I'll be fine."

"If Justice Hampton and his goon squad have returned, you'll need my help."

"You're right. I was thinking burglars, but it's more likely ghosts."

"We should probably plan for anything."

"Stay behind me," said Heath as he walked toward the kitchen in the back of the castle. Rome followed closely, picking up a long handled umbrella along the way.

As they moved from room to room, they noticed more items were missing along the way. Listening closely, they heard voices coming from the servants' entrance in the back.

"Do you hear that, Heath?" whispered Rome.

"Yes."

"Then it's definitely not ghosts."

"Correct," spoke a low, raspy voice from behind.

Rome and Heath froze in their tracks unsure of what to do.

"Drop the umbrella and keep moving," ordered the voice.

Rome leaned the umbrella against the wall then instantly felt the comfort of Heath's hand take hold of hers. Together they continued down the hallway toward the other voices.

Once inside the servants' entranceway, they saw Sheldon, Miss Lemmons, George and Gladys the cook, all tied to the chairs they were occupying. Even more shocking was the sight of Max lying on the floor near their feet. Heath immediately squatted down to make sure he was still alive. Feeling the pulse in his neck, he was relieved to find he was only unconscious.

"I'm afraid this is the result of a bad hire on my part, sir," Sheldon exclaimed.

"Shut up, butler," said a man holding a gun as he struck him across the face with the back of his hand.

"Don't you touch him!" warned Heath as he lunged toward the man who hit his friend.

Before he could reach him, he was abusively restrained by two of the other gunmen and knocked to the floor by the butt of one of their weapons. Just then, a man entered through the outside door, oblivious to the fact that anything had gone wrong. "I got the last of it in the truck." Seeing the presence of Rome and Heath, he began to grow nervous. "We better get out of here, while we still can."

"It's thanks to you, idiot, that we have witnesses."

"Without me working here you never would have known the code to the gate."

"Let me guess, plumbing?" asked Rome, assuming he was the dimwitted husband of Bev's cousin.

"How do you know that?" responded the dimwit.

"I'll make sure to give Beverly your regards," replied Rome as she watched a look of horror come over his face.

"Shut up, already!" said the boss, hoping to end the conversation. But he didn't know Rome London.

"Do you seriously think you're going to get away with this?"

"Who's going to stop us, lady? The only question left is whether or not we end you here or take you somewhere else to finish the job."

"This was just supposed to be a robbery. You said no one would get hurt!" anxiously responded the dimwit.

"You should have checked our resumé better before you signed on."

To the shock of everyone, a gun fired and the dimwit dropped to the ground, his once life-giving blood creating a puddle around his head.

"His time was short lived anyway. He just didn't know it. Who's next?"

"Wait! Release us and I'll give you more money than anything you've taken is worth."

"Have you ever heard of identity theft?"

"Of course."

"My IT guy in the truck already has your laptop and all the personal and account information he needs to hack into your life. We'll have you drained of every dollar before anyone even finds your bodies."

Thinking there were no other options, Heath looked up at Rome apologetically for not being able to save her from harm. As their eyes met, however, he found himself surprised by Rome's response: a simple wink.

Without a second thought, Rome turned and knocked the gun from the hands of the raspy-voiced man behind her. As she continued to attack with some pretty impressive fighting skills, Heath leaped from the floor, taking down the two men near him as their attention was diverted to Rome.

Sheldon and the others stood up and tried to fight, while still being tied to their chairs, turning the room into a hotbed of chaos. A semi-automatic rifle began shooting at the ceiling, causing everyone to stop and cower.

"Enough!" yelled the man, as he lowered his rifle, taking aim at Heath's staff in the chairs. George quickly positioned himself between the gunman and Miss Lemmons as the shooter placed his forefinger on the trigger.

"No!" screamed Heath and Rome in unison.

Much to everyone's surprise, the man's rifle was yanked from his hands and tossed out the open door. William had arrived just in time and no one else could see him but Rome.

A fight ensued, but this time they had a ghost named William on their side. As Rome continued to fight, she noticed Lady Jones out of the corner of her eye, untying the ropes holding the staff on the far side of the room. Her attention quickly returned to the fight at

Block by Block

hand, delivering a series of kicks and punches until a cast iron skillet struck her opponent on the back of the head.

William lowered the skillet and tilted his head to Rome, denoting how impressed he was with her fighting skills.

"Oh, I'm just getting started!"

She put out her hand and he handed her the skillet. "Would you mind stopping the man in the truck from getting away?" asked Rome of William.

"I have centuries of anger to unleash. It would be my pleasure," William responded, then instantly disappeared.

Rome rushed to Heath's aid as he continued to take on the two robbers. A skillet to the side of the head ended the fighting of one of his opponents, leaving the other one in Heath's capable hands. From there she moved to the aid of Mr. Burns and the rest of the staff, noticing along the way that Lady Jones had taken an interest in Mr. Snavely's condition. Kneeling on the floor next to him, she gently patted his face in an attempt to wake him from his unconscious state. Briefly opening his eyes to the chaos around him, the chauffeur responded to the fighting in true Maximillian fashion. "This is one crazy party," he said, then slipped back into his incognizant state.

Rome's attention quickly returned to the fight as she saw a thief pick up his gun from the floor and aim it at Mr. Burns. Rome grabbed a wooden chair and without hesitation nailed the thief across the back of the head and shoulders, busting the chair to pieces.

"That was an antique, Ms. London!" cried Mr. Burns, "But thank you all the same." Then he quickly ran to the aid of Miss Lemmons, Gladys and George, who were busy fighting off their own bad guy, a large man with a whole lot of muscle.

Next, Rome glanced at the floor seeing a loose gun being kicked around unintentionally. Just as she was about to dive for the gun, the boss pushed her aside, knocking her against the wall. With great pleasure he reached down, picked up the gun and pressed it against her forehead. "You should have stayed away, rich girl."

Like a bull running toward a red piece of cloth, Heath intercepted the head thief and slammed him backwards to the floor. Rome quickly jumped on top of them both and fought to get the gun from the bad guy's hand as Heath struggled to keep him down. Standing up, gun in hand, Rome aimed it at the boss. "Now who's the one that should have stayed away?"

Heath grabbed a piece of the rope that was used to restrain the staff and tied the head thief's hands behind his back, then slowly crawled to his feet. On the other side of the room, most of the burglars lay on the floor, either unconscious or held down by the staff as Mr. Burns worked to tie their hands as well.

"We've taken back the castle," yelled Heath as the adrenaline continued to pump. The rest of the staff cheered in response as they basked in the glory of their underdog victory as Heath turned his attention back to Rome. "Where did you learn to do that?"

"Do what?"

"Go all 'Rocky Balboa' on the bad guys."

"My dad boxed in the Navy. He hated the idea of leaving his wife and teenage daughter unprotected when he was at sea, so he taught me a lot of moves when he was home. We used to spar at the naval base gym all the time, then after college, when I began my career as a travel writer, Dad insisted I take some self-defense classes. Later I got into kickboxing as a form of exercise and I've been doing it ever since."

"It probably doesn't hurt dating a secret agent either."

"Enough with the secret agent shtick. It's not that funny anymore."

"I'm pretty sure it's still got some mileage," Heath said with a cheeky smile, then turned to address everyone else in the room. "Does anyone have a mobile I can borrow?"

Just then a phone began to ring, causing everyone to search for the source. Heath knelt down to Max's unconscious body and not-so-gently rolled him over. His lack of gentleness didn't fare well with Lady Jones, so she reached out and popped him in on the forehead. Heath reacted to the slap by springing sideways and rubbing his forehead with his fingers. He looked to Rome for answers, but all he got was advice in return. "Don't be so rough with Max. He's out cold, not dead. You should probably apologize."

Heath leaned down toward Mr. Snavely's ear and told him that he was sorry as he reached into the inside pocket of his chauffeur's suit jacket and answered his phone. "Max will have to call you back." Then he disconnected the call and walked out of the room, dialing the police emergency number on his way.

Max reached up and touched the back of his sore head as he slowly began to regain consciousness and sit up. Pushing himself back toward the wall, he leaned up against Lady Jones and closed his eyes to rest. Lady Jones placed a finger on either side of his head and began massaging his temples.

Next, Rome noticed Mr. Burns carefully examining the faces of each of the thieves and wanted to know why. "Are you looking for something, Mr. Burns?"

"Two days ago, I caught one of the movers in the electrical room. The same room which houses the main control to the security system, but none of these men look like him."

"Why would someone be in the electrical room?"

"A good question, Ms. London. One I do not have an answer for, yet."

Heath re-entered the room and approached Rome, suddenly remembering the identity thief. "The guy in the truck!"

"He may be the one," said Mr. Burns as he ran for the door.

Heath started to follow but was stopped immediately by Rome, who whispered in his ear, "William took care of him," then she took hold of his hand and led him across the room.

Prepared to do battle, Mr. Burns was surprised to find the man's hands tied to the steering wheel of the truck. He didn't recognize him as the mover from the electrical room, so he left him behind and re-entered the house. Excited to report his discovery, he looked about the large room for Heath and Rome, finding them engaged in what appeared to be a conversation with the wall. Curiously, he observed their strange behavior, slightly bothered by the fact that he wasn't privy to the secret they were hiding.

Sheldon was not used to being kept out of the loop when it

came to Heath's life. He'd been his confidant for far too long, but the arrival of Rome had moved him to the rear. He knew this day would come but did not expect to feel the sting of loss so profoundly. Although he hoped Heath's current path would lead to a happy ending, his gut was speaking a different language. At this point, all he could do was watch and wait, a feat much easier said than done.

After thanking William for his help during the fight, Heath had more questions. "Why did you come back, William?"

"I don't rightly know," he responded, confused by his mixed emotions, "I feel a need for conversation but have no idea what to say."

"Maybe your mother could help with that," added Rome.

Seeking clarification, William looked at Rome as she motioned in the direction of Lady Jones. Astonished, William stepped back, uttering her name. "Mother?"

Shocked by the sight of her son, Lady Jones leaned Mr. Snavely's head against the wall, rose to her feet and made her way toward William. Finding herself hesitant to get too close, she examined him from head to toe and finally found the ability to speak. "Is that you, William, or a figment of my imagination?"

"It is I, Mother."

Lady Jones slowly reached out and gently wrapped her arms around William. "You've come home at last," she said, scared to squeeze too tightly for fear he would break. Unable to resist any longer, William wrapped his own arms around his mother, just as he had done countless times in his youth.

"We must find your father at once. He will be so happy to see you?"

"Will he, Mother?" asked William as he pulled away.

"Of course. You're his son."

"I've brought you both such great shame."

"You've caused no shame to be found in my eyes nor the eyes of your father."

"How can you feel that way after all that I've done? You had a reputation to uphold, an image to protect, a status to maintain and I ruined that for both of you. I destroyed the family name."

"When a family name is based on how we appear in society or climbing the ladder of hierarchy, maybe it needs to be destroyed, so we can rise from the ashes and be built anew. Unfortunately, it took a tragedy to make us realize that all the pretense found in the words we shared with others, as well as the family secrets we worked so hard to conceal, were nothing more than meaningless signs of arrogance. It was only after they were stripped away and truth became our banner that we truly understood what was most important."

"And what was that, Mother?" desperately enquired Heath.

"Love."

"Any love I once felt was replaced by anger years ago."

"No matter how much darkness we allow in, a spark always remains, but you must search for it. Love is never fully extinguished, William."

"I want to believe that, but I fear it's been too long."

"Nonsense. We'll get you moved back into your room and everything will be as it once was at Forest Gate," replied his mother, before the realization hit that Forest Gate was no longer their home. With fear in her eyes, she looked to Rome for the help necessary to get back on track.

In response, Rome rubbed her hand over the back of her shoulder, reassuring Lady Jones that all would be well. "Moving beyond a certain event or time in our lives can be difficult, but with a little help we can find our way through it," said Rome lovingly.

William nodded to Rome, acknowledging that he understood, then wrapped his mother's arm around his and led her to the door. "Come for a walk with me, Mother. I have much to tell you."

A tear rolled down Rome's cheek as she watched mother and son leave the room together. Feeling a need to share in the afterglow, Heath wrapped his arm around her as they continued to watch them walk away.

"You truly have a gift."

"I may have a gift, but they're the ones doing all the work."

"With a little help from you."

"Maybe a little."

"That's my family, Rome."

"They are indeed, Heath."

As the sound of sirens grew closer, Mr. Burns walked toward them, wanting to know more, but deciding to keep it light. "Have you two gone into shock?" he asked facetiously.

"Excuse me?" responded Heath.

"You seem to be acting rather peculiar, 'staring off into space' as it were."

"Just enjoying the moment," said Rome happily.

"You certainly deserve it, Ms. London, after such bravery and skill."

"Right back at you, Mr. Burns."

"Shall I be the one to welcome the police officers to the castle, sir?"

"If you would, Sheldon."

"Of course."

"By the way, I think I displayed some pretty decent skills as well," remarked Heath, searching for a compliment.

"Splendid skills indeed, sir!"

"Impressive, for sure," concurred Rome.

"Quite impressive," reiterated Mr. Burns.

"First-class, all they way," added Rome.

"All right, that's enough, thank you," responded Heath rolling his eyes at the overkill.

"Then I shall see to the police."

"Was the man in the truck the one you were looking for, Mr. Burns?" asked Rome.

"I'm afraid not."

With that said, Mr. Burns turned and walked through the cluttered crime scene.

"I'm sure the police will need to talk to me," remarked Heath, with little enthusiasm.

"You are the king of the castle."

"That I am."

"If possible, can you leave my name out of the report? I am supposed to be touring other convict sites right now."

"Your wish is my command, my lady."

"This lady's going to take herself up to the master suite, draw herself a bath and soak her sore body in hot lavender and chamomile-scented water."

"What about the late night snack we had planned?"

"This is probably the only time you'll ever hear me say this, Heath, but I think I'm too tired to eat." Rome turned and left the room just as Mr. Burns entered from the outside, followed by several policemen, a fireman and a couple of paramedics. Heath took one last look in Rome's direction, smiled, then made his way toward the emergency responders.

ROME ENTERED the master suite and walked directly into the bath. She sat down on the side of the tub, turned on the water and waited for it to reach the right temperature. "Perfect," Rome thought to herself as she painfully began to undress, her body feeling like one big bruise. She couldn't wait to soak in the hot water as she put on Heath's robe and lit the candles nearby, creating a peaceful environment to help with her relaxation. She picked up the Moonlight Lavender and Chamomile bath soak and poured some into the water, then sprinkled an extra dose for good measure. As the aroma-filled steam rose to meet her nostrils, Rome knew she was well on her way to tranquility.

Unexpectedly, she heard a noise come from the bedroom, a muttering of sorts. She peeked out the doorway to find the source was Lord Hubert, pacing the floor and talking to himself. She watched him walk back and forth between the bed and the window, staring out at the grounds each time. Rome looked at the tub which was nearly full, then back at Lord Hubert, who was clearly in distress. She lowered her head as she considered her options: a relaxing soak in the tub or a conversation with what appeared to be a somewhat arrogant ghost. At this point, any other person would have shut the door and chosen the tub, but not Rome. She turned off the taps, tightened the belt on her robe and entered the bedroom, much to the surprise of Lord Hubert.

"Good heavens, madam. Where is your clothing?"

"I'm about to jump in the bath."

"I shall leave you to your privacy."

"Stop! Do not disappear on me!" yelled Rome as though giving an order.

"A refined lady would never speak in such tones!"

"I'm an American, the rebels from across the pond. What you see is what you get."

"Clearly," Lord Hubert said with a hint of disapproval.

"Would you like to talk about what's bothering you?"

"Of this I cannot speak."

"Why?"

Lord Hubert walked toward the window and looked down at the ground below. "My son has returned. At this very moment, he walks the grounds of Forest Gate with his mother."

"After all this time, I'd think you would be excited to join them."

"I want nothing more, but I fear the look of betrayal I shall see in his eyes. It will cut me to the core."

"Betrayal?" enquired Rome, hoping to learn more.

"It was in no way premeditated. I had no idea the course my actions would chart."

"What did you do?"

"Something deplorable that shall vex my soul for eternity. No lesser punishment will do."

"I recently had a conversation with someone on an island near here who once shared in your same philosophy of self-inflicted punishment."

"Once?"

"He's in the process of letting go."

"My crime is far too serious."

"Why not let someone else be the judge of that?"

"And would that be you?"

"I'm only offering to help. It's up to you to accept."

Lord Hubert began to nervously pace the floor, searching for the courage to share his inner demons. "I was entrusted with a secret. In my attempt to achieve a certain outcome, I shared that secret with the wrong person."

"And this led to what?"

Lord Hubert approached the window once again and looked toward the grounds below. "The destruction of my son's life."

"What did you do, Lord Hubert?"

"The agony of my shame. I cannot speak of it."

"Then you'll never resolve the problem."

"There is no undoing of the damage I have caused."

"Go to William. Talk to him. Give him the opportunity to forgive you."

Summoning the courage necessary, Lord Hubert asked the painful question that continued to plague his mind. "Why should he forgive me? It was my pride that led me down this path. It was my arrogance that allowed me to believe that I had the right to control the outcome of my own son's life."

"No matter what you've done, the only cure is your son's forgiveness."

"Is it really that simple?"

"I don't know about simple, but I do know it's the only path to happiness, for yourself and for your family."

"I shall heed your advice, come what may," exclaimed Lord Hubert as he disappeared from the room.

Rome hurried across the room and looked out the window in time to see him approach his family, wishing she could hear the conversation. She watched as Lord Hubert took his son in his arms and held him tightly. William had finally returned home and for the first time in over a century and a half the Jones family was reunited. But the happiness was short lived once Hubert began to share the dark secret he'd kept hidden for years. William staggered backwards in disbelief and quickly turned his back on his father. Lady Jones appeared to go into shock as she covered her mouth with her hands and lowered herself to the ground. Immediately, her husband dropped to the ground beside her, pulling her toward him and holding her tightly as she sobbed.

The reaction to Lord Hubert's secret was more than Rome

expected. Uncertain as to what course his son would take, Rome pressed her hands against the glass, whispering as though he were in earshot. " Don't go, William. Don't you disappear. Stay and fight for your family. You're the only one who can end this."

After a moment, William glanced up toward the window as though he had heard Rome's pleading, then turned his attention back to his father. He appeared angry at first, dramatically responding to his father's admission of the truth. Although Rome couldn't hear the words being spoken, it was clear that William was expressing years of emotional pain. Time slowed to a crawl as she watched a broken family face the bitter truth that had kept them apart for so long.

But then something wonderful happened. William fell to his knees and hugged his father. Lord Hubert instantly returned the embrace as Lady Jones leaned over and placed her arms around her son and husband's shoulders. This was the beginning of what Rome had been hoping for since her first conversation with William. Feeling victorious, she raised her fists in the air and yelled a triumphant "yes," then rolled away from the window and wrapped herself in the curtain surrounding her. She had watched truth and forgiveness bring together a family torn apart by a tragedy of epic proportions. The intensity of what she witnessed was overpowering and Rome needed a moment to let her emotions run their course. Although she wanted desperately to fill in the blanks with Lord Hubert's secret, the satisfaction of what she witnessed would have to suffice for now.

With that in mind, she turned her attention to the tub. "And now for the cherry on top," she thought to herself as she walked toward the bathroom, removed her robe and immersed herself in the soothing water. She couldn't have asked for a more perfect environment to replay the days events as she laid her head back and closed her eyes. Peace and contentment were in the air and Rome wanted to savor it for as long as she could. Almost instantly, however, her eyes popped wide open as one word escaped her mouth. "Helen."

Rome knew there was still one member of the Jones family

missing from the reunion and that was William's wife. "I'll take care of that tomorrow," she whispered as she closed her eyes and basked in the tranquility of that gloriously scented tub of water.

After sufficient time in the bath, Rome dried herself off, wrapped her hair in a towel and put on her robe. Entering the bedroom, she saw a tray setting on the bed containing a scoop of trifle arranged beautifully in a glass dish. She picked up the note lying next to it and read: "No one should go to bed hungry. Sweet dreams. Heath." Rome sat down on the bed and took a bite, allowing her taste buds to play sweet music as she relished in the deliciousness of an Australian trifle. If her day was a fairy tale, this dessert would be her happily ever after. Resting the empty spoon against her bottom lip, she paused for a moment to consider if that would make Heath her Prince Charming. Probably not the best thought to have before drifting off to sleep... or was it?

Chapter Seventeen

Morning came as it always does and Rome slowly opened her eyes. In the quiet dawn of day, she took in the master suite, the room she had grown to love, allowing herself to briefly fantasize of a future with Heath. After a long sigh, she climbed out of bed, walked to the window and greeted the sun as it made its debut. She wondered if anyone else was up that early. Why was she up that early? It had barely been five hours since she crawled into bed. Rome knew the answer to her question before she even considered it. Sunday had finally arrived, the last day she would spend in the castle with Heath. Time was of the essence and she wanted to make the most of every second she had left. She walked to the armoire, pulled out the perfect outfit, brushed her teeth and hair and left the room.

The castle was quiet, making the dark hallway that much longer. Once she reached the stairs, she looked down and saw Mr. Burns on the couch in one of the sitting rooms engaged in reading the paper. Rome skipped down the stairs, crossed the floor and sat next to him, conforming to his silence. Without a word, Mr. Burns handed her the paper.

The bold headline plastered across the front page jumped at

Rome like a coiled snake. "Castle Jones: The Devil's Playground for Evil Spirits." The picture beneath captured the castle at night with two glowing silhouettes standing in the windows.

"This is ridiculous!" exclaimed Rome. "No one's going to believe this is real."

"It's not about the truth."

"Clearly it's been doctored."

"Sensationalism sells, especially if it's in Sergio Arturo's column."

"Is the article just as bad?"

"Worse. I lost count of how many quotes he shared from 'trusted ex-employees.'"

"This is going to hurt him, isn't it?"

"Not just him. Jones Shipping company will take another hit and that's exactly what Roger Ash wants."

"Heath's uncle?"

"And COO of Jones shipping. One would think achieving that title would be enough for the incompetent parasite, but he wants it all. This may be exactly what the board needs to hand it to him on a silver platter."

"I can't believe anyone would take these ghost stories seriously."

"It gets worse. Arturo paints Heath as a mentally unstable recluse and questions his ability to run a billion-dollar company."

"Causing stock prices to drop."

"And forcing the board to make a change to save the company's reputation in the business community," confirmed Mr. Burns.

"Do you think Roger and this columnist are working together?"

"I can't prove it, but I sure would bet on it and I'm not a betting man."

"Has Heath seen the paper?"

"No, he's still sleeping."

"Are you going to show it to him?" asked Rome.

"Of course he is. That's what he gets paid to do," said Heath as he descended the stairs.

"You're up early, Heath," said Mr. Burns, standing to greet him.

"Looks like I'm not the only one."

"Perhaps a glass of juice before you read the paper."

Heath reached the floor and zeroed in on one thing. "I think I'll read the paper first. May I?" Heath took the paper from Rome's hand, then began studying the picture and scanning the article while Rome and Mr. Burns waited for his reaction. Folding the newspaper in half, Heath walked toward the staircase and sat down.

"I think I'll check on breakfast," said Rome, hoping to give Heath some private time with his confidant, but she didn't get far. Grabbing onto her arm, Mr. Burns changed the plan. "I think it is I who will go to the kitchen," replied Mr. Burns. "You're needed here." Without giving Rome time to refute his decision, the butler exited the room, leaving her to step into his role as advisor. Taking a deep breath, she walked over and sat on the stairs next to Heath. Unsure of what to say, Rome resorted to her favorite tactic, humor. She picked up the paper and pointed to one of the ghostly silhouettes in the picture, asking, "Lady Jones or Lord Hubert?"

Heath lifted his head from his hands and looked at Rome in disbelief. "Really?"

"They do have a similar shape," continued Rome.

"Let me see that," said Heath, taking the paper back. Heath stared at the picture for a while, then pointed his finger to the ghostly silhouette in the top window.

"This one's got to be Lady Jones."

"I think you're right," responded Rome.

"Joking around is not going to lessen the impact this article will have on my company."

"I'm more interested in the impact it's having on you."

"Roger warned me that things could get worse. I didn't take him seriously."

"Have you asked yourself how he might know that?" asked Rome, hoping Heath would take the bait.

"I know what you're implying, but I can't believe he would be behind something like this. He's my uncle, Rome. Roger and I are pretty much the only family we have left."

"So what now?"

"I'll start by making some phone calls to the board members.

I'm meeting with them tomorrow, but a little reassurance in advance should help," responded Heath as he leaned over and kissed her on the cheek. "Thank you for being a friend," he said as he stood up and crossed the grand hall in the direction of the library. Disappointed that her last day with Heath had taken a turn for the worse, she decided to leave the castle and go for a walk. Once outside, Heath's final words echoed in her mind. "Thank you for being a friend," a simple statement that hit Rome like an avalanche. It appeared as though Heath had finally given up on trying to convince her to stay. A flood of mixed thoughts swirled around her head, then her heart added its two cents to the conversation by beginning to ache inside her chest.

"Breathe in the good air, let out the bad," she reminded herself as she walked toward the memorial, trying to process this new development. This was a win for Rome, the successful ending she had been working toward. A home run hit out of the park. A triumph of mind over matter. 'Mind over matter.' A phrase Rome never fully understood until that moment, a victorious moment, void of applause, fulfillment or even satisfaction.

"You worry for your husband," said Helen as she appeared next to Rome.

"I am worried for him, but he's not my husband."

"Yet you live here together?"

"I'm only visiting from America."

"That would explain the difference in the way you speak. Do you like it in America?" enquired Helen.

"Yes, I do."

"I had a cousin who sailed to the American continent in 1836. His correspondence welcomed me to come and offered to pay my passage."

"Why didn't you go?"

"I fell in love."

"William."

"If I hadn't loved him so dearly, I would have been tempted. But never mind."

"Love does tend to complicate things."

"I have watched you and the man of this house..."

"Heath."

"There appears to be more between the two of you than just friendship."

"Heath and I come from two very different worlds. Not to mention the fact that I live thousands of miles away and am involved with another man."

"I once knew a couple from two different worlds who lived with a distance between them. One was promised to another, but despite it all, they fell in love."

"Not to seem insensitive, Helen, but your story didn't end happily ever after."

"True, but yours can."

"After all this time, you still haven't given up on love."

"Without love, the world would be in great peril."

"May I ask how you and William met?"

"My cousin was a clockmaker and I was at work in his shop one day. He used to pay me to carefully dust the clocks each afternoon. William entered holding a pocket watch that his parents had given to him for his fourteenth birthday. He had broken it by accident and was hoping to have it fixed. My cousin examined the timepiece, concluding that it could be fixed but would take at least a week. Being the only clockmaker in town, he was behind schedule as usual. William agreed and every afternoon he returned to check on the watch, or so he said. He would spend the hour following me around the shop as I dusted, telling me all about his life in London. Having never traveled from my small town, I found it fascinating. Once his watch was fixed, we began meeting for walks in the countryside. We grew closer with each passing summer until we were certain of our love for one another. The rest of our story you already know."

"Helen, would you meet me here later, when the sun is directly above us?"

"To what end?"

"You're going to have to trust me."

"You've given me no reason to choose otherwise."

"Then we'll meet again at noon."

"When the sun is directly above us," agreed Helen.

"Until then," said Rome as she turned to walk away.

"Rome?"

"Yes."

"I will never regret falling in love with William. The short time we spent together was the happiest of my life." With that said, Helen disappeared, leaving Rome in the same place she was before their conversation, consumed with mixed thoughts and feelings.

Rome entered the kitchen, finding Gladys busily preparing breakfast for the staff. Looking around she spotted Miss Lemmons and George, reading the paper together as they waited at the small table in the corner. She walked toward them and sat down as George quickly moved the newspaper from the top of the table to his lap.

"Can we help you, Ms. London?" enquired Miss Lemmons.

"Do you mind if I eat with you guys? Heath's tied up with business this morning and I'm starving."

"Not at all," replied George as he quickly got up and fetched Rome a plate, a glass and some utensils.

Gladys placed the final food item of their modest breakfast on the table and sat down next to Rome. "Eat up while it's hot," the cook insisted.

As they began dishing up their plates, George could control himself no longer. "We don't believe a word of it, Ms. London, what they said about Mr. Jones in the paper. He's none of those things."

"I agree, George. Let's hope he can turn this bad publicity around."

"I've never liked that *Arturo: Off the Wall* column. There's something shady about that man," said Gladys.

"Unfortunately, I think you're in the minority," responded Rome.

"So what can we do to help?" asked Miss Lemmons.

"I'm not sure what can be done at this point."

"I'm going to tweet about this, right after breakfast," pointed out George.

"Social networking is a good idea," agreed Rome.

"I'll do it too," Miss Lemmons replied, "we both have a lot of followers."

"Awesome. Keep it simple and don't give out any details, especially about ghosts."

"Sounds good," replied both Miss Lemmons and George.

"I'm sure Mr. Jones will appreciate anything you can do to help."

"He's a good boss and we really like working here, even with the ghosts."

Rome smiled as they all began to eat. The food was delicious, but what she really enjoyed was listening to George and Miss Lemmons make plans for what they would post on social media. As she looked around the table, Rome realized that there was more to Heath's family than his Uncle Roger.

Mr. Burns entered the kitchen and took a seat at the table. "This looks lovely as usual, Gladys," then he began to dish up his plate. In return, everyone greeted the man in charge while Mr. Burns took the opportunity to share his feelings with his loyal staff. "Thank you for working so hard to get this house up and running. You've gone beyond the call of duty and Mr. Jones is very appreciative of your performance. As am I. In light of your valiant efforts, Mr. Jones had decided to give the entire staff the day off."

Rome watched as George and Miss Lemmon's eyes lit up in anticipation of spending their day together. Mr. Burns went on to thank them for their heroics from the night before and assured them that there would be a bonus in their upcoming paychecks. Needless to say, Sunday had just become the best day of their week.

FOLLOWING BREAKFAST, Rome and Mr. Burns departed the kitchen together and walked toward the grand hall. Much to the butler's disapproval, Rome carried a tray of breakfast for Heath. "Ms. London, I really wish you would let me carry the tray."

Block by Block

"Not this time, Mr. Burns. Heath gave you the day off, so go and enjoy it."

"I do have some personal errands to run, but in light of this morning's circumstances..."

"I promise to take good care of him until you return."

"Of that, I have no doubt. Let Heath know that I'll be back in plenty of time to get him packed for his flight to Sydney," replied Mr. Burns as he left Rome standing in the middle of the grand hall.

"Will do," she responded, her voice echoing throughout the empty castle.

Before continuing to the library, Rome took a moment to look around her surroundings. "I will miss being lady of the castle," she commented to herself as she continued across the floor and down the long hall toward the library. Opening the door, she peaked into the room, expecting to find Heath on the phone. Instead, she saw him staring out the far window, deep in thought. Clearing her throat, Rome entered the room.

"You don't have to wait on me, Rome," said Heath as he made his way back to the desk.

"And you didn't have to leave dessert on my bed last night. Thank you, by the way. I wasn't sure what you'd be in the mood for this morning, so I brought a bit of everything."

"First, I have some news that I think you're going to find very interesting. I received a response to the email I sent to my dad's genealogist in regard to Meredith Hampton."

"So soon?"

"I stressed the importance of finding out quickly and I may have mentioned the possibility of extra compensation."

"And you think I'm a force to be reckoned with."

"You got to pay to play, Rome."

"So what did you buy us?"

"A death date. Meredith Hampton died in 1901."

"Wow! She certainly had a long life."

"It gets better," said Heath as he sat down at the desk and started picking grapes off the tray and popping them into his mouth. "She's buried in Boston."

"Massachusetts?"

"She emigrated to America in eighteen..."

"Let me guess... 1840."

"You got it."

"Are you thinking what I'm thinking?"

"That maybe sweet little Miss Hampton wasn't the sad victim of Helen and William's love affair at all."

"What if she had something to do with Helen's alleged crime?"

"And her father, the magistrate, shipped her off to America to keep anyone from finding out."

"That would explain why he keeps haunting the castle."

"To keep us from digging further into the past."

"And to keep the Jones family from finding out."

Rome sat back in her chair and pondered what their assumption may mean as Heath picked up his fork and knife and dove into his breakfast like he hadn't eaten in days. "I suppose I am a little hungry."

"A little hungry?"

Heath smiled at her sarcasm knowing he totally deserved it, then returned to business. "Is the staff gone for the day?"

"Yes, and Mr. Burns wanted me to inform you that he would be back in time to pack your bags for Sydney."

"Good."

"You seem a bit old to have someone else packing your bags."

"Says the woman who can't possibly understand because she has no butler of her own."

"Touche'."

"Honestly, I don't even know where he stores the luggage."

"We definitely live in two different worlds."

"A point you've made abundantly clear and one I've finally taken to heart."

Rome picked up a knife, carved deep into his butter, grabbed a croissant and sat back down. Splitting it open, she pondered the subtext to his words as she spread the butter generously over the bread. Before taking a bite, Rome turned the discussion back to business, his business. "So how did the board react to the article?"

"It's not good."

"Don't they believe your side of the story?"

"They want to, but they're in a tough spot."

"Once you're in the same room with them tomorrow they'll come around."

"I hope so."

"I had a visit from Lord Hubert last night."

"And how is good old Hubert these days?"

"He was 'vexed.'"

"What was he 'vexed' about?"

"Something he'd done in the past that he believes led to the destruction of William's life."

"That does sound vexing. What did he do?"

"I don't know, but I encouraged him to talk to his son about it."

"Do you think he will?"

"He already did. I watched the exchange from the bedroom window."

"It sounds like Forest Gate may be losing some of its ghostly visitors."

"Do I detect a tone of sadness?"

"More like melancholy," replied Heath.

"There's just one relative missing from the reunion."

"Helen."

"She's meeting me at noon today."

"What's the plan?" enquired Heath.

"What makes you think I have a plan?"

"You always have a plan."

"You seem to know me so well."

"How is that possible? It's only been a week," responded Heath sarcastically as he lobbed another shot over the bow, a shot that today would go unanswered. With her defenses down and out of ammunition, Rome conceded the win. Standing up, she began pacing in front of the desk, continuing with the details of the plan. "Somehow, we need to lure William and his parents back to the castle at the same time as my meeting with Helen."

"I didn't think you could summon spirits."

"That doesn't mean I can't try."

"That's reassuring."

"I'd never had a conversation with a spirit before my visit to the Isle of the Dead, let alone seen one in person. This trip has opened me up to more possibilities than I ever thought possible."

"You're not the only one. Can I help?"

"I'm certainly not doing it alone."

"I was hoping you'd say that."

"These are your ancestors, Heath. I'm just here to help."

"What do you want me to do?"

Rome pulled out her cell phone to check the time, inadvertently noticing she had a couple of voicemails from Jamie, her boyfriend.

"That's interesting."

"What?"

"Just a few missed calls."

"A certain secret agent, by chance?"

"Why don't you finish eating while I take a walk and try to locate either William or his parents."

"Where do you want me to meet you?"

"I think the best place to hold the reunion is in the grand hall. I'll meet you there."

Rome took a drink from Heath's glass of juice and walked across the room, sharing one last bit of information before her departure. "I got an email from Bev. She left Western Australia last night and made it to Sydney. She's spending today and tomorrow touring the convict sites around Sydney and Cockatoo Island."

"Should I even ask if she's having a good time?"

"She's having a blast!" said Rome as she continued to the door.

Heath waited for her to leave, then laid his fork and knife down and leaned back in his chair. Heath Jones had everything money could buy, but all he really wanted was more time with Rome. Unfortunately, time was not something he could purchase.

ROME HAD SPENT the better part of a half hour walking the

grounds in search of a spirit. She started out looking for Lady Jones and Lord Hubert, but at this point she'd take anyone. Well, maybe not Justice Hampton. Rome pulled out her recently charged cell phone and checked the time. She had two and a half hours left before her planned meeting with Helen.

Little did Rome know that Lady Jones was playfully waiting for her around the corner of the castle. "Boo!"

"Very funny!" Rome responded, trying to catch her breath.

"Isn't that what the ghosts of your day say?"

"Only on All Hallows' Eve."

"My apologies. With my heart now lightened I could not resist having a bit of fun."

"I'm glad to hear it."

"I came to thank you, Rome. You helped to save our family."

"Not your entire family, Lady Jones."

"There has only ever been the three of us."

"Until William married."

"He has not mentioned one word of that girl. I simply assumed she had become a distant memory."

"That girl's name is Helen and he still loves her with all his heart. Unfortunately, he feels solely responsible for what happened to her and he will never forgive himself. That's why he hasn't mentioned her."

"That will not do. None of that was his fault."

"He refuses to see it that way."

"You must tell him."

"Nothing you or I can say will change his mind. I've already tried."

"What can be done?"

"We need to bring William and Helen together. They're the only ones who can free each other from the pain and guilt they both carry."

"I will do it to help my son."

"And Helen?"

"Of course."

"Do you mean that, Lady Hampton?"

"Yes. I have blamed her for far too long."

"This is not about forgiving Helen. You and Lord Hubert must accept her into your family, like you should have done in 1840. Helen has agreed to meet me in a little over two hours. I need you to make sure William arrives in the grand hall at the same time. Can you do that?"

"I will go to my husband and explain everything."

"How do you think he'll take it?"

"Thanks to you, my husband is a changed man. It's as though we're newlyweds again, looking forward with hope and wonder. Together we will make certain that William is there waiting. You have my word."

"Two hours then?"

"I will watch for you and Helen," agreed Lady Jones before she disappeared from view. Rome wanted nothing more than to share her victory with Heath, so she took off running, eventually arriving at the service entrance in the rear of the castle. Walking through the door, she immediately noticed that the staff had cleaned up the majority of the mess from the night before. The nearly-stolen items were all stacked against the walls, waiting to be put back in their original spots. Rome picked up a painting that once hung in the grand hall and hurried out of the room. As she entered the grand hall, she saw Heath sitting alone on the stairs.

"Well?" he asked, rising to his feet.

"Lady Jones is on board, which means we have two hours to decorate this room."

"Decorate. How?"

"I need you to pay, so I can play."

"Your wish is my command."

"Find the number for a wholesale floral shop in town. We need flowers. Lots of flowers."

"Are you thinking what I think you're thinking?"

"Recreating the wedding chapel?"

"That's what I thought you were thinking," said Heath as he left the stairs.

"We'll need ribbon too. And maybe an archway!" hollered Rome.

"We saw the wedding memory together, remember?" Heath hollered back just before he disappeared down the hallway toward his library.

"Yes, I do!" Turning her attention back to the job at hand, she began to hang the paintings and returned for more. What better way to distract oneself than to help two star-crossed lovers find happiness at last. Although their timetable and circumstances were not ideal, there was no question in her mind that they could make it happen. Together, Heath and Rome had proven to be unstoppable, so why would reuniting two spirits for eternity be any different?

ROME PACED BACK and forth near the grave site. "Come on, Helen," she said to herself, "Please be on time." Although she still had a few minutes, Rome was about to burst at the seams with excitement, making it difficult to stand still. Finally, Helen appeared in front of her.

"I hope I'm not late," enquired Helen after seeing Rome's impatience.

"Not at all. Would you mind coming into the castle with me?"

"I'm trusting you have my best interest at heart."

"That and more, Helen."

As they entered the castle, Heath stood near the doorway. Rome extended her hand to Heath and the three of them walked into the grand hall together.

"It's so beautiful," responded Helen as she looked about the room. Garlands made of flowers and ribbon crisscrossed the span of the grand entranceway, creating the look of a false ceiling. Off to the side, near the bottom of the stairs, was a beautiful white archway decorated with flowers and greenery. An abundance of flower bouquets and lit candles were scattered about, helping to soften the large room, while a layer of flower petals created a trail leading to the archway.

"It reminds me of my wedding day," whispered Helen.

"Heath and I wanted to make this special for you."

"It is truly breathtaking, but without William, there is a sadness to it as well."

All at once, William and his parents appeared at the top of the staircase.

Helen gasped as she stared up at her husband, recognizing him instantly. It took every bit of control she had not to run toward him and fall into his arms, those same arms that held her tight as a younger woman. But she knew her heart could not handle another betrayal, so she chose caution and waited.

The look on William's face showed no less of a surprise as he stared down at Helen. No longer in his prison uniform, he now wore a loose, white shirt and white pants. Although the sadness of his eyes, the fatigue of his posture and the look of torture on his face had softened, there was still an emptiness, a longing. The aching of his heart immediately slowed to a stop and he wanted nothing more than to hold her once again. But would she forgive him? Could she forgive him? He looked at his parents, who smiled at him reassuringly and pointed to the staircase with their hands. William slowly made his way down the stairs, never once taking his eyes off his beautiful bride. Arm in arm, Lady Jones and Lord Hubert followed in silence.

Now it was Helen's turn and Rome waited patiently for her to make a move.

"What shall I say to him?" she asked nervously.

"He's your husband. You'll know what to say," advised Rome.

Sensing Helen's fear, Heath leaned in and offered his two cents. "Trust me, Helen. He's just as nervous as you are." Then together the three of them walked down the aisle. As they neared the archway, Rome let go of her hand and she and Heath made their way to the bottom of the stairs, taking their place next to William's parents. Whispering to Rome, Lady Jones shared one last thought with her new friend as they watched Helen walk toward her husband. "When all the constraints of life are removed, the only thing left is the truth. And it's the truth that sets us free. Thank you for that."

The student had become the teacher and Rome considered her words as she turned her head toward Heath. Just over a week ago she sat on a plane, secretly wanting to know what it felt like to be unrestrained. She had found that with Heath. She had tasted a freedom she never thought possible. But even now the truth of how she felt about him was clouded by the circumstances that brought them together. Had she fallen in love with the man or the main character in the adventure they shared? Feeling her gaze, Heath turned and looked at her, raising his eyebrows in curiosity. Rome smiled at him, then they turned their attention back to the main event.

As Helen neared the archway, William slowly reached out and took her hands in his. He raised them to his face and gently kissed the back of each one. Lost for words, he studied her face while trying to find a way to express what was in his heart.

"I see you finally came for me," said Helen as she looked deep into William's eyes.

"I should have come sooner, but I was afraid of what you would think of me," responded William.

"Think of you?"

"I failed to save you on the streets of London and then again at the docks."

"You could not have saved me, William."

"If I hadn't been so presumptuous and selfish to ask for your hand in marriage, you could have traveled to America and lived a happy life there."

"You are mistaken."

"You read to me from your cousin's invitation. On what point am I mistaken?"

"That I could have been happy without you."

"At least you would have been free."

"Enough talk of a past we cannot change. Tell me of your life. I assumed you married?"

"Then you don't know?"

"Know what?"

"I was sent to the convict prison at Port Arthur in Van Diemen's land."

"No!"

"We shared the same fate, Helen." I died while in prison. That's why I never came for you."

"Your father was a Baron. Could he not save you?"

"I only recently learned that my father died in an accident the day I was sent to Australia, as well as my mother. I was as alone in the world as you were."

"But I wasn't alone. I had our son to keep me company."

"A son I never knew."

"I've wanted so much for you to know him, yet my search for you has been in vain."

"I did not want to be found, Helen. My heart was cold and my thoughts were consumed with anger and grief."

"And now?" asked Helen, as she placed her hand on his chest, covering his heart.

"I am free of the darkness. My heart is yours if you will have it. It always has been," replied William as he placed his hand over hers.

"Only the truest kind of love could survive the separation that our hearts have endured," responded Helen as she leaned in and gave her husband a kiss, a kiss nearly two centuries in the making. Immediately, William wrapped his arms around his wife and kissed her back.

Rome and Heath smiled at each other as they watched William and Helen reunited in each other's arms. "What a wonderful ending," whispered Heath as he wiped away an unexpected tear.

"Or a wonderful beginning," said Rome quietly as she watched two broken hearts, torn apart by forces beyond their control, finally mended. Theirs was an epic love story that spanned both life and death, and it all began with a damaged pocket watch.

Lady Jones and Lord Hubert joined in the splendor of the moment as they walked toward their daughter-in-law and welcomed her to the family with hugs of their own. The moment Helen and William had hoped to experience all those years ago was finally taking place.

All of a sudden, a terrible wind began to twist about the grand hall, causing Rome, Heath and the Jones family to huddle together in the center of the room. The fierce, encircling wind extinguished the light of the candles and ripped the garlands from overhead, catching them in the tornado-like pattern. The archway was knocked onto its side and the flower bouquets were destroyed as they hit the ground, one after the other. The flower petals were sucked from the floor and began to rotate with the wind as well.

"What is this? What's happening?" yelled Heath.

"I have no idea!" replied Rome.

"Allow me to enlighten you!" boomed Justice Hampton's voice as he appeared at the top of the stairs. Immediately, his ghostly relatives stopped flying in a circle and dropped to the floor, surrounding the Jones family and Rome in the center of the room. "You will never know happiness, William Jones, not as long as I'm around to end it. You destroyed my daughter's opportunity for happiness and for that you must pay!" warned Justice Hampton from the top of the staircase.

"You already destroyed my happiness," responded William defiantly, "you were responsible for sentencing my wife and sending her to the Australian Colony. My father told me that he went to you for help following our conversation about my marriage to Helen, but he did not expect you to go to such lengths."

"Your father was a fool!" responded Justice Hampton.

"I was a fool," agreed Lord Hubert. "I thought because you were a magistrate, we could simply get the marriage annulled. That was what you told me. Following that, my son would have been betrothed to Meredith and Helen would return to her life in the country. I was wrong to come to you."

"You came to me because you were weak, so I took it upon myself to remedy the situation. I called an emergency court session and did what needed to be done," proclaimed Justice Hampton.

"You sent an innocent woman to prison in a faraway land, just to serve your own interests," replied William.

"Innocent? She was found with a stolen brooch in her possession. I simply dealt the verdict and sentence she deserved."

"I did not steal that brooch, sir. I am not a thief!"

"How did the brooch end up in your bag without the ability to prove ownership?"

"For that I have no answer," responded Helen.

"But I do," said a voice from behind.

Everyone in the room turned their heads to look at the female spirit standing alone, near the inner entranceway.

"Meredith?" asked William. "Is that you?"

"Yes, William," responded Meredith Hampton, the woman who was promised to wed William so many years earlier.

"I have remained silent for too long. This will no longer do," said Meredith as she began walking through the crowd of spirits. "I was near to the court that day as Lord Hubert left my father's office. He did not see me in the crowded lobby. Before I reached his office, I saw my father call a man from the crowd, so I waited outside for him to finish his business. Unfortunately, I overheard the conversation."

"Stop at once, Meredith!" demanded Justice Hampton.

"I will not, Father. I can no longer carry the knowledge of your deceit."

"Please continue, Meredith?" enquired William.

"I heard my father concoct a plan with the man who entered his office. It involved the appearance of a woman committing a crime. He went on to tell the man where he could find this woman and told him to follow her until an opportunity arose to put the plan in motion. Feeling confused by what I heard, I ran from the building and returned to our home. Days later when I heard Father tell the story of what had happened to William and his new bride, I knew she had been the woman they plotted against. I should have said something to someone, but I was young and no match for a magistrate."

"Our family's union with the Jones family would have elevated and sealed your place in society, as well as provide you the kind of property and wealth that we could not. I absolutely refused to let a girl with no station take what was rightfully yours," responded Justice Hampton with not a sign of remorse.

"Rightfully mine? It was you who wanted it so desperately, to elevate your own self."

"And what of William's sentence?" enquired Lord Hubert of Justice Hampton, "If your plan was to do away with Helen in order for him to marry Miss Meredith, why not stop your fellow magistrates from sending William to the Australian Colony as well?"

"You served in parliament, Hubert. Do you not remember how congested the prisons were? Do you not recall the amount of prisoners crammed into all the decommissioned prison ships awaiting transport to the Australian Colony? All those prison hulks, anchored in the waters of England and elsewhere, were evidence of how desperate we were to alleviate the overcrowding and get the criminals through the courts and out of England as fast as the ships could sail."

"But William was of a different station. That should have made a difference," cried Lord Hubert.

"He foolishly attacked a policeman with an intent to harm or kill. From that point, it was completely out of my hands. I could do nothing to stop it. William's sentence became the first cruel irony of my plan," explained Justice Hampton.

"We were the best of friends, Henry. What happened?" asked Lord Hubert.

"We may have been friends, Hubert, but I was never your equal. All I really wanted was to stop living in your shadow and for my family to be seen in the same light as yours. But in the end I lost my family as well, the cruelest irony of all." With that said, Justice Hampton disappeared along with all the spirits that had arrived with him.

After a moment of silence, Meredith continued her account. "When my mother and I came to the entire truth of my father's involvement, we took what jewelry we had and a few other things of value and sold them to buy passage to America. We had enough left over to make a new beginning for ourselves once we reached Boston. We packed our steamer trunks while Father was away at work and left without saying goodbye." Then Meredith walked toward William and took hold of his hand. "William, my dear friend. When I think of the small part I played in your tragedy, it cuts me to the quick. By the time my mother and I put all the pieces together, your father and mother had already passed. Having no evidence of the role my father played in Helen's conviction, there was nothing we could do. I am so sorry for the pain our family caused you and your wife," apologized Meredith.

"It is done, Meredith. Put your mind at ease. Helen and I are united once again and now we will continue together throughout eternity."

"And for that, I am grateful," responded Meredith.

"But what of your life in America?" asked William.

"You would have been very proud of me, William. You remember the young Irishman, Robert O'Brien, the son of the baker, who worked at that little bake shop we loved so much?"

"I do. We used to play a bit of cricket together when we were boys. I used to wait on the street outside my father's office for him to finish work. Robert and his friends always had a cricket match going in the park nearby. One day he invited me to play and the rest was history."

"Robert and his father had booked passage on the same ship as my mother and I. It seemed they had grown tired of working eighteen to twenty hours a day in a London bakery, only to take home a sparse wage and worn-out bodies each night. They made the bold decision to travel to America in the hopes of one day owning their own bakery. By the time our ship reached Boston, we were engaged to be married. With our financial help and their knowledge of baking, we opened and operated one of the finest bakeries in all of Boston. We raised eleven wonderful children in that bakery and lived a very happy life."

"I could hear nothing from you that would make me more happy," responded William.

"I shall take my leave, knowing our friendship continues beyond the grave," replied Meredith, nodding her head and disappearing from sight.

"And to you my great-great-great-great-grandson..." said William, as he walked toward Heath and Rome.

"Grandson?" replied Lady Jones in great surprise.

"Yes, Mother. This is our descendant, your fifth great-grandson, Heath Jones. I am indebted to both of you. I've been rescued from my own prison and now I am free."

Next, Helen approached and took hold of both Heath and Rome's hands. "I wish to thank you as well. I've waited a long time for this reunion and now my son will finally meet his father... and his grandparents. Without the two of you this would not have been possible."

"It's been a pleasure to get to know my family," replied Heath.

"Enjoy your happiness. You've definitely earned it," added Rome.

"We shall bid you both farewell until we meet again," announced Lord Hubert as he and Lady Jones disappeared from sight.

Despite what appeared to be the remnants of a natural disaster, William couldn't help but make one last comment. "I really like what you've done with the place. You should both be very happy here." Then he took hold of Helen's hand and they departed the room, leaving Heath and Rome with some food for thought. Finally, Rome broke the awkward silence. "We did it, Heath, we actually did it."

"You can do anything you put your mind to. That's just one of the things I love about you," replied Heath sincerely, taking advantage of their 'heightened emotional state' by taking her into his arms and dipping her backwards. Caught up in the moment, Rome showed no hesitation as they began to kiss. The moment was nothing less than magical, until the unexpected sound of a knock on the door pulled them apart.

"Are you expecting someone?" asked Rome.

"Only Sheldon, but he wouldn't be knocking," replied Heath as he returned Rome to her feet. Clearly frustrated by the interruption, Heath walked to the door as Rome turned her attention to the mess surrounding her.

"Hello. I'm looking for Rome London," spoke a familiar American voice causing Rome to freeze in place, her arms overflowing with garlands. "My name is Jamie Webb."

Although confused, Heath welcomed him into the castle, noticing the sculpted physique beneath his tailored, dark suit. Jamie's arrival couldn't have come at a worse time for Heath. He had reached a peak moment with Rome only to see it now dissolve into an anticlimactic ending.

"This is quite the place you have here," remarked Jamie, taking in every detail.

"Thank you," he responded, shutting the door and following him into the grand hall. Heath stopped a ways back and watched Jamie approach Rome and give her a kiss on the cheek as they greeted each other.

"Jamie, what are you doing here?"

"We just wrapped up the final stop in Canberra on our South Pacific tour. I've called several times and left voicemails, but no answer and no return call."

"I've just been really busy."

"I got worried so I used the locating software that we put on your new phone and it showed me your location."

"That certainly came in handy," responded Rome.

"I know you can take care of yourself but the lack of communication had me worried."

"So you flew all the way down here from the Australian capital just to check on me?"

"After I received this morning's security briefing and heard about the breaking and entering at a castle near Hobart, I checked the addresses and they were both the same. I sent the rest of my security detail back with the state department reps this morning and caught the next flight to Hobart. Is this the crime scene?"

"No. We're just cleaning up after a... wedding of sorts."

"That must have been some wedding. It wasn't yours was it?" said Jamie, jokingly, yet suspicious of the circumstances.

"No! Just a couple of Heath's relatives," responded Rome, turning Jamie's attention toward Heath. "Jamie Webb, meet Heath Jones, the owner of the castle or 'king of the castle' as we like to call him," joked Rome, but neither of the men laughed as they shook each other's hand, launching an unspoken competition.

"You're also the owner and CEO of Jones Shipping and Ship Manufacturing," responded Jamie.

"You've done your homework," said Heath.

"Just part of the job."

"And how did I become part of your job?"

"It's protocol to gather intelligence when visiting a country. For security purposes."

"I seem to be at a disadvantage. Rome and I have spent the entire week together and I don't know near as much about you as you seem to know about me," replied Heath."

Much to Rome's delight, Mr. Burns entered from the back hallway, stopping in his tracks at the sight of the enormous mess in the grand hall. "I leave you and Ms. London alone in the castle for one morning and this is what I come home to? Do I dare ask?"

"Jamie Webb. And you must be Sheldon Burns."

"I'm sorry, Mr. Webb, have we met?" replied Mr. Burns.

"We're just part of the recent intelligence he's gathered. For security purposes," responded Heath with a touch of sarcasm.

Feeling the intensity grow, Rome again tried to change the subject. "I believe you and Heath have some packing to do. And don't worry about this mess. I'll have it cleaned up in no time."

"I'll help. Just point me in the direction of the broom and dustpan," responded Jamie.

"Very well," said Mr. Burns as he and Jamie left the room, leaving Heath and Rome by themselves.

"So that's the secret agent boyfriend?"

"Believe me, Heath, I'm as shocked as you are."

"Does he often just show up like that?"

"Sometimes we'll meet up with each other if we happen to be in the same corner of the planet. His itinerary is usually top secret."

"For security purposes," interjected Heath with a hint of cynicism.

"Yes, for security purposes."

Before Rome could finish her sentence, Jamie re-entered the

room carrying a broom, a dustpan and a box of garbage bags, while singing a line from the Mighty Mouse theme song.

"Here I come to save the day."

"He has a thing for Mighty Mouse. It's this cartoon from the 1940's and 50's," explained Rome as she pulled a large garbage bag from the box. "He has the entire collection of DVDs. He even dressed up as Mighty Mouse last Halloween," added Rome.

"A secret agent in a superhero costume..."

"Actually, I'm a diplomatic security agent."

"Sounds like the perfect job for Mighty Mouse," responded Heath.

Seeing the direction the conversation was headed, Rome opened the garbage bag and nonchalantly began filling it as their sparring continued. Matters escalated when Jamie removed his suit jacket and began rolling up the sleeves to his perfectly tailored white shirt. "I was always the smallest kid on the team when I played little league baseball, but I could hit the ball farther than anyone else. During one of the games, my coach started calling me Mighty Mouse and it stuck. That was my nickname for years, until I finally had a growth spurt."

"You definitely appear to have had a growth spurt," acknowledged Heath. Unsure of how to respond, an awkward silence occurred between the two of them. Fortunately, Mr. Burns re-entered the room and saved their pride. "When you're ready, sir, I'll be in the master suite packing," announced the butler before he turned and walked up the stairs.

"So you're heading back to Sydney," said Jamie.

"Yes. I'm surprised Mr. Burns mentioned that."

"Your butler is a steel trap. I was informed this morning when your pilot filed a flight plan."

"More intelligence gathering."

"For security purposes."

"Of course. May I ask how long you're planning to stay in Tasmania?"

"That will depend on Rome and her schedule."

"She's grown fond of Forest Gate, so any friend of hers is welcome to stay here as well," invited Heath.

"That's very generous."

"We have more than enough rooms to accommodate another guest."

"One room should be fine for the both of us," responded Jamie.

"I should probably get to packing," said Heath as he reached out to shake Jamie's hand. "It was nice to meet you."

"You as well."

Heath turned and walked toward the stairs, approaching Rome on his way. Leaning in, he whispered one last comment before leaving her alone with her boyfriend. "And you thought I was formidable."

Rome watched as Heath ascended the stairs and disappeared into the second floor. The time to say goodbye had finally arrived, but with the complication of Jamie's arrival, Rome knew she wouldn't have an opportunity to say the type of goodbye she had hoped. "It can't end this way," she thought to herself. They had shared and extraordinary week together and to say goodbye in passing seemed like a travesty.

"Shall I hold or stuff?" asked Jamie, pulling Rome's attention back to the task at hand.

"What?"

"The bag. Do you want me to hold it or would you like to?"

"I'll hold the bag, you stuff," responded Rome, with a pasted-on smile.

It took everything she had to hold back the tears that were so close to escaping. She'd known all along that it would be difficult to say goodbye, but she did not expect the complication of her boyfriend's arrival.

As Jamie bent up and down, picking and stuffing, he knew something was off with Rome. Even before arriving in Tasmania he had his suspicions with all the unanswered calls. After seeing her together with Heath, he now suspected more to their relationship than a newly formed friendship, but decided to postpone that discussion until after

Heath's departure. The idea of losing Rome was not one he welcomed, so the decision to play it carefully was the right option to take. The best thing for now would be to distract her with light conversation concerning the subject of her article and that's exactly what he did.

MR. BURNS HAD two pieces of luggage lying open on the bed of the master suite. He carefully chose the right suits to go with the right shirts and ties and gently packed them away as he'd done hundreds of times over the years.

Heath entered the room, walked directly to the bathroom and began splashing cold water onto his face until he achieved the result he needed. Leaning over the sink, he let the water drip from his face as he tried to make sense of what just happened. Grabbing a towel he wiped himself off, then caught a glance of Sheldon in the mirror, leaning against the door frame behind him. "Don't say it, Sheldon."

"What shouldn't I say?"

"That I was a fool to let her into my life."

"I've known you since you were a boy, Heath, and I can honestly say that I've never known you to be a fool. Even when you decided to buy a castle and ship it to Tasmania."

"You're probably the only one."

"Your feelings for Ms. London are good for the heart."

"My heart would disagree with you right now."

"Has she made her final decision?"

"She made it days ago. I'll leave for Sydney as planned and she'll return to the States with her boyfriend. Why couldn't he have been a jerk?"

"Clearly, Ms. London has a type."

"I really thought I could convince her, Sheldon."

"That's not how it works, Heath."

"Well, it should."

"I'll pack your rowing clothes. That's always a good way to work out one's frustrations."

"There isn't enough water in Sydney," concluded Heath as he walked past Sheldon and left the bathroom.

"I'll need your shaving kit and toothbrush from the other room," hollered Sheldon as he watched Heath leave the bedroom. "Beverly and I are going to have much to discuss tonight and she's not going to be happy." Muttered Sheldon as he returned to the precise business of packing Heath's bags.

THE MOOD APPEARED much lighter in the grand hall as Jamie and Rome put the final touches on their massive cleaning project. Functioning together like clockwork, they performed like a well-oiled machine, a by-product of their long term relationship. Just as Rome was about to declare victory over the disaster zone, Jamie reached over and picked several pieces of debris from her messy hair and placed them in the dustpan. "Thank you. I probably look like a wreck," admitted Rome, recognizing that Jamie still looked perfectly polished, without a drop of sweat to be found.

"You've never looked more beautiful," responded Jamie, knowing exactly the right thing to say. Rome rolled her eyes at his kindhearted fib, then tried to comb her fingers through her tangled hair. Needless to say, she didn't get far. She knew it would take a massive dose of conditioner to free the knots spun into her hair by the ghost-induced windstorm.

Rome leaned the broom against the wall and sat down on the stairs, grateful for the respite. From her court-side seat, she watched Jamie empty the dustpan into the last bag, tie it shut, pack it to the door and stack it next to the others. Admittedly, watching Jamie do anything was an activity that never got old for Rome.

On his way back, he picked up a white flower that he'd previously set aside and twisted the stem off about three inches from the bloom. As he sat down next to Rome, he tucked it into her hair, letting the palm of his hand slowly slide down the back of her hair. She gently touched the flower and smiled at Jamie as she lowered her arm and placed her hand on top of his thigh. There was no doubt of their strong affection for each other or the devotion they felt, but things had grown complicated. Rome's emotions felt like they were in a blender set to "puree," while Jamie had bigger fish to fry. He came on a mission to take Rome back and that's exactly what he planned to do.

"What's your ETA for heading home?"

"I haven't decided yet."

"You have no plan? How is that possible? What have you done with the real Rome?"

"Point taken. I'll book a flight this evening. It's going to cost me an arm and a leg, but I'm the one who made the choice to stay."

"I'll take care of it for you," generously offered Jamie.

"You gave up a free flight home and now you want to purchase my flight as well as yours? I don't think so."

"At least let me pay for the upgrade. I'm not sitting in coach all the way back to the States."

"We do have a lot in common, you and I."

"You're just now realizing this?"

"I know how well we work together."

"I've been getting the feeling these past couple of months that that might not be enough for you anymore," commented Jamie.

"Let's save that conversation for another time."

"Speaking of time, we both have some vacation days saved up, so why don't we take that scuba diving trip we've been planning for the past year?"

"Return to work or go on a sunken treasure hunt in the Caribbean. That's a tough choice."

"If I didn't have to go back to D.C. and fill out an enormous stack of paperwork to report on this latest assignment, I'd say let's go from here."

"I have several more articles to write before my deadline."

"Soon things will be back to normal."

"That they will," responded Rome with a touch of melancholy in her voice. "But you're still not paying for my ticket home."

"That's because I'm paying for it," interjected Heath.

Happy to hear his voice, Rome looked up in time to watch him walk down the stairs, carrying both of his bags as Mr. Burns followed.

"That was part of the deal we made, remember?"

"Deal?" enquired Jamie.

Heath reached the floor, pulled a credit card out of his wallet and handed it to Rome. "As promised."

"You don't have to do this, Heath."

"Blame it on the sunset or the full moon. Either way, I owe you."

Jamie couldn't help but notice the way Heath looked at Rome, but more alarming was the way she looked back.

"I expect nothing less than two first-class tickets to the States. If I see you've booked anything less, I'll know you learned nothing from our time together," added Heath.

"One first-class ticket. I'll take care of my own," demanded Jamie.

"Not after cleaning up this mess. Consider the ticket payment for services rendered."

"For that kind of money, I'd quit my job and come work for you."

"Fortunately, I have Sheldon to clean up all my messes."

"In more ways than you can imagine," responded Rome as she winked at Mr. Burns.

"Now, if you'll excuse me, Mr. Snavely is waiting."

Heath bent down, picked up his bags and began to walk toward the door as Rome watched him leave. With desperation in her eyes, Rome looked to Mr. Burns, who immediately sensed her distress. "Mr. Webb. You have yet to see the castle in its entirety. If you'll accompany me to the top of the stairs, I'd be delighted to give you a tour."

"Actually..."

"That's a great idea, Mr. Burns. I think Jamie would love that," encouraged Rome.

"Are you coming on the tour?" asked Jamie.

"I need to take care of something, then I'll catch up with you."

"Come along. Don't dawdle," insisted Mr. Burns as he started up the stairs.

Jamie hesitated, suspecting Rome needed more time with Heath, but stood up anyway and followed Mr. Burns to the second floor. Rome mouthed the words 'thank you' to Mr. Burns, who glanced back toward her from the top of the stairs. He gave her a wink, then began the tour with some historical facts about the castle.

Rome waited until they were out of sight, pulled the flower from her hair, laid it on the step and ran for the door. As she left the castle, she found Mr. Snavely putting the last bag in the trunk of the car. She hurried around the side of the car and grabbed Heath's arm before he stepped into the back seat. "After all we've been through, you're just going to leave without a proper goodbye?"

Mr. Snavely, realizing they needed some privacy, shut the trunk and made up an excuse to remove himself from the situation. "I must have dropped my driving gloves inside. Can't drive without them." Max hurried into the castle, leaving them alone in the driveway.

"Are you going to say something?" asked Rome.

"What else is there to say, Rome?"

"Something. Anything."

"I've got nothing left. For the past week, I've said everything I could think of to get you to stay and it hasn't been enough. The truth is you were right. You and Jamie work well together. I see that now. He's a good guy, Rome."

"He is a good guy."

Heath took his fingers and tucked Rome's messy hair behind her ears as he stared deep into her eyes. "You know your hair's a wreck."

"What's new?" responded Rome as she placed her hands over his, pulling them down to her jaw line and cupping his hands in hers.

"I don't want to say goodbye, Heath, but I can't stay either. It's been a whirlwind week and I can't make a decision while everything is spinning around me. I have to stop the ride and get off for a while. I need time to consider the circumstances, to look at things logically from the outside."

"Then stay here while I go to Sydney for a couple of days. That should give us enough time apart."

"You may be gone physically, but you'll be everywhere in the castle. Everywhere I walk on the grounds. Everywhere I drive down the road. I need to get away from here and clear my head in order to know what I want. Home is the best place to do that."

"And your heart has no say in the matter?"

"Passion has never been my thing, Heath."

"I disagree. I've seen plenty of passion this week. Maybe it's never been your thing, because you haven't found the right person to share it with."

"A point that may warrant future consideration," admitted Rome.

"Once you return home to your scheduled life of logistics, itineraries, deadlines and the ticking of the clock, how long will it take you to logically talk yourself out of a having a future with me?"

Speechless, Rome stared at Heath knowing he was right and unable to respond to the contrary. Heath leaned in and kissed her on the lips one last time, but this time it was him who pulled away. "Goodbye, Rome." Then he stepped into the back seat and shut the door behind him.

No longer able to contain her tears, Rome turned her back to the car and hurried into the castle. Once inside, she nearly collided with Mr. Snavely, who was pacing back and forth waiting for them to finish.

"I'm sorry, Max," apologized Rome as she ran down the hallway toward the library.

"No worries, Ms. London!" Feeling sympathy for both Rome and his employer, Max shook his head as he walked through the open door. "It's going to be a long ride to the airport."

Inside the library, Rome shut the door behind her just in time to let down her guard. She hurried to the window, leaned up against the wall and watched the car make its way down the driveway and through the gate. Then she turned her back to the wall, slid to the floor, pulled her knees into her chest and let the tears pour, unrestrained.

Chapter Eighteen

Sydney, Australia

Heath walked down the hallway of his office building, dressed in a suit and tie and ready for business. Halfway down, Roger entered the same hallway and walked alongside Heath as they continued toward the boardroom. "I thought we had a meeting scheduled before the board meeting to go over the agenda."

"I went rowing this morning with some guys from the club and didn't get back in time."

"Well, at least you're here. That's all that matters to the board."

Roger opened his leather binder and pulled out a copy of the agenda. "Do you want the highlights?"

"I'm the CEO and President of this company, Roger. I'm pretty sure I can keep up," said Heath as he entered the boardroom.

Roger paused before entering, allowing him enough time to utter what he really thought beneath his breath. "Not for much longer."

Once inside, Heath walked to the front of the room, faking a smile and nodding his head at several members of the board seated around the long table.

Roger followed him to the front of the table, handing out copies of the agenda as he passed by each member. Once at the front of the room, Roger took a seat and Heath stood at the end of the table.

"I realize this isn't on the agenda, but I'd like to apologize for my absence this past week or so. I had some personal business to take care of in Hobart and it took longer than I had anticipated."

One of the board members tossed the front page of Sunday's edition of the Sydney newspaper onto the middle of the table. "These days, your personal business is looking more public than private, Heath, and it's reflecting on the company."

"I'm fully aware of the aggressive columnist who seems to have developed an interest in regard to the acquisition of my family home in England and its transfer to Tasmania."

Not buying Heath's well-worded excuse, another board member decided to speak his mind. "Cut the crap, Heath. You bought a bloody castle, broke it down and shipped it block by block across the North Atlantic Ocean to the Southern Atlantic Ocean, and across the Indian Ocean! Ship, after ship, after ship. Did you think no one would notice? No wonder he's obsessed with you. It looks like you've lost your mind!"

"With all due respect, what I do with my money is my own business."

"And what about these ghost rumors, Heath," demanded another board member. "Is the castle haunted or not?"

"Of course it's not. Anyone with a brain in their head can tell these pictures were doctored. I've already contacted our legal team and they're pursuing a slander case against the newspaper who published it."

"What?" responded Roger, obviously surprised by the new information. "I was not informed of this."

"Well, consider yourself informed," barked Heath in an angry tone.

"Everybody calm down," said a third board member as she rose from her chair and took the floor. "We're not going to accomplish anything by arguing with each other. What we need is a solution. I agree with pursuing legal action, but in the meantime, we need to calm the public's obsession with your castle and all these ghost stories."

"Agreed!" said Heath. "I have a meeting scheduled with our PR department right after this one to begin a campaign that should help fight what this Arturo is writing in his column. He may have the power of the pen, but I have the financial power to create an advertising campaign that will dwarf any future attempt at sensationalizing and slandering my name and the name of Jones Shipping."

"And when were you going to tell me about the PR move?" asked Roger.

"When I felt you needed to know."

"Am I invited to the meeting?"

"As far as I'm concerned, there's no reason for you to be there."

Frustrated, Roger threw his hands in the air then slammed his leather binder shut on the agenda. "Obviously, there's no reason for me to be here either."

"There's the door, Roger."

"Heath! I don't know what's gotten into you, but you need to calm down. Roger is only trying to help," inserted another board member.

Taking a deep breath, Heath leaned his hands on the table and took a moment to think. As he looked out at the disapproving faces staring back at him, he realized that he may have gone overboard. He pulled the chair toward him, sat down and folded his hands together on top of the table. "I began this meeting with an apology and I apologize again. I had a lot of unexpected things take place this week and yesterday was very difficult."

One by one the board members began to soften and offer their thoughts and suggestions in an attempt to solve the problem at hand.

"We understand that it's been difficult, Heath, especially with that ridiculous article and picture plastered across the front page of the Sunday paper. But we need to get out ahead of this thing before the company's image and stock take another hit."

"I think you're on the right path with legal action and a PR blitz, but what about Roger's fundraiser idea?"

"Yes, Heath, have you given any more thought to hosting an open house charity event at your castle?"

"It would certainly give credence to the fact that the relocation of your family's castle was simply a labor of love and not the crazy obsession that this reporter is making it out to be."

"Normalizing the situation may very well take the wind right out of Arturo's sails."

Silence filled the room as the board members waited for Heath to reply. After a moment of deliberation, Heath stood again at the head of the table to share his thoughts. "When Roger originally proposed the idea, I was dealing with a situation that was up in the air, but that problem has now been resolved," announced Heath.

Roger smiled sheepishly to himself as he slowly reopened his leather binder, pleased to see things changing in his favor. Now it was his turn to take the floor and drive the idea home.

"Does that mean you're going to do it?" asked Roger.

"That means I'm considering it," responded Heath.

"The more time that passes, the more difficult it will be to sway public opinion back to our favor."

"I'm no party planner, Roger, but a fundraiser of this magnitude isn't something you just throw together at the last minute, especially with the list of guests you're thinking of inviting."

"In my enthusiasm, I may have already got the ball rolling."

"And just how far have you rolled this ball, Roger?"

"I already sent out the invitations."

"You did what?"

"I knew you had a lot on your plate, so I figured the least I could do is set a date, put out some feelers and see who might bite."

"I can't believe you went behind my back like that!"

"I was only trying to help."

"This is my problem to deal with, not yours."

"We're family, Heath. Your problems are my problems."

"I highly doubt that."

"What was the response?" inserted one of the board members.

"I've received an RSVP for nearly every invitation."

"And how many was that?"

"We invited around two hundred of Hobart's finest and most influential. If each of them show up with a plus one, we could have over four hundred guests."

"That's a lot of people," responded Heath.

"That's a lot of the right people," concluded Roger.

"What date have you chosen?"

"Saturday."

"This Saturday?"

"Just in time for the Sunday edition of the paper."

"You really think we can pull this off in a week?"

"I also took the liberty of retaining an event planning and catering service in Hobart. They've already got the wheels rolling."

"It appears you've thought of everything."

"All we'll need is open access to the castle."

"Limited access, no more. I want to know who's coming and who's going. No one gets in without proper identification."

"I'll get someone on it."

"No! I need someone I can trust. Sheldon will handle it."

"If you think the old man's up to it."

"You do realize Sheldon's younger than you?"

"Must be the clothes. They do make the man."

"The final okay for everything goes through me. Is that understood?"

"You are the CEO, Heath."

"And I plan to keep it that way. Now what's next on the agenda?"

FOLLOWING THE MEETING, Heath left the boardroom and started down the hallway, checking emails on his phone as he walked. Roger quickly caught up to him in the hopes of worming his way into the PR meeting. "Are you sure you don't need me at your meeting?"

"You have more important things to do, Roger."

"I meant what I said about us being family."

"As your nephew, I can only hope that's the case."

Heath turned a corner, leaving Roger standing at the intersection of two hallways. As he entered the office of their company's top-notch, public relations manager, Donna Oak, greeted him with a handshake and friendly smile. "I've been looking forward to this meeting, Heath. It's been a while since I've seen you."

"I can't remember the last time we met together."

"It was last year, over that sticky situation in Johannesburg."

"That was awful."

"But you handled it brilliantly as usual."

"I couldn't have done it without you."

"Thank you, Heath."

Without uttering another word, Donna spun her desk chair around, picked up a stack of newspapers from the table behind her and spun back to face Heath. She dropped them on the desk and turned her attention back to her boss.

"You've been a busy boy."

"I see you've done your homework."

"Painstakingly so. I used to enjoy reading, *Arturo: Off the Wall*, but that was before he decided to take aim at my friend."

"He's done a number on me, that's for sure."

"Fortunately, 'reverse engineering' is my specialty."

"Due to his popularity, it's not going to be easy."

"Where there's a will there's a way. And you, my friend, have a will of iron when it comes to making things happen."

"In business, maybe."

"Your father once told me that 'business is warfare.' He was right. It'll take some doing, but eventually we'll get your private life back to being private," assured Donna, accompanied by a wink.

"Thank you. I could use a friend I can trust about now."

"I've already purchased a week's worth of ad space in every metropolitan paper throughout Australia and New Zealand. Each day's ad will build on the one before it, sharing a message that will show the importance of pursuing a person's individual passions and dreams. Our research shows that this type of message resonates with the twenty-something demographic who are in the process of pursuing their own goals."

Donna laid several pages of copy on the desk in front of Heath while she continued with her pitch. Heath examined each one closely. "We're going to build a narrative, with slogans like... 'A Labor of Love,' 'Connecting with the Past,' 'Roots Grow Deep,' 'Righting a Wrong,' and on and on."

"Writing a wrong? What made you choose that phrase?"

"We're using it in conjunction with the story of your fourth great-grandfather who was sent to Port Arthur so young and died in prison. By the time we wrap up a week's worth of heartstring-tugging ads, the people of Australia are going to be cheering for you and your castle. Your story is our story. It's part of our country's heritage. The readers are going to eat it up!"

"You've done a great job, Donna, and with such short notice."

"When the CEO calls me on a Sunday, I know it's important."

"Thank you."

"And of course, the entire campaign will culminate with the coverage of the charity fundraiser in next Sunday's edition."

"So you've heard about that already."

"Roger mentioned it in our emergency meeting last week."

"Emergency meeting?"

"About the eco-friendly ad campaign you guys are running in that international travel magazine."

"Which travel magazine?"

Donna shuffled through the papers on her desk until she found a copy of the most recent edition.

"Here it is. *Trekking the Globe*," she said, tossing the magazine across the desk.

As he looked at the magazine cover, Donna wheeled her office chair away from the desk, picked up another set of papers from the table to her left and wheeled herself back. "As you can imagine, the short notice of the magazine's deadline has had my people working overtime just to get it finished."

Donna laid the copy pages out in front of Heath, overtop of the castle ad pages. "Roger found out the magazine is planning a series of articles covering Australia's convict prison sites, and the next thing you know, we're buying a massive and expensive ad campaign in the same edition."

"What day was your meeting?"

"Late Thursday afternoon. As soon as he got back from Hobart."

Heath instantly realized that Roger was the one behind Rome's editor's request to cover more sites for the magazine. He wanted her away from him and Heath wanted to know why.

"Are you all right, Heath?" asked Donna, noticing he'd drifted away.

"I'm fine."

"Since you and Roger just met that morning, I assumed you'd signed off on this."

"Go ahead and run it. I'll look at the figures later."

"The ad can only help with the company's publicity, but the urgency seemed a bit strange. Usually that kind of money requires a crisis of some kind."

"You're very perceptive, Donna."

"Funny! That's what your dad said when he made me head of PR."

"He certainly made the right choice."

"Thank you, Heath."

"Everything looks great," proclaimed Heath as he stood up from the chair and buttoned his suit jacket.

"My team and I put our heart and soul into it, not to mention my entire Sunday."

"Allow me to repay you by taking you to lunch. I went rowing this morning and didn't have time for breakfast so I'm starving."

"Your timing is perfect. I was about to start gnawing on the desk."

Donna put on her suit jacket and grabbed her bag as Heath waited to escort her to the door. They left the office and walked down the hallway, not noticing the presence of Roger lurking around the corner.

Roger waited until they were out of sight, then entered Donna's office and quickly walked toward her desk. He looked through the ad copy for the travel magazine and noticed the castle ad campaign below it. Uncovering the rest of the pages, he perused each one, growing more and more angry at what he saw. Slamming his fist on the desk, he turned and stormed out of the office.

Chapter Nineteen

*R*ome rolled her bags across the master suite and placed them in the hallway, then turned back to take one last look at the room she had fallen in love with. Throughout her career, she had stayed in renovated castles and five-star hotel rooms that would take a person's breath away, but luxury wasn't what made this place special to Rome. It was here that she discovered herself on a deeper level than she had ever dared to delve. It was in this space that she found a tranquility that surpassed any spa, beach house or country cottage. It was from this room that she saw heartbreak healed through forgiveness, and tragedy overcome by love. The memories she would take with her were unique and irreplaceable, and as she said her last goodbye, a sad melancholy came to rest upon her heart.

Down the hallway, she heard a door close and the sound of footsteps walking toward her. Jamie approached from behind and looked over Rome's shoulder as he gently placed his arms around her waist.

"It's a beautiful room."

"Yes, it is," replied Rome. "How did you sleep?"

"The bed was very comfortable, but lonely," said Jamie as he kissed Rome's neck. "Soon we'll be back to work and back to our normal lives. Come on. We don't want to be late for the flight."

Jamie grabbed onto the handle of Rome's largest bag and walked down the hallway, picking up his overnight bag on the way. He paused for a moment and looked back at Rome, still standing in the doorway, staring into the master suite. Jamie knew the sooner he got her away from the castle, the better it would be for both of them.

Rome shut the door, took hold of her carry-on and rolled it down the long hallway for the last time. As she and Jamie approached the top of the stairs, she was surprised to see Mr. Snavely waiting for her. "Good morning, Ms. London. May I help you with your bags?"

"That would be wonderful, Max."

As Rome watched Mr. Snavely pick up her bags and carry them down the stairs, she was delighted to see Mr. Burns, Miss Lemmons, George and Gladys standing near the foot of the stairs, waiting to say goodbye. Surprised she had any tears to hold back, Rome felt a lump forming in her throat as she descended the stairs. Determined to control her emotions and keep her departure on an upbeat note, Rome cleared her throat several times, causing a physical reflex known to halt tear production.

Rome waited as Jamie thanked the staff for their generosity, then followed Mr. Snavely to the door. Taking a moment to ensure her composure, Rome engaged her new friends with a hug. She'd only known them for a week, but they had become precious to her. As they said their goodbyes, the staff slowly exited the grand hall, allowing Rome to say a private farewell to Mr. Burns. "I think I'll miss you most of all."

"...Said Dorothy to the scarecrow as she prepared to leave OZ," sentimentally responded Mr. Burns. "As the week progressed, I'd dared to hope that saying goodbye would not be necessary."

"Reality bids my return."

"Einstein taught that 'reality is merely an illusion, albeit a very persistent one.'"

"My editor would strongly disagree."

"Perhaps," observed the butler. "But she is not the master of your destiny, Ms. London, you are."

Abruptly, Rome wrapped her arms around the butler's neck, allowing herself a moment to breathe. Touched to the quick by the truthfulness of his words, she held on tight, silently expressing her response. The safety of his arms made everything all right and allowed an opportunity to experience the important role he played in Heath's life. "He's fortunate to have you, Mr. Burns. I will miss you," whispered Rome as memories of Forest Gate flooded through her mind.

"Please, call me Sheldon. You're not saying goodbye to a butler, you're bidding adieu to a friend."

"I feel the same way," said Rome as she pulled away. "Although, 'Ms. London' does sound pretty cool when you say it with that British accent."

"Then I shall 'mix it up' for the next time you visit. You brought life back to an old castle and a struggling friend. You will be missed."

Across the room, Jamie re-entered the grand hall. "We need to leave now to make the flight."

Sheldon cleared his throat, pulled a hanky from his pocket and discreetly wiped a tear from Rome's cheek. The time had come for her departure from Forest Gate and it was left to Mr. Burns to do what she could not. "Have a safe flight, Rome, and to you as well, Mr. Webb." Lifting his chin, he tugged on the bottom of his vest and walked toward the kitchen as though it were any other day.

FOR ROME, the ride to the airport was one of quiet introspection. The opposite was true of Jamie, who used the time to secretly study her body language. Fortunately, Mr. Snavely used his rearview mirror to read the situation as well and offered enough trivia to randomly deflect Jamie's attention to the passing sights.

At first, the flight home was more of the same and Rome was grateful to have a window seat for the distraction it provided. On her flight to Australia, she had fantasized of being unrestrained and doing summersaults in the clouds. Now, eleven days later, she never felt so trapped. Rome had no idea how much her trip down under had changed her until once again she found herself strapped into a seat that could also be used as a floatation device.

Rome got a glimpse of something in Tasmania. She dipped her toe in the waters of reckless abandon and was forced to open her mind to the wonder of wanton breezes. For the first time in her adult life, she felt the buckles of her bridle being loosened, a bridle controlled by her own tight grip.

Her plan was to wait until she got home to consider the circumstances, to look at things logically from the outside, to clear her head in order to know what she wanted. But she knew Heath was right. Once she returned to her scheduled life of logistics, itineraries, deadlines and the ticking of the clock, she would sink back into it like stepping on quicksand. Short of their plane crashing into the ocean, there was not a lot she could do about it.

Jamie was not as patient, and with a simple question regarding her time with Heath, he opened a dialogue that would continue throughout the rest of the flight. Jamie had questions and she had the answers, so there was no point in dragging out the inevitable. She told him everything that had happened, with the exception of the midnight grave robbing and her encounters with the spirits of Heath's ancestors.

There were times when they held hands and bared their souls and other times when words were spoken in quiet anger. At one point, Jamie simply disappeared for a while to collect his thoughts, allowing Rome the privacy to do the same. It was a necessary discussion that neither of them wanted to have: honest, painful and real. Maybe the conversation had been a long time coming or maybe it was completely the result of Rome's time with Heath. That's a verdict for another day and possibly another conversation. But for now, Rome's heart was filled with two types of love for two different men and she needed distance and time to sort it all out.

NEW YORK, New York, USA.

When the plane landed at JFK, they made plans to part at the airport, and much to Jamie's relief, he was able to catch a redeye down to D.C. that night. They hugged goodbye and Rome found herself riding home alone in a taxi like she had done countless times before.

Barely able to walk, Rome unlocked her door and entered the apartment, pulling her bags behind her. She parked them next to the wall where they would stay for the night and planted herself in the nearby desk chair. The tough conversation she'd had with Jamie on the flight back was grueling to say the least. She was already spent thanks to her difficult departure from Forest Gate, so peeling away another layer left her raw and vulnerable.

As Rome sat alone in her apartment, completely drained by the physical and emotional journey she had just experienced, she knew it was only the beginning. Miles of untraveled road lay ahead, yet somehow she would find the strength to keep going. In the meantime, the short distance between the chair she was occupying and the bedroom seemed impossible to traverse. An irony worthy of an exhausted chuckle, if she had the strength. She should never have sat down.

Unexpectedly, Rome heard the ringing of a phone. She turned around and noticed someone was calling through the computer. Although she wanted to ignore it, Rome accepted the call and when she saw who it was she was glad she did. Beverly Hucker's gorgeous mug instantly popped up on the screen, helping Rome to realize how much she needed to see a friendly face.

"G'day, mate!" joked Bev with a big smile.

"It's so good to see you, Bev. Where are you?"

"I just wrapped up my second day of convict sites in New South Wales. Tomorrow I catch my flight out to Norfolk Island to tour the Kingston and Arthur's Vale Historic Area."

"It sounds like you're having a blast."

"I have not had this much fun in years, Rome. I can't thank you and Heath enough for this opportunity."

"I'm the one who should be thanking you. You're saving my neck."

"What do you think of the pictures I've sent so far?"

"The ones I've seen look really good. Tomorrow, I'll be in the office, where I'll download everything and start writing the articles and picking through the photos."

"Sheldon told me you left Forest Gate this morning. What were the odds of your boyfriend showing up like that?"

"That was a bit of a surprise."

"Heath's back in Sydney and you're back in the States."

"Looks like everything is back to normal," said Rome with a touch of melancholy.

"So how's 'normal' feeling these days?"

"That's a conversation for a later date."

"Speaking of dates, Sheldon asked me on a date this weekend."

"Sheldon. As in, Mr. Burns, Heath's Butler?"

"The one and only."

"When? How?"

"I'm pretty sure I hooked him with my alphabetizing skills that first night in the castle and I've just been reeling him in ever since."

"That's fantastic! I'm so happy for you guys."

"It's a black tie affair, so I'll need to go shopping for something that's not khaki."

"Where's he taking you?"

"I'm his date for the charity fundraiser Heath's holding at the castle on Saturday night."

"Heath's going through with his uncle's plan?"

"From what I hear all the muckety-mucks of Hobart are going to be there."

"Sounds like the social event of the year."

"And Beverly Hucker will be in attendance. I'm going for lots of bling, Rome. I want to stand out in the crowd."

"You don't need bling to do that, Bev."

"Thank you. I think."

"I hate to cut this short, but I'm wiped out from the flight."

"Looks like more than just jet lag?"

"Let's talk in a couple of days when you get back to Tasmania."

"Sounds good. I should have the Norfolk Island photos and notes to you by my Thursday morning, your Wednesday afternoon."

"I'll make it work."

"Get some sleep, Rome."

"Will do. Thanks, Bev."

Rome ended the call and sat back in her chair. The apartment was silent. She was alone for the first time in over a week. She picked up her cell phone and located Heath's number. Stopping herself from dialing, she tossed the phone back onto the desk. More time passed. She picked up her cell again, this time locating Jamie's number. Again, she tossed it onto the desk. Finally, Rome stood up from the chair and walked into the bedroom, glad to say goodbye to a lousy day.

Tuesday morning arrived and Rome entered the offices of *Trekking the Globe* and walked to her desk. She put down her bag and woke up the computer, but before she could sit down, Angelica Fontaine appeared in the doorway.

"The prodigal writer finally returns home."

"I'm sorry the budget for the Port Arthur trip went a little overboard, but 'prodigal?' Really?"

"A little overboard?"

"I can explain."

"Please, allow me."

Angelica opened the budget sheet file in her hand and began to read from it.

"You upgraded to business class, rather than flying coach as we had budgeted."

"It's a twelve hour flight, Angelica, and I've done it one too many times."

"Seven days at a hotel for a trip originally scheduled for four."

"My research took longer than expected."

"Several hundred dollars to fix a vehicle's water pump?"

"That was not supposed to be included."

"One ferry fee across the Bass Straight, plus fuel."

"It was less than a connecting flight from Melbourne."

Angelica closed the budget sheet file and slammed it on Rome's desk.

"What happened down there, Rome?"

"A person cannot anticipate and budget for everything."

"Yet you do, every month. Logistics are your thing. So what happened?"

"I got sidetracked."

"We go to print on Thursday, which means..."

"The usual Wednesday afternoon deadline. I have been doing this for a while."

"Today's Tuesday. Are we going to make it?"

"I'm not the one who decided to change things up at the last minute and double my assignment!"

"The money from the Jones Shipping ad campaign will be well worth it."

"Did you say Jones Shipping?"

"Yes. Have you heard of them?"

Rome stood up and walked toward the window as the realization hit. "This wasn't about an eco-friendly ad campaign. It was about getting rid of me," Rome whispered to herself, contemplating Heath's company's motivation.

"What did you say?" responded Angelica.

"Nothing. Once I meet the deadline for this issue, I'm going on vacation for a while."

"You don't vacation, Rome."

"I need a vacation, Angelica. I need to clear my head."

"Your career is a series of non-stop vacations."

Shocked that Angelica could be so ignorant to what she does for the magazine, Rome turned away from the window and responded to her in no uncertain terms. "The very definition of a vacation is to take a holiday from work. A holiday devoted to rest and relaxation. I don't vacation! I go where other people vacation and watch them while they vacation. I'm busy taking pictures and doing interviews and writing down notes so other people can plan their vacations. Then I take those notes and photographs and turn them into outstanding articles for your magazine. That's not vacationing, Angelica, that's a job!"

"I thought you loved your job."

"I do! And I want to keep loving my job, but right now, I feel like I'm going to explode!"

"Okay, okay! I don't know what happened down under, but it's obvious you need some time to decompress. I still have that standby article you did on Toronto last year. Consider that your article for next month's edition. We'll do some... Canadian theme."

"Thank you, Angelica."

"You're the best travel writer in the business. The last thing I need is for you to have a meltdown. Just out of curiosity, where does a travel writer choose to vacation?"

"Some place where I can't hear any voices talking in my ear."

"And where would that be?"

"Under water."

"Of course, the scuba diving get-away you and Jamie have been talking about doing for the past year."

"It's now a get-away for one."

"I see."

"It'll be more relaxing that way."

"Just out of curiosity, how did you cover all the convict sites in such a short amount of time?" enquired Angelica.

"I didn't. I had a friend cover the ones I couldn't get to."

"A friend?"

"You're the one who wanted the impossible."

"You got two days till print, London, make them count," ordered Angelica as she walked out of Rome's office.

Rome sat back down at her desk, breathed a sigh of relief, then did exactly what her boss told her to do. She knew she'd be pulling an 'overnighter' that would extend into a forty-eight-hour marathon as she sprinted toward her Wednesday night deadline. But she'd been here before and she was up for the challenge. So she went to work.

THE FOLLOWING DAY found Rome asleep on her desk. She could hear a noise that sounded like knocking but was too tired to acknowledge it.

"Rome? Rome."

In an attempt to wake up, Rome tried to focus her eyes on the nearest image, slowly lifting her head to find Jamie standing in her office. Wondering if she was awake or dreaming, Rome decided to find out. "Jamie," whispered Rome, "is that you?"

"Don't tell me you've already forgotten what I look like."

"What are you doing here?"

"I went by your apartment and you weren't there, so I figured I'd find you at your second home."

"Deadline was this afternoon."

"Did you make it?"

"Barely."

"How long since you slept?"

"A couple days, if you don't count my nap on the desk just now. What are you doing in New York?"

"I'm taking some of that vacation time we've talked about for so long."

"In the city?"

"I needed to pick up a few things from the house so I routed my flight through New York."

"Mask and fins?"

"You better believe it."

"Are you going after it alone?"

"Why let all the planning we've done go to waste?" responded Jaime.

"I hope you find the ship or what's left of it."

"It's about time someone does. She's been setting on the bottom of the ocean for a lot of years."

"I'm leaving on vacation tomorrow as well."

"Scuba diving?"

"I need the solace," expressed Rome.

"Caribbean?"

"Still undecided."

"You know where I'll be staying if you want some company."

"Yes, I do."

"But that's not why I'm here. When I had my team in Australia gather intelligence on Heath last week…"

"For security purposes?" inserted Rome with a touch of sarcasm.

"Cut me some slack! My girlfriend, at the time, was shacked up in a castle with a billionaire."

"You have a point."

Jamie placed a manila envelope on the desk in front of Rome. She picked it up, pinched the clasp shut and pulled out the contents as Jamie continued to explain. "We inadvertently discovered a link between the columnist, Sergio Arturo, and an employee of Jones Shipping and Ship Manufacturing."

Rome sorted through the items of the envelope containing copies of newspaper clippings, phone records and surveillance photos, eventually coming across a photo of Arturo entering the Jones Shipping office building.

"Wow. You guys are thorough. Are you sure you're not a secret agent?"

"Not officially," Jamie said, winking at Rome. "I didn't notice the connection until I was typing up my report yesterday morning."

"Please don't tell me Heath and I are part of an official State Department report."

"No, I was shredding all non-essential intel when that picture caught my eye. I cross referenced Arturo's phone records and they came back to the COO of Heath's company, Roger Ash."

"Heath's uncle."

"Correct. According to flight records, both he and Arturo were also in Tasmania at the same time last week."

"Heath's butler suspected his uncle might be involved with Arturo."

"Oh, they're definitely in cahoots."

"Is this mine to keep?"

"Do what you want with it, as long as it doesn't get traced back to me."

"I'm going to forward it to Sheldon Burns."
"The British butler with a nose for the truth."
"Thanks, Jamie. You didn't have to do this... considering."
"You know how much I hate it when the bad guy wins."
"Yes, I do."
"I hope you also know how much I still want you in my life, even if it's just as friends."

Rome stood up, walked around the desk and took Jamie in her arms. As they hugged, Rome used the opportunity to whisper a personal response. "Not just a friend. Best of friends."

As they slowly pulled away from each other, Jamie nodded his head in agreement then left her office. Just as she turned to walk back to her desk she heard his voice holler a familiar reminder from down the hallway. "Don't work too late."

Rome smiled to herself as she returned to the desk, but the smile was quickly replaced by the contents of Jamie's envelope. "I don't like it when the bad guys win either." She pulled a new manila envelope out of her desk, addressed it to Sheldon Burns along with the castle's address and placed the contents inside. She put the envelope in her large bag, turned off the desk light and left the office, shutting the door behind her.

OAHU, Hawaii

Rome made her way through the boarding gate of the Honolulu Airport, then merged into the group of passengers, all moving in the same direction. She pulled her carry-on behind her with a smaller bag strapped to the top. Rome couldn't help but smile at all the tropical shirts, dresses and beautiful leis she saw passing by in the opposite direction. She was just arriving in paradise and they were leaving, tanned and relaxed. She continued along with the flow of passengers until she saw a sign directing her to the Business Center of the Overseas Terminal. She knew they offered mailing services there and she had yet to post the envelope to Tasmania.

Once again, she found herself in a long queue waiting to make her way to the counter. She pulled out her wallet and the manila envelope containing the contents that Jamie had given her. Unexpectedly, she heard a familiar Australian voice whisper in her ear. "It would arrive more quickly if you took it with you."

Looking behind her and seeing no one confirmed that it was a ghost. A ghost she would choose to ignore.

"It would arrive more quickly if you took it with you," repeated the ghostly voice.

"That's not going to happen," Rome said in response to the spirit's suggestion, causing the customer in front of her to glance back. Rome smiled and smiled then returned to patiently waiting her turn, until the voice repeated his advice a third time.

"It would get there more quickly if you took it with you."

"I'm not flying to Australia! I'm going to express mail it and he'll have it in a couple of days," Rome said sternly, causing the passenger in front of her to scoot forward as far as he could.

Frustrated and embarrassed, Rome left the line, eventually finding herself standing in front of the international flight departure screens.

"There's a flight that leaves in less than an hour."

Rome turned around to argue with the voice of the ghost but was surprised to see a male spirit standing behind her.

"I recognize your voice. You're the one who locked the door and spoke to me on the castle tower. The one who told me not to give up."

"You're as good as other spirits say you are."

"People talk about me on the other side?"

"In some circles."

"Then you probably know that I took your advice. I didn't give up and now the Jones family has been reunited."

"What makes you think I was referring to them?"

Taken aback by his response, Rome began to piece things together.

"You were talking about Heath. He was the one you didn't want me to give up on."

"What you did for our family, for William and Helen, was a big part of the reason I sent for you."

"It wasn't the Isle of the Dead calling me, it was you. You're Heath's father, Marshall Jones."

"It's a pleasure to finally meet you, Ms. London."

"You orchestrated this whole thing."

"When Heath discovered our family's tragic past, I knew he'd take an interest. But I didn't think he'd go out and buy a castle, creating the perfect opportunity for my brother-in-law to discredit him publicly and steal the company right out from under him."

"So you sent me to fix it."

"I sent you to save him, by saving his family. Our family."

"You're also the one who called me to the water's edge at Port Arthur and left me there as a target for the convict's anger."

"The only way you could help Heath and the rest of the family was by accessing the full extent of your ability. That required extreme circumstances. A shock to the system, so to speak."

"It was more than a shock. How did you know to do that?"

"I may have received guidance from your Great-Grandma Rome."

"Are you two on a matchmaking committee or something?"

"When I called to you for help, I did not anticipate a relationship forming between you and my son."

"One of the reasons I'm in Hawaii is to clear my head and consider my options."

"Is there a better option than spending your life with the one you truly love?"

"Isn't there a rule up there against spying on people's personal lives?"

"Not when it comes to family."

"I love my life, Mr. Jones, and nothing frightens me more than the idea of turning it all upside down. I'm not the type who throws caution to the wind."

"Yet you long to know what it feels like to be unrestrained."

"How do you know that?"

"I can see it in your eyes. Being on the other side gives us a sixth sense for certain things. A new perspective."

"As much as I appreciate the insight, I need time to think."

"If you say so. It appears Heath may have moved on already anyway."

"What do you mean?"

"He's invited a lovely woman to accompany him to his charity fundraiser. She's been with the company for years."

"Well... good for him."

"They've been friends for a long time. Who knows what will come of it?"

"He's really taking a date. And so soon."

"Speaking of dates, I'm supposed to be meeting my wife for a very special date we have planned. So I will say goodbye, Rome London, and thank you for all you did for Heath and our family. I am eternally in your debt."

"Honestly, it was my pleasure," replied Rome.

"Enjoy your stay in Hawaii. I always loved coming up to my beach house and sailing the waters here."

"Of course you'd have a beach house in Hawaii," said Rome with a touch of sarcasm.

"It belongs to Heath now. By the way, sorry for dumping the bucket of muddy water over your head. I knew Sheldon would never let you in the castle otherwise." On that note, Marshall winked at Rome then disappeared from sight, leaving her to contemplate their conversation, before whispering one last thought into her ear. "I hope all that logical thinking leads you to the happiness you seek."

"Wherever that is," Rome responded out loud.

Just then, the passenger from the previous line walked by observing her talking to herself again.

Rome smiled and waved, took hold of her bag and rolled it back toward the postal service line. Rome had chosen Hawaii as a place to clear her head. She needed to analyze her time in Tasmania with Heath from the outside looking in and that's exactly what she planned to do. But in the back of her mind, she couldn't escape the curiosity she felt over Heath's date for the charity event.

Chapter Twenty

Hobart, Tasmania

The castle was abuzz with activity as preparations for the fundraising event that evening were well underway. In the grand hall, lights and decorations were being hung, furniture was being replaced with tables and chairs and the musicians were setting up the bandstand. The kitchen was even more commodious as the catering service prepared the dinner buffet and put their final touches on the dessert items.

Hundreds of dishes, pieces of silverware and glasses were being hauled in, unpacked and placed on rolling carts, then rolled from the kitchen. Mr. Burns nearly collided with one as he entered the kitchen. Quickly he stepped aside, avoiding a disaster as the young man continued his push through the door. Mr. Burns took one look around, turned and left the kitchen.

He was very familiar with coordinating the behind-the-scenes preparations of events such as these, but that didn't stop the pit in his stomach from continuing to grow as things progressed. As he walked down the hallway, he reminded himself of all the catered events Marshall Jones used to host when he was alive. They all turned out successfully, but even those memories didn't alleviate his concern about Roger Ash's involvement. Heath had made a decision and it was up to him to carry it out. As he reached the grand hall, he noted that everything was progressing as planned.

He would like to have had a chance to speak with his employer personally about his concerns, but Heath unexpectedly extended his stay in Sydney for the entire week and wouldn't be arriving until today. Looking to the door, Mr. Burns noticed the arrival of Max, carrying and rolling luggage through the door. He grew curious at the number of bags in his possession. Max carried two more pieces of luggage than what Heath had taken with him to Sydney. Soon Heath entered the door, holding the hand of the woman following him.

Mr. Burns quickly recognized her as Donna Oak, a woman who worked for Heath at Jones Shipping. He hadn't seen her for years but recognized her from company parties held in the past. Once inside the grand hall, Mr. Burns watched as Heath began telling Ms. Oak about the castle, using his finger to point out different aspects of the architecture.

He took a deep breath and walked toward them as Max make his way up the stairs to with their luggage.

"Welcome home, sir."

"It's good to be home, Sheldon."

"Is it, sir?" asked Mr. Burns, questioning his long stay in Sydney.

Without skipping a beat, Heath ignored his butler's implication and continued the introduction. "You remember Donna Oak from the office."

"Of course. You work in publicity."

"Head of publicity and marketing," she said as she extended her hand in a very businesslike manner.

"Welcome to Forest Gate, Ms. Oak."

"Donna will be staying with us for the weekend."

"I'll have a room prepared at once."

"That would be lovely."

"And now for that tour I promised you," Heath said as he

escorted her back toward the door. "We'll be on the grounds if you need me, Sheldon."

Heath shut the door behind them and was gone as quickly as he had arrived. Mr. Burns shook his head in confusion at this new development, which unfortunately added to the size of the pit growing inside his gut. Ms. London had been gone for less than a week, which made him even more concerned. Seeing Miss Lemmons approaching the top of the stairs from the second floor, he charted a course through the obstacles and intercepted her before she reached the bottom.

"We have a female guest staying with us tonight, so we'll need to make up a room."

"Has Ms. London returned?" she said with great enthusiasm.

"No. Mr. Jones is accompanied by a co-worker. She'll be with us until Monday."

"I'll get right on it, sir."

Miss Lemmons hurried up the stairs as Mr. Burns turned back toward the grand hall, taking in the organized chaos playing out on the floor. All he really wanted to do was sit down on the stairs, put his head in his hands and drift off to a quiet place for a while. But that would not do. The event was only a few short hours from beginning, so it was back to business as usual. Looking across the floor, he saw one of the decorators removing a painting from the wall. He quickly descended the stairs and crossed the floor, hoping to ensure the safety of the piece of art currently in the hands of a plebeian.

THE HOURS FLEW by quickly and the charity fundraiser was at hand. Mr. Burns put the final touches to his bow tie, checked himself out in the mirror and left his room. He walked down the long hallway, past the top of the stairs and continued moving in the same direction, eventually reaching the master suite. Entering the room, he found Heath, struggling with his bow tie, as expected.

"Allow me."

Mr. Burns took hold of the tie and began forming a bow.

"Perfect timing as usual, Sheldon."

"Practice makes perfect, Heath."

"And you've had plenty of practice."

"Indeed."

"I hope Donna's presence didn't throw you off too much."

"It was a bit of surprise, especially with the departure of Ms. London being so recent."

"Donna and I have been friends for years and what's wrong with having another friend around?"

"Is that a rhetorical question, Heath, or would you like me to answer?"

"Rhetorical. For now."

"Do you have your welcoming remarks prepared?"

"Yes. It won't be as good as Dad would have done, but I'll do the best I can."

"Your best is all that matters. If your father were here, he would say the exact same thing." Mr. Burns finished tying the bow and stepped back to take a look at Heath. "It's been years since you've dressed for an occasion."

"And I'm as uncomfortable tonight as I've always been."

"Would it make a difference if it were Ms. London waiting for you at the bottom of the stairs?"

"It's been nearly a week and not even a phone call. I'm not going to hold my breath, Sheldon. It's back to business as usual." Heath turned to leave the room, but Sheldon could not let the conversation end on that note. "It doesn't have to be."

Heath opened the door, but his curiosity kept him from leaving the room. "Meaning?"

"You were a changed man with her around."

"She's gone, Sheldon. And so is that man." Heath left the room and slowly walked down the hallway toward the party. He knew Sheldon was right. The presence of Rome in his life had effected him in ways he never imagined possible. For one week, he dared to envision more to his life than the role of CEO. It was Rome who opened him up to a whole new world of possibilities and now all that was gone. In her absence, he'd chosen to return to the only place he felt safe, the world of business.

Deep down, he knew he could never be the philanthropist or charismatic party host that his father had been. Not by himself, anyway. Did he wish, as Sheldon had asked, that Rome would be waiting for him at the bottom of the stairs? Absolutely, but he also knew that was impossible.

Heath reached the top of the stairs and stared down at his guests. As he waited for a member of the catering staff to approach, he glanced to the side and saw Sheldon, standing out of sight, nodding his head in support. Heath took the glass from the caterer's tray and the knife next to it and began clinking the crystal, gaining the attention of everyone in the room. "Good evening and welcome to my home," his voice being broadcast through a microphone located at the top of the stairs.

The crowd applauded Heath and lifted their glasses in the air.

"Tonight you have the privilege of visiting Forest Gate without having to travel to the shores of England."

Again, the crowd applauded.

"Many have asked me why I bought a castle and had it shipped to Tasmania. I didn't know the exact reason until recently, when a good friend helped me to see into my family's past. I originally bought the castle and brought it here to right a wrong that was done to my family over a century and a half ago, but I have since discovered the reason to be so much more than that. In a very real sense, this castle has become a link to my family. A place to learn more about them and in turn to learn more about me. It's also become a place of refuge. A place of solace. A place of new beginnings and old friendships. And as difficult as it has been to see my home mocked by the press, week after week, lie after lie, my decision to purchase my ancestors' home and rebuild it in Australia is one I will never regret. So in the spirit of unity and community, let us join together this evening in raising money for a wonderful cause. Thank you and enjoy your evening."

The crowd applauded with great fervor as Heath descended the stairs and met up with Donna, waiting near the bottom. With great pride, Mr. Burns walked to the top of the stairs and watched Heath mingle with his guests.

That is until his eye caught sight of Beverly Hucker in the center of the crowd, wearing a sparkly evening gown that outshone everyone on the floor. As Sheldon began to descend the stairs, Bev began to climb, the sequins on her dress reflecting the light of the room. Sheldon became instantly mesmerized by her beauty and she was equally smitten by his handsome dress and demeanor.

Sheldon took hold of her hand, holding it out in front as he descended the stairs by her side as though they were royalty. Just as their feet touched the floor, the band began to play. "I fear I'm a bit rusty at this," said Mr. Burns as he wondered what to do next.

"I didn't get all dressed up to stand on the sidelines, Sheldon."

"May I have this dance?"

"You certainly may."

Sheldon and Bev danced their way into the center of the floor, forcing the circle of guests to widen, and prompting others to join them as well.

The night was off to a great start as Heath continued to fulfill his role as host, employing the art of small talk as he made the rounds with Donna. The food was lovely and the catering was very professional. Heath had invited the entire staff to be in attendance and he couldn't help but think of Rome as he saw Miss Lemmons and George dancing and laughing with Max and his punk-rock-styled girlfriend and Gladys and her husband sampling the dinner and dessert tables.

Rome had united them all as a family of sorts and brought a certain spirit to the castle that was not present before she arrived. But what really warmed his heart was watching his life-long friend, Sheldon, dance with Beverly Hucker, the blonde bombshell and take-charge guide from Port Arthur. If only Rome could seem them now. If only she could see the unique family of misfits that they had become.

"Heath. Heath?"

Heath's focus returned to the party as Roger called for his attention.

"Is everything all right?"

"Yeah."

"The reporter we invited would like to ask you a few questions."

"Is it Sergio Arturo?"

"Yes."

"That's a definite no," said Heath as he turned away from Roger.

"What harm could it do?"

"You've seen the kind of harm he can do."

"Just answer the questions you want to answer and skip the rest."

"Why him?"

"He's the only reporter here."

"Exactly. Why did you invite him?"

"To end his suspicions and in turn the suspicions of his readers. That's why we planned this event in the first place."

"Fine."

Roger quickly lifted his hand above the crowd and motioned for Arturo to come his way. Heath and Roger watched as Arturo signaled to his photographer to follow him through the guests.

"We're doing this now?"

"Might as well get it over with so you can get back to enjoying the party."

"Is that what you think I'm doing?"

"You're a natural at this, Heath. A chip off the old block. Philanthropy may be a part of your future after all."

Arturo busted through the last set of guests and stood eye to eye with Heath as though he were the MVP of the party. "Sergio Arturo: Off the Wall." He extended his hand in greeting as he introduced himself, but Heath declined to remove his hand from his pocket or introduce himself. Arturo withdrew his hand and signaled to his photographer to take some pictures of him interviewing Heath.

"You've got two minutes, Arturo."

As the cameraman snapped a few photos, Arturo pulled out his digital recorder. "This makes it easier to gather the facts I need for my column."

"And here I thought you just made everything up."

Arturo bit his tongue, knowing that revenge would be his as he pointed the digital recorder toward his own mouth and began the interview. "Mr. Jones, it appears your open house charity event is a huge success. How do you feel about that?"

"I'm pleased that so many people were able to support this important cause by attending tonight."

"Do you plan to make this an annual event?"

"That has yet to be decided."

"Do you plan to host other activities and events at your castle throughout the year?"

"Again, that has yet to be decided."

"Do you believe the reports of your castle being haunted?"

"Of course not!"

"Have you seen any ghosts yourself?"

"This interview is over," said Heath as he walked away.

Roger watched Heath disappear into the crowd, then shared his assessment of the situation with Arturo. "That lasted longer than I thought it would."

"Long enough," replied Arturo as he flashed his conniving smile. "We got everything we need. Let the games begin." Arturo pulled out his phone and sent a quick text.

At the top of the stairs appeared the image of a ghost staring down at the guests below. The band stopped playing and the dancing came to a halt as everyone's attention turned to the ghost and the evil sound of his voice, booming throughout the grand hall. "I warned you to stay away from my castle, but you refused to listen! Now you will pay with your lives!"

Images of ghosts began filling the air and circling around the ceiling, diving down toward the crowd and back up again. Their ghostly howls caused the crowd to scream and run for the door. In the middle of the chaos, Arturo stood for a photo as the photographer took a shot with him in the foreground and the crowd running from the ghosts behind him.

Confused by what he was seeing, Heath ran to the door to stop the people from leaving the castle, but he was surprised to find Bev and Max already blocking the door. As the crowd tried to physically remove Heath and the others, he tried in vain to calm the panicked crowd. "Stop. Everybody calm down. I can explain everything."

A man tried to grab Bev and move her out of the way, but she made it very clear that would be an enormous mistake. "You touch the dress or mess with the hair, you'll pay the price and it's not cheap." Unfortunately, they were highly outnumbered and losing the battle, until a voice sounded over the microphone, louder than the howls of the ghosts. "May I have everyone's attention! Please, calm down and listen to me!"

Heath instantly recognized the voice and began fighting his way through the crowd for a better view as Gladys, her husband and Miss Lemmons took his place guarding the door. A flood of emotions slammed Heath as he saw Rome standing at the top of the stairs, next to the image of the ghost, while the other frightening images continued to swirl around the room. She was dressed for the occasion in a long, black Hawaiian dress, covered in a silver hibiscus print. Her only accessory was a red hibiscus flower holding her hair back on one side. It wasn't long before her presence began to calm the crowd's hysteria and turn their attention away from the ghosts.

"I thought you got rid of her," Arturo said to Roger, angry at the possibility of his plan being thwarted.

"Clearly, that's not the case," Roger replied as they made their way out of the grand hall toward the service entrance.

Once outside the castle, the two men ran toward the local news van that Arturo's photographer-on-loan had used to pick him up from the airport and transport him to the castle. "Get in. I'll drive," Arturo yelled to Roger as they quickly approached the rear of the van.

Abruptly, the back doors flew open and they were picked up and thrown into the back of the van. Unseen by Roger and Arturo, Lord Hubert and William brushed their hands together, signaling their great delight in taking out the trash. Then they crawled into the back of the van and shut the doors as Lady Jones appeared in the driver's seat with Helen as her copilot. Helen pushed down the automatic lock, signaling the men's doom and sending chills throughout their spineless bodies.

"Let the party begin, my dear," said Lord Hubert, giving his wife the green light.

With a wink to Helen, Lady Jones started the engine and floored it. The van sped recklessly down the driveway, slamming the two men from side to side and bounced onto the road as Roger and Arturo screamed for help. But no one heard their cries.

Inside the grand hall, the ghosts were still swirling about, but the crowd had turned their attention to Rome at the top of the stairs. "On behalf of Mr. Jones, we would like to apologize for the confusion this evening's entertainment has caused. We thought it would be fun to use some special effects to play on the rumors of the haunted castle, but clearly, an introduction should have been in order."

"So they're not real," yelled a voice from the crowd.

"Of course, they're not. A fact which Mr. Burns, who is standing by in the electrical room, will now prove with the flick of a button."

With that said, the ghostly images and the howling noises immediately disappeared, causing a collective sigh of relief to be heard throughout the room, especially from the staff and friends guarding the door.

"Again, we apologize for the oversight and ask that you rejoin the party and continue with your evening."

Uncertain of what to do, the band slowly returned to the bandstand and picked up their instruments as the guests attempted to regain their composure. To Rome's surprise she was quickly joined by the Lord Mayor of Hobart, who borrowed her microphone to speak to the guests. "I don't know about the rest of you, but I haven't had that much excitement and fun at a charity event in years. I think a round of applause is in order." The Lord Mayor began to clap and one by one the guests followed suit, until the entire room was clapping and smiling with each other. "The night is young, my friends," the Lord Mayor continued, "And now that we know our hearts are still beating, let's trip the light fantastic." On that note, he handed the microphone back to Rome and descended the stairs. Building on the Lord Mayor's enthusiasm, the band started to play and the guests couldn't help but gather together to express their excitable reactions with one another.

Rome placed the microphone in the stand, then looked down at the dance floor to see Heath standing in the center staring up at her in awe. As she began to confidently walk down the stairs, Heath made his way through the crowd of guests, all patting him on the back. "What are you doing here?"

"I'll show you," said Rome as she took hold of Heath's hand and led him down the hallway to the electrical room. Rome opened the door to find George and Mr. Burns standing over a man sitting on a milk crate with a computer on his lap and surrounded by other equipment. "Well done, gentlemen," said Rome as she greeted them both.

"Just like clock work, Ms. London," responded George.

"Will someone please explain what is going on here?"

"Shall I do the honors or would you like to, Ms. London?"

"It would sound so much better with a British accent."

"Very well. I had an uneasy feeling about this open house, due to the fact that your uncle was behind it, but per your request, I did my part to make it happen."

"Wait," inserted Rome. "Start with finding our new friend."

"Sorry, I got ahead of myself. Must be the adrenaline pumping."

"That tends to happen when Ms. London's around," added George.

"Agreed. On the day the movers were here, I found this man in this very room, examining our electrical system. Although I was suspicious, I allowed him to leave but never forgot the encounter. During the burglary attempt, I thought he may have been involved with the planning, but that proved not to be the case. During Beverly and Rome's last conversation, however, she mentioned that she had evidence that your uncle was working with Arturo and was somehow involved with the barrage of negative press."

"Jamie actually found the connection," mentioned Rome.

"So Jamie's still in the picture?" said Heath in disappointment.

"If it weren't for Jamie, this night would have turned out quite differently."

"Mighty Mouse saves the day. I'm surprised he isn't here with you now. Or is he?"

"Actually, he's in the Caribbean."

"On assignment?"

"On vacation."

"By himself?"

"Yes."

"Yet, you're here."

"Yes, Heath, I'm here."

"If I may continue," asked Mr. Burns. "Between the pit in my stomach and Rome's new information, the three of us concluded that Arturo and Roger were planning something for tonight. The final nail in your coffin, so to speak."

"Hold on a minute, Sheldon. Why didn't you call me with this information, Rome?"

"Because you would have cancelled the event and that would have made you look even worse in the eyes of the public."

"Rome was correct, Heath. Although we had no idea what they were planning, we figured we had enough evidence to counter and hopefully stop whatever might occur," added Mr. Burns.

"You could have at least told me she was coming, Sheldon."

"I had no idea she was coming. She just showed up out of the blue."

"Maybe not out of the blue," said Bev as she approached, followed by Gladys, Max and Miss Lemmons.

"I had to make sure someone knew I was coming," said Rome.

"At any rate, right before the ghost show began, Rome entered through the staff entrance..." Mr. Burns paused for a moment and looked at Bev. "That explains why you dragged me off the dance floor to the kitchen. There was no emergency."

"Yet."

"Secrets are no way to begin a relationship, my dearest Beverly."

"It'll never happen again," she said, winking at Rome.

"When we heard the loud voice come from the grand hall, we knew something was wrong. We ran to the end of the hallway and saw the ghostly image at the top of the stairs and the others flying about the room. Somehow Rome knew right away that the ghosts were not real, so she sent George and I to the electrical room."

"And myself to guard the door. Thanks for the help by the way, Heath," said Bev, with a pat to Heath's back.

"Then Ms. London ran for the stairs and saved the day, or the evening, as it were," concluded Mr. Burns.

"How do we tie this to my uncle?"

"Fortunately, our new friend here decided to fully cooperate and told us that Arturo hired him to do the job and the amount of money he was paid is staggering."

"That still doesn't implicate Roger."

"No, but these do."

Rome handed Heath the envelope addressed to Sheldon and he removed the contents into his hand. His face showed the great disappointment of realizing how far his own uncle would go to take control of Jones Shipping and Ship Manufacturing.

"I'm sorry, Heath."

"I suppose the old saying that blood is thicker than water isn't always the case. It's time my uncle and I have a talk."

"He's no longer here," said Miss Lemmons. "I saw him and the reporter sneak out the door as Rome began to speak."

"He can't go far. Neither of them can. But that's a problem to be solved tomorrow. Tonight, we have a party to get back to. Thank you, my friends. I'll never forget what you did for me tonight."

"There you are. You must have snuck out on me during the ghost show. That was quite the spectacle. A heads up would have been nice," said Donna as she approached the electrical room.

Everyone stood in silence, not knowing what to say until Rome, completely oblivious to the situation, introduced herself. "My name's Rome London."

"I'm Donna Oak. 'Rome London.' Why is that name so familiar to me?"

"She's the feature writer for *Trekking the Globe*," responded Heath.

"Of course, I read your article every month. I could only dream of a job as splendid as yours."

"It has its moments."

"Speaking of moments, I think this is a good time to steal my friend away," said Bev as she wrapped her arm around Rome's and led her back down the hallway, followed by Gladys, Max and Miss Lemmons. Unsure of what to do, George awkwardly reached over and shut the electrical room door, with him and Mr. Burns still inside, leaving Heath and Donna alone in the hallway.

"You certainly do have a tight-knit staff," remarked Donna.

"Yes, I do."

Heath placed his hand on the small of Donna's back and started her down the hallway.

"Rome's not just a travel writer, is she, Heath?"

"A half hour ago, I would have disagreed with that."

"And now?"

"I'm not sure."

"Well, until you decide, I think you owe this old friend a dance or two."

"With pleasure, Donna." The two entered the grand hall, made their way through the guests and began to dance.

BEV AND ROME entered the library, carrying plates piled high with an assortment of buffet items. They both kicked off their heels, put down their food on the coffee table and plopped down on the couch. Rome reached down and touched the back of her heel. "I think I'm getting a blister."

"I've got some mole skin in my purse. We'll put some on before we head back to the dance floor."

"Don't make me go back."

"Who knew that Max was an animal on the dance floor?"

"I had my suspicions."

"I'm starving," said Bev as they both began to eat.

"Napkin?"

"Thank you."

"This is amazing."

"Try the stuffed crab."

"That's delicious. I was too nervous to eat on the plane, if you can imagine that. Granted I was crammed in the worst seat that coach had to offer."

"That's what happens when you buy a last-minute ticket at the airport. Why did you do it?"

"When I landed in Hawaii, I met somebody who changed my mind. Next thing I knew I was standing at the ticket counter booking a connecting flight to Australia. That's when I called you."

The door opened and Heath entered the room. He walked up behind one of the chairs facing the couch and rested his arms on the back. "I hope I'm not interrupting."

"Not at all. We just wanted a comfortable and quiet place to eat," responded Rome.

Bev discreetly removed the cream puff from her plate and placed it on a napkin beneath the coffee table. "Wait a minute. Where did you get those cream puffs?" enquired Bev, trying to give herself an excuse to leave the room.

"They were on the dessert table. You were the one who pointed them out. I thought you picked one up."

Bev quickly stood up and placed her feet in her heels and walked toward the door. "I must have gotten distracted."

"You can have one of mine."

"You'll need both of those. I'll be back in a while. Unless I get detained... or distracted... or Sheldon just wants to smother me with kisses in some dark corner of the castle." Leaving Heath and Rome stunned, Bev shut the door. Before they could speak, the door opened back up, just enough for Bev to speak through. "You're welcome to whatever you want on my plate, Heath." The door quickly shut again, leaving them in silence. They both started to chuckle at the obvious absurdity of what just happened as Heath walked to the couch and took Bev's place. "So why is Jamie vacationing by himself?"

"We had a long talk on the flight home and decided that we'd try it as friends for a while."

"You both decided that?"

"I may have started the ball rolling."

"Where does that leave us?"

"The problem between us wasn't just Jamie."

"Logistics."

"Something I'm usually pretty good at navigating."

"I can't believe you flew all the way down here to help me."

"How have you survived without me for so many years?"

"I'm wondering the exact same thing. Remember when you told me about soulmates?" asked Heath.

"You said you didn't believe in soulmates."

"No. I said I didn't believe that everyone has a soulmate."

"And I said that maybe not everyone is lucky enough to find their soulmate," reminded Rome.

"Will I freak you out if I told you that I think we're two of the lucky ones?" said Heath, completely opening his heart to Rome once again.

Not prepared to have the conversation Heath wanted to have, Rome got up and walked across the room to pour her a glass of water.

"I threw myself back into running my company this week, but it wasn't enough. It all felt hollow." Heath rose to his feet and walked toward Rome, who stood with her back toward him. "When I'm with you, Rome, it feels real. Tangible. Like somehow we're a part of each other. I don't know if that's the definition of a soulmate, but I'm certain it's what my dad was talking about when he told me that someday, if I was lucky enough to meet the right woman, I would understand." Heath placed his hands around her waist and leaned down to whisper in her ear. "I understand now."

"Do you realize the type of work this is going to take?"

"It just so happens that work is one of the things that I'm very good at."

"That's one thing we have in common."

Heath turned Rome in his arms, coming face to face with the

woman he loved. "I'm more interested in what makes you different."

Before she could respond, Marshall and a female spirit Rome had not met appeared across the room behind Heath. Rome saw them over his shoulder, then looked Heath in the eye and took hold of his hand. "It appears a couple of very important guests have arrived at the party."

"How do you know that?"

Rome walked around Heath, turning him in the opposite direction as she went. "Dad? Is that you?" asked Heath in great surprise, as he realized who was standing next to him. "Mum?"

"Yes, Heath. It's me."

Tears instantly filled Heath's eyes as he stared at his parents, unable to utter a single word. Squeezing Rome's hand, he hung on for dear life, scared to even blink for fear of losing sight of them.

"So this was the big date you had planned," remarked Rome, trying to buy time for Heath to collect himself. "For a billionaire, you're kind of a cheap date."

"You have a good memory."

"You knew I'd come back to Tasmania, didn't you?"

"No, but I hoped you would."

"You two have met?" enquired Heath, surprised by the news.

"We ran into each other at the Honolulu Airport. I just can't seem to escape the Jones family."

"I had some business there," responded Marshall.

"You're still involved in business in the next life?" asked Heath.

"Family business. Rome can explain later. We haven't much time."

Heath's mother walked toward her son followed by her husband, Marshall. She touched Heath's face and examined every detail. "You grew up to be a handsome and wonderful man. I couldn't be more proud of you."

"Thank you, Mum. I think of you often, especially since I moved back to Tasmania."

"And my thoughts of you never cease."

Marshall stepped forward and rested his hand on Heath's shoulder, just as he had done so many times throughout Heath's life. "I'm sorry that I was taken so unexpectedly, Heath, but it's the one thing I couldn't negotiate."

"I miss you, Dad, but I'm doing all right now."

"Nothing could make us happier. Well, maybe one thing."

Marshall tilted his head in Rome's direction and smiled.

"You think running a multi-billion-dollar company is a lot of work..." said Heath jokingly.

"Then it's goodbye until we see you again," responded Marshall as he and his wife took one last look at their son and disappeared from the room.

Although Rome had a whole lot of one-liner responses floating through her head, she decided to patiently wait for Heath to process his parents' visit. Now was not the time nor the place for her brand of humor. After a few minutes had passed, Heath surprised Rome by changing the subject entirely.

"So what's in Hawaii?"

"Excuse me?"

"I thought you were headed home."

"I was on vacation."

"Why choose Hawaii when the Caribbean is closer?"

"What are you insinuating?"

"That it's closer to Australia."

"Or I just enjoy scuba diving in Hawaii. You ever been?"

"To Hawaii?"

"Scuba diving."

"Why? You know a good instructor?"

"I might know of someone."

"Would she be open to lessons?"

"If you happened to be in Hawaii at the same time."

"That could be arranged."

"You'd need a boat."

"Would a sailboat do?"

"It's my understanding that this particular instructor would like to learn to sail."

"It just so happens that I know a pretty decent sailing instructor."

"With access to a boat?"

"And a beach house on Kauai."

"Which would allow the instructors more privacy."

"For educational purposes."

"To learn from each other."

"And about each other."

"A good place for two novices to try that 'starting point' idea you keep kicking around," admitted Rome.

"Agreed," said Heath as he took Rome into his arms and kissed her.

She had no idea where things would go from there, but she was open to the possibility. Rome London was ready to feel what it was like to be unrestrained. And this time logistics would have to take a back seat.

The End

Sea to See

BOOK TWO IN THE ROME LONDON SERIES

Caribbean: 1722

Captain Locke of the Maiden's Return and his crew are lost in battle. But are they really?

Caribbean: Modern-day

Jamie Webb disappears and Rome is his only hope. Too bad they broke up…

Just kidding.

Rome and Heath arrive to save him and Heath is not happy.

Not kidding.

Suddenly, the female spirit she had been searching for appeared next to her in the water. "They're coming for you. Get to shore!"

"Who's coming for me?" Before she received an answer, Rome felt something wrap around both of her ankles and begin pulling her down. Panic struck as she fought to keep her head above the water. She screamed for help, but there was no one to hear her cry. The only thing she could do was breathe deep before being pulled beneath the surface.

Once submerged, she bent toward her feet, surprised to see the ghosts of two men pulling her toward the bottom. Rome worked feverishly to escape their grasp as the air in her lungs had all but dissipated. Finally free, she fought her way to the top, filled her lungs with oxygen and began swimming toward shore.

Again, she felt their grip on her legs and this time around her waist, forcing her down. Once beneath, she saw more ghosts swimming in every direction, pulling her one way then the other, causing her to briefly lose her frame of reference. Again, she burst out of the water with only enough time to gasp for air, then back to the fight of her life. Although much of her strength had been drained, she continued her struggle for survival, each time finding it more difficult to reach the surface and uncertain as to how much longer she could last.

Eventually, her need to rest, to close her eyes and float away in the warm waters of the Caribbean, chipped away at her stamina until Rome did the unthinkable—she conceded defeat. Releasing the last bit of air from her lungs, she gave up the fight, allowing the ghosts to freely take hold of her body.

About the Author

Xann-shapella Smith had the opportunity to study playwriting and screenwriting at Brigham Young University and has brought her plays to the stage on many occasions. Her love for great storytelling has produced scripts that span many genres, including: drama, romance, comedy, fantasy, adventure and science fiction. After making the decision to pen her most recent screenplay idea in novel form, she has broadened her horizon in terms of storytelling. She's extremely excited about her first novel and looks forward to future books in the series. Xann resides on a small farm where the beauty and solace that surround her provide the perfect atmosphere for creating stories as far as the expanse of her imagination. Writing has been one of the great loves of her life and telling a good story is one of her passions. Xann-shapella's writing is a skill that rewards her in abundance each and every day and a passion she loves to share with audiences everywhere.

For more books and updates:
www.xannsmith.com

Made in the USA
Monee, IL
31 October 2020